T0090748

Recasting Lin Shu

Wanlong Gao

Order this book online at www.trafford.com
or email orders@trafford.com

Most Trafford titles are also available at major online book retailers.

© Copyright 2009 Wanlong Gao.
All rights reserved. No part of this publication may be reproduced, stored in a retrieval system, or transmitted, in any form or by any means, electronic, mechanical, photocopying, recording, or otherwise, without the written prior permission of the author.

Printed in Victoria, BC, Canada.

ISBN: 978-1-4251-9221-1

Our mission is to efficiently provide the world's finest, most comprehensive book publishing service, enabling every author to experience success. To find out how to publish your book, your way, and have it available worldwide, visit us online at www.trafford.com

Trafford rev. 11/17/2009

 www.trafford.com

North America & international
toll-free: 1 888 232 4444 (USA & Canada)
phone: 250 383 6864 ♦ fax: 812 355 4082

Acknowledgements

I would like to thank School of Languages and Linguistics, Griffith University for providing resources and research funding for this study. I am also grateful to the libraries of Griffith University, Queensland University, Auckland University, Stanford University, Beijing University, Auckland University, Taizhou University and Beijing National Library, Shanghai Library for assisting me to find the research data and reference books I needed for working on this book.

There are many people to thank for their support and encouragement, without whom this book would not have been possible.

Firstly I am greatly indebted to Dr. Debbie Cao and Professor Mary Farqhuar from Griffith University for their valuable advice. It was on Debbie's advice that I began to view modern Chinese translation through target-oriented translation theory, thus laying a theoretical frame for this book. She deeply impressed me with her sagacious critical perception as well as her conscientious attitude to my study. Mary's advice suggested that my research interest focus on Lin Shu's translation instead of the corpus of modern Chinese literary translation. She also coined the term "poetic equivalence' in our discussion of Lin Shu's translation method and my work in this regard has become the major extension of translation theory, i.e. dynamic equivalence. Their unquenchable curiosity and love for the subject are probably the most valuable lessons I have learned from this research, and their continual support and encouragement have kept me going over the last three or so years.

My thanks also go to Professor Nick Knight for suggesting me to refer to the section regarding Lin Da's translation in his work 'Lin Da and Marxist Philosophy in China', which greatly inspired me. I would also like to thank all my friends and colleagues in China, Australia, UK, USA and New Zealand, especially Professor Zhao Xinggen, Professor Liu Nianzi, Professor Guo Yanli, Dr Frances Knight, who have offered me a great number of advices and academic and technical supports. Without their generous assistance, everything would have been a great deal harder.

ii

Finally I am also extremely appreciative of my wife Linda Chen and my daughter Cathy Gao for putting up with my long hours away from home and taking on household duties as well as their continuous encouragement.

W. Gao

CONTENTS

Chapter 1

Introduction

This study is an examination and re-evaluation of Lin Shu's translations. Lin Shu (alias Lin Qinnan, 1852-1924) is best known for his translations of Western literary works into classical Chinese. Yet his translations have long been denigrated as 'unfaithful' by subsequent scholars wedded to a narrow view of translational faithfulness that focuses on the original text, not the target culture. Recent Western works on translation theory that focus conversely on the target culture can allow a recasting of Lin Shu's works and their impact in China. From this perspective, Lin Shu's works epitomise a translation practice that privileges reception, not original. The present study will contribute to both the study of Lin Shu's translation and to contemporary translation studies.

The study is that Lin Shu's translations influenced not only Chinese, changing the traditional Chinese perception of Western literature as 'low' art, but also a new generation of Chinese writers and reformers during the May Fourth period. The May Fourth New Culture Movement (1917-1924) is recognised as a watershed in Chinese literary, political and national life, ending the dominance of the Confucian tradition in the classical language and ushering in a transition to modernity. Lin Shu belongs to a previous generation whose translations could be said to form a distinctive genre in the classical language. Certainly, Lin Shu's insistence on classical, not vernacular, language in his translations later earned him widespread criticism. The subsequent politics of literary criticism in China saw Lin Shu's formidable contribution to transitional Chinese culture being denigrated until the 1970s when scholars began re-evaluating his works. This study is part of that re-evaluation. Firstly it defines a theoretical framework that precisely targets the cultural milieu in which Lin Shu's works were devoured by a hungry intelligentsia eager for Western ideas in a Chinese linguistic form. The theoretical framework is best understood as a cultural approach. Secondly, the study undertakes a detailed textual analysis of Lin Shu's translations within the cultural milieu informed by the framework.

Lin Shu and his translations have been a controversial topic since his first translation, *Bali Chahuanü yishi* (*La Dame aux Camélias* by Alexandre Dumas fils),

2

appeared in 1899. As soon as this translation was published, it caused a national sensation among the Chinese reading public. Its success inspired Lin Shu's ongoing introduction of foreign literature. For approximately twenty years thereafter, namely, from the late Qing period to the May Fourth New Culture Movement, Lin Shu translated more than 180 foreign literary works into Chinese.

However, Lin Shu did his translations without any knowledge of foreign languages. He had to collaborate with his friends who had first-hand knowledge of foreign languages and orally relayed the original to him. Therefore, translators or critics after him, both Chinese and foreign, have found faults with his work, even claiming that he was not really a translator but a second-hand storyteller. This is because the majority of translators today abide by such principles of translation as 'faithfulness' and 'translation equivalence', emphasizing that the target text (TT) must be faithful to the source text (ST). Critics claim that 'Lin adopted an approach of his own, which is widely different from what is practised by translators today'; 'Lin seems to have been more concerned about spinning his own yarn than acting as a faithful intermediary between the Western writer and his Chinese readers. Retelling the story in his own way, he often took liberties with the original, making changes and adaptations here and there to suit his purpose.'[1] Given modern translation protocols, Lin's translations are barely accepted by linguistics-oriented or source-oriented translators or critics. I argue that Lin Shu must be acknowledged as a translator due to the role he played in both translational practice and in the development of Chinese literary translation, and that Lin's works must be accepted as translation, especially given their quantity, reception and ongoing impact. Therefore, translation theories need to extend to accommodate the translational phenomenon of Lin Shu.

What interests me is this contradiction. On the one hand, most scholars in China and elsewhere have acknowledged that Lin Shu, as one of the most important translators in China, occupies a prominent position in the history of Chinese translation. He was a well-known translator, essayist, fiction writer, painter, and calligrapher. Of his works, his translations are the best known, covering both foreign literature and foreign reviews concerning political,

---

[1] Wong, Laurence, 'Lin Shu's Story-retelling as Shown in His Chinese Translation of La Dame aux camélias', Babel, 44: 3, 1998, pp. 208-209.

economic, military and social areas. His literary translations are considered the most influential. It is widely acknowledged that Lin Shu is unsurpassed in terms of output and impact of his literary translations; no Chinese translator, past or present, can match him. Yet, on the other hand, it is quite difficult to find a significant critique that can clarify why Lin Shu's translations enjoy such a prominent position in China's history of translation and why they created such a huge impact on modern Chinese culture and literature. It seems that nearly all critics are merely concerned with linguistic analysis and subjective judgement of Lin's translated texts while neglecting the enormous cultural significance and influence of Lin's translations.

As stated, because Lin Shu knew no foreign languages, he adopted a rather unique approach to translation. It can be argued that Lin Shu preferred a reader's reception oriented approach with due consideration to the target culture to a linguistic equivalence approach that gives priority to the source text and stresses the linguistic matching between the source and target texts. He preferred free translation to literal translation. Therefore, a narrow linguistic analysis and judgement is insufficient to discern and give adequate recognition to Lin Shu's achievements or to locate his place in the history of Chinese translation and of the cultural transformation in China's modernity. For this reason, I will examine Lin's translations from the perspective of the target culture and reception. The approach adopted in this study is significant. Firstly, it contributes to a more balanced judgement and evaluation of Lin Shu and his translations. Secondly, the approach presents the new result from a case study of Lin Shu in the light contemporary translation theory.

1. Lin Shu: a controversial figure in Chinese translation history

The focus of the study is Lin Shu's literary translations. The research questions are: How can we evaluate Lin Shu's literary translations and his contributions to modern Chinese literature and culture in the light of contemporary translation theories? What were the historical and cultural variables that contributed to the type of translation Lin produced? What were Lin Shu's translational motives and strategies in dealing with the source texts for the purpose of the target culture? How can we interpret the translational phenomenon of Lin Shu in the historical context and in terms of contemporary

2. Significance of the Research on Lin Shu

(1) Need for Re-evaluation of Lin Shu's Translations

Lin Shu and his translations have been a controversial topic in translation studies. Owing to his ignorance of foreign languages, Lin Shu's translations were often sternly criticised both during his lifetime and after his death. In the postscript to his translation *Xiliya junzhu biezhuan* (*For Love or Crown* by Arthur W. Marchmont), Lin Shu explained:

> In my hurriedly written works, I cannot say for sure that there are no errors. Recently, some bosom friends of mine wrote to me to enumerate my errors as an object lesson, I feel very grateful. However, as I did not understand Western languages, I could only take down what I heard, so I was completely ignorant even if some errors occurred.[1]

Owing as well to Lin Shu's opposition to the use of the vernacular language in literary writing and in the Movement of Literary Revolution (1917–1919) later in his career, some scholars from cultural circles so vehemently depreciated him that he was castigated as an obstinate defender of feudal culture and a formidable enemy of social progress. Lu Xun (1881–1936) called him 'a present murderer' of China's 'future'.[2] Qian Xuantong (1887–1939) called him 'an old fogy'.[3] Some critics attempted to negate his achievements in literary writing and translation, and often mocked him through finding inappropriate words and faulty expressions in his writings and translations or labelling him a

---

[1] Zhu Xizhou 朱羲冑, Chunjue zhai zhushu ji 春觉斋著述记 (Works from the Chunjue Study), Vol. 3, Shijie shuju, Shanghai, 1949, p. 45.

Note: In this book, all quotations from Chinese reference books and articles have been translated into English by myself unless an indication is given.

[2] Lu Xun 鲁迅, 'Xianzaide Tushazhe'现在的屠杀者(A Murder of the Present), New Youth (新青年), 6:5, 1919, in Lin Shu yanjiu ziliao 林纾研究资料（Research Materials on Lin Shu）, eds Xue Suizhi 薛绥之 & Zhang Juncai 张俊才）, Fujian renmin chubanshe, Fuzhou, 1982, p.148.

[3] Qian Xuantong 钱玄同, 'Xie zai Bannong gei Qiming de xin de houmian'写在半农给启明的信底后面 (Writing after Bannong's Letter to Qiming), Yusi（语丝）, No.20, March 30, 1925, in Research Materials on Lin Shu）, eds Xue Suizhi & Zhang Juncai, Fujian renmin chubanshe, Fuzhou, 1982, p.165.

'badly-written' writer and translator. After the May Fourth New Culture Movement, the name of Lin Shu seemed to have disappeared. In the history of Chinese literature, he was either rarely mentioned or attacked as a negative figure. However, Zheng Zhenduo (1898–1958), a modern Chinese writer, commemorated Lin Shu in 'Mr Lin Qinnan': 'It seems unfair, only due to his temporary conservative view that   his standing in the literary world of China is thoroughly repudiated, and the fact that he worked hard in these respects for several decades has been neglected'[1]; 'In China, apart from Mr Lin, probably, nobody has translated more than 40 masterpieces in world literature' (see Chapter 3 for detailed discussion).[2] A Ying, a famous Chinese critic, claimed that the attacks were unfair:

> As we know, after the Republic of China was established, Lin Shu was a man who strongly opposed the New Literature Movement, which provoked some new type people. When those people attacked Lin Shu, his translations frequently became the major object of their attack. They spared no effort to satirise them. But for ordinary and reasonable people, the majority of Lin's translations preserve the spirit of the original. Even though there are some errors, perhaps the collaborators should be more responsible for them. On the ground that he could not drift with the tide and   'his mind was ill-timed', Lin Shu, whose life spanned the late Qing and the Republic of China, made important literary contributions, but he has been labelled as 'a feudal fogy'. Actually, he was a worthy person.[3]

It is obvious that the attacks on Lin Shu and his translations were mostly based on Lin's attitude towards the New Literature Movement. The main evaluation of Lin and his works was politically prejudiced. During the five decades from Lin Shu's death to the end of 1970s, especially after 1949 and during the Cultural Revolution (1966–1976) in China, his reputation suffered an unredressed injustice mainly due to political bias.

Since the 1980s, an interest in Lin Shu and his translations has revived in China. The significance and influence of his translations in Chinese culture and

---

[1] Zheng Zhenduo 郑振铎, 'Lin Qiannan xiansheng' 林琴南先生(Mr Lin Qinnan), Lin Shu's Translations, Shangwu yinshuguan, Beijing, 1981, p.1.
[6] Ibid., p.14.
[3] A Ying 阿英, Wan Qing xiaoshuo shi 晚清小说史(A History of the Late Qing Fiction), Zhonghua shuju, Hong Kong, 1973, pp. 676-677.

6

literature has been gradually affirmed. In 1981, Shangwu Yinshuguan (the Commercial Press) in Beijing reprinted *Lin yi xiaoshuo congshu* (*Lin Shu's Translated Novel Series*), which includes ten of Lin Shu's most important literary translations. The reprint of Lin Shu's translated novels indicated the beginning of comprehensive re-evaluation of Lin Shu and his works. In 1982, *Research Materials on Lin Shu*, edited by Xue Suizhi and Zhang Juncai,[1] appeared as one of the national literary research projects, which has greatly contributed to studies on Lin Shu in China. Soon afterwards, Lin Shu's other translations, novels, poems and essays, as well as biographies and reviews on Lin Shu, appeared in succession. Yet most of them were more inclined to reverse the verdict on Lin Shu than provide a systematic and detailed examination of Lin Shu's translations, especially from fresh perspectives. In fact, Lin Shu's achievement and his historical position are mainly based on his literary translations. Therefore, in order to re-evaluate Lin Shu and his status, it is essential to start with an examination of his translations. A study of Lin Shu in the West seems to show a different focus. Western scholars are more interested in Lin Shu's translations than in his attitude towards the New Literature Movement of the time. Before the 1960s, Western studies are generally hampered by the insufficient introduction to Lin Shu's translations in the West. However, in the 1960s and 1970s, scholars such as Leo Ou-fan Lee and Robert W. Compton, conducted comprehensive studies of Lin Shu's translations and provided a fresh view points(see chapter 3 for further discussions), although their evaluation of Lin Shu and his translations were influenced more or less by Chinese scholars' views.[2]

Therefore, we argue that the study of Lin Shu's translations is inadequate both inside and outside China. From the perspective of modern translation theory, a historical and cultural criticism is required to systematically reappraise Lin Shu's translations and their influence.

(2) Lin Shu, Father of China's Modern Literary Translation

---

1 Xue Suizhi 薛绥之 & Zhang Juncai 张俊才, (ed.), Lin Shu yanjiu ziliao 林纾研究资料 (Research Materials on Lin Shu), Fujian renmin chubanshe, Fuzhou, 1982.
2 In 1965, Leo Ou-fan Lee published his article 'Lin Shu and His Translations: Western Fiction in Chinese Perspective' in Papers on China, Vol. 19. In 1971, Robert W. Compton completed his PhD thesis 'A Study of the Translations of Lin Shu, 1852 – 1924' in Stanford University.

One of the considerations for the study of Lin Shu's translations in this study is Lin's pioneering status in the history of modern Chinese translation. This fact has long been ignored. Two famous translators appeared during the late Qing and early Republic. One is Yan Fu (1854-1921),[1] the other Lin Shu. Kang Youwei (1858–1927) praised them as 'the two outstanding geniuses for translation coexisting in this world'.[2] Both of them enjoyed a reputation as 'the genius for translation' in the translation circles in China, and both used classical Chinese in their translations. The difference is that Yan did not translate any foreign novels, although he had a good command of English and was aware of the importance of novels. Instead, he rendered Western works of social science into classical Chinese.[3] It is Lin Shu who was continually engaged in translating Western novels although he had no knowledge of foreign languages. He was praised as 'the King of the translation world'. His translations were very popular and influential in China. As a result, they both occupy prominent positions in China's translation and culture. Indeed, Lin's works are a unique literary phenomenon in China's history of translation and deserve further study.

It is under the influence of Lin's translations that the translation of foreign literature in China was really initiated. It can be said that Lin Shu's translation of *La Dame aux Camélias* was the first influential translated novel in China. As soon as it was published, it attracted a large number of the Chinese readers. 'The novel became a bestseller for a period of time, and was popular throughout the country.'[4] Although he was unable to read any foreign language, during the late Qing and early Republican periods Lin Shu succeeded in rendering more than 180 works of foreign literature into Chinese with the help of collaborators.

---

[1] Refer to Benjamin Schwartz's In search of wealth and power : Yen Fu and the West, :Belknap Press of Harvard University Press, Cambridge, 1964.

[2] Kang Youwei 康有为, 'Qinnan xiansheng xie wanmu caotang tu, tishi jian zen fu xie'琴南先生写《万木草堂图》, 题诗见赠赋谢'(A Poem to Thank Mr Qinnan for His Painting of Trees and the Thatched Cottage with a Inscribed Poem), Yongyan 庸言(Trite Remarks), Vol. 1, No, 7, 1972, quoted in Guo Yanli 郭延礼, The Modern Translated Literature of China: An Introduction, Hubei jiaoyu chubanshe, Wuhan, 1998, p. 263.

[3] Yan Fu 严复 rendered eight famous Western works of social science into Chinese from 1892 to 1912, especially his translation of Evolution and Ethics (天演论) by T.H. Huxley exerted a tremendous influence on Chinese intellectuals of that time.

[4] Hanguang 寒光, Lin Qinnan 林琴南, Zhonghua shuju, Shanghai, 1935, p.5.

Among these translations, there are more than 40 famous literary works. He was 'the first person who translated Western novels in a classic style in China'[1]. On the basis of the previous scholars' investigation, his translations are tabled as follows (see also Reference Matters).

Table/Figure 1:1 Lin Shu's Translated Works

Country of Origin	Number of Works	Authors
Britain	105	59 authors including Defoe, Fielding, Swift, Scott, Stevenson, Dickens, Haggard, Conan Doyle, etc.
America	23	13 authors including Irving, Stowe, Alden, O Henry, etc.
France	28	18 authors including Hugo, Dumas, Dumas fils, Balzac, etc.
Switzerland	2	Wiss
Russia	11	Tolstoy, etc.
Belgium	1	Conscience
Spain	1	Cervantes
Greece	1	Aesop
Norway	1	Ibsen
Japan	1	Kenjiro Tokutomi
Unknown origin	7	
Total	181	

In terms of both date and output of translation, Lin Shu should be regarded as a pioneer who introduced Western literature into China through translation.

(3) The Influence of Lin Shu's Translations

Lin Shu's translations were also a unique cultural phenomenon. Translation is a product of cultural exchange and translating activity is a cultural activity. The latest cultural translation research lays special stress on the significance and

---

[1] A Ying, 1973, p. 182.

influence of translation on a national culture and the analysis and exposition of various translation phenomena and events from the view of cultural dissemination. This research examines the role and influence in cultural exchange rather than the quality of a translation. One of its characteristics is that the truthfulness of a translation is not in direct proportion to its role and influence in cultural exchange. From the view of cultural dissemination, the he translation phenomenon of Lin Shu is worth discussing. The discussion below is about the literary and ideological significance of Lin Shu's work.

Lin Shu's literary translations broadened Chinese readers' outlook on life and art and changed their low opinion of foreign literature. After Lin's translation of *La Dame aux Camélias* appeared in 1899, Liu Bannong (1891–1934) and Xia Kangnong translaed the same novel, but these had little influence. Liu Bannong, an advocate of the New Literature, looked down at and satirized Lin Shu's translation in 'A Letter in Reply to Wang Jingxuan' and thus decided to re-translate *La Dame aux Camélias*, but his attempt failed in popularity. [1] Lin Shu's translation was the most popular throughout the country at that time. Its unexpected success greatly inspired Lin Shu's enthusiasm for translation. He went on to translate over 180 foreign novels. It is through Lin's translated novels that Chinese readers not only learned about the exotic natural scenery, customs and habits of Western civilisation, but also more importantly, changed their deep-rooted prejudice against foreign literature. Early modern[2] Chinese intellectuals had originally thought that the West was advanced in natural science and political theory, but Western literature was too inferior to bear comparison to famous works of Chinese literature such as Sima Qian's *Shi ji* (*Records of the Grand Historian*), Li Bai and Du Fu's poems and Cao Xueqin's *Hong lou meng* (*The Dream of the Red Chamber*). This notion was quite common among the Chinese intellectuals at that time. For example, Feng Ping, a poet, stated in the preface to the *Collection of Mengluofuguan Ci*:

> It is regretful that since the European wind blew to China, all men of letters have been bent on Byron's poems, Shakespeare's sonnets and Voltaire's

---

[1] 新青年 Xin qinqnian (New Youth), 4:3, 1918, quoted in Xue Suizhi & Zhang Juncai, 1982, p.145.

[2] Here the 'early modern' period of China, refers to the period from 1840 to the occurrence of the May Fourth movement; the 'modern' period is from the May Fourth movement till 1949.

verses. They claimed that no one in China can match them. Alas! Ignorant! In terms of science, China is truly inferior to the West, but in terms of literature, China should be the best in the world. Foreign writers such as Byron, Shakespeare and Voltaire, cannot compare favourably with our sages such as Shaoling, Taibai, Jiaxuan, Baishi.[1]

Differing from most of Chinese literati, after rendering *La Dame aux Camélias*, Lin Shu realised that the value of Western literature was not inferior to that of Chinese literature. Consequently, he devoted himself to translating foreign literary works, initiating the translation of foreign literature in China. These foreign writers and works opened a new window for Chinese readers. Zhu Xizhou said: 'Until Lin Shu introduced innumerable famous works, Chinese people had not known the names of the European writers such as Scott, Dickens, Irving, Dumas and Haggard. Until Lin Shu asserted that Scott and Dickens's works are not inferior to Sima Qian, Chinese people had not known that there was literature in the West too.'[2] Lin's translated novels introduced new ideas, new customs and new literary concepts. Lin Shu stated in the preface to his translation *Feizhou yanshui chou cheng lu* (*Allan Quatermain*):

The European people aim at reform and modernisation, so they only learn from new things. To create a new world, they even consider something negligible like a novel, and abandon writing about outdated things. If we stubbornly adhere to ancient things, how can we learn any new ideas throughout our lives?[3]

Hence, Lin Shu used translations to enable the Chinese people to learn the value of Western literature in content, style, structure, language and expressive technique, and greatly widened Chinese writers' outlook. For example, his work initiated the changes in literary structure. The publication of his Chinese version of *La Dame aux Camélias* broke the Zhanghui style of traditional Chinese fiction

[1] Shaoling (少陵) is another given name of the Chinese poet of the Tang dynasty Du Fu (杜甫); Taibai (太白) is the given name of the Chinese poet of the Tang dynasty Li Bai (李白); Jiaxuan (稼轩), the given name of the Chinese poet of the Song dynasty Xin Qiji (辛弃疾); Baishi (白石), the given name of the modern Chinese painter and poet Qi Baishi (齐白石). Collection of the Southern Society (南社丛刻), Vol. 21, 1910. quoted in Guo Yanli, 1998, p. 279.
[2] Ibid.
[3] Zhu Xizhou, 1949, p.26.

(with each chapter headed by a couplet giving the gist of its content). Consequently, a number of Chinese writers such as Su Manshu's (1884–1918) and Lin Shu began to learn the structure from *La Dame aux Camélias* in their respective novels such as Duan hong ling yan ji (The Lone Swan) and Jian xing lu (The Stench of the Sword). In these novels, Western-style chapters replaced traditional Chinese chapters, and conventional introductory phrases such as '话说' and '且说'(Now let's turn to…), '且听下回分解'(…will be told in the following chapter) were also omitted.

The happy ending in traditional Chinese fiction was broken by Lin's translated novels as well. Zhang Jinglu (1898–1969) stated: 'Since Lin Qinnan translated French writer Dumas's sentimental novel *La Dame aux Camélias*, a new path for the novel was hewed out and the happy ending of the gifted scholars and beautiful ladies (caizi jiaren) was overthrown. Chinese fiction circles were greatly affected by his translations.'[1] Besides, the novels of this period such as Su Manshu's *Sui zan ji* (*The Tale of a Broken Hairpin*) and *Fen jian ji* (*The Tale of Burning the Sword*), He Zou's *Suiqin lou* (*Broken Strings Tower*), and Xu Zhenya's *Yu li hun* (*The Soul of Jade Pear Flower*) used the techniques in Lin's translated novels for reference. It is through Lin's translations that the modern Chinese novelist Zhang Henshui (1895–1967) realized the advantages of Western novels: 'From these translations, I learned many techniques of description, especially psychological description, which is insufficient in Chinese novels.'[2]

The literary significance of Lin's translations also lies in extending the range of subject matter of modern Chinese novels and introducing the literary styles and creative methods of Western novels into China. The subject matters of Lin Shu's translated novels are very wide-ranging. His translated novels include nearly all types of fiction in Western literature. See the table below for some representative samples.

---

[1] Zhang Jinglu 张静庐, Zhongguo xiaoshuo dagang 中国小说史大纲 (An Outline of the History of Chinese Fictions), Taidong tushuju, Shanghai, 1920, p.280.
[2] Zhang Henshui 张恨水, Xiezuo shengya huiyilu 写作生涯回忆录 (Memories of My Writing Career), Renmin wenxue chubanshe, Beijing, 1982, p.8.

Table/Figure 1:2 Types of Lin Shu's Translated Novels

Genre	Original Title	Translated Title
Love Stories	*La Dame aux Camélias*	巴黎茶花女遗事
	Joan Haste	迦茵小传
Family Novel	*Nami-ko (It Is Better to Return)*	不如归
Social Commentary Novel	*David Copperfield*	块肉余生记
	The Old Curiosity Shop	孝女耐儿传
Historical Novel	*Ivanhoe*	萨克逊劫后英雄略
Adventure Novel	*Life and Strange Surprising Adventures of Robinson Crusoe*	鲁滨逊漂流记
	Der schweizerische Robinson	鹯巢记
Novel of Ghosts	*She*	三千年艳尸记
	Black Heart and White Heart, and Other Stories	蛮荒异志
Detective Novel	*The Quests of Paul Beck*	贝克侦探谈
	A Study in Scarlet	歇洛克奇案开场
Ethical Novel	*The Dove in the Eagle's Nest*	鹰梯小豪杰
	Jimmy Brown Trying to Find Europe	美洲童子万里寻亲记
Military Novel	*Histoire d'un conscrit de 1813*	利俾瑟战血余腥记
	Hindenburg	德大将兴登堡欧战成败鉴
Industrial Novel	*Le tour de la France par deux enfants*	爱国二童子传
Political Novel	*Uncle Tom's Cabin*	黑奴吁天录
Satirical Novel	*Don Quijote de las Mancha, I*	魔侠传

The extension of subjects is one of the features of modern Chinese novels. Lin's translated novels are rich and varied, compared with the old fiction, which takes gifted scholars and beautiful ladies, chivalrous swordsmen, legal cases and history-telling as the subject matter. Accordingly, it may be said that Lin's translated novels made contributions to the development of the genres of modern Chinese novels.

Although Lin Shu knew nothing of foreign languages, he had the ability to discern the schools of Western literature owing to his long engagement in literary writing and translation. In his preface to his translation of The Old Curiosity Shop, Lin Shu said:

> I was often alone in a room for several months. No need to look, I could easily discern my family's footfall out of the window. Now some gentlemen who cherished the same ideals as me showed me the Westerners' literary works. Although I did not know any Western languages, when I listened to their oral interpretations, I could discern their literary schools just as I could discern my family's footfall. Among them, some are very serious, some illusory, some sentimental, some magnificent, some sorrowful, some obscene .... [1]

It is with a power of subjective discernment that Lin's translated novels reproduced the styles of the originals. Dumas fils's romantic sentiment, Scott's colour of heroic legends, Dickens's humour, Cervantes's exaggeration and absurdity can all be found in Lin Shu's translations.[2] Lin Shu had not only the ability to discern schools and styles of Western literature, but also the ability to make judgements between different Western authors and to critically evaluate their works. In the postscript to his translation *Sanqian nian yan shi ji (She)*, Lin Shu distinguished between excellent writers and inferior writers. In his opinion, Haggard's works are far behind Dickens's.[3] He said of Dickens's *David Copperfield*, 'I have translated more than forty books. This book is the best of them.' [4]

Lin's literary translations convey his patriotism and spread new ideas about Western democracy and freedom. During the late Qing period, with the invasion of the Western powers, China and the Chinese people became weaker

[1] Zhu Xizhou, 1949, p.5.
[2] Qiu Weiyuan 丘炜爰, 'Hui chen shi yi'挥尘拾遗'(Whisk the Dust To Pick Up) in Wanqing wenxue congchao: xiaoshuo xiqu yanjiu juan 晚清文学丛钞：小说戏曲研究卷(Late Qing Critical Papers on Fiction and Drama), ed A Ying, Zhonghua Shuju, Shanghai,1960, p.408. Zheng Zhenduo 郑振铎, 'Lin Qinnan xiansheng'林琴南先生'(Mr Lin Qinnan), Zhongguo wenxue yanjiu 中国文学研究 (Studies of Chinese Literature), Guwen shuju, Hong Kong, 1970, pp. 1226-1227; Qian Zhongshu, et al, 1982, pp.25-27.
[3] Zhu Xizhou, 1949, p.34.
[4] Ibid., p. 255.

and poorer. Many intellectuals tried to find ways to strengthen the country and enrich the people. The patriotic spirit catered to these demands and efforts. Lin Shu always instilled patriotic ideas into his readers through his prefaces and postscripts to his translations. His translation *Hei nu yutian lu* (*Uncle Tom's Cabin*) is an obvious example. His original intention of translating this novel is that 'the yellow race will be subjugated soon'. He claimed in the postscript: 'I translated this book with Mr Wei, not in order to skilfully tell a tragic story to cause readers' tears for no reason, but especially because the momentum of slavery has pressed upon our race, I cannot but cry out for the people.'[1] He saw black slaves being maltreated in *Uncle Tom's Cabin*, and associated this in his mind with the humiliation and torture suffered by Chinese labourers in the USA. He wrote in his translation of *Aesop's Fables* (*Yisuo yuyan*):

> If a country with inhuman laws takes advantage of its power to bully its people, is there anything it does not dare to do? This is happening before my eyes. Observing what happened in Honolulu, the grievances of the overseas Chinese overseas cannot be impartially solved owing to a total absence of justice. The USA is a civilised country, but they do not regard what they have done badly as a wrong thing while other big powers look on unconcerned and do not see it as a torture. All of them treat the overseas Chinese like cattle ... Justice cannot be promoted a bit further. This suffering is much bigger than it is in hell. Our compatriots are still in a dream. I will die with a grievance![2]

Lin Shu was unwilling to see the Chinese nation submit to stronger neighbouring countries, and hoped to use his translation to express his patriotic ideas regarding saving the nation from subjugation and ensuring its survival. In the preface to his translation *Buru gui* (*Nami-ko*, published in 1908), he stated, 'I am getting on in years and there are no more years left for me to serve this country, so I would rather act as a cock crowing every morning in order to arouse my compatriots.'[3] The reason he translated *People of the Mist* (*Wu zhong ren*, published in 1906) was to warn: 'since white people may annex Africa, they may

[1] Lin Shu, Hei nu yu tian lu 黑奴吁天录 (Uncle Tom's Cabin), Shangwu yinshuguan, Beijing, 1981, p. 1.
[2] Lin Shu, Yisuo yuyan 伊索寓言(Aesop's Fable), Shangwu yinshuguan, Beijing, 1903, pp. 21-22.
[3] Zhu Xizhou, 1949, p.36.

annex Asia'; 'I am an old man, without both wisdom and bravery, without learning. Everyday I talk with patriotic tears to my students about the situation, I cannot stop. Therefore I try my best to translate novels everyday.'[1]   He translated *Eric Brighteyes* (*Aisilan qing xie zhuan*, published in 1904) in an attempt to advocate militarism: 'The reason why I selected and translated it is that I paid particular attention to its military spirit, and hope it can help our people get rid of their decline and weakness and rouse themselves to become brave.'[2] The heroes in Lin Shu's translated novels such as *Shizijun yingxiong ji* (*The Talisman*, published in1907), *Sakexun jie hou yingxiong lüe* (*Ivanhoe*, published in1905), *Jian di yuanyang* (*The Betrothed*, published in1907) are full of courage and mettle, fighting a bloody battle and showing unyielding heroism. Through them, Lin Shu advocated militarism. He translated *Waterloo: suite de conscrit de 1813* (*Huatielu zhan xie yu xing ji*, published in1904), because he was impressed by the French people. All of them 'were aware of national humiliation', so could unite to fight. If everyone can be aware of national humiliation, the nation will not be subjugated in the end. He said in the preface: 'The people who are reading this book should know that I have shed my endless tears into it.'[3] Under the circumstances of the West's invasion of China, these prefaces and postscripts of Lin Shu had an immediate significance and an inspiring power on readers. It is mainly because of this patriotic aim in translating foreign literature that his translated novels were immediately and overwhelmingly accepted by the Chinese reading public.

Lin Shu's literary translations also to some extent spread the ideas of democracy and science, and contained some anti-feudal elements. This was the focus of the May Fourth Movement in 1919. As far as his translation of *La Dame aux Camélias* is concerned, the descriptions of love in the novel involve Western ideas such as the emancipation of individuality, the independence of personality, and the equality of men and women. The love stories that Lin Shu translated thus run counter to traditional Chinese moral concepts. The most obvious instance is *Jiayin xiaozhuan* (*Joan Haste*, published in 1905). The British writer Haggard's *Joan Haste* was hardly mentioned in the history of world literature at that time, but the publication of Lin's version greatly extended its

---

[1] Ibid., p. 27.

[2] A Ying 阿英, (ed.), Wanqing wenxue congchao: xiaoshuo xiqu yanjiu juan 晚清文学丛钞：小说戏曲研究卷(Late Qing Critical Papers on Fiction and Drama), Zhonghua Shuju, Shanghai, 1960, p. 205.

[3] Zhu Xizhou, 1949, p. 18.

influence. It provoked attacks from the defenders of traditional moral principles and a heated controversy in the late-Qing literary world. Before Lin's version, there was another version of *Joan Haste* with the same Chinese title *Jiayin xiaozhuan* (*Joan Haste*), translated by Pan Xizi and Tian Xiaosheng. But the two translators merely translated half of the original, omitting the description of Joan's passionate love for Henry and her resulting illegitimate child in order to preserve Joan's chastity. Lin Shu provided a full version. Yin Bansheng, a conservative critic, wrote in 'After Reading the Two Versions of Joan Haste':

> When I read *Jiayin xiao zhuan* (*Joan Haste*) in the past, I exclaimed in admiration that Joan preserves her purity and refuses to be contaminated, that she is willing to sacrifice herself to aid someone in doing a good deed. She is really a goddess in the love world. When I read *Jiayin xiaozhuan* now, I know that Joan is licentious, base, and shameless. She abandons her obligation of life and sacrifices herself for pleasure. In fact, she is a person harmful to the country and people. It is not owing to my mental contradiction, but owing to the versions I read. After Pan Xizi's translation was published, Joan's status suddenly rose to the highest of heaven, but after Lin Shu's translation, Joan's status suddenly dropped to hell.
>
> Pan Xizi's *Jiayin xiaozhuan* presents her virtue, so all the descriptions against her virtue were deleted, but Lin's *Jiayin xiaozhuan* presents her licentious, base and shameless conduct .... [1]

From Yan Bansheng's attack, we can clearly see Lin's stance on traditional morality. Through a comparison between the two versions, we can see Lin's descriptions of love are 'modern'. Guo Moruo's (1892–1978) experience of reading Lin's *Jiayin xiaozhuan* in his youth shows the Chinese response among a younger generation:

> Lin Qinnan's translated novels were popular at that time and were also my favourite readings. What I read originally is Haggard's *Joan Haste*. The heroine Joan roused my deep sympathy and moved me to tears. I felt a tender affection for her and I also very much admired her lover Henry. When I read that Henry climbed the old pagoda to get hold of the young crow for her and fell from the roof of the pagoda, and she stretched her

---

[1] A Ying, 1960, pp.285- 287.

arms to catch him, it appears that it is me who fell from the roof of the pagoda on Mount Lingyun. I imagined, if I possessed the pretty and kind girl Joan who loves me so much, I would be most willing to fall from the roof of the pagoda on Mount Lingyun and die for her.[1]

Such a sense of love aroused sympathetic responses among young Chinese readers. Yet the descriptions of love in Lin's translated novels differ from the ones in the classic Chinese works. Lin Shu lived in the times of the new replacing the old. On the one hand, he still believed in the Confucian doctrine: 'to start from emotion, and control oneself by etiquette'. On the other hand, he was a man full of sentiment and was influenced by the Western sense of love. He embraced aspects of modernity. In the preface to his translation *Xiang hu xian ying* (*Dawn*, published in 1906), he satirised the Confucian moralists: 'The scholars during the Song dynasty had a liking for a sanctimonious expression. They would rather bow to show their etiquette all day long, although they were privately thinking of beautiful women'.[2] In the preface to his translation *Hong jiao hua jiang lu*(*Beatrice*, published in 1906), he approved of some feminist views and stood for freedom of marriage: 'Freedom of marriage is a benevolent policy. If this policy is carried on, women will never sigh because of their withered marriage... It is a guiding principle to initiate feminism and women's education.'[3] It may be seen from this that Lin Shu was influenced by Western ideas regarding democracy. The new ideas in Lin's literary translations were rapidly spread and accepted in China and contributed to the occurrence of the May Fourth New Culture Movement. From this point, Lin Shu might as well be regarded as a precursor to the advocates of the New Culture Movement in the May Fourth period such as Liang Qichao (1873-1929) and Lu Xun.

In brief, it is through his translations and the relevant prefaces and postscripts that Lin Shu made an indelible contribution, not only to the occurrence of the May Fourth New Culture Movement, but also to the form and development of modern Chinese literature. Therefore, the significance of Lin's literary translation should not be underestimated.

---

[1] Guo Moruo 郭沫若, Shaonian shidai 少年时代 (My Early Youth), Renmin wenxue chubanshe, Bejing, 1997,   p. 113.

[2] Zhu Xinzhou, 1949, p.10.

[3] Ibid., p. 43.

Lin Shu's literary translation had a profound influence on modern Chinese writers and literature. When Lin Shu started his translation work, few other people were engaged in translating novels. At that time the ancient prose of the Tongcheng School dominated China's literary scene, so Lin's translation of foreign novels was no doubt a new thing in both content and form, and thus attracted a great number of readers. To their surprise, the Chinese people discovered that excellent literary works also existed beyond China, thereby becoming interested in foreign novels. During the two decades before the May Fourth Movement, many famous Chinese writers, inspired by Lin's translations, began the translation of foreign literature. Lu Xun and his brother Zhou Zuoren (1885–1967) were well known examples. In the essay 'My Experience of Studying Chinese', Zhou Zuoren recalled: 'We were so enthusiastic about Lin's translated novels that as soon as one of them was published and distributed in Tokyo, we went to buy it in Shentian Chinese Bookshop.'[1] Other modern Chinese writers such as Guo Moruo, Maodun (1896–1981), Hu Shi (1891-1962), Zhu Ziqing (1898–1948), Bingxin (1890–1999), and Lu Yin (1898–1934) devoured Lin's translated novels. The first Western novel that Guo Moruo read in his early youth was Lin's version of *Joan Haste*, and he wept over the heroine in the novel. At the age of eleven, Bingxin was fascinated by Lin's version of *La Dame aux Camélias*. This was her beginning for 'doing her best to collect Lin's translated novels and seeking to read Western literary works'.[2] Lu Yin acknowledged that she read all Lin's translated novels.[3]   Qian Zhongshu said:

> The two small boxes of Lin Shu's Translated Novel Series published by the Commercial Press was one of my discoveries at the age of twelve and attracted me to a new world, a new world beyond Chinese novels such as *Water Margin*, *Journey to the West* and *Strange Stories from Liaozhai*. I had read Liang Qichao's translation of *Deux Ans de Vacances* by Jules Verne, and Zhou Guisheng's translated detective novels before, but felt they were dull and drab. It was only after reading Lin Shu's translated novels that I have

[1] Zhou Zuoren 周作人, Zhitang wenji 知堂文集(The Selected Essays of Zhou Zuoren), Tianhai shudian, Shanghai, 1933, pp.239-240.
[2] Bingxin 冰心, Bingxin xuanji 冰心选集(Selected Works of Bingxin), Vol.2, Sichuan renmin chubanshe, Chengdu, 1984, p.328.
[3] See Yan Chunde 阎纯德, 'Wusi de chan'er' 五四的产儿'(A Newborn Baby of the May Fourth), Xin wenxue yanjiu ziliao 新文学研究资料(Materials Concerning New Literature), No.4, 1981, p.141.

started to know that Western novels are so fascinating. I tirelessly read Haggard, Dickens, Irving, Scott and Swift's works over again and again.[1]

Zhou Zuoren wrote in the article 'Lin Qinnan and Luo Zhenyu': 'To tell the truth, it is due to Lin Shu's translated novels that most of us learned that there are novels abroad, and we began to become interested in foreign literature. I devoted major efforts to imitate his translation.'[2] Guo Moruo said, Lin's translated novels not only were a kind of reading he was fond of, but also greatly affected his later literary writing, especially Lin's translation of Scott's Ivanhoe.[3] It is obvious that Lin Shu's translations influenced the later May Fourth generation of major great modern Chinese writers.

In short, Lin's translated novels inspired many famous modern Chinese writers such as Lu Xun, Guo Moruo and Bingxin, influencing their literary translation and creation, although during the May Fourth period Lin Shu was viewed as an out-of-date person by virtue of his opposition to writings in the vernacular.[4]

3. Contribution of the study to Translation Studies

Lin Shu's translation is now recognized as a special translation phenomenon. The development of modern cultural translation theories offers the feasibility of re-evaluating Lin's translations. Toury's translation theory, for example, attaches great importance to the influence of the target culture and norms on a translator and his translation. Target/culture-oriented translation studies lay stress on the cultural significance of a translation, and reader-response criticism emphasizes the reception of the target readers. Lin's case illustrates and supplements target-oriented translation studies or the cultural translation studies from a literary viewpoint.[5] Moreover, Lin's translation is not an isolated phenomenon, for in Lin Shu's contemporary translators or in the later translation circle in China, we can see his successors.

---

[1] Qian Zhongshu, 1981, p.22.
[2] Zhou Zuoren, 'Lin Qinnan yu Luo Zhenyu'林琴南与罗振玉(Lin Qinnan and Luo Zhenyu), Yu si 语丝(Thread of Talk), No. 3, 1924.
[3] Guo Moruo, 1979, p.114.
[4] Refer to Chapter Four of this book.
[5] Refer to Chapter Two of this book.

Even in the history of Western translation, we can also see translators of the same school.

The value of research into Lin Shu's translation should not be underestimated. The works on the role and function of translation in national culture and the influence of the target culture in its process have been seen elsewhere (e.g. Toury's *Study Of the Translation Of Western Literature Into Hebrew*), but not in relation to China. Furthermore, little consideration is given to the influence of translated texts on the target culture in China. This study makes conceptual contributions in the following areas.

First, a re-evaluation of Lin Shu's literary translation will not only re-define Lin Shu's position in the history of China's translation and modern Chinese literature but also clarify the roles of Lin Shu's translation in remoulding Chinese cultural identity in a specified period.

Second, the cultural, linguistic, literary and ideological roles and functions of translation in China will be illustrated in detail with Lin Shu's case, which will enrich the study of contemporary translation theory.

Third, Lin Shu's translation methods are seldom acknowledged by some translation critics, but are favourably received by a great number of Chinese readers. On the whole, he truthfully relayed the spirit and style of the original, but he also made some adaptations with a view to making his translations more readable in the target cultural environment. From the view of a target-oriented theory, Lin Shu's translation methods and strategy are acceptable and commendable.

Fourth, this study of Lin Shu's translations, will contribute to showing that literary translation may serve target readers and culture, although it also involves linguistic transformation, and that a translation that is rejected by target readers may not be a successful product, although it may literally stick to the original. Therefore, this study contributes to substantiating the target-oriented translation theory: the needs of target culture and readers are a prerequisite for the success of a translation.

Fifth, in terms of literary studies, the integration of the two skills of Lin Shu both as a writer and translator shows that literary translation is not only a linguistic activity of the transformation between two languages but also in a sense a literary re-writing activity. However, the latter has been long ignored in translation studies. Lin Shu's case study contributes to highlighting the dual nature of the translation activity.

4. Structure of the Book

This book is composed of seven chapters. Chapter 1 is an introduction to Lin Shu and his translation. It consists of the research focus and rationale, and the contributions of this study. The chapter highlights the Lin Shu translation phenomenon as a research issue and the necessity and significance of re-valuating Lin Shu and his translations.

Chapter 2 outlines my target-oriented approach to Lin Shu's translations, combining target-oriented/culture-oriented translation theories and readers-oriented criticism with my analysis of Lin Shu's translations. Differing from source-oriented translation theory and linguistic criticism, target/culture-oriented translation theories pay attention to a translator's role in a target culture, and the mutual influence between a translation and the target culture. Lin Shu insisted on accessibility by Chinese readers, privileging the target text, language and culture over source text, language and culture. As a result, his translations achieved a huge success in China at that time, influencing and changing Chinese culture and literature. Target/culture-oriented theories offer the feasibility of theoretically explaining and supporting Lin Shu's translation strategy, practice and method. These theories constitute a theoretical framework and approach for my re-evaluation of Lin Shu and his translations.

In Chapter 3, I trace the previous assessments and reviews on Lin Shu and his translations from Lin Shu's lifetime up to the present both in China and in the English-speaking world. These evaluations, favourable or unfavourable, political or linguistic, are insufficient to fully explain and identify the Lin Shu translation phenomenon, thus unable to offer a comprehensive assessment of Lin Shu as a translator. I will then focus on two key issues in the previous assessments: Lin Shu's attitudes towards the constitutional reforms of 1898 and the New Culture Movement (i.e., his attitude towards wenyanwen). The revolutionary movement in China from the early twentieth century means that Lin Shu's oeuvre – called *Lin yi xiaoshuo* - has been evaluated in political terms that devalue his work, especially in the People's Republic. The Chinese 'politics of translation' included a twentieth-century push for language reform that replaced literary Chinese (wenyanwen) with a written vernacular (then called baihua). Thus Lin Shu seemed to occupy a politically and linguistically conservative position in China's fraught history of modernisation. This diminished view of Lin Shu is no longer tenable on the facts, because the view is more on political grounds. Scholars are now reassessing Lin Shu and his works, affording him a revolutionary status in terms of modern Chinese translation and its cultural effects. In the chapter, I will re-examine and re-assess the relations between Lin Shu and the relevant political and cultural events, redressing earlier political verdicts imposed on Lin Shu.

Chapter 4 is a substantial examination of Lin Shu and his translations in the trans-cultural context to discern the relation between Lin Shu's translation and Chinese culture and translation, the cultural influence of his translations as well as his status as a translator in the history of Chinese translation. Lin Shu was an intellectual between two eras – imperial and modern China – whose work is a bridge between old and new China, between China and the West, and between prose and poetry. Lin Shu was the father of modern Chinese literary translation in terms of translation output and cultural impact. Lin Shu's translations resulted from the cultural needs. His choice and response to the original not only reflected his translation goal, but also embodied his consideration for the needs of the target culture and the expectation of the target readers. It is one of the reasons that his translations were so well received. In this chapter, to go further into Lin Shu's translations from the angle of the relations of Lin Shu and his translations to the trans-cultural context. I take Lin Shu's *Bali chahuanü yishi* (*La Dame aux Camélias*) as a case to explore the influence of this translated work on Chinese fiction. This translated novel brought in new ideological content, literary style and techniques, transfiguring Chinese novel writing among his contemporaries and later generations of writers. The analysis shows that Lin Shu played an important role in transforming Chinese fiction from traditional to modern.

Chapters 5 and 6 are comparative analyses of the target texts and the source texts. Through this textual comparison, I attempt to interpret Lin Shu's 'truthfulness' to the original and his adaptation of the original from a perspective of target/culture-oriented, culture-oriented theories.

In Chapter 5, aiming at the claim that Lin's translations lack of fidelity/ truthfulness to the original, I argue that Lin Shu translated the spirit, style and content (and sometimes the language itself) of the original works, rather than seeking a superficial and technical imitation. Lin Shu transcends translation as transmission, turning translation into an art. He is a translation poet, using China's classical heritage over two millennia to enrich his translations linguistically at a time when that same heritage was about to come under fierce attack. Lin Shu's truthfulness is primarily embodied in masterly use of classical Chinese to seek a poetic equivalence between ST and TT. It is a second reason for the success of his translations.

Chapter 6 concentrates on Lin Shu's translation strategy beyond the equivalence between ST and TT termed 'Poetic Equivalence', namely Lin Shu's adaptation of the original. It includes adaptation, omission, addition, alteration and abridgment, which is often regarded as untruthful to the original and is thus often criticized. In fact, the translation strategy of Lin Shu was mostly based on his attention to the needs of the Chinese culture and the acceptability by the Chinese readers. Besides, Lin Shu as a writer / translator saw translation as a literary re-writing. His strategy was to serve the literary effects of his translations. This strategy ensured him as a translator to play a most important role in affecting the Chinese readers, remoulding modern Chinese literature and initiating literary translation undertakings in China. We can find theoretical supports from recent cultural translation studies for Lin Shu's translation strategy and methods. Therefore Lin Shu's efforts in this respect ought to be acknowledged from the view of target/culture-oriented translation and readers' acceptance.

In Chapter 7, a conclusion is reached: Lin Shu was the father of modern Chinese literary translation. His translations not only reshaped the ideas of the intellectuals of his time in China, but also changed the Chinese culture and literature of that time. Therefore, Lin Shu's contributions and achievement in translation should be reaffirmed.

Chapter 2

Lin Shu's Works within
a Target/Culture-oriented Framework

This study is informed by translation theories that can offer an insight into the translational phenomenon of Lin Shu. The aim is to re-evaluate Lin Shu's translations. The study will make comprehensive use of target-oriented and culture-oriented translation theories as a basic theoretical framework for the evaluation. This chapter therefore discusses the background to various theoretical strands in translation studies that contribute to our target-oriented/culture-oriented approach. These strands are (1) target-oriented, (2) culture-oriented and (3) readers-oriented, etc.

1. Target/Culture-oriented Translation Theories

This study of Lin Shu's translations is approached through target-oriented and culture-oriented translation theories. The current dominant evaluation of Lin Shu's translations is mostly based on various linguistic criticisms; as a result, it is hard to avoid a negative attitude towards Lin Shu's translations. Target/culture-oriented translation theories, however, offer a possibility and a theoretical base for re-evaluating Lin Shu's translations through a different framework. Therefore, it is the first step of my study to elucidate these theories.

Target-oriented and culture-oriented translation theories overlap. One of the obvious features they share is their emphasis on the target or receptive culture. On the basis of the previous translation theories, target-oriented translation theory as a functionalist trend took shape in the 1970s, and ultimately superseded equivalence as a central concept in translation studies due to their orientation to the receptor. The main contributors to this theory are Itamar Even-Zohar, Gideon Toury. In 1978, Even-Zohar first introduced the concept 'polysystem' for the aggregate of literary systems.[1] Later Gideon Toury

---

[1] See Even-Zohar, Itamar, Papers in Historical Poetics, Porter Institute, Tel Aviv, 1978.

adopted this concept and developed it into the target-oriented descriptive translation theory.[1] Even-Zohar and Toury, in their respective essays, theorize literature as a 'polysystem' of interrelated forms and canons that constitute the 'norms' constraining the translator's choices and strategies.[2] According to the polysystem theorists, the social norms and literary conventions in the receiving culture ('target' system) govern the aesthetic presupposition of the translator and thus influence ensuing translation decisions.[3] In 'The Position of Translated Literature within the Literary Polysystem', Even-Zohar points out:

> Translated works do correlate in at least two ways: (a) in the way their source texts are selected by the target literature, the principles of selection never being uncorrelatable with the home co-systems of the target literature (to put it in the most cautious way); and (b) in the way they adopt specific norms, behaviors, and policies – in short, in their use of the literary repertoire – which results from their relations with the other home co-systems. These are not confined to the linguistic level only, but are manifest on any selection level as well.[4]

Even-Zohar's main contribution to translation theories is the establishment and development of the polysystem theory.[5] His polysystem theory is designed to treat translation as a complex and dynamic activity governed by system relations rather than by a priori fixed parameters of comparative language capabilities. This has subsequently led to studies on literary interference, viewed as intercultural relations. The significance of this theory lies in its emphasis on individual texts within their cultural context. Differing from earlier theorists' views that a text is totally autonomous, Even-Zohar argues that a text is always

---

[1] See Toury, Gideon, Search if a Theory of Translation, Tel Aviv University, Tel Aviv, 1980.

[2] See Even-Zohar, Itamar, 'The Position of Translated Literature within the Literary Polysystem', Poetics Today 11:1, 1990, and Toury Gideon, 'The Nature and Role of Norms in Translation' in Literature and Translation: New Perspectives in Literary Studies, eds. James S Holmes, José Lambert, Raymond van den Broeck. Leuven: acco,, 1978, pp.83-100.

[3] Gentzler, Edwin, Contemporary Translation Theories, Poutledge, London and New York, 1993, p.107

[4] Even-Zohar, 1990, pp.45-51.

[5] Even-Zohar, Itarmar, Papers in Historical Poetics, Tel Avi, 1978, and Polysystem Studies, a special issue of Poetics Today, 11:1, 1990.

correlated in many ways to various systems and elements of a given culture, and that translation is no longer a phenomenon whose nature and border are given once and for all, but an activity dependent on the relations within a certain cultural system. [1] According to Snell-Hornby, in this approach, 'translation is seen essentially as a text-type in its own right, as an integral part of the target culture and not merely as a reproduction of another text.' [2] Even-Zolar transcends the traditional translation theory that is largely based on linguistic models, and puts translated texts into a larger cultural context, thus carrying translation studies a major step forward. Keeping in step with Even-Zohar, Toury began to explore a new theory of translation: target-oriented translation theory, initially in his innovative book In Search of a Theory of Translation in 1980, and developed further in *Descriptive Translation Studies and Beyond* published in 1995. [3] He envisaged a descriptive and fundamentally target-oriented approach to translation (on which there is an elaboration later). Lefevere, on the basis of the seminal work of Even-Zohar and Toury, redefines their concepts of literary system and norm, thus strengthening this target orientation. Lefevere sees translation as 'refraction' or 'rewriting'. As he explains, 'a refraction (whether it is translation, criticism, historiography) tries to carry a work of literature over from one system into another'[4], and whether a foreign writer or text is accepted is determined or dependent on the need of the native or target system which is composed of 'patronage', 'poetics' and 'ideology'.[5] He concludes that a system approach to literary studies 'aims at making literary texts accessible to the reader by means of description, analysis, historiography, translation'.[6] The development of these translation theories is the framework for the re-interpretation of the translational phenomenon of Lin Shu.

(1) Toury's Target-oriented Translation Theory

---

[1] Even-Zohar, 1990, p.51.
[2] Snell-Hornby, Mary, Translation Studies: an integrated approach, John Benjamins Publishing Company, Amsterda/Philadelphia, 1988,p.24
[3] Toury, Gideon, Descriptive Translation Studies and Beyond, John Benjamins, Amsterdam/Philadelphia, 1995.
[4] Ibid., p.237
[5] Ibid., pp.237-238.
[6] Ibid., p.248.

Gideon Toury's target-oriented translation theory is highly applicable to Lin Shu's case, to explain the translational phenomenon of Lin Shu. Toury is the main proponent of the target-oriented descriptive translation theory, expounded in his major works, *Translation Norms and Literary Translation into Hebrew*[1], *In Search of a Theory of Translation*, and *Descriptive Translation Studies and Beyond*. Toury's basic view is that translators' main goal is to achieve acceptable translations in the target culture. They do not work in ideal and abstract situations nor desire to be innocent, but have vested literary and cultural interests of their own, and want their work to be accepted by another culture. Thus they manipulate the source text to inform as well as conform to existing cultural constraints. [2] It is evident that Toury's view orients towards the target text, readers and culture. Instead of attending to each and every aspect of Toury's theory, I concentrate on facets that can be applied in my work on Lin Shu.

Translators' main goals

In *In Search of a Theory of Translation*, Toury clearly states that the main goal of the translators is to have their translations accepted in the target culture, but they are not indifferent to the source text.[3] On the one hand, it is hard to find examples of translation considered 'inadequate' in the target culture; on the other hand, it is also hard to find the examples of translation that are the full linguistic equivalent to ST. The reason is that the translators' main goal is to make their translations accepted in the target culture. Therefore, the practical decisions in the translation process naturally resulted from a preference for the translators' initial intention; the changes are dominated by the cultural conditions of the receiving system.[4] Besides, he points out that no translation is entirely 'acceptable' to the target culture because it will always introduce new information and forms to that system, nor is any translation entirely 'adequate' to the original version, because the cultural norms cause shifts from the ST structures.[5]

---

[1] Toury, Gideon, Translation Norms and Literary Translation into Hebrew, Tel Aviv University, Tel Aviv, 1977.
[2] Edwin Gentzler, 1993, p. 134.
[3] Toury, 1980, p.137.
[4] Ibid., p.137.
[5] Ibid., p.94.

In Search of a Theory of Translation successfully pushes the concept of a theory of translation beyond the margins of a model restricted to faithfulness to the original, or of single, unified relationships between the ST and TT. Translation becomes a relative term, dependent upon the forces of history and culture. The role of translation theory is correspondingly altered, ceasing its search for a system from which to judge the product and now focusing on the development of a model to help explain the process that determines the final version.

In his *In Descriptive Translation Studies and Beyond*, Toury expands his target-oriented views on translation. Toury views the main goal of descriptive translation studies as a discipline to describe, explain and predict translational phenomena in a target culture. The subject matter of this discipline is the fact of real life rather than merely speculative entities resulting from preconceived hypotheses and theoretical models. Therefore it is empirical by its very nature and should be worked out accordingly. He believes that descriptive studies have been made within the disciplines other than translation studies, e.g., contrastive linguistics, contrastive texttology, comparative literature, [1] and focuses on 'function-process-product-oriented'. [2]

In this work, Toury intensifies his target-oriented position on translation. He believes that target culture factually governs the shape of the target product, for after all, the translations are designed to meet certain needs in the target cultural environment, and 'translations are indeed intended to cater for the needs of a target culture.' [3] Therefore the translators necessarily take the cultural needs into consideration in the process of translation: 'translators may be said to operate first and foremost in the interest of the culture into which they are translating, however they conceive of that interest.' [4]

Through his field study, documented in 'The History of Literary Translation into Hebrew', Toury finds that most source texts are selected for ideological reasons rather than linguistic and aesthetic reasons. [5] In other words,

---

[1] Toury, 1995, p. 1.
[2] Ibid., p.9.
[3] Ibid., p.28.
[4] Ibid., p.16.
[5] This field study was undertaken at the University of Tel Aviv in the 1970s. It catalogued the translations of fiction from five foreign languages into Hebrew and generated quantitative data.

linguistics and aesthetics play a very small role in the process of translation. The target texts, though inconformity with the principle of translation equivalence according to the linguistic criticism of translation, were accepted in the target culture as translations and occupied all positions from the centre to the periphery (still functioned as translations in the Hebrew polysystem).[1]

The role and function of translation

Toury claims that he centres his study on the position and function of translations (as entities) and translating as a kind of activity in a prospective target culture, and accordingly, he offers a definition of the term 'target-oriented':

> Translations have been regarded as facts of the culture which hosts them, with the concomitant assumption that whatever their function and identity, these are constituted within that same culture and reflect its own constellation. To be sure, it was by virtue of such a methodological starting point that this approach to the study of translations and translating in their immediate contexts earned the nickname of 'target-oriented'.[2]

In a detailed discussion of the role and function of translation in the target culture, Toury is aware of the cultural impact of translation: translation activities and their products not only can, but do cause changes in the target culture, yet he asserts that cultures resort to translating precisely as a major way of filling in gaps, whenever and wherever such gaps manifest themselves.[3]

Translation strategies

Toury also argues that translators of different periods produce different (more or less) translations owing to different strategies adopted when translating the same work. This difference is largely affected by different target cultural conditions. He says, 'at any rate, translators performing under different conditions (e.g., translating texts of different kinds, and / or for different audiences) often adopt different strategies and ultimately come up with

---

[1] Gentzler, 1993, pp.126-127.
[2] Ibid., p.24.
[3] Ibid., p.27.

markedly different products. Something has obviously changed here.'[1] Accordingly, he doubts that there exists a translation that is totally equivalent or identical to the original.

In Toury's views, translators' different stances in the source norms or target norms lead to their different pursuits for the product, because 'adherence to source norms determines a translation's adequacy as compared to the source text, subscription to norms originating in the target culture determines its acceptability.'[2] It is evident that Toury values 'acceptability', and regards it as the basis of translation strategies and methods that translators adopt. To make the target text acceptable in the target culture, it is inevitable to modify or sacrifice certain features of the source text, for 'the novelty of an entity derives from the target culture itself, and relates to what that culture is willing (or allowed) to accept vs. what it feels obliged to submit to modification, or even totally reject,'[3] on the ground that it reflects the source too closely.[4]

Toury's following summary is constructive here:

As we have observed, translation is basically designed to fulfil what is assumed to be the needs of the culture which would eventually host it. It does so by introducing into that culture a version of something which has already been in existence in another culture, making use of a different language, which – for one reason or another – is deemed worthy of introduction into it. The introduced entity itself, the way it is incorporated into the recipient culture, is never completely new, never alien to that culture on all possible accords. After all, much as translation entails the retention of aspects of the source text, it also involves certain adjustments to the requirements of the target system. At the same time, a translation is always something which hasn't been there before: even in the case of retranslation, the resulting entity – that which actually enters the recipient culture – will definitely not have been there before.[5]

It is believed that Toury's theory and model can be used to view Lin Shu's translation from a new perspective, contributing to the re-evaluation of Lin's

---

[1] Ibid., p.54.
[2] Ibid., pp.56-57.
[3] Ibid., p.166.
[4] Ibid., p.169.
[5] Ibid., p.166.

translation on a theoretical basis, turning critical interest to the relations between Lin Shu and the target cultural context, the cultural influence, reception and significance of Lin Shu's translations rather than the fidelity of Lin's text to the source text. Undoubtedly, it is of great significance to re-assessing Lin Shu as a translator and his translations. Yet, Toury's theory only partially explains the translational phenomenon of Lin Shu, namely, that the target culture dominated Lin's original intention and his translation process, and that Lin Shu paid more attention to making his translations acceptable to the reading public and to the target culture. Toury seems to lay only stress on the norms for translation, which social-culturally constrain 'the translator's choice and strategies'.[1] But, he rarely touch on the issue that how the translator influence the target culture. It is a fact that in the period of the transition from the old to the new in China, the target culture embodied two different orientations: a traditional culture and a newly emerging culture. Lin Shu did his translation in the period of the transition from the late Qing to the early Republic. Therefore the question is: how did Lin Shu's translations fit in with the traditional culture and the newly emerging culture? How did Lin Shu's translation influence or change the target culture? Toury's theory and model are insufficient to explain them. Yet the significance of Lin Shu's translations lies more in the influence of Lin Shu's translation on the target culture. An argument in this study is that, through Lin Shu's main translations, particular emphasis is laid on illustrating how translation creates possibilities for cultural acceptance, resistance, innovation and change. I will therefore introduce the cultural translation approach as a complement in the study.

(2) Culture-oriented Translation Studies

Lin Shu's translation practice is a phenomenon related to the target culture. A culture in transition. In this respect, culture-oriented translation theory offers a persuasive theoretical support for our understanding and assessment of Lin Shu's translations.

Culture-oriented translation theory is the combination of translation studies and culture studies, or more precisely, the introduction of culture studies into translation studies. Around the 1980s, translation studies began to shift

---

[1] Venuti, Lawrence, (ed.), Translation Studies Readers, Routledge, London and New York, 2000, p.123.

emphasis towards interdisciplinary culturally oriented, target oriented and reader-oriented approaches. In fact, target-oriented theory and culture-oriented translation theory overlap. These new trends are a reaction against the views of the early, more linguistic and source-oriented translation studies. First of all, the culture-oriented theorists argue that translation studies should be interdisciplinary and cultural. Bassnett views translation studies as 'bridging the gap between the vast area of stylistic, literary history, linguistics, semiotics and aesthetic'.[1] Snell-Hornby says: 'translation studies, as a culturally oriented subject, draws on a number of disciplines, including psychology, ethnology, and philosophy, without being a subdivision of any of them.'[2] Leppihalme identifies the main feature of the culture-oriented translation studies:

> As a result, much of the work that is currently being done in translation studies foregrounds social and cultural aspects of translation, with the emphasis on text in their macro-context; instead of simply pondering the translatability of source text, there is concern with the functioning of the target text in the target language and cultural context.[3]

A similar theoretical foundation is explored by Lefevere and Bassnett. They define translation as:

> A rewriting of an original text. All rewritings, whatever their intention, reflect a certain ideology and a poetics and as such manipulate literature to function in a given society in a given way. Rewriting is manipulation, undertaken in the service of power, and in its positive aspect can help in the evolution of a literature and a society. Rewritings can introduce new concepts, new genres, new devices, and the history of translation is the history also of literary innovation, of the shaping power of one culture upon another.[4]

---

[1] Bassnett, Susan, Translation Studies, Routledge, London and New York, 1991, p.6.
[2] Snell-Hornby, 1988, pp.2-3.
[3] Leppihalme, Ritva, , Culture Bumps: An Empirical Approach to the Translation of Allusions, Multilingual Matters Ltd, Clevedon, 1997, p.2.
[4]Lefevere, Andre and Bassnet, Susan, 'The Preface to Translation/History/Culture', Translation/History/Culture, ed Lefevere, Andre, Routledge, London and New York, 1992, p. ix.

If translation is a rewriting, as argued by lefevere and Bassnett, rewriting means deviating from the original to some extent in order to adapt the original to the target culture, making the translation more effectively function in the target culture. In terms of the basic function of translation, Lefevere lays stress on the impact of translation on the receptive culture:

> Translation is not just a 'window opened to another world', pious platitude. Rather, translation is a channel opened often not without a certain reluctance, through which foreign influences can penetrate the native culture, challenge it, and even contribute to subverting it.[1]

Lefevere also touches on the question of the receptiveness of translations. First of all, he emphasises readers' relation to translations: 'Readers decide to accept or reject translations'.[2] He argues that in order to make a translation acceptable to the receptive culture, the translator necessarily makes adaptations of the original. He says that 'not all features of the original are, it would seem acceptable to the receiving culture' and 'to make a foreign work of literature acceptable to the receiving culture, translators will often adapt it to the poetics of that receiving culture.'[3]

More important for this study is Lefevere's definition of a prose translation. In Lefevere's view, translation is divided into two types: 'a generous translation' and 'a servile translation'. The former clings closely to the ideas of its original, tries to match the beauty of its language, and renders its images without undue austerity of expression, even where it takes the greatest liberties; as a result, 'it becomes not just the faithful copy of the original, but a second original in its own right'. The latter tries to be scrupulously faithful, ruining the spirit by trying to save the letter', thus becoming 'very unfaithful'.[4] Evidently, Lefevere's 'a generous translation' means free translation. It shows his preference for free translation, for in his view, free translation is more truthful to the original.

Lefevere's views on translation are based on his examination and discussion of the historical fact of translation. When discussing Etienne Dolet (1509-1549), a French poet and translator, Lefevere concludes that translators

---

[1] Ibid., p. 2.
[2] Ibid., p. 5.
[3] Ibid., p. 7, 8.
[4] Ibid., pp. 12-13.

often 'try to recast the original in terms of the poetics of their own culture, simply to make it pleasing to the new audience and, in doing so, to ensure that the translation will actually be read.'[1] Upon discussing Nicolas Perrot d'Ablancourt(1606-1664), a French translator, Lefevere expresses his view on fidelity in translation:

> In most cases translators do not reject outright, but rather rewrite, both on the level of content and on the level of style since, as the Earl of Roscommon observes: 'Words in one language eloquently used/ Will hardly in another be excused.' 'Fidelity' in translation can therefore be shown to be not just, or even not primarily a matter of matching on the linguistic level. Rather, it involves a complex network of decisions to be made by translators on the level of ideology, poetics, and Universe of Discourse.[2]

Thus, Lefevere arrives at a conclusion: translation involves much more than the search for the best linguistic equivalent. Everybody would agree that 'the translator's first duty is to be faithful,' but the question at issue between them is, in what faithfulness consists. That question cannot be answered on purely linguistic grounds.[3]

Indeed, Lefevere's criticism and views on translation are quite pertinent to Lin Shu's case. If perceived from Lefevere's stand, Lin Shu's translations may be seen as rewritings of the originals, reflecting 'a certain ideology and a poetics', introducing 'new concepts, new genres, new device', and thus helping 'in the evolution of a literature and a society'.[4] Lefevere's statement — it is necessary for a translator to adapt the original to make his translation acceptable to the receptive culture — also applies to Lin Shu's case. Lin Shu often made additions, omission and abridgments of the originals to meet the needs of the Chinese culture or the acceptance of the readers of the time, which is one of the grounds for some critics' negation of his translation (see Chapters 3 and 6). Lin Shu's method of free translation can also be supported by Lefevere's claim that 'a generous translation' (free translation) is more faithful to the original, for Lin Shu's translations through free translation can 'cling closely to the ideas' of the

[1] Ibid., p. 26.
[2] Ibid., p. 35.
[3] Ibid.
[4] Ibid., p.ix.

originals, and match the beauty of their language and render their images 'without undue austerity of expression' (as seen in this study in Chatpter 5). It is obvious that applying culture-oriented translation theory to Lin Shu's case helps subvert the negative views on Lin's translations, and offers a perspective on culture and reception to the study of the translational phenomenon of Lin Shu.

(3) Readers' Response and Reception Theory

As mentioned in Chapter 1, Lin Shu's success in literary translation is primarily embodied in the fact that his translations evoked enormous repercussions among the Chinese reading public. Therefore, the application of readers' response and reception theory also helps our assessment of Lin's translations. In reality, target/culture-oriented translation theories embrace target-readers' response to and reception of translated texts. It is the combination of reader-response criticism with translation studies. Reader-response theory is one of the important recent developments in literary analysis as target culture translation theory develops. As Leppihalme states:

> As the current trend in translation studies increasingly focuses on how translations work in the target language culture, it is, inevitably, and despite the logistical problems involved, to readers that we must go to learn how they receive target texts. If there is a subtext to my efforts, it is that readers deserved the best. It is a plea for creative and varied use of strategies, and striving to produce a target-language version that will enable the target-text readers to participate in text production in their own way, see-ing connections and meaning instead of stumbling over culture bumps.[1]

Reader-response criticism arose from reception theory as a reaction against the New Criticism, or formalist approach. Reception theory is seen in two major fields: phenomenology and semiotics. Phenomenology focuses on the interaction between the act of reading and textuality: the reader should be seen as a creative and pro-active agent in the function and analysis of the text, and reading is a highly dynamic process, and the range of possible interpretation is as wide as the reading audience itself. As Ingarden argues, 'we can say that, with regard to the determination of the objectivities represented within it, every literary work is in principle incomplete and always in need of further

---

[1] Leppihalme, 1997, p.X.

36

supplementation; in terms of the text, however, this supplementation can never be completed.[1] The semiotic approach concentrates on the social and cultural constructions that take place in reading.[2] It is from these two fields that the reader-response criticism derives. The principal theorists of reader-response criticism are Wolfgang Iser,[3] Norman Holland[4] and Stanley Fish. Though there is no complete agreement among the theorists, they share the following basic views: their emphasis on the effect of the literary work on the reader, hence the moral-philosophical-psychological-rhetorical emphases in reader-response analysis. The second feature is that the text is relegated to secondary importance and the reader is of primary importance.[5] Among them, Fish's views, seen in his compilations of essays entitled *Is There a Text in This Class?*, are rather representative. [6] Fish's concern is with what 'is really happening in the act of reading'.[7]

In Fish's view, meaning inheres not in the text but in the reader, or rather the reading community. 'In the procedures I would urge,' he writes, 'the reader's activities are at the centre of attention, where they are regarded not as leading to meaning but as having meaning.'[8] It is the reader who determines the shape of text, its form, and its content. 'Different interpreters will see different intentions because they are a creation of the reader and not the author.'[9] As Booth points out, according to the reader-response theory, the text in literary interpretation is not the most important component; the reader is. In fact, there is no text unless there is a reader. The reader is the only one who can say what the text is; in a

---

[1] Ingarden, Roman, The Literary Work of Art: An Investigation on the Borderlines of Ontology, Logic and Theory of Literature, Northwestern University Press, Evanston, 1973(1931), pp.18-19.
[2] See Eco, Umberto, Semiotics and the Philosophy of Language, Indiana University Press, 1984.
[3] Refer to Iser, Wolfgang, The Act of Reading, Johns Hopkins University Press, Baltimore, 1978.
[4] Refer to Holland, Norman, The Dynamics of Literary Response, Oxford University Press, New York, 1968.
[5] Wilfred, L.Guerin, et al. A Handbook of Critical Approaches to Literature, Oxford University Press, New York and Oxford, 1992, p. 342.
[6] Fish, Stanley, Is There a Text in This Class?: The Authority of Interpretive Communities, Harvard University Press, Cambridge, 1980.
[7] Ibid., p.7.
[8] Ibid., p.158.
[9] Ibid., p.16.

sense, the reader creates the text as much as the author does. Critics should reject the autonomy of the text and concentrate on the reader and the reading process, the interaction that takes place between the reader and the text.[1]

The concern of reader-oriented theory with readers and reading process has attracted translation theorists' attention. They have introduced this theory into their translation studies. Leppihalme combines his translation study with reader-response criticism. He remarks that on the one hand, translators need to take the TT readers' needs, expectations and background knowledge into consideration so as to decide their appropriate translation strategies; on the other hand, the reader (even the reader of translations) is not just passive receiver of the text but a participator, even a co-author.[2] Both Leppihalme and Snell-Hornby touch on the double capacity of a translator both as a reader of the ST and a creator/producer of the TT. Leppihalme remarks: 'Translation complicates the communicative situation in that the translator, a receiver of the ST, becomes the text producer of the TT.'[3] Influenced by reception theory, Snell-Hornby argues:

> Equally important for literary translation in particular is a more recent development, also with roots in Germany, known as Rezeptionsäs Thetik, investigating the role of the reader .... For our purposes it must be emphasized that the role of the translator as reader is an essentially active and creative one, and that understanding must not be equated with a passive 'reception' of the text.[4]

In their work, Nida and Taber also introduced a reader-response approach to translation equivalence under the name of dynamic equivalence:

> Dynamic equivalence is therefore to be defined in terms of the degree to which the receptors of the message in the receptor language respond to it in substantially the same manner as the receptors in the source language. This response can never be identical, for the cultural and historical settings are too different,

---

[1] Booth, Wayne C., The Rhetoric of Fiction, The University of Chicago Press, Chicago and London, 1983, pp.37-39.
[2] Leppihalme, 1997, pp.20-21.
[3] Ibid., p.15.
[4] Snell-Hornby, 1988, p.42.

38

but there should be a high degree of equivalence of response, or the translation will have failed to accomplish its purpose.[1]

It is noticeable that their notion of reader's response lies in an understanding of the 'correctness' of the message.[2] According to them, the measure of the correctness of the message in the target text form is not in the form itself, but in how the target readership responds to the translated text. They illustrate their notion of reader's response through the diagram below:

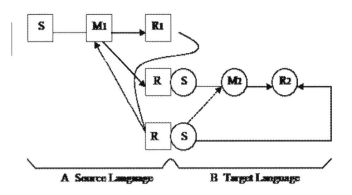

S = Author,   M = Message,   R = Receptor

Figure 2:1[3] __

In the diagram, the first message M1 was designed by the author S not for the bilingual person, but for the monolingual R1. The translator, who is both receptor and source (the R next to the S), first receives M1 as if he were an R1, and then produces in a totally different historical-cultural context a new message M2, which he hopes will be understood by the final receptor, R2. It is the original receptor's comprehension, R_1, which is to be compared with that of R_2 by scholarly judge (the bottom R next to the S). Moreover, it is the comprehension of M2 by R2, which must ultimately serve as the criterion of

[1] Nida, Eugene A. and Taber, Charles, and Taber, Charles Taber, The Theory and Practice of Translation, (United Bible Societies), E.J. Brill, Leiden, 1969, p.24.
[2] Ibid., p.23.
[3] Ibid.

correctness and adequacy of M_2. Obviously, the diagram shows a reasonable orientation that focuses on the crucial aspect of reader-dependency in translation.

In *Medio-translatology*, Xie Tianzhen shares the above-mentioned views. He states that in a broad sense, in literary translation, the receptor ought to include both the translator and the reader. The translator with the double capacity is either a reader of the ST or a receptor of the messages in the ST, but also a sender of the TT. Referring to Nida's ethnolinguistic model of translation,[1] he presents the diagram below to illustrate the double capacity of a translator:[2]

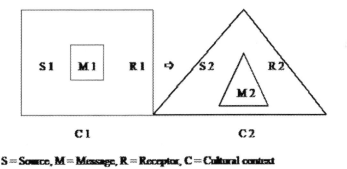

S = Source, M = Message, R = Receptor, C = Cultural context

In the diagram, S is source, namely, the sender of message; M is message, R is receptor. C represents the cultural context where message spreads. In C1—the cultural context where the original spreads, the translator is R1 – receptor; yet in C2 – the cultural context where the translation spreads, the translator becomes S2 – sender. From this diagram, the double roles that the translator plays can be clearly displayed. On these grounds, Xie Tianzhen first argues that 'the translation without readers is a pile of waste papers, totally valueless, for only by readers' reception can literary translation achieve its goal of literary

---

[1] Nida, Eugene A., Toward a Science of Translating, E. J. Brill, Leiden, 1964, pp.146-149.
[2] Xie Tianzhen 谢天振，Yi jie xue 译介学 Medio-translatology, Waiyu jiaoyu chubanshe, Shanghai, 1999, p.164.

40

communication'.[1] He lays further stress on the creative rebellion of the translator as a receptor/reader against the original. This creative rebellion seems to indicate that literary translation is a re-creation or re-writing. In this process of re-creation, the translator applies his own knowledge and experience in the process of re-creation in his own way. In addition, re-writing or re-creation is embodied as well in the fact that now and then the translator has to make adaptations of the original in order to adapt his translation to the receptive culture.

Certainly, reader-response criticism is valuable for the analysis of the translational phenomenon of Lin Shu. As a matter of fact, in his translating process, Lin Shu acted as both a reader (a member of the audience) and a writer. He both 'read' (though through another person) a text and created a text. As a reader (translator), he created (rewrote) the text as much as the author did, and at the same time, as an author (translator), he made full use of rhetorical strategies to ensure his texts to attract, capture and affect his readers. The relationship between them is illustrated below:

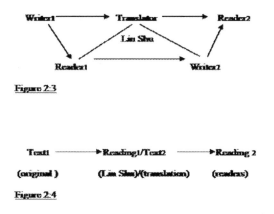

Figure 2:3

Figure 2:4

In terms of my analysis of Lin Shu's works, Figure 2:3 displays the relations between Lin Shu and Writer, Translator, Reader. In the process of translating, Lin Shu successively plays three roles: Reader1, Translator and Writer. First, he is Reader of Writer's work; then as a translator, he renders Writer's work into Chinese, thus becomes Writer. Finally, he provides Reader with his final work

---

[1] Ibid., p.165.

(translation), while Reader's positive response to his work guarantees him to be a successful translator. Figure 2:4, corresponding to Figure 2:3, shows the relations between text and reading: first, Lin Shu conducts his Reading (through a collaborator) of Text (the original); then through translating he produces Text (translation). Finally Text leads to Reading. Noticeably, in the process of translating, reader's response takes place twice: one is the Chinese reader Lin Shu's response to the text of the original writer, the other is the Chinese readers' response to the translator Lin Shu's translated text. These two responses in fact are the embodiment of the Chinese readers' understanding and interpretation of the original text and translated text in the target cultural context. As reader1/translator, Lin Shu interpreted the text1 from a perspective of Chinese culture. As a translator/writer2, Lin Shu rewrote the text1 and produced text according to the needs of the reader. As a result, the text achieves success due to the positive response of the reader. As far as Lin Shu's case is concerned, the process protrudes the reader (Lin Shu) and reader (Lin's readers)'s orientation to the target culture, which is beyond Nida's model, as Nida's notion of reader's response ultimately focuses on seeking the dynamic equivalence between the ST and TT.

Thus it is believed that target/culture-oriented translation theories as well as readers' response translation criticism will contribute to the analysis and understanding of Lin Shu's translations.[1]

---

[1] It is generally acknowledged that Lin Shu adopted a method of 'free translation' in literary translation, which has been long criticised by the linguistic scholars who have an inclination to literal translation, and has also been one of the main reasons for their belittling or even negating Lin Shu's translations. However, Lin Shu's approach to translation can be supported by the translation practice and theories in the history of Western translation. Target/culture-oriented translation theories have their own historical origins. The history of translation theory can be retraced from two major threads of the protracted debate on translation: word for word translation and sense for sense translation. The development of translation from sense for sense to dynamic equivalence shows that free translation has been a principal translation practice in the West (the sense for sense translators such as Cicero (106-43 B.C.), St Jerome, William Tyndale(1494-1535), Wyatt(1503-1542) and Surrey(1517-1547), Philemon Holland(1552-1637), William Morris(1834-1896) and Edward Fitzgerald, the advocates and theoreticians of the sense for sense translation such as Horace(65-68, B.C.), Etienne Dolet(1509-1546), George Chapman(1559-1634), John Denham(1615-1669), Abraham Gowley(1618-1667), John Drydon(1631-1700) and Alexander Fraser Tytler(1748-1813), and the theoreticians of equivalence in translation such as Eugene Nida). It helps explain

2. Cultural Translation Studies in China

Before the 1990s, linguistic criticism was nearly the only approach to assessing a literary translation. But the late 1990s, Chinese scholars have gradually started to view literary translation from a cultural perspective according to modern Western translation theories. A series of theoretical works pertaining to cultural translation appeared in succession such as Wang Bingqin's *Cultural Translatology*,[1] Wang Kefei's *A Critical History of Translational Culture*,[2] Liu Miqing's *An Outlined Theory of Cultranslation*,[3] Xie Tianzhen's *Medio-translatology*, Zhou Yi and Luo Ping's *A Critical View on Translation*,[4] Guo Jianzhong's *Culture and Translation*,[5] Zheng Hailing's *Literary Translatology*,[6] Wang Hongzhi's *Translation and Creation*.[7] They provide a fresh cultural perspective to view literary translation, particularly Chinese translation.

---

and support Lin Shu's case. Lin Shu mostly adopted free translation instead of sticking to the original word for word and sentence for sentence. Especially in early modern Chinese literary translation, due to the lack of translation theory and practice, free translation was a universal translational phenomenon. Like his contemporary translators, Lin Shu probed into literary translation according to his personal conditions, adopting free translation. As a result, he achieved great success in literary translation, initiating modern Chinese literary translation. Lin Shu's practice bears a strong resemblance to the methods of the translators in Western translation such as Cicero (106-43 B.C.), the early translators of Bible, George Chapman (1559-1634), Philemon Holland (1552-1637), Antoine Galland (1646-1715), William Morris(1834-1896), Edward Fitzgerald (1809-1863). Lin Shu's free translation belongs to this long history of free translation, therefore, ought not to be much censured.

[1] Wang Bingqin 王秉钦, Wenhua fanyi xue 文化翻译学 (Cultural Translatology), Nankai daxue chubanshe, Tianjin, 1995.

[2] Wang Kefei 王克非, Fanyi wenhua shi lun 翻译文化史论 (A Critical History of Translational Culture), Shanghai waiyu jiaoyu chubanshe, Shanghai, 1997.

[3] Liu Miqing 刘宓庆, Wenhua fanyi shi gang 文化翻译史纲 (An Outline Theory of Cultranslation), Hubei jiaoyu chubanshe, Wuhan, 1999.

[4] Zhou Yi 周仪 and Luo Ping 罗平，Fanyi yu Piping 翻译与批评 (A Critical View on Translation）, Hubei jiaoyu chubanshe, Wuhan, 1999.

[5] Guo Jianzhong 郭建中, (ed.), Wenhua yu fanyi 文化与翻译 (Culture and Translation), Zhongguo duiwai fanyi chuban Gongsi, Beijing, 2000.

[6] Zheng Hailing 郑海陵, Wenxue fanyi xue 文学翻译学 (Literary Translatology), Wenxin chubanshe, Zhengzhou, 2000.

[7] Wang Hongzhi 王宏志, (ed.), Fanyi yu chuangzhuo 翻译与创作(Translation and Creation), Beijing daxue chubanshe, 2000.

A relevant point here is that many of the Chinese commentators use Lin Shu as an example in their discussion of cultural translation. In *A Critical View on Translation*, Zhou Yi and Luo Ping include a section entitled 'The Translational Phenomenon of Lin Shu', in which they particularly argue in defense of Lin Shu's translations. They argue that some of Lin's translations are superior to the originals: 'striving to make the translation superior to the original should be the goal that translators are in pursuit of. Isn't it good to create a translation that can compare favorably with, even be better than its original so as to add a new exhibit to the world culture treasure-house?'[1] They also propose that the vitality of a translation should be one of the criteria of judging whether it is good or not. If it can entrance generations of readers, this translation is a treasure despite errors.[2] Obviously, the authors treat readers' acceptance and the target orientation of a translation as one of the criteria for assessing a literary translation. They also quote Xu Yuanchong's statement to strengthen their view: 'It may be said that translation is a contest between two cultures. In the contest, the translation should try to surpass the original it comes from. If a culture can learn from the strong points of other cultures to offset its weakness so as to develop the culture of all mankind, it should be the highest goal of a translator.'[3] Evidently, their views are similar to the target/culture-oriented translation theory.

In the preface to his *Translation and Creation*, Wang Hongzhi points out that, as far as early modern Chinese translation of foreign fiction is concerned, we cannot or should not judge whether a translation is truthful to its original simply by contrasting the former with the latter, because it is certain that 'infidelity' was common in the translations of that period from a linguistic view, but these translations exerted a great impact on Chinese culture. If the whole generation of translations is rashly demoted as 'reckless translations', it seems to be of little help to understand the translations of this period.[4] For this reason, Wang Hongzhi introduces a new cultural translation theory: translation is regarded as an activity with an intense political nature. The new ideas introduced by

[1] Zhou Yi and Luo Ping, 1999, pp.75-76.
[2] Ibid., p.125.
[3] Xu Yuanchong 徐渊冲, 'Yiwen neng shengguo yuanwen ma?' 译文能胜过原文吗? (Can the Translation Surpass the Original?), Fanyi de yishu 翻译的艺术(The Art of Translation), Beijing: Zhongguo duiwai chuban gongsi,1984, p.3.
[4] Wang Hongzhi, 2000, pp. 1-2.

translation can either subvert the present power structure or help establish a new social order and structure in the receptive culture, causing a great shock to politics, society and culture.[1] This translation outlook is actually based on the emphasis on translation itself and the receptive culture. On the one hand, it can be against the translation outlook that centers on the original; on the other hand, it can open up a new prospect for translation studies. Although Wang takes Lin Shu's translation of *Uncle Tom's Cabin* as an example to expound on the function of translation in the receptive culture, there is full examination of Lin Shu's translations in the new light. The editor provides a first-step for the re-evaluation of Lin Shu's translations, but he could not make further steps.

In *Literary Translatology*, Zheng Hailing believes that most scholars define translation from the perspective of linguistics. Their definitions cover literary translation, but ignore the particularity of literary translation.[2] Upon discussing the relations between translation and creation, he points out that in the West, from the Roman times to today, there have always been scholars who emphasize that literary translation is a literary creation, and have their eyes on its creativity. As well, Zheng Hailing takes Lin Shu's translation as an instance, believing that Lin Shu's achievement in literary translation 'gives the best evidence to Cicero's views on translation.'[3]

In *A Critical History of Translation Culture*, Wang Kefei responds to the culture-oriented translation studies in the West, introducing the concept of 'cultural translation' into China. He states that cultural translation studies emphasize cultural transmission. Translation plays an important role in this link-up, as language is the most important carrier of culture. Therefore, translation is the product of cultural exchange, and translation activity cannot do without culture. Cultural translation also pays special attention to the influence of translation on the target culture, the role of translation in the cultural history, particularly its role and goal in absorbing foreign culture.[4] Wang Kefei distinguishes cultural translation studies from other translation studies: 'As far as the fact of translation in history is concerned, we not only consider the quality of a translation, but also examine its role and influence in cultural

---

[1] Ibid.
[2] Zheng Hailing, 2000, p.36.
[3] Ibid.
[4] Wang Kefei, 1997, pp.2-3

exchange.'[1] In Wang's view, cultural translation embraces three features: First, from a perspective of cultural translation, the truthfulness of a translation is not in direct proportion to its role in cultural exchange. Second, a translator's motives and cultural needs are of vital importance to translation undertakings. Third, cultural translation studies emphasize the analysis and explanation of various translational phenomena and events from the view of cultural dissemination. Wang Kefei also argues that the history of cultural translatology focuses on the study of the significance and influence of translation on culture (especially the receptive culture), and the mutual relations between translation and culture. Wang Kefei does not apply his general theory to Lin Shu or use Lin Shu's case to illustrate his theory. However, he cites Qian Zhongshu's whole essay, 'The Translations of Lin Shu', in his work, which shows in reality his attention to the cultural significance of Lin Shu's translations. These cultural translation works in Chinese are the important reference for a re-evaluation of Lin Shu's translations.

Overall, Target-oriented translation theories since the 1970s in the West and cultural translation studies since the late 1990s in China offer an valuable theoretical foundation for re-evaluating Lin Shu's translations, helping expound the influence and significance of Lin Shu's translations in cultural dissemination, and the success of Lin's translations and his translation strategies. Therefore it may be used as a theoretical framework for an analysis of Lin Shu's translation motives and strategies as well as clarify the effectiveness of Lin Shu's translation method. The above-mentioned theories should be concretely applied and fulfilled through the following approaches.

(1)Target/culture-oriented translation approach: target/culture-oriented translation theories are designed to be a theoretical framework for this study. Target-oriented translation theory, especially Toury's theory, will provide a theoretical foundation in order to assess how the target culture influenced Lin Shu's translational motive and his choice of the originals, the role of Lin Shu as a translator in the target culture, the effects of Lin Shu's target text. Culture-oriented translation theory will guide the investigation of the impact of Lin Shu's translations on the target culture, the cultural significance of Lin Shu's translations, and the new cultural factors introduced by Lin Shu's translations as well as the response of Lin Shu as a reader to the originals and the response of

---

[1] Ibid., p.6.

the target readers to his translations so as to show the popularity and success of Lin Shu and his translations.

(2) Contextual analysis: contextual analysis is helpful for viewing and understanding Lin Shu's translation from a target/culture translation perspective. In this study, it will include the investigation of the cultural context in which Lin Shu lived and translated, Lin Shu's role and intellectual activities and the relations between Lin Shu and his cultural context, the context, in which various important political, cultural and translational events interweaved and in which Lin Shu's translations were produced. By examining the prefaces and postscripts Lin Shu wrote for his translations, I will outline Lin Shu's attitude towards the relevant political and cultural events, which partly contribute to the controversy in the assessment of Lin Shu and his translations.

(3) Textual analysis: comparative textual analysis of the selected translations by Lin Shu and the originals will be conducted. Some of Lin Shu's most influential translated works such as *Bali Chahuanü yishi(La Dame aux Camélias)*, *Heinu yu tian lu(Uncle Tom's Cabin)*, and *Kuai rou yusheng shu(David Copperfield)* will be selected as samples of textual analysis. Through such a comparative analysis, the features and strong points of Lin Shu's translations can be illustrated and highlighted and a further understanding of such issues can be acquired, e.g. the 'fidelity' or equivalence of Lin Shu's translated texts to the original texts, Lin Shu's translation approaches to the source text such as adaptation, addition, omission and abridgement.

Before applying this theoretical framework to Lin Shu's work, I turn to over a century of critical literature on Lin Shu in the next chapter.

Chapter 3

Critical Literature Review on Lin Shu

Since target/culture-oriented translation theories attach due importance to the role, function, influence and significance of translation in the target culture, it is necessary to examine scholars' various critical response to Lin Shu's translations during different periods since he first began his translation in 1899. Lin Shu is best known as a translator, although his classical Chinese prose, fiction, poems, paintings and calligraphy are also of considerable importance. My concern here is the reviews and criticisms of Lin Shu as a translator. No sooner had his translation *Bali Chahuanü yishi* (*La Dame aux Camélias*) appeared in 1899 than it became a best seller in China. His success in literary translation offered him a major reputation. Unfortunately, for various reasons, Lin Shu was involved in the heated debates that took place in the New Culture Movement in China, in and after which, Lin Shu was labelled a reactionary man of letters and a representative figure who upheld old Chinese culture. Thus, Lin Shu's merits and achievements in literary translation were ignored or even negated for political reasons. In fact, a political judgment on him replaced a professional evaluation of his translations. Since then Lin Shu has been a controversial figure in the history of Chinese literature and translation, both personally and professionally. One of the main reasons is that the political climate of the different periods in China influenced the evaluation of Lin Shu and his translations. In this chapter, I will review the criticisms of Lin Shu to set the context of my re-evaluation.

1. Chinese Criticism

In China, from Lin Shu's lifetime till now, there are numerous reviews and criticisms of Lin Shu and his translations, favourable and unfavourable. These literatures are scattered in various newspapers, journals and books from literary, cultural and translation circles. There are also some influential monographic studies such as Zheng Zhenduo's 'Mr Lin Qinnan', Han Guang's *Lin Qinnan* and

Qian Zhongshu's 'The Translations of Lin Shu'. These works are invaluable to our study, and are discussed in details in this section.

(1) Affirmation by Lin Shu's Contemporaries

The appearance of Lin Shu's *Bali chahuanü yishi* (*La Dame aux Camélias*) in 1899 first attracted reviewers' attention to Lin Shu's translation. Its publication succeeded beyond Lin Shu's expectation, and had an intense sympathetic response among the Chinese readers. In 1904, Yan Fu made his famous remark: 'a book titled *Chahuanü* has thoroughly broken the hearts of China's young people in love.' [1] Kang Youwei also praised Lin Shu: 'The two talents for translation in this world are Yan Fu and Lin Shu.'[2] In 'A Biography of Lin Shu', Chen Yan (1856–1937), one of Lin Shu's students, said, 'After *Bali Chahuanü yishi* was published, ten thousand copies of the book were sold, for Chinese had never seen it before.'[3] Qiu Weiyuan, a well-known writer, widely publicized this book in the newspapers of that time. He thought that Lin Shu's translation most vividly depicts the temperament of the Europeans in a Chinese style, and shows great ingenuity. 'The wonderful descriptions in his translated work are subtle and skilful, very pathetic and stirring so that readers can see that Marguerite's charming soul, Armand's tears, Dumas fils's literary conception and Lin Shu's understanding and writing style at the same time, which are the acme of perfection.'[4] Indeed, a great number of reviews on *Bali Chahuanü yishi* at that time showed that the Chinese readers were loud in their praises and how *Bali Chahuanü yishi* aroused their sympathy for the heroine and influenced the generation of writers. Judging from the reviews, the success of this translation by Lin Shu established his reputation as a translator. It was also because of the success of *Bali Chahuanü yishi* that Lin Shu started to devote himself to literary translation. His later translations such as *Heinu yu tian lu* (*Uncle Tom's Cabin*)，*Jiayin xiao zhuan* (*Joan Haste*), *Sakexun jie hou yingxiong lüe* (*Ivanhoe*) and *Kuai rou*

[1] Yan Fu 严复, Yan Fu ji 严复集 (A Collection of Yan Fu's Works), Vol.2, Zhonghua shuju, Beijing, 1986, p.365.
[2] A Ying 阿英, 'Guanyu Bali chahuanü yishi'关于《巴黎茶花女遗事》(On Bali chahuanu yishi) in Lin Shu's Translations, Shangwu yinshuguan, 1981, p.53.
[3] Fujian tongzhi 福建通志（General Annals of Fujian）, The Republic of China edition, Vol.9, 1918, p.26.
[4] Qiu Weiyuan 邱炜爰, Hui chen shi yi 挥尘拾遗(Cleaning and Finding), quoted in A Ying, 1960, p.408.

yusheng shu (*David Copperfield*) further strengthened his reputation as the most influential literary translator in China.

(2) Condemnation during the May Fourth New Culture Movement

Despite the overwhelming success of Lin Shu's translations and favourable reception by the literary critics earlier as discussed above, the occurrence of the New Culture Movement in the second decade of the 20th century signalled the turning point in the evaluation of Lin Shu and his translations. Such leading political and literary figures as Chen Duxiu (1879–1942), Li Dazhao (1889–1927), Hu Shi, Qian Xuantong, Lu Xun and Zhou Zuoren opposed 'old morality' while advocating 'new morality', and opposed classical Chinese while advocating vernacular Chinese. Lin Shu could not agree with them, because from their radical views Lin Shu detected a tendency towards total the repudiation of traditional Chinese culture. Lin Shu was versed in classical Chinese writing, so he opposed the radical positions of the leading figures of the Movement on abolishing classical Chinese and superseding it with vernacular Chinese. He published two articles 'Should Classical Chinese Be Abolished?'[1] and 'On the Growth and Decline of Classical Chinese and Vernacular Chinese'[2] to defend classical Chinese, which incurred the disfavour of the advocates of the New Culture Movement. These advocates of the New Culture Movement were determined to provoke a cultural debate with Lin Shu. Originally, Lin Shu had no intention of opposing the New Culture Movement and just wanted to express his different opinions from more radical views, but he was finally trapped into heated debates on new and old cultures. Qian Xuantong, by the alias of 'Wang Jingxuan', published a letter in *New Youth*,[3] pretending to oppose New Literature. Meanwhile Liu Bannong published his letter in reply, in which he refuted Wang's views.[4] They all made pointed allusions to Lin Shu in their letters. Actually, it was their scheme to provoke and challenge Lin Shu. As Lydia H. Liu said:

---

[1] Published in 1917. The journal where this article was first published remains unknown.

[2] Published in Wenyi congbao 文艺丛报(Literature and Art Series), No.1, April 1919.

[3] See Xin qingnian 新青年(New Youth), 4:3, 1918.

[4] The Horizon Publishing Co. (eds.), Essays on May Fourth Movement, The Horizon Publishing Co., Taipei, 1975, p.22.

The episode, well known to literary historians, involved two radical thinkers impatient with the general indifference of old-style literati to their call for literary revolution who wanted to provoke a reaction. To the end, Qian Xuantong fabricated a Wang Jingxuan, who attacked progressive thinkers in the voice of an old-style literatus. This fictional challenge was countered by his friend Liu Bannong, who was instantly jointed by others until the debate escalated to the famous battle between the defenders of classical Chinese headed by Lin Shu and the *New Youth* advocates of the modern vernacular language.[1]

First, in 'A letter to the Editors of *New Youth*', Qian Xuantong used classical Chinese on purpose and pretended to worship Lin Shu, having the greatest esteem for Lin Shu's views and translations. The passage concerning translation is quoted below:

> Mr Lin [Shu] is a contemporary literary giant. He is expert in adopting the style of the fiction of Tang dynasty in the translation of foreign novels. Their content is about Westerners, but the literary style in the translations is Chinese, which makes readers almost forget that these novels relate to Westerners' life. It is beyond the reach of those ordinary writers, yet against all expectations; your journal defamed him on the pretext of incoherence that has happened in his translations. According to my observation, Zhou [Zuoren]'s translation of Dostoevski's novel, published in your journal (No.3, Vol.4), may be really regarded incoherent. I don't understand foreign languages, so I don't know the original. If the original were also so incoherent as this translation, it would be better not to be translated. If Lin Shu simply wants to translate it, he should do it in coherent Chinese. He ought not to make his translation fragmented and make the literary style and atmosphere incoherent. You thought that Mr Lin's excellent classical Chinese translation is incoherent while publishing Zhou's awkward

---

[1] Liu, Lydia H., *Translingual Practice: literature, national culture, and translated modernity – China, 1900 –1937*, Stanford University Press, Stanford & California, 1995, p.233.

translation. It is really not a wise move.[1]

In spite of the sarcasm, Qian Xuantong clearly stated some features of Lin Shu's translation as distinguished from Zhou Zuoren's.

Liu Bannong's 'A Letter in Reply to Wang Jingxua' appeared in the same issue of *New Youth*. In the letter, Liu Bannong ostensibly rebutted Wang Jingxuan, in reality, to belittle and attack Lin Shu and his translations. He claimed that Lin Shu's literary translations could only be seen as 'light readings' rather than literary works. His main censures are that firstly, 'it happened frequently that he translated those exceedingly worthless foreign works, but never concerned himself with those really excellent works';[2] secondly, there were too many errors in Lin's translations. 'If his translation is compared with the original, the spirit of the original has been distorted beyond recognition due to his wilful deletion and alternation';[3] and thirdly, Lin Shu adopted a Chinese style to translate foreign novels. Liu Bannong added,

It must be understood that literary writing differs from translation. Literary writing should take itself as the principal part while translation should take the original as the principal part. Thereupon, translation can only make the native language close to the foreign language rather than alternating the meaning and spirit of the foreign language so as to be close to the native language.[4]

However, Liu Bannong's rebukes were rebutted by other scholars such as Zheng Zhenduo, Han Guang and Qian Zhongshu. They acknowledged that at least more than forty works among Lin Shu's translations belonged to world masterpieces, and that until then nobody but Lin Shu had achieved such a great deed in literary translation. Even those so-called second-rate foreign works that Lin Shu translated were not worthless. Therefore, Liu's first charge of Lin Shu is quite arbitrary. Indeed, Lin Shu often made some alterations to the original, primarily because he was influenced by his collaborators' oral interpretation as

---

[1] As quoted in Zhang Ruoying 张若英, (ed.), Xin wenxue yundong shiliao 新文学运动史料(Research Materials concerning the History of the New Literature Movement, Guangming shuju, Shanghai, 1935, p.113.
[2] Xue Shuizhi and Zhang Juncai, 1982, p.149.
[3] Ibid.
[4] Ibid., p.146.

well as trying to make his translations readily acceptable to the Chinese readers. Moreover, we should consider the historical contexts. Zheng Zhenduo, Han Guang, Qian Zhong Shu, Mao Dun thought that many of Lin Shu's translations preserve the spirit and style of the originals, and those scholars such as Hu Shi and Zhou Zuoren, who had opposed Lin Shu, also had to acknowledge these points. Therefore, Liu's second sensure of Lin Shu is quite wilful as well. Liu's third censure of Lin Shu is arguable. In fact, it involves the debates about target-oriented translation versus source-oriented translation. Undoubtedly, Liu Bannong's criticism of Lin Shu's translations reflected his emphasis on the source text. The main problem with Liu Bannong's rebukes is that they ignored the great cultural influence and significance of Lin Shu's translations. Such advocates of the New Culture Movement as Qian Xuantong and Liu Bannong tailored criticism of Lin Shu and his translations to the requirements of a cultural revolution. Their criticisms, however, reflected the central feature of Lin Shu's translation: an attention towards the target culture and target readers.

The supporters of *New Youth* achieved their desired results: Lin Shu was provoked to anger. He published two short stories 'Jingsheng'[1] and 'Yao meng' (A Dream of Demons)[2] to attack the advocates of the New Culture Movement. Then he published his open letter to Cai Yuanpei (1868–1940), the president of Peking University, in which Lin Shu reproached Peking University for 'seeking pleasure from overturning Confucius and Mencius and uprooting traditional moral principles'.[3] On 18 March, 1919, Cai Yuanpei wrote a letter in reply in which he rejected Lin Shu's censure, clearly expressing his disapproval to Lin Shu's attack on vernacular Chinese, arguing in favour of vernacular Chinese and its advocates like Hu Shi, Qian Xuantong and Zhou Zuoren. [4] When talking about translation, Cai argued:

> Vernacular Chinese and classical Chinese are different only in form but the same in content. The original languages of *Tianyan lun* (*Evolution and Ethics*), *Fa yi* (*Spirit of Law*), *Yuan fu* (*An Inquiry into the Nature and Cause of the Wealth*

---

[1] It appeared in New Shen Bao 新中报，No.17-18, Febuary, 1919.
[2] It appeared in New Shen Bao 新中报, No.18-22, 1919.
[3] Zhang Ruoying, 1935, p.101.
[4] The letter was published in Beijing Daxue Rikan 北京大学日刊(Beijing University Daily), 21 March, 1919.

of Nations) and so on are vernacular, but Yan Fu translated them in classical Chinese; the novels of Dumas fils, Dickens, Haggard and so on are also in vernacular, but you (Lin Shu) translated them in classical Chinese. Can you say that the translations of you and Yan Fu are better than the originals?[1]

On affirming the principle of 'ideological freedom', Cai Yuanpei cited the relation between Lin Shu's translating and teaching as an example:

> You have translated the novels such as *Chahuanü* (*La Dame aux Camélias*), *Jiayin xiaozhuan* (*Joan Haste*) and *Hong jiao hua jiang lu* (*Beatrice*). Moreover, you have also lectured on classical Chinese and ethics in different schools. If someone censures you for teaching literature by this sort of novels, and for teaching ethics by the novels relating to prostitution, adultery and chasing a married woman, will it be worth laughing?[2]

Thus it can be seen that Lin Shu did not think that the love stories in his translated novels against his conception of literature and ethics.

Cai Yuanpei's letter actually backed up the advocates of the New Culture Movement. Lin Shu's short stories offended them. Henceforth, Lin Shu was seen as the representative of opposing new culture and new literature, and was fiercely attacked by the new school of scholars, although Lin Shu made concessions to avoid further debates. Lu Xun, Zhou Zuoren and Qian Xuantong continued to write articles for *New Youth* to assail Lin Shu. They also tried to belittle Lin Shu's translations. Qian Xuantong said in his letter to Chen Duxiu: 'The eminent writer [Lin Shu] adopted the writing style of *Liaozhai zhi yi* (*Strange Stories from Liaozhai*) and worked with others to translate foreign novels. His translations mostly deviated from the original meanings, and contained his pedantic and wrong comments. It would be best not to read this kind of translation.'[3]   Liang Qichao, in *An Introduction to the Learning of Qing Dynasty*, also stated,

> Lin Shu translated more than one hundred foreign novels; they were very popular for a while, although all his translations are from the second or

---

[1] Zhang Ruoying, 1935, p.108.
[2] Ibid., p.109.
[3] Han Guang 寒光, Lin Qinnan 林琴南, Zhonghua shuju, 1935, p.37.

third-rate writers' works. Lin Shu was expert in the classical prose of the Tongcheng School. Whenever he translated a book, he always write an article to propagate traditional morality, which is irrelevant to the new ideas.'[1]

Obviously, the negative views on Lin Shu's translations were mainly initiated by a number of noted Chinese scholars, primarily on the basis of the so-called Lin Shu's conservative views on the New Culture Movement. Their views are mostly political, lacking impartiality and objectivity. As a result, Lin Shu's reputation suffered a disastrous decline. His paramount position in the literary world, which had been established through his translations, collapsed. His conservative views in later years also brought sully to his achievement in translation. His translations were depreciated, mocked, and negated.

(3) Assessment after Lin Shu's Death

Sympathetic and affirmative reviews on Lin Shu and his translations revived after Lin Shu's death. Among them, the most important and influential are Zheng Zhenduo's 'Mr. Lin Qinnan' and Han Guang's *Lin Qinnan*,[2] as well as the comments of those who had attacked Lin Shu in the earlier stage. These comments affirm the influence of Lin Shu's translations on Chinese culture and readers in varying degree.

<u>General reviews</u>

In *An Outline History of Chinese Literature,* Tan Zhengbi addressed the criticism that Lin Shu's translations were mostly the works of the second or third-rate foreign writers, and untruthful to the originals. He argued that Lin Shu's success in translation lies in the fact that he could select and translate the works of famous foreign writers in the light of classical Chinese writings and apply the original Chinese tone and classical Chinese while retaining the meaning of the original, and that Lin Shu's early translations were celebrated for

---

[1] Ibid., pp.37-38.

[2] Han Guang's Lin Qinnan records some important reviews on Lin Shu and his translations, favorable or unfavorable, most of which are valuable references for us, as it is extremely hard to find them now due to the lapse of time. Some scholars' comments in this section are quoted from this work.

their faithfulness.[1]

In 'To Commemorate the century of the Death of Walter Scott', Ling Changyan affirmed the achievement of Lin Shu in translating Scott's *Ivanhoe* by saying that Scott's novel was his first step in knowing Western literature. He continued that 'for modern Chinese culture, the significance of introducing it into China is under no circumstances inferior to *Tianyan lun* (*Evolution and Ethics*) and *Yuan fu* (*An Inquiry into the Nature and Cause of the Wealth of Nations*). Scott has let the Chinese know that excellent literature exists beyond China too, spurring us to walk towards literary revolution.'[2]

In *My Childhood*, Guo Moruo stated that, compared with the original, Lin's translations were more attractive to the Chinese readers. For example, Lin Shu's translation of *Joan Haste* (*Jiayin xiaozhuan*) was considered better of the original due to his mastery of classical Chinese as well as his ability to appreciate literature. On discussing Lin's *Sakexun jie hou yingxiong Lue* (*Ivanhoe*), he affirmed that 'Lin's translation concretely and vividly presented the romantic spirit of the original to me in spite of quite a few errors and abridgments'.[3] Moreover, he felt that Lin's translation *Yin bian yan yu* (*Tales from Shakespeare*) made a stronger impression on him than Shakespeare's originals. Guo Moruo also touched on the problem of the unfair treatment of Lin Shu:

> Several years ago, when we fought for vernacular Chinese, Lin Qinnan was our enemy. At that time, the criticism on him naturally had the inclination to negate him totally, but his historical position cannot be blotted out. His contribution to literature is the same as Liang Qichao's contribution to cultural criticism. Both of them were representatives of the period of the bourgeois revolution and persons with great achievements.[4]

Guo Moruo, one of the advocates of the New Culture Movement, frankly admitted the unfair criticism on Lin Shu during the New Culture Movement. Guo Moruo confessed that Lin Shu's translated novels had a decisive influence on his literary inclination.[5] Guo Moruo's remarks paid more attention to the impact of Lin's translations on a reader, or rather, a reader's reception as well as

---

[1] Ibid., pp.28-29.
[2] Ibid., p.41.
[3] Ibid., p.43
[4] Ibid., pp.42-43.
[5] Ibid., p.43

56

their impact on the target Chinese culture.

In *A History of Chinese Literature in the Last Thirty Years*, Chen Bingkun (1898–1990) emphasized one of the main features of Lin Shu's translation: Lin Shu liked to express his views, reviewing literature in the prefaces to his translations, among which there were many bold comments. Chen Bingkun said, 'these comments really stunned the old scholars who looked down on Western literature and asserted that there was no literature in the West'[1]. Indeed, thanks to Lin Shu's comments in the prefaces to his translations, today's critics can have a better understanding of Lin Shu's ideas.

Many scholars considered Lin Shu an initiator of the literary translation undertakings in China. Zhang Jinglu thought that since Lin Qinnan translated Dumas fils's sentimental novel *La Dame aux Camélias*, an unprecedented path to fiction writing was opened up, and the happy ending in the story of 'talent meets beauty' was broken through. [2] The world of Chinese fiction was greatly influenced by this translate novel, and thus Chinese scholars became interested in translation. Gu Fengcheng also stated that in China, people's interest in translation was aroused by Lin Shu.[3]

However, such advocates of the New Culture Movement as Hu Shi and Zhou Zuoren who had treated Lin Shu as an opponent and foe, to some extent, realized and rectified their extreme views on Lin Shu later on. It is worth mentioning here that during the New Culture Movement, Lin Shu was attacked by Hu Shi and others for defending classical Chinese. After Lin Shu's death, Hu Shi gave a relatively objective appraisal of Lin Shu and his translations. In *Chinese Literature in the Last Fifty Years*, Hu Shi believed that Lin Shu's translations have their special 'flavour', and that he had a penetrating grasp of the humour in the originals. Lin Shu's main defect, according to Hu Shi, was that he could not read the original text. Yet after all he was a man of literary genius, therefore if he worked with a good assistant, his understanding of the literary interest of the original was often much more profound than many who could read foreign languages.[4] Hu Shi pointed out that many of the critics could not thoroughly

---

[1] Ibid., p.46.

[2] Ibid., p.51.

[3] Ibid., p.58.

[4] Hu Shi 胡适, Wushi nianlai Zhongguo zhi wenxue 五十年来中国之文学 (Chinese Literature in the Past Fifty Years) in Hu Shi wencun 胡适文存 (The Selected Essays of Hu Shi), Vol.2, Yadong Tushuguan, Shanghai, 1930, p.122.

grasp the original, or use vernacular Chinese as well as Lin Shu use classical Chinese, they nevertheless wanted to criticize Lin's translations, and Lin Shu was really wronged.[1] Then Hu Shi concluded:

In all fairness, on the whole Lin Shu made achievements in his experiment in applying classical Chinese to the translation of foreign novels. Classical Chinese had been never used in the writing of a novel, but to one's surprise Lin Shu rendered over one hundred novels in classical Chinese and encouraged lots of people, who modeled themselves on him, to translate many novels in classical Chinese as well. Classical Chinese lacks a style of humor, but to one's surprise, Lin Shu translated Irving and Dickens's works. Classical Chinese is not good at the description of love, but to one's surprise, Lin Shu translated *La Dame aux Caméllias*, *Joan Haste* and so on. Since Sima Qian, there has never been such a great achievement in the application of classical Chinese. [2]

In his letter of February 21, 1928 to Zeng Mengpu (1872–1935), Hu Shi was amazed to find that the young generation could not surpass Lin Shu in the translation of foreign literature:

The Chinese may have read Western literature for nearly sixty years, but the translated famous works have not reached 200 kinds. Among them, most came from Lin Shu who knew no foreign languages. It is really a surprising thing! In the last thirty years, more people can read English literature, yet nobody dares to translate famous English works.[3]

Zhou Zuoren's views on Lin Shu also underwent a dramatic change. During the New Culture Movement, he mocked and attacked Lin Shu and his translations with Qian Xuantong, Liu Bannong and others, although his own early translations were influenced by Lin's translations. For example, in the magazine *Yu Si* (No.4), he said, Lin Shu did translation just for contribution fee:[4] 'During the May Fourth Movement, the reactionary literati under the leadership of Lin Shu, due to their hostility towards the views of *New Youth*, attempted to urge Xu

---

[1] Ibid.
[2] Ibid.
[3] Huang Jiade 黄嘉德, Fanyi lun ji 翻译论集(Essays on Translation), Xifeng she, Shanghai, 1940, p.33.
[4] Han Guang, 1935, p.15.

Shuzheng (a warlord) to repress them'.[1] In his *Zhitang's Reminiscences*, Zhou Zuoren also said that Lin Shu 'considers himself to be a defender of the holy morality, and attempted to strike against Beijing University with the aid of the military force', and Lin Shu's short stories 'attempted to destroy dissident thought with the help of outside forces'.[2] It seems that these statements were not supported by any facts. After Lin Shu's death, Zhou Zuoren also to some extent rectified his views, as the trend to re-affirm Lin Shu and his translations appeared in the Chinese literary world. However, unlike Hu Shi, Zhou acknowledged Lin Shu's outstanding achievement and influence in literary translation, but he continued with some of his negative views on Lin Shu till his later years.

In November 1924, soon after Lin Shu's death, Zhou Zuoren wrote a short article in memory of Lin Shu, in which he acknowledged that it was because of Lin Shu that the Chinese writers learnt about foreign literature beyond China, and imitated his translations.' Then he pointed out the fact:

> After the Literary Revolution of 1919, everyone is entitled to condemn Lin Shu, but nobody has tried one's best to introduce foreign literature and has translated world masterpieces as Lin Shu did. Today even the rickshaw men can speak English, and there are numerous experts in the English language who are keen on showing off on public occasions, but where are the translations of the English masterpieces? Is there anything else apart from Lin Shu's translated works in classical Chinese? Let us look back. Mr Lin had obsolete ideas and an eccentric writing style and knew no foreign languages, yet he unexpectedly translated more than 100 novels, excellent or poor. Let us also look back at those youth who are lazy and swollen with arrogance. We feel extremely ashamed for them. Mr Lin did not know what literature and 'ism' is, yet owing to his devotion to the undertaking, he might be our teacher. I must say that my love for the truth surpasses my

---

[1] Zhou Qiming 周启明, 'Lu Xun he wan Qing wenxuejie' 鲁迅和晚清文学界 (Lu Xu and the late Qing Literary World', in Research Materials on Lin Shu, eds. Xue Shuizhi & Zhang Juncai, 1998, p.240.

[2] Zhou Zuoren 周作人, Zhitang huiyilu 知堂回忆录 (Zhitang's Reminiscences), San Yu Stationery & Publishing Co., Hong Kong, 1974, pp. 336-337.

love for our teacher.[1]

Compared with his early remarks on Lin Shu, Zhou Zuoren's statement seems relatively sincere. However, about ten years after Lin Shu's death, as the trend to commemorate Lin Shu appeared again in the literary world, Zhou Zuoren became discontented with the positive memorial articles on Lin Shu. He still thought Lin Shu was a person 'who argued in defence of both traditional moral principles and classical Chinese and who annihilated the heterodox views on ideology as well as literature and art with the aid of military force.'[2]

Zheng Zhenduo's 'Mr. Lin Qinnan'

Zhen Zhengduo was the most important among the scholars who re-assessed Lin Shu and his translations. Soon after Lin Shu's death, on 11 November 1924, Zheng Zhenduo wrote his commemorative article titled 'Mr Lin Qinnan'.[3] Most probably it is the first article to give a relatively fair evaluation of Lin Shu after Lin Shu's death. In the article, aiming at the current negative assessment of Lin Shu and his translations, Zheng Zhenduo articulated the following views:

First, Lin Shu's conservative views should not become the reason for negating Lin Shu's contributions and influence in literary translation and writing. He stated that Lin Shu was well known as a translator and classical Chinese writer in the literary world of China for three or four decades, but during the New Culture Movement 'many scholar saw him as a representative of old tradition, trying to find mistakes in his views on morality, his classical Chinese writings and his translations'. Henceforth, 'in ordinary youth's eyes, Lin Shu's standing in the literary world of China had been shaken.' Dissatisfied with the common practice of the advocates of the New Culture Movement who negated and dismissed Lin Shu's contributions on the basis of his conservative politics, Zheng pointed out that 'Lin Shu's view is one question, but his standing in the literary world of China is another. It appears unfair to thoroughly overturn his standing in the literary world and blot out his laborious work merely because of

---

[1] Zhou Zuoren 周作人, Ku cha suibi 苦茶随笔 (Bitter Tea Jottings), Beixin shuju, Shanghai, 1935, pp. 256-257.
[2] Ibid., p.258.
[3] This article was first published in Xiaoshuo yuebao 小说月报(Fiction Monthly), 15:11, 1924.

60

his transient conservative views.'[1]

Second, Lin Shu's political ideas were not conservative for all time. Zheng took Lin's three poems in *The New Yufu Poems in Fujian* as instances to affirm Lin Shu's new political ideas in his early stage: 'In his *The New Yufu Poems in Fujian*, we may see Mr Lin's approval to the new reformist party. Fifty poems in *The New Yufu Poems in Fujian* were written in the middle period of Qing Emperor Guangxu's reign, before the Constitutional reforms. At that time, he still lived in Fuzhou, talking with his friends about new political reforms, so he wrote these poems to voice his views.'[2] In the first poem, Lin Shu conveyed his position on enlightening children with new knowledge in order to strengthen the nation. In the second poem, Lin Shu criticized the gender discrimination against women in Chinese society and advocated initiating and running girls' schools. In the third poem, Lin satirized pedantic scholars who were too addicted to ancient books and lost the ability to bring their learning into any relation with actual facts. This poem conveys Lin's view: saving the nation lies in social reforms, one can be only addicted to old learning and stubbornly stick to the tradition. Zheng Zhenduo remarked: 'Before Kang Youwei submitted his memorial to the court of Qing dynasty, with these views, Lin Shu should be regarded as an advanced member of the reformist party.'[3] Zheng Zhenduo said that Lin Shu's views had not become conservative until his later years, which was unrelated to his contributions and achievement in translation.

Third, the majority of the errors in Lin Shu's translations should be imputed to the oral interpreters whom he collaborated with. The main problems with Lin Shu's translations according to later scholars were that Lin Shu translated many second or third rate, even worthless foreign works, ignored the difference between literary forms in his translation, and wilfully abridged the originals. In Zheng Zhenduo's opinion, these should be mostly attributed to the oral interpreters' ignorance of foreign literature. 'Because Lin Shu knew no foreign languages, the selection of the originals was completely dominated by the oral interpreters who worked with him.'[4] Zheng Zhenduo's analysis of the reasons for the errors in Lin Shu's translations had not been seen in the

---

[1] Zheng Zhenduo, Zhongguo wenxue yanjiu 中国文学研究 (Studies of Chinese Literature), Guwen shuju, Hong Kong,1970, p.1214.
[2] Ibid., p.1219.
[3] Ibid., p.1221.
[4] Ibid.

previous criticisms on Lin Shu. Although some minor errors resulted from his speedy translation and some abridgments were due to his consideration for the Chinese readers, it is improper to impute all the errors to Lin Shu.

Fourth, Zheng Zhenduo gave a positive appraisal of Lin Shu's achievement in literary translation. Lin Shu's translations amount to 180 works or so, which include at least forty world masterpieces, and 'more than 40 works are regarded perfect'. Not only in the past but also up to now, nobody in China can compare with him as far as the number of translations is concerned. 'Therefore, we should be greatly indebted to Mr Lin indeed for his laborious work'. [1]

Fifth, the major translated works of Lin Shu were excellent, most of which were loyal to the spirit and style of the originals. Zheng Zhenduo quoted Mao Dun's remark on Lin Shu's translation of *Ivanhoe*:

> Except for several minor mistakes, *Sakexun jie hou yingxiong lue* (*Ivanhoe*) considerably retains the style of the original. The depiction of the characters in the translation is the same as the characters in the original, and has no major changes.[2]

Then Zhen quoted one passage from Lin Shu's translation of *The Old Curiosity Shop* (*Xiaonü Naier zhuan*) to show his opinion in agreement with Mao Dun's. He remarked:

> If we read the original text without a break, and then read the translated text, we cannot feel any changes. In some places, even humour, which is the most difficult to express in translation, have also been expressed in Mr Lin's translation. Sometimes, he can also present those words that were ingeniously used in the original.[3]

Zheng Zhenduo also compared Lin Shu with other translators of that time, especially the translators in Shanghai. In Zheng's opinion, the works of the translators in Shanghai were not very truthful to the originals. When translating a foreign work, they did not indicate the name of the author, and sometimes changed the names of the characters and places in the original so as to turn the original into their own work. Zheng Zhenduo pointed out that the adaptation

---

[1] Ibid. p.1226
[2] Ibid.
[3] Ibid. p.1227

of the original was a common phenomenon in translation circles of that time, but 'he [Lin Shu] did not slide into the bad habits. Even though he translated an unknown work, he would indicate the name of the author. Moreover, he never changed the sounds of the names of the characters and places in the original work. A truthful translator like Lin Shu was very rare at that time.' [1]

Most of the previous reviewers, who mostly echoed the views of others, directed the attacks at Lin Shu's untruthfulness to the original, but Zheng Zhenduo reversed the judgement through a careful comparative reading of the original and its translation as well as the comparison between Lin Shu and other translators of that time.

Finally, Zheng believed that Lin Shu's translations exerted a great influence on Chinese literature. Lin's translations broadened the Chinese readers' outlooks, letting them learn about the social and family life of the Westerners. At that time, the Chinese people had a very narrow knowledge of the world. They always viewed the Westerners in a different light, thinking that the Chinese people were totally different from them. But until Lin Shu 'diligently and unceasingly introduced more than 150 European and American novels into China', most of the Chinese intellectuals 'did not understand the conditions of their families and the society, and their national nature'.[2]

Lin's translations dispelled the Chinese people's preconceived ideas that Chinese literature is the best in the world, and Western literature was much inferior to Chinese literature. As Zheng Zhenduo said,

> At this time, in the eyes of the majority of intellectuals, China's backwardness is no more than the corrupt political structure. As to Chinese literature, it is still the most high-level and the most beautiful in the world. None of Western literary works can compare with our Sima Qian, Li Bai and Du Fu's works. Until Lin Shu introduce a great number of Western literary works into China, claiming that Scott's works were not inferior to Sima Qian's, they had not known that there was also so-called literature in Europe and America, where there are also writers who can compare favourably with our Sima Qian.[3]

---

[1] Ibid.
[2] Ibid., p.1228.
[3] Ibid., pp.1228-1229.

Lin Shu broke with the Chinese literati's prejudice against the novel, thus raising the status of novel. Chinese literati had invariably looked down on fiction and fiction writers, but Lin Shu's efforts in translating and writing novels changed this long-standing prejudice. Zheng Zhenduo affirmed that 'Mr Lin completely broke free from the traditional views', and that 'since him, some Chinese literati have considered themselves as novelists', and that 'in the recent twenty years, so many persons have engaged in translating foreign novels, it may nearly be said that they were influenced and changed by Mr Lin's translations'.[1]

Zheng Zhenduo, with his defence and praise of Lin Shu and his translations, laid the foundation for a wider comprehension and objective evaluation of Lin Shu's translations.

Han Guang's *Lin Qinnan*

In the ninth year after Lin Shu's death, Han Guang published his *Lin Qinnan* in1935, a more detailed study of Lin Shu's life, thought, translations, writings, literary value and contributions.

In his preface, Han gave the reason for writing this book. He stated that Lin Shu was the most prolific translator, and was venerated as 'the king of the translation world'. His first-rate translated works amount to forty kinds and more, and nobody 'has translated this amount of foreign works up to now'. Moreover, Lin Shu 'propped up the banner of literature, acting as a chief general for old literature while hewing a path beyond China for a new literature. He kept a foothold in the literary world of China for two or three decades'. For these reasons, Han Guang thought, 'it is worth discussing in detail such an established figure'. Yet, Han regretted that 'nearly ten year after Lin's death, we have not yet seen any systematic special study of Lin Shu and his translations except Zheng Zhengduo's article "Mr Lin Qinnan"'. [2]

Being aware of the problems in the assessment of Lin Shu and his translations as well as their extraordinary cultural significance, Han Guang was determined to provide an overall, systematic detailed discussion of them for a fair and objective appraisal.

First of all, Han Guang discussed whether or not Lin Shu was a representative of the opponents of the New Culture Movement. He argued:

[1] Ibid., p.1229
[2] Han Guang , 1935, p.1.

As far as the conflict between the new and the old is concerned, although the discussion of this question has lasted a long time, there is not yet a relatively fair conclusion. I vigorously support the New Culture Movement, but I feel it necessary to give a re-examination because Lin Shu has been suffering an unredressed injustice.[1]

The conflict between the new and the old at that time was evident in the debates between Chen Duxiu's faction (the supporters of *New Youth*) and Lin Shu. Han Guang accepted that opposite views on morality and literature might peacefully coexist in some modern countries like Britain, Germany, and made out that this conflict between the new and the old could only take place in China. In his views, the conflict between the new and the old as well as the mutual attack between the both sides completely 'ran wild'[2].

Like Zheng Zhenduo, Han Guang went along with those people who negated Lin's contributions and influences in both literary writing and translation merely according to his transient conservative views. He quoted some of Lin Shu's early articles and poems to bear out Lin Shu's new ideas, refuting the negative views on Lin Shu. He argued:

As long as we read Lin Shu's early articles and his *The New Yuefu Poems in Fujian*, we will know that he was a man full of ideas on social and political reforms. Otherwise, it was impossible for him to turn his attention to translating foreign literature. What a pity that at that time Lin Shu was condemned by the ignorant people as a 'diehard conservative' and a member of the 'national cultural heritage party', even his laborious introduction of foreign literature was wantonly attacked through enumerating various errors.[3]

Second, Han Guang also debated the notion of 'faithfulness' in Lin's translations. In the beginning, he said that translation was Lin Qinnan's great achievement as well as a very great event in the previous decades of the literary world and the society in China, but 'recently the people who criticized him always like to say that in many places his translation does not correspond to the

---

[1] Ibid., pp.12-13.
[2] Ibid., p.14.
[3] Ibid. p.15.

original, making many errors. In my opinion, this view is a bit overcritical.'[1] Han Guang had some quotations from Lin's translations to prove that Lin Shu's translation, on the whole, is truthful to the original, especially in spirit and style. After quoting a passage from Lin's *Zei shi* (*Oliver Twist*), he commented:

> As for the original text, when reading the description of Giles and others who attempt to shift responsibility onto each other and their fearful mood, the reader cannot help laughing. Of course it is the beauty of Dickens' writing; yet as for the translation, in faith, it could catch the verve of the original text so that it can nearly be said that it is just right! So long as the reader carefully read the original text once, and then read the translated text, he will know how the translated text caught the verve of the original text. It is hard to find the translation like this…; yet it is easy to find it in Lin Shu's translations. [2]

Han Guang also took a passage from Lin Shu's translation of Washington Irving's *Westminster Abbey* as an example. He said that the readers 'should not rigidly read the translated text word for word or sentence for sentence against the original text', because Lin Shu abridged the original text, but 'Lin Shu's translation can catch and present the cream of the original'.[3] Then Han quoted Yan Jicheng's remark on the translated text to support his own view:

> The translator made abridgments. Luckily this sort of description about meditation on the past originally had no well-knit composition, so there is no harm in making a little abridgment. The translated text can keep the spiritual reflection and aesthetic feeling of the original intact.[4]

Obviously, Han Guang's judgment of the truthfulness of Lin Shu's translation was heavily based on whether the TT is truthful to the ST in spirit and literary style, not in word and sentence. It is a very significant re-assessment of Lin Shu's translations.

Third, Han Guang identified another alleged feature of Lin Shu's translation: sometimes his translation is better than the original is, especially his

---

[1] Ibid. p.65.
[2] Ibid., p.128.
[3] Ibid., p.130
[4] Ibid., pp.130-131.

translation of Haggard's novels. Lin Shu was aware that Haggard's works were not so good as Dickens', but by reason of his proficiency in classical Chinese, the target language, as well as his aim at making his translations acceptable, he incorporated an artistry that improved the original. Han Guang quoted Guo Moruo's remark on Lin's *Jiayin Xiaozhuan* (*Joan Haste*) to prove it: 'This work has no place in the history of world literature, but after it was translated into Lin Shu's succinct classical Chinese, it gained a lot of lustre.' However, in Han's opinion, 'it is either his strong point or his mortal wound.' [1]

In the end, Han Guang came into a conclusion that after Lin Shu's translation of *La Dame aux Camélias*, the world of Chinese fiction became more farsighted, breaking free from many traditions and old ideas. The translator made Chinese people value foreign literature, enhanced the social status of novelists, and thus promoted international views in the Chinese literary world. Lin Shu was not only 'a revolutionary figure with foresight in the world of early modern Chinese literature', but also 'a founder of new literature'.[2] Even if he made a lot of errors and absurdities, his contributions should not be totally negated, because he could yet be regarded as 'a Columbus of the new culture'.[3]

To sum up, Han Guang reversed and refuted the current negative views on Lin Shu and his translations, re-affirming Lin Shu's contributions. But Han Guang did not consider the relationship between Lin Shu's translations and the originals in the light of translational culture. His affirmation of the faithfulness of Lin's translation is still limited to the framework of linguistic translation theory. He still took the source text as the objective of translation activity.

However, when arguing the question about literal translation and free translation, Han Guang stated that the first principle of translation is that a translation is to be provided for the readers who do not know foreign languages. In this case, the translation should have a Chinese style to accord with the Chinese readers' habit. For the Chinese readers, the advantage of Lin's translation is that 'it is clear at a glance without the defects of incompatibility and awkwardness'.[4] It is a pity that Han Guang did not develop this argument.

It should be noted that in this section, I give a detailed introduction of

---

[1] Ibid., p.123.
[2] Ibid., p.200.
[3] Ibid.
[4] Ibid., p.33.

Zheng Zhenduo and Han Guang's affirmative views on Lin Shu and his translations, but in fact, their views were not recognized by later scholars and never became dominant until the 1990s.

(4) Negative Criticism from 1949 to 1979

Between 1949 and 1979, Lin Shu was invariably regarded a negative figure in various authoritative critical works. When his name was mentioned, he was labeled a reactionary scholar, a man of back-to- the ancients, a defender of the feudal culture and moral principles. Lin Shu was once again negated as a man devoid of any merits. These authoritative critical works conveyed the official views of Chinese authorities. As these books were officially approved as textbooks for university students in China, the negative views on Lin Shu became authoritative. They not only influenced both several generations of Chinese intellectuals after 1949 and foreign Sinologists.

Liu Shousong's *The First Draft of the History of New Chinese Literature*[1] and *A History of Modern Chinese Literature*[2] compiled by seven universities and colleges in southern China are among the most authoritative and influential books on modern Chinese literature in the 1970s. The authors produced the books mainly under official ideology. As far as Lin Shu is concerned, in addition to parroting the advocates of the New Culture Movement, their criticisms on Lin Shu are political, denying Lin Shu's literary status.

In Chapter One, Section 5 of *First Draft of the History of New Chinese Literature*, Liu Shousong maintains that Lin Shu was both a defender of feudal moral principles and a vanguard of opposing the New Literature. Liu labeled Lin Shu 'a feudalist back to the ancients'. He claimed that Lin Shu hoped that 'the feudal warlord at that time could set up a "literary inquisition" to round up the promoters of the New Literature Movement at one fell swoop'.[3] He also quotes Lu Xun's 'Jotting 15' and 'Jotting 47' as well as Chen Duxiu's 'A Reply

---

[1] Liu Shousong 刘绶松, Zhongguo xin wenxueshi chugao 中国新文学史初稿 (First Draft of the History of New Chinese Literature), Zuojia chubanshe, Beijing, 1956.
[2] The Compiling Group of the Seven Universities and Colleges in Southern China, (comps. & eds.), Zhongguo xiandai wenxueshi 中国现代文学史(A History of Modern Chinese Literature), Changjiang wenyi chubanshe, 1979.
[3] Liu Shousong, 1956, p.47.

to the Charge against this Journal' in his arguments against Lin Shu. He concluded,

> The literary debate during the period was basically on vernacular Chinese and classical Chinese, which resulted from the Chinese people's struggle against feudal culture and the feudal literati's defense of feudal culture. In the debate, these feudalists of 'back to the ancients' did not display their strength, but their attitudes were quite indomitable. They did not hope to see the feudal culture 'dying in bed of old age'; therefore, they posed as apologists to put up a last-ditch struggle.[1]

In *A History of Modern Chinese Literature*, the authors also maintained that as far as political ideology was concerned, Lin Shu belonged to the adherents of the Qing dynasty, which was reactionary at that time. From the beginning, they claimed that Lin Shu adopted a hostile attitude to the New Culture Movement and the Literary Revolution, and attempted to put down the movements by his position and reputation in the world of old literature. In their eyes, 'Lin Shu's short stories actually exposed the vicious intentions of the school of feudal back-to- the ancients': gang up with the feudal warlords to attempt to suppress the New Culture Movement and Literary Revolution.'[2]

It is not hard to see from the above quotations that the criticism was coloured by the Cultural Revolution. Their views and critical style were representative in the Chinese critical circles between 1949-1979.

(5) Revival: 1980s onwards

Around 1980, ideological emancipation was officially initiated and encouraged in China. Against the background of 'let a hundred flowers blossom and a hundred schools of thought contend', which included redressing mishandled historical cases as well as rethinking and reassessing some historical events and figures, albeit cautiously, Qian Zhongshu's article 'Lin Shu's Translations', written in the 1960s, was published around 1980, initiating the re-evaluation of Lin Shu and his translations. Although this revival was still restricted due to political factor in China, it offered a chance for reassessing Lin Shu and his works.

---

[1] Ibid., p.52.
[2] Xue Shuizhi & Zhang Juncai, 1982, pp.382-383.

Qian Zhongshu's 'Lin Shu's Translations'

Qian Zhongshu's 'Lin Shu's Translations' is the most important criticism on Lin Shu's translation since 1949. It first appeared in an academic journal that had limited distribution in 1963, but had not been published and put on sale throughout the country until in the late 1970s after the Cultural Revolution (1966–1976) ended. This fact seems to show that it was hardly possible to put in a good word for Lin Shu during the Cultural Revolution before 1978 (the year marked the beginning of the era of reforms and opening to the outside world in China). 1979 was the year of ideological emancipation in China, which made it possible to publish the article written in the 1960s.

Differing from his predecessors, Qian Zhongshu's 'Lin Shu's Translations' concentrated on Lin Shu's translations while avoiding the arguments about the rights and wrongs of Lin Shu during the New Culture Movement. He took some passages and sentences from Lin Shu's translated works as instances to support his views on Lin Shu's translations so that his arguments seem more substantial and convincing.

In the article, Qian Zhongshu made a detailed analysis of Lin Shu's translations from a linguistic viewpoint. He put forward his criterion of translation:

> A translated work is to transform a work from the language of one country into that of another. If this could be done without betraying any evidence of artifice by virtue of divergences in language and speech habit, while at the same time preserving intact the flavor of the original, then we say that such a performance has attained 'the ultimate transmutation'.[1]

In other words, a translation should be truthful to the original, but it should not read like a translation.[2] Of course, it is an ideal. Therefore, Qian also accepted that it is unavoidable that infidelity occurs in a translated work.[3] It is on the basis of this criterion that Qian examined Lin Shu's translations.

Qian believed that Lin Shu's translations could induce the readers' interest in the original. In his views, a good translation is self-defeating, and leads the

---

[1] Qian Zhongshu, 'Lin Shu's Translations', trans., George Kao, Renditions, No.5, 1975, pp.8-9.
[2] Qian Zhongshu, 1981, p.9.
[3] Ibid., pp.18-20.

readers to the original, while the inferior translation has the effect of destroying the original.[1] He took his own experience in reading Lin Shu's translations as an example to prove this point:

> I for one became increasingly interested in learning foreign language after reading Lin's translations. ...it was not until I came into contact with Lin Shu's translations that I realized how captivating Western fiction could be. I tirelessly perused the works of Haggard, Washington Irving, Scott and Dickens in the Lin translations. If I was in any way self-consciously motivated toward learning English, it was so that one day I could gorge myself on the adventure stories of Haggard and company without hindrance.[2]

Qian Zhongshu also found that Lin Shu's translations have not lost their appeal to the Chinese readers even now, and many of them still deserve to be read again. As far as the translation of the same original work is concerned, after comparing Lin's translation with later translators' ones, he found that he preferred reading Lin 's translations although the latter's ones were much more truthful to the original than Lin's from a linguistic point of view.[3]

On discussing the unfaithfulness of Lin Shu's translations, Qian Zhongshu paid special attention to Lin Shu's additions and supplements to the original text. It often happened that Lin Shu was ready to make some addition and polish when he saw blemishes in the original depiction. As Qian pointed out, 'when he was translating, if he happened to see a weak or faulty expression in the original, he would have an itch to grab the author's pen, writing for the author'[4] Qian argued that Lin Shu's additions and supplements often had a better effect: to make the expression more concrete, more vivid, and more substantial.

Besides, Qian tried to clarify critics' arguments on Lin Shu's use of classical Chinese, *guwen*, in his translation of foreign novels. He argued that Lin Shu's classical Chinese writing style, strictly speaking, did not tally with the rule of '*guwen*'. In fact, what he used in his translations is a more popular, more informal, more flexible classical Chinese. His writing form retains some

---

[1] Ibid., p.21.
[2] Qian Zhongshu, 1975, p.10.
[3] Qian Zhongshu, 1981, pp.23-24.
[4] Ibid., p.26

ingredients of '*guwen*', but is much freer than '*guwen*'. In vocabulary and grammar, it is short of strict rules and embraces a wider range of expression. Therefore, he maintained that Lin Shu's classical Chinese is not completely opposite to vernacular Chinese, *baihua*.[1]

Finally, in Qian Zhongshu's opinion, Lin Shu's 'target language' is better than the original author's 'source language' sometimes. After a comparative reading of Haggard's novels and Lin's translations, he concluded: 'in addition to Dickens and Irving, Lin Shu's early translations of Haggard's novels have distinctive features. This time, I prefer reading Lin's translations to reading Haggard's originals. The reason is very simple: Lin Shu's Chinese writing is much more brilliant than Haggard's English writing.' He thought that this phenomenon has frequently happened in the history of world translation.[2]

Qian's article, on the basis of Zheng Zhenduo and Han Guang's studies, involved some controversial questions about Lin Shu's translations. Its publication provoked a new round of research interest in Lin Shu and his translations in China. It is evident that Qian examined Lin Shu's translations principally from a traditional view of translation — in other words, he only made a linguistic analysis of Lin Shu's translated text — but he touched on some principal translational phenomena and facts, e.g., the creativity of a translator, how a translation influences a reader, a reader's preference for the translation to the original, a better use of the target language than that of the source language and so on. He was aware that these phenomena and facts are worth carefully consideration,[3] but he did not couch them in terms of cultural translation. However, his linguistic criticism is a beginning to post-Mao re-evaluation of the translational phenomenon of Lin Shu.

New critical interest

After "Lin Shu's Translations' was published as one of the articles in Qian Zhongshu's *My Four Old Articles*[4] in 1979, the Commercial Press in Beijing reprinted this article and some of Lin Shu's translated novels in 1981. This indicates the occurrence of a new wave of research interest in Lin Shu and his

[1] Ibid., pp.37-39.
[2] Ibid., p.45.
[3] Ibid., p.24.
[4] Qian Zhongshu 钱锺书，Jiu wen si pian 旧文四篇(My Four Old Articles), Shanghai guji chubanshe, 1979.

translations. Some authoritative works on the history of Chinese literature or Chinese translation have started to give Lin Shu and his translations wide coverage such as Chen Yugang's *A Draft History of China's Translation Literature*,[1] Guo Yanli's *The Modern Translated Literature of China: an introduction*, Ma Zuyi's *A Short History of Chinese Translation*.[2] In addition, biographies, critical biographies and critical works on Lin Shu have been reprinted or published such as Kong Li's *Lin Shu and His Translated Novels*;[3] Xue Suizhi and Zhang Juncai's *Research Materials concerning Lin Shu*, Han Guang's *Lin Qinnan*,[4] Zhu Bisen's *The Man's Tears in the Women's Kingdom: A Biography of Lin Qinnan*,[5] Lin Wei's *Vicissitudes in a Century: A Summary of Lin Shu Studies*,[6] Zhang Juncai's *A Critical Biography of Lin Shu*,[7] Kong Qingmao's *A Biography of Lin Shu*,[8] Feng Qi's *A Critical Biography and Selected Works of Lin Shu*.[9] More papers on Lin Shu and his translations have appeared in home and overseas.

The new wave of research interest in Lin Shu and his translations includes repeating the 1920s-40s criticisms. In other words, most of the views simply repeat or extend Zheng Zhenduo, Han Guang and others. In their criticism, they laid more emphasis on Lin Shu's achievements, influence and significance in literary translation, but their critical yardstick is still linguistic to a great extent.

---

[1] Chen Yugang 陈玉刚, Zhongguo fanyi wenxue shigao 中国翻译文学史稿(A Draft History of China's Translation Literature), Zhongguo duiwai fanyi chuban gongsi, Beijing, 1989.

[2] Ma Zuyi 马祖毅, Zhongguo fanyi jianshi 中国翻译简史(A Short History of Chinese Translation), Zhongguo duiwai fanyi chuban gongsi, Beijing, 1998.

[3] Kong Li 孔立, Lin Shu he fanyi xiaoshuo 林纾和翻译小说(Lin Shu and His Translated Novels), Zhonghua huju, Beijing, 1981.

[4] Han Guang 寒光, Lin Qinnan 林琴南, Zhonghua shuju, Beijing, 1985.

[5] Zhu Bisen 朱碧森, Nü guo naner lei: Lin Qinnan zhuan 女国男儿泪：林琴南传 (The Man's Tears in the Women's Kingdom: A Biography of Lin Qinnan), Zhongguo wenlian chuban gongsi, Beijing, 1989.

[6] Lin Wei 林蔚, Bainian chenfu: Lin Shu yanjiu zongshu 百年沉浮：林纾研究综述(Vicissitudes in a Century: A Summary of Lin Shu Studies), Tianjin jiaoyu chubanshe, Tianjin, 1990.

[7] Zhang Juncai 张俊才, Lin Shu pingzhuan 林纾评传(A Critical Biography of Lin Shu), Naikai daxue chubanshe, Tianjin, 1992.

[8] Kong Qingmao 孔庆茂, Lin Shu zhuan 林纾传(A Biography of Lin Shu), Tuanjie Chubanshe, Beijing, 1998.

[9] Feng Qi 冯奇, (ed.), Lin Shu pingzhuan jiqi zuopin xuan 林纾评传及其作品选 (A Critical Biography and Selected Works of Lin Shu), Zhongguo wenshi chubanshe, Beijing, 1998.

It seems that they were aware that Lin Shu has been unfairly treated and assessed mainly due to the fact that the advocates of the New Culture Movement and Literary Revolution were the official voice of translation criticism. As well they realized that those positive views on Lin Shu and his translations before and soon after Lin Shu's death had been stifled for a long time. Along with the appearance of the relatively free critical atmosphere in the last decades of the last century, they re-excavate or reiterate preceding positive appraisals of Lin Shu. In fact, they pay more attention to reversing the previous 'unfair' verdict on Lin Shu than re-evaluating Lin Shu's translations through a concrete and substantial analysis.

A typical example is Guo Yanli's study of modern Chinese translations, *The Modern Translated Literature of China: an introduction*. This work on modern literary translations was officially sponsored as one of the 1995-2000 National Research Programs in Social Science.[1]   One chapter is entitled 'Lin Shu's translations and His Historical Position'. It offers a detailed exposition of Lin Shu's life, his translating activity, his representative translated works, and the historical position, weakness and influence of 'Lin Shu's translated novels'. As a matter of fact, Guo Yanli's exposition is merely a summation and supplement of the works such scholars as Zheng Zhenduo, Han Guang, Qian Zhongshu. In the conclusion of the chapter, he wrote:

> In brief, 'Lin Shu's translated novels' not only directly influenced early modern literature, but also enlightened many famous modern writers, and to some extent influenced their later engagement in literary translation and literary writing as well as the formation of their artistic method and personality. Later, Lin Shu, owing to his opposition to vernacular Chinese, was cast aside by the youths of the May Fourth New Culture Movement. It is a historical fact that the aspect of Lin Shu was behind the times. However, his contribution to the New Culture in the May Fourth period should be acknowledged and re-evaluated on the basis of the facts.[2]

---

[1] Chinese Government approves some research programs pertaining to social science every five years. The approved programs will achieve research fund, and the result of the research will be officially regarded authoritative.

[2] Guo Yanli, 1998, p.303.

It is a common characteristic that the 1980s onwards appraisals of Lin Shu and his translations shared or repeated their predecessors' views, favorable or unfavorable. However, this new wave of research interest has led to the re-evaluation of Lin Shu as a translator. It should be acknowledged that my re-evaluation of Lin Shu and his translations is built on these works and subsequent research.

2. Western Criticism

No Western scholar who touch on modern Chinese literature can overlook Lin Shu. However, there are few monographs on Lin Shu's translations. Comments on Lin Shu are scattered in Western scholarly works on Chinese literature. Some scholars are aware that Lin Shu, who had long been negated in his homeland, played an important role in remoulding modern Chinese literature. They pay special attention to Lin Shu and his translations.

Differing from the study of Lin Shu in China, Western scholars seem to pay little attention to Lin Shu's attitude towards the New Literature Movement. Instead, they are more concerned about Lin Shu as a translator. There are two kinds of reviews on Lin Shu in the West. One is by Western scholars, the other by overseas Chinese scholars. As far as Western scholarship is concerned, insufficient introduction to Lin Shu's translations in the West and Lin's use of classic Chinese in his translations may have to some extend hindered a comprehensive study of Lin Shu's translations. However, scholars who have devoted themselves to a study of Lin Shu, have significance for our study owing to their being based within a different cultural context and beyond Chinese political influence. Some positive remarks on the influence and contributions of Lin's translations can be easily found in Western criticism. Among them, Arthur Waley's views on Lin Shu may be the most noticeable.

Waley was a well-known translator of Chinese literature into English. Waley had a good command of classical Chinese and could read Lin Shu's classical Chinese texts. He was the earliest and only Westerner we have found so far who fully affirmed Lin Shu's translations. In his 'Notes on Translation',[1] Waley spoke highly of Lin Shu's translations. He first affirmed Lin Shu's use of

---

[1] Waley, Arthur, 'Notes on Translation', The Atlantic Monthly, the 100th anniversary issue, 1958.

classical Chinese in his translations:

> The translator must use the tools that he knows best how to handle. And his reflection reminds me at once of what Lin Shu, the great early 19th-century translator of European fiction into Chinese, said when he was asked why he translated Dickens into ancient Chinese instead of into modern colloquial. His reply was: 'Because ancient Chinese is what I am good at.'[1]

He believed that Lin Shu was an extraordinary man, from whom there are indeed so many lessons about translation to be learned.[2] He compared Lin Shu's translations with Dickens' originals and concluded that Lin Shu's translation had improved Dicken's works:

> To put Dickens into classical Chinese would on the face of it seem to be a grotesque undertaking. But the results are not all grotesque. Dickens, inevitably, become a rather different and to my mind a better writer. All the overelaboration, the overstatement and uncurbed garrulity disappear. The humour is there, but is transmuted by a precise, economical style; every point that Dickens spoils by uncontrolled exuberance, Lin Shu makes quietly and efficiently. [3]

Then Waley provided an explanation of Lin Shu's translation. He argued that in the case of the Dickens novels it would be misleading to use such terms as 'paraphrase' or 'adaptation'. Lin Shu was the transmitter, on the grandest possible scale, of European fiction to China, and through him Chinese fiction was revitalized when it was at its last gasp. The effect of his prodigious life-work was in fact to revolutionize Chinese fiction.[4]

R.W.Compton is the first person who conducted a comprehensive study of Lin Shu's translations. In the late of the 1960s, he chose Lin Shu's translations as the topic of his PhD dissertation. Originally, he envisaged examining Lin Shu's role in his society, but soon his study was diverted into Lin Shu's translations, for he realized that the latter should be the starting point of his

---

[1] Waley, Arthur, 'Arthur Waley on Lin Shu', Renditions, No.5, Hong Kong University, 1975, p.29.
[2] Ibid.
[3] Ibid., p.30.
[4] Ibid., p.31.

more ambitious undertaking.[1] In his thesis, Compton, for the most part, did some basic but important work for his further study but he communicated established views of Lin Shu as a 'minor' figure. For instance, he gave a brief introduction to Lin Shu's life and investigated the quantity and quality of Lin Shu's translations and Lin Shu's collaborators. Compton's investigation was primarily based on Chinese scholars' work. Although he concentrated his research interest on Lin Shu's translations, his basic appraisal of Lin Shu as a translator was relatively low. In the beginning of his thesis, he stated:

> It must be conceded that Lin Shu was not destined to play a major role in the intellectual or literary currents of modern China. Although he was well-known and his translations were widely read in the last years of the Ch'ing dynasty, his contributions proved to be minor in view of the tremendous upheavals that have shaken the Chinese literary world since his time. [2]

His comments on Lin Shu's translation more or less repeated the views of the advocates of the May Fourth New Culture Movement on Lin Shu and his translations. He primarily saw Lin Shu as a conservative and traditional writer. On explaining the reason why Lin Shu did translation, Compton asserted:

> With his serenity and faith in traditional Confucian values, Lin saw no danger from the West in the form of ideas or technology; there was no conceivable way that these things could affect the universally valid truths of Confucianism. There was nothing to fear, therefore, from such ideas as might come to China in the pages of foreign books or novels. This goes far to explain why it was possible for Lin to translate foreign novels of all kinds without any qualms.[3]

In Compton's view, Lin Shu's translation of Western literature was not in order to introduce new elements into Chinese culture or to change it, but to highlight Chinese cultural tradition by assimilating Western literature. He believed that Lin Shu's interest in Western fiction could be seen as 'an attempt to uncover

---

[1] Compton, Robert W., A Study of Lin Shu's translations, 1852 – 1924, Ph.D thesis, Stanford University, 1971, p.iii.
[2] Ibid., p.1.
[3] Ibid., pp. 98-99.

sources of inspiration or new ideas which might be incorporated into the Chinese literary tradition'.[1] Compton thought that a second reason why Lin Shu translated was 'find moral lessons' from his translation of Western fiction.[2] Undoubtedly, Compton's basic work can further the study of Lin Shu, yet his low assessment of Lin Shu and his translations is now open to question. I argue that Compton's study overlooked and underestimated the cultural significance and influence of Lin Shu's translations.

Other Western scholars' brief comments on Lin Shu can be seen in their critical works on Chinese literature. For example, Kaltenmark remarked that it was thanks to Lin Shu that the Chinese first became acquainted with Scott, Dickens, Hugo, Dumas, Tolstoy and many others.[3] Dolezelova-Velingerova mentioned the impact of Lin Shu's literary translations:

> Lin Shu, the most prolific and most influential of the late Qing translators, made a deep impression on the Chinese literary world. ... Lin Shu made the remark (outrageous for the time) that Scott's novels were as sophisticated as the phenomenal history by Sima Qian, the second century BC founder of Chinese historiography. This statement left the elitist, Sino-centric Chinese literary men in a profound state of bewilderment; but it forced them to re-evaluate the status of fiction, and encourage China's novelists to write, and translators to continue rendering foreign fiction into Chinese.[4]

In terms of Lin's translated texts, some Western scholars, probably influenced by Chinese scholars, regarded his translations as the products of story-telling and rewriting rather than translation.[5] In their view, Lin Shu translated foreign novels in order to maintain classical Chinese. Tagore said, 'classical scholars like Lin Shu tried to maintain the popularity of the classical written language by translating Western literary masterpieces into classical Chinese'; 'Lin Shu had

[1] Ibid., pp. 99-100.
[2] Ibid., p.125.
[3] Kaltenmark, Odile, Chinese Literature, Walker and Company, New York,1984, p. 132.
[4] Dolezelova-Velingerova, Milena, The Chinese Novel at the Turn of the Century, University of Toronto Press, Toronto, 1980, p. 32.
[5] McDougall, Bonnie S., The Introduction of Western Literary Theories into Modern China 1919 –1925, The Centre for East Asian Cultural Studies, Tokyo, 1971.

not been attracted by the style or grammar of a Dickens or a Zola and he maintained his loyalty to his classical training.'[1]

However, some overseas Chinese scholars in the West have a relatively deeper understanding of Lin Shu's translations. Leo Ou-fan Lee, a scholar at Harvard University working on modern Chinese literature, is the first overseas Chinese scholar who was aware of the importance of Lin Shu as a translator. As early as in the 1960s, when negative views on Lin Shu prevailed in China, Lee published his monographic study: 'Lin Shu and His Translations: western fiction in Chinese perspective' in the Harvard's journal *Papers on China*. In the paper, Lee discussed Lin Shu's thought and personality in some detail and his major translated works. In the beginning, Lee gave a high appraisal of Lin Shu as a translator: Lin Shu was 'China's first prolific translator of Western fiction. Like Yan Fu for Western thought, he stands out as a pioneering genius who for the first time introduced a considerable volume of western literature into China' and 'this was a noteworthy achievement'.[2] Then Lee further examined three subject matters in Lin's translated novels: sentiment, ethics and adventure primarily through Lin Shu's prefaces and comments in his translations, which pointed to the social, ideological, spiritual and cultural needs of the Chinese at that time. In Lee's view, the impact of Lin's translations does not rest on his style alone; Lin not only brought his fellow intellectuals to appreciate the literary achievements of Western literature, but also opened the eyes of his Chinese readers to a glittering new world, which considerably differs from the traditional image of the Western 'barbarians'. He wrote that 'it is a world shining with the legacy of Western romanticism in its Protean appearances: sentimentalism, vitalism, dynamism, even racism and nationalism'.[3] He believes that Lin Shu and Yan Fu 'have come along different paths to a similar destination'.[4] In fact, Lee's analysis already involves the function of translation in a target culture. Yet, it is arguable that Lee thought that Lin Shu's treatment of the subject matters of the originals was based to some extent on his Confucian views. The content of this paper was partly absorbed into his critical works *The Romantic Generation of*

---

[1] Tagore, Amitendranath, Literary Debates in Modern China 1918 – 1937, The Centre for East Asian Cultural Studies, Tokyo, 1967, p. 14, p. 41.

[2] Lee, Leo Ou-fan, 'Lin Shu and His Translations: western fiction in Chinese perspective', Papers on China, Vol. 19, 1965, p.159.

[3] Ibid., p.187.

[4] Ibid., p.182.

Modern Chinese Writers (1973). In the preface, Lee states that for thematic purposes, he chose to begin with Lin Shu, a precursor who embarked upon his literary careers before the emergence of the May Fourth literary scene but who nevertheless had an enduring impact on the May Fourth generation.[1] This indicates that Lee affirms Lin Shu's impact on modern Chinese literature. However, inspiration may be drawn from Lee's conclusion at the end of the third chapter 'Lin Shu'. He wrote that 'later historians can readily perceive how Lin was inevitably engulfed in the temper of his times. They also have the vantage of hindsight to assess Lin's influence both on his generation and on subsequent ones. The Pandora's box of Lin Shu's translations has released a swarm of legacies of which he himself was unaware.'[2] Lee's views exerted a certain influence on Compton's study on Lin Shu's translations.[3]

Henry. Y. H. Zhao particularly emphasises the impact of Lin Shu's translations in his examination of the Western influence on Chinese fiction:

Although Western literature began to appear in Chinese translation much earlier, it did not attract any serious attention until around 1900 when it began to be published in astonishing quantities. According to A Ying's statistics, among the 1,107 books of fiction published between 1882 and 1913, 628 – almost two thirds of the total – were translations. This wave was ushered in by Lin Shu, the great translator of the late Qing, with his remarkable rendition of *La Dame aux Camélias* in 1899. Chen Xiying tells us 'a well-noted scholar said that the Chinese Revolution was brought about by two Western novels *La Dame aux Camélias* and *Joan Haste*. Lin Shu's translation certainly gave these two novels a disproportionate influence.[4]

Zhao's three points of view should be mentioned here. First, the translators of that time, almost without exception, adapted the original. This adaptation was to sinicize their translation. 'The purpose of this adaptation was to increase the readability so as to boost sales.'[5]   Second, another reason why abridgement was favoured during this period was that more than half of the translations used

---

[1] Ibid., p. ix .
[2] Ibid., p. 53.
[3] Compton, 1971, p.iv.
[4] Zhao, Henry Y.H., The Uneasy Narrator: Chinese Fiction from the Traditional to the Modern, Oxford University Press, Oxford and New York, 1995, pp. 288-289.
[5] Ibid., p.229.

' literary language rather than the vernacular. 'As a dead language burdened with cultural associations, the literary language was not flexible or 'innocent' enough to recast foreign narrative without colouring it with Chinese culture.'[1] Third, Lin Shu 'thought that turning foreign fiction into elegant literary language would strengthen the claim that these works of fiction were refined enough to be considered literature of high status'.[2] In fact, Zhao's views involve the reception of translation in a target culture, but he did not develop these ideas.

In her article on Lin Shu, Hu Ying pays close attention to the initial constitution of the figure of Lin Shu as a translator and its gradual transfigurations. Hu examines Lin Shu and his translation in his cultural context and argues that Lin's translation is not a 'case of a failed translator who laboured in an outdated mode of translation'. On the contrary, it is 'interesting because it is closely tied up with the cultural crisis of his time'.[3] Disagreement with some scholars' censure on the infidelity of Lin Shu's translation, Hu points out that 'the significance of Lin Shu's translations has more to do with the transformation of the source language original than with the degree of fidelity to it. It has more to do with the function that the translated texts played, which come from the productive difference rather than the assumed transparency of the translation.'[4] However, on the whole, Hu's views are not beyond those of the 1920s-1930s. For example, he states that in order to make his translations authoritative at that time, Lin Shu insisted on using classical Chinese in his translation and identified foreign works by comparison with classic Chinese works, and that Lin Shu treated the originals primarily from a perspective of traditional Chinese culture.

3. Key Issues in dispute Concerning the Assessment of Lin Shu

From the Chinese and Western criticisms, it is evident that Lin Shu has been a controversial figure. The evaluation and controversies about Lin Shu and his translations concentrate on three aspects: Lin Shu's political attitude toward the constitutional reforms and constitutional monarchy, his defense of classical

---

[1] Ibid., p. 230.
[2] Ibid., p. 230.
[3] Hu Ying, 'The Translator Transfigured: Lin Shu and the Cultural Logic of Writing in the late Qing', Positions: East Asian Cultures Critique, 3:1, 1995, p.70.
[4] Ibid., pp. 70-71.

Chinese or literary Chinese (*wenyanwen*) during the New Culture Movement, and his 'unfaithfulness' to the original in translation. How should we look at these controversies and evaluations? Target/culture-oriented translation theories open a window for re-examination, as they pay regard to the relationship between a translator and the target culture. One of these important aspects is to examine how the target culture influences, even dominates a translator's work and his strategy in dealing with the original, as Toury argues that translations have been regarded as 'facts of the culture which hosts them' and the translation is 'as good as initiated by the target culture'.[1] On the other hand, since Lin Shu was involved in some historical and cultural events such as the constitutional reforms of 1898 and the May Fourth New Culture Movement and since the scholars have different views on the events, it is important to investigate these events in context. This section is largely designed to respond to the above criticisms through a detailed investigation of the relations between Lin Shu and his politico-cultural contexts.

Lin Shu's thought and writing were closely related to the political and cultural changes and events of his time. For this reason, Lin Shu and his translations have been criticized. The key issues are Lin Shu's attitudes towards the Constitutional Reform and Modernization of 1898 and the May Fourth New Culture Movement. Hu Ying states that 'like many scholars of his generation, he professed fierce loyalty to the two emblems of what he saw as an endangered tradition, the Qing emperor and *guwen*.'[2] Lin Shu's nostalgia for Emperor Guangxu and his approval of constitutional monarchy as well as his defence of classical Chinese led to censure as 'an old fogy',[3] a conservative or a reactionary man of letters. The political1 negation resulted in a political repudiation on Lin Shu's translations. Therefore, his unfaithfulness to the original and some errors in his translations were frequently ridiculed and attacked as a consequence. In fact, Lin Shu's free translation is also an controversial issue. As we have seen in Chapter 2, Western translation theories and practices can powerfully support Lin Shu's translation strategy and method.

---

[1] Toury, 1995, p.24, p.27.

[2] Hu Ying, 1995, p.69,

[3] In the article 'My Late Remark on Liu Bannong's Letter to Zhou Qiming' (Yu Si 语丝, No.20, 25 March, 1925), Qian Xuantong called Lin Shu 'an old fogy', which has been long used by some Chinese scholars in disapproval of Lin Shu's political positions.

This issue will be discussed in Chapters 5 – 6 in detail. This chapter focuses on redressing the negative judgments on Lin Shu and his translations through an analysis of Lin's relations to the major political and cultural events of his time.

(1) Lin Shu's Thought: Conservative or Reformist?

The political reason for negating Lin Shu is that Lin Shu was among such royalists as Kang Youwei and Liang Qichao who supported Emperor Guangxu and the constitutional reforms of 1898. It was for this reason that Lin Shu was called an 'old fogy'. The constitutional reforms around 1898 were initiated and promoted by Kang and Liang who advocated constitutional monarchy, a matter of controversy among Chinese scholars to this day. In the past, owing to the official approval of the Republic Revolution initiated and led by Sun Yat-sen (1866–1925), the institutional reform of 1898 was commonly viewed as conservative, even reactionary. Sun maintained that the monarchy must be thoroughly overturned in order to establish a republic in China while Kang maintained that a constitutional monarchy was more fitting for the conditions of China through constitutional reforms instead of a radical revolution. It is because of his advocacy of the constitutional reforms and his doubt about the republican revolution that Lin Shu and his works were officially dismissed in China. In recent years, an obvious change has taken place in the assessment of the constitutional reforms of 1898 in China and overseas. On 28, August 1998, the Chinese People's Political Consultative Conference held a conference to commemorate the 100th anniversary of the constitutional reforms of 1898, which affirmed the movement as one of reform, patriotic national salvation and ideological emancipation. The conference affirmed that it had a deep influence on the awakening of the Chinese nation and the reform of modern Chinese society. In the Chinese official views, the constitutional reforms of 1898 is that 'Chinese people with lofty ideals arduously sought the way of saving the nation and its people', and this 'exploration pushed forward the progress of China', though it failed.[1] Some scholars in China and overseas have begun to re-assess the political reforms. This re-evaluation suggests that Lin Shu and his work also require re-assessment.

---

[1] Remin zhenxie bao 人民政协报(People's Political Consultation Paper), 2 July 2001, Beijing.

In China, there have existed dual views on the movement of constitutional reforms. On the one hand, it is affirmed as historical progress; on the other hand, it is viewed as conservative or even reactionary in comparison to the Republican Revolution of 1911. One authoritative view is that:

> The bourgeois reformers, who Kang Youwei represented, facing the raging waves of imperialism attempting to extinguish China, stepped forward bravely to go around campaigning for reform and national salvation, demanding to defend national dignity and develop capitalism. Obviously it was a patriotic action that accorded with the developing trend of China's history. They advocated new bourgeois knowledge and attacked old feudalistic knowledge, which had a huge impact in the ideological sphere. After the constitutional reforms around 1898, more people began to doubt the old knowledge while favorably receive new knowledge. All these showed that under the historical condition, the movement of bourgeois reform was progressive.
>
> Chinese bourgeois reformers, who launched the movement of the Constitutional Reforms, aimed not at overturning the reactionary power of the Qing dynasty and dared not offend imperialism. Relying on an emperor without real power, they attempted to enforce the reforms from top to bottom in a 'peaceful' and 'legal way'. Finally, their efforts met a rebuff and suffered defeat. Henceforth, the bourgeois reformers split up. Some of them, quickly waking up from the lessons of the defeat of the reforms, stepped on a revolutionary road while Kang Youwei, Liang Qichao and other reformers still obstinately persisted in political reforms. As a result, they became royalists and obstacles to democratic revolution. [1]

This evaluation of the constitutional reforms around 1898 is quite representative of dominant Chinese views. In recent years, however, a more positive assessment has appeared in China and overseas. As Fairbank says,

> Informed mainly by the self-serving writings of Kang and Liang, many have viewed the fiasco of the Hundred Days of 1898 in black and white terms, seeing Kang, Liang, and the emperor as heroes defeated by evil reactionaries. The opening of the Palace Museum Archives in Taibei and

---

[1] The compiling group of A Modern History of China, 1988, pp. 280-281.

the Number One Historical Archives at Bejing have now allowed a revisionist like Luke S.K Kwong (1984) to reinterpret the events of 1898 and specialists like Benkamin Elman to question some of his questionings. The Beijing politics of 1898 require fuller appraisal.[1]

These changes necessarily lead to a change in the political assessment of Lin Shu and his writings.

In his life, Lin Shu lived through the Opium War(1839-1842), the Taiping Rebellion(1851-1864), the Sino-Japanese War(1894-1895), the Constitutional Reforms of 1898, the allied forces' invasion of Bejing, the Republican Revolution of 1911, the establishment of the Republic of China in 1912 and the wars among the warlords. All these historical events had a huge impact on his thought. Like many thinkers of his generation, such as Yan Fu, Lin Shu advocated political reforms and modernization. Like most contemporary reformist intellectuals in China, Lin Shu was a patriotic scholar. He believed that the Chinese nation was in dire peril. He placed his hopes of saving the nation from subjugation on constitutional reforms and modernization. Therefore, his ideas were quite radical at that time.

Lin Shu's political ideal was to establish the constitutional monarchy in China as advocated by Kang Youwei and Liang Qichao. In the preface to his translation of *Jimmy Brown Trying to Find Europe* (*Mei tongzi wanli xun qin ji*), he stated: 'I am old and obtuse, and am getting obstinate day by day, but whenever I hear young people talking about political reforms, I always nod consent.'[2] In the preface to his translation of *The Scarlet Pimpernel* (*Yingguo daxia Hongfanlu zhuan*), Lin Shu added, if constitutional monarchy can 'make rulers and people link up and make everything in conformity with the law of thing or generally acknowledged truth, people will feel at ease and justified and China will be in order and at peace. Both rulers and people should be limited by constitution and they should behave within laws and norms'.[3] In the preface to his translation of *Le tour de la France par deux enfants* (*Aiguo er tongzi zhuan*), he expressed his political hope for constitutional reforms:

---

[1] Fairbank, John King, China, A New History, The Belknap Press of Harvard University Press, Cambridge, Massachusetts, London, England, 1992, p.229.
[2] Xue Suizhi and Zhang Juncai, 1982, p.391.
[3] Zhu Bisen 朱碧森，Lin Qinnan zhuan 林琴南传 (A Biography of Lin Qinnan)，Zhongguo wenlian chuban gongsi, Beijing, 1989, p. 227.

As far as autocracy is concerned, if a person in high position is patriotic, what he does will be more effective and faster than what common people do. However, as far as constitutional monarchy is concerned, if common people have patriotic aspiration, their suggestions that are beneficial to the country can reach the parliament. It is for this reason that members of the parliament should be elected from the representatives of all the provinces and counties. As for this country, the authority solely relies on memorials from lower levels, yet these memorials give the higher government a bad headache. Objectively speaking, all these so-called memorials are about protecting the sender-self and seeking promotion, little to do with loving this country and making it strong. Alas! When will the reforms start? When will constitutionalism be achieved? If Heaven shows sympathy for this nation, the day when the river becomes clear can be expected.[1]

It is apparent that Lin regarded constitutional reforms as the best scheme for saving China. Therefore, he saw Emperor Guangxu, Kang Youwei, Liang Qichao and other reformers as national heroes. In his argument with his colleague, Lin Shaoquan, over the political affairs in 1899, Lin Shu expressed his endorsement of promoting reforms and introducing new knowledge and his disagreement with abolishing the monarchy and realizing republicanism. He was apprehensive that it would be likely to lead to a great turmoil if republicanism was realized in China, while he was confident that that if the constitutional reforms had succeeded and the constitutional monarchy had been established in China, the nation would have become richer and stronger and chaos would have been avoided.[2] The reality after the revolution of 1911 seemed to bear out Lin Shu's apprehension. After the republican revolution of 1911 under Sun Yat-sen's leadership, China underwent the wars among warlords and then a civil war. The Chinese people lived in extreme misery and China was still in utter disorder and darkness. In 1912, Lin wrote a poem for Kang Youwei:

历历忠言今日验，滔滔祸水发端微。
万木萧森秋又暮，飞鸿谁盼我公归。[3]

[1] Feng Qi 冯奇, (ed), Lin Shu pingzhuan ji zuopin xuan 林纾评传及作品选(A Critical Biography of Lin Shu and His Selected Works, Zhongguo wenshi chubanshe, Beijing, 1998, p.184.

[2] Ibid., p.242

[3] Ibid., p.284.

(The early earnest advice has been affirmed by today's reality,
the surging flood of the trouble has bee expanding from small to large.
The trees withered up in late autumn,
the swan longs for your return.)

The lines truly expressed his disappointment in the reality and his nostalgia and expectation for the constitutional reforms.

Then, what is the nature and content of the constitutional reforms Lin Shu endorsed? In terms of the historical context, did the reforms actually play a positive role or a negative role in remoulding the Chinese society? Let us look at the initiator and promoter of the constitutional reforms Kang Youwei. Kang's ideas on political reforms were based on the theory and practice of Western political system and Japanese Meiji Reform (1868) model. As M.D.David says of Kang's main argument:

> The national policy, political and administrative structures of China were meant to serve the need of China in the medieval times when China was a most powerful country and her supremacy remained unchallenged. During the 19th century the circumstances had changed entirely and China had to restructure her political, social and economic system to suit the changing needs of industrialization and foreign relations. [1]

Kang's political ideas include establishment of a national assembly, adoption of a constitution, creation of a parliament and division of powers between the executive, the legislature and the judiciary as well as reform of education, development of industry, trade and commerce and defence forces. In practice, his ideas were partly accepted and were absorbed into the reform edicts issued by Emperor Guangxu. Apparently, Kang's political reform is a constitutional reform, namely, to learn from the West and capitalize China while preserving monarchy in consideration of the condition of China.

According to Kang's position, beyond doubt, the constitutional reforms of 1898 were a progressive reform movement at that time. For that reason, I argue that Lin Shu's endorsement of the reforms and his respect for Kang, Liang and Emperor Guangxu should not be negative criteria in the evaluation of Lin Shu's

---

[1] David, M. D., The Making of Modern China, Himalaya Publishing House, Bombay, 1993, p. 97.

translational achievement.

(2) A Pioneer or an Opponent of Modern Chinese Culture?

Another reason often used for negating Lin Shu is his attitude towards the New Culture Movement. It is primarily on the ground of Lin Shu's resentful attitude towards the leading figures of the New Culture Movement who, totally repudiated traditional Chinese culture, and his defence of Classical Chinese, *guwen*, that he was labelled 'an apologist of feudal moral principles' and 'a representative of the 'back to the ancients' school.[1] These appraisals lasted from 1915 till of the late 1970s. A typical appraisal is quoted below:

> Lin Shu's political ideas were very reactionary at that time, as they were identical to the ones of those old fogies of the Qing dynasty. From the beginning, Lin Shu adopted a hostile attitude to the New Culture and Literary Revolution, and attempted to make use of his position and prestige in the literary world to defeat them.[2]

It is obvious that in some scholars' eyes, Lin Shu was an opponent of the New Culture Movement. But in reality, he contributed a lot to the movement through his writings and translations, which has been gradually recognized by today's critics. Lin Shu's works had a positive influence on the occurrence of the New Culture Movement.

Like most of the initiators and advocates of the New Culture Movement, Lin Shu was a patriotic scholar. After the Sino-Japanese War of 1894, Lin Shu became more concerned with national affairs and longed for reform. As early as 1887, with his friends who advocated constitutional reforms and modernization, Lin Shu discussed new political systems and criticized current malpractices. According to Gao Mengdan's recollection, 'whenever talking about China and foreign affairs, we could not help sighing. Lin Shu thought that speaking of changing the current tendencies in society, nothing was better than enlightening younger generation. Therefore, he wrote our discussion into his poems in a

---

[1] Liu Shousong, 1979, p.52.

[2] The compiling group of A History of Modern Chinese Literature of the seven universities in the middle south of China, 'A Struggle against the Feudal school of 'Back to the Ancients represented by Lin Shu', A History of Modern Chinese Literature, Changjiang wenyi chubanshe, 1979, in Xue Shuizhi and Zhang Juncai, 1982, p.382.

short time.'[1] This is Lin Shu's first famous poetry anthology *The New Yufu Poems in Fujian.*

The New Yufu Poems in Fujian, consisting of 32 poems, embodies a bold innovation in poetic content and form and is characterized by a distinctive style of the day, and strongly shows Lin Shu's inclination to reform and modernization. To put it briefly, he advocated the following:

(a) Keep the national hatred in mind, and loudly appeal to the public to arouse the Chinese people to save the nation from subjugation ('The National Hatred').

(b) Attack in writing the Eight-Legs essay and advocate learning from the West and enlightening the populace ('Village Teacher', 'Worn-out Blue Robe', 'Initiate Girl's Schools').

(c) Expose the corruption in the officialdom of the late Qing.

It may be said that *The New Yufu Poems in Fujian* is a gush of Lin Shu's patriotic zeal. Its radical ideas and popular form attracted the readers' attention. It is notable that Lin Shu, a scholar with a full traditional education, could give such a strong patriotic cry.

This was repeated in the prefaces and postscripts to many of his translations. Lin Shu's early translations in particular aimed at propagating patriotic ideas. In his preface to *Wu zhong ren (People of the Mist)*, he said: ' I am old, neither intelligent and courageous nor erudite, and cannot do all I can to avenge our nation. My eyes are brimming with patriotic tears every day. Whenever I talk to my students about this, I cannot contain my feelings, so I spare no efforts to translate foreign novels.'[2] His aim of translating *Uncle Tom's Cabin* was 'not at skilfully telling a tragic story so as to draw readers' tears for no reason, but particularly on account of the situation that our nation will be forced into slavery soon, I have to cry out to the public.'[3] He also hoped that this work could help rouse the Chinese people to safeguard the nation. Obviously, Lin Shu's translation was motivated by nationalism, as were the advocates of the New Culture Movement.

Like the advocates of the New Culture Movement, Lin Shu's thought

---

[1] Gao Mengdan 高梦旦, 'The Postscript to New Yufu Poems in Fujian', in Xue Shuizhi and Zhang Juncai, 1982, p.127.

[2] A Ying 阿英, 1960, pp.232-233.

[3] Lin Shu 林纾, He inu Yu Tian Lu Ba 黑奴吁天录(The Postscript to Uncle Tom's Cabin), Shangwu yinshuguan, Beijing, 1981, p.206.

embodied reformist notions of democracy and science, which can be seen from the prefaces and postscripts to his works and translations. These prefaces and postscripts, together with his translations, duly influenced the New Culture Movement that took democracy and science as its two great banners. At the end of the 19th century, most intellectuals looked down on labouring people, but Lin Shu had an understanding of the sufferings and hardships of ordinary people. The poem 'The Old Man Who Sells Rushes' in his *The New Yuefu Poems in Fujian* describes the miserable experience of an old man who sells rushes, showing compassion for the labouring people. In the poem 'Sigh under the Light', he wrote of servant-girls with 'too many rod wounds on the back', recounting their inhuman plight of 'new wounds are added before the old ones heal up, the big rods are used so many times that they snap'. He was indignant over the brutal maltreatment. The lines such as 'I hear that there are prohibitions against slavery in Western Europe' and 'all human beings are on an equal basis regardless of their social status'[1] reflect both his expectation for democratic politics and his ideas of anti-slavery and advocating equality.

Similarly, in the poem 'Fallen Flowers' in *The New Yuefu Poems in Fujian*, Lin Shu showed deep sympathy for prostitutes who 'feel miserable in the dark'. In his preface to *A Legend of Lusugelan (Lusugelan xiao zhuan)*,[2] he wrote:

> When I translated *La Dame aux Camélias*, I cast my pen aside three times. I think that women in this world are more steadfast than worthy men. Only those worthy men like Longpang and Bigan who were extremely loyal and steadfast, can compare favourably with Marguerite.[3]

Here Lin Shu placed Marguerite as a prostitute and the well-known Chinese figure on a par. It shows how deeply Lin sympathized with unfortunate women. His sympathy was based on modern ideas of democracy and equality. In this respect, he surpassed his contemporary novelists such as Li Boyuan (1867–1906) and Wu Jianren (1866–1910),[4] as well as the literati such as Liu E[1] who treated

---

[1] Lin Shu, Minzhong xin yuefu 闽中新乐府(New Yuefu Poems in Fujian), Wei han keben, Fuzhou, 1897.

[2] The original title is unknown.

[3] Xinling Qike 信陵骑客, Lushugelan xiaozhuan 露漱格兰小传(A Legend of Lusugelan), Putong xueshu shi, 1902.

[4] Li Boyuan 李伯元 (1867-1906) and Wu Jianren 吴趼人(1866-1810) were noted writers of Reprimanding Fiction during the late Qing. Li Boyuan's major work is

women as playthings. Hence, his translation of *La Dame aux Camélias* evoked a strong response among the readers. To be sure, one of the reasons why the translation could cause a sensation throughout China seems to be the ideological content of the novel.

Moreover, Lin Shu believed that women should have the right to education like men, and that women's foot-binding should be banned, and women should have the right to their marriage. All of these embody his preliminary ideas of democracy. Lin's views have something in common with the positions of the advocates of the New Culture Movement. Running girls' schools and abolishing women's foot-binding was not realized until the May Fourth Movement, but Lin Shu had expressed these positions before the Constitutional Reforms of 1898. Evidently, Lin Shu was a man ahead of his times.

Lin Shu also regarded the lack of democracy in China as one of the reasons for national subjugation. His approval to the constitutional reforms was based on his discontent with autocratic monarchy. In 1905, in the postscript to his translation of *Montezuma's Daughter (Ying xiaozi huoshan baochou lu)*, he stated, 'The subjugation of Maxico resulted from the veneration of the monarchical power' and 'in an uncivilized country, a monarch always regards his power supreme, how could this country escape from subjugation?'[2] Like Kang Youwei and Liang Qichao, Lin Shu's ideal society is a democratic one under constitutional monarchy rather than autocratic monarchy. His support of the constitutional monarchy was qualified by his reformist ideology. In the preface to his translation of *Waterloo: A Sequel to the Conscript*, Lin Shu also said, 'As French people's learning has gradually increased, the democratic system has been established already'.[3] Although Lin Shu's democratic ideas were still in the making, they played an active role in the introduction of the democratic ideas through translation from the West into China.

Lin Shu asserted that education could save China from peril, and he

---

Guanchang xianxing ji 官场现形记(The Bureaucrats: a revelation) and Wu Jianren's is Ershi nian mudu zhi guai xianzhuang 二十年目睹之怪现状(Strange Events Witnessed in the Last Twenty Years).

[1] Liu E 刘鹗(1857-1909), the late Qing novelist. His main novel is Lao Can youji 老残游记(The Travels of Lao Can).

[2] Lin Shu, Ying xiaozi huoshan baochou lu 英孝子火山报仇录(Montezuma's Daughter), Shangwu yinishuguan, Shanghai,1905.

[3] Lin Shu, Hutielu zhanxue yu xing ji 滑铁卢战血余腥记(Waterlo: Aequel to the Conscript), Wenmin shuju, Shanghai, 1904.

earnestly hoped that the young generation could diligently study. In this respect, he also prefigured central May Fourth ideas. He wrote: 'The yellow race is in imminent danger now! I want to exhort my compatriots to pursue their studies. Only in this way can this nation dispel his slavery, otherwise, the whole nation will be reduced to the status of slavery which is not different from a donkey's.'[1] He related learning to wiping out the humiliation of the nation. In the preface to his translation of *Waterloo: A Sequel to the Conscript*, he pointed out that the reason why France could free itself from peril and survive was that all the French people devoted themselves to learning, so all of them knew national humiliation.[2] In his views, science and culture must be introduced from the West into China, if China wants to become as strong and powerful as Western countries are. He maintained that the Chinese nation should abandon the content of traditional Chinese education: 'The traditional etiquette that exists in name only, and those essays on integrity and loyalty are not helpful to saving China now'.[3] Instead, education involves learning science and culture from the West. In the preface to the translation of *People of the Mist*, he advocated, 'We should use sword and rifle against a robber who is attempting to loot our things. We should deal with a robber who is attempting to extinguish our race by education. Learning what the robber has learned is not in order to become a robber but to guard against robbery. Only in this way can the robber's capacity be limited.'[4] Clearly, Lin Shu aimed at making China powerful so as to guard against the invasion of foreign powers. He continued, 'Europeans aim at reforms and modernization, only pursuing new things and knowledge, even of novel, a genre that has been regarded as insignificant, they give a consideration from a new vision, and remove old things. If our generation is pedantic, and is exceedingly fond of antiquities, how can we get to know new truths in our lives?'[5] He also criticized some of well-known scholars who 'never learn about Western learning, and prefer digging into deep, musty old books throughout

---

[1] Lin Shu 林纾, 'Dan pian shi yu 14' 单篇识语十四, Yisuo yuyan 伊索寓言 (Aesop's Fables), Shangwu yinshuguan, Shanghai, 1903.

[2] Lin Shu, Hua   tielu zhanxue yu xing ji 滑铁卢战血余腥记 (Waterlo: Aequel to the Conscript), Shangwu yishuguan, Shanghai, 1904.

[3] Lin Shu, Wu zhong ren 雾中人 (People of the Mist), Shangwu yinshuguan, Shanghai, 1906. p.1.

[4] Ibid.

[5] Ibid.

their lives'.[1] He asserted: 'if the ruler rejects western learning, how can it flourish in China?'[2] In order to urge his students to study Western learning diligently, he cited his own experience as an example. He sighed that he was too old to join his students to learn from Western teachers, and saw it as a great misfortune of his life. At that time, most of the feudal literati were parochial, arrogant and conservative, but Lin Shu actively advocated learning Western science and culture. It indicates that he was far from conservative for his times. Although his starting point is not exactly the same as the advocates of the New Culture Movement, it is undeniable that the movement was influenced by Lin's ideas.

Lin Shu's contribution to the New Culture Movement is especially significant in terms of literary translation. Lin Shu occupied a prominent position among modern Chinese translators. Though Lin Shu had no clear reformist purpose when he translated *La Dame aux* Camellias, his later translations consciously disseminated and introduced new Western culture in China. He is therefore one of the early initiators of bourgeois new culture in China.

Lin Shu started his translation from the late 19th century. During the period, Kang Youwei and others were attempting to save China through political reforms while Sun Yat-sen and others were attempting to do it by overthrowing the Qing dynasty in a radical revolutionary way. Lu Xun thought that the first step of the revolution was to change people's spirit. In his *On the Spirit of the Romanticist Poets* (*Molu shi li shuo*, 1907), Lu pointed out, 'The enhancement of the national spirit is related to the extensive knowledge of the world'.[3] Although Lin Shu was not in favour of revolution, he wanted to introduce the Chinese people to the political and social conditions of the foreign countries so as to wake up his compatriots and make them realize the danger of the national subjugation and genocide.

Lin Shu's translation and introduction of foreign novels were influenced by Yan Fu and Liang Qichao's positions. Around the Constitutional Reforms, Yan

---

[1] Ibid.
[2] Ibid.
[3] Lu Xun 鲁迅, Fen 坟(The Grave), Lu Xun quanji 鲁迅全集(The Compete Works of Lu Xun), Vol.1, Remin wenxue chubanshe, 1973, p.58.

Fu and Xia Huiqing's 'The Origin of Printing Novels in This House'[1], Liang Qichao's 'The Preface to the Translation and Publication of Political Novels'[2] and 'On the Relation between Novel and Governance of the Masses'[3] were published, which greatly raised the position of the novel in society. They stressed that the 'novel is the best in all the literary forms', and its effect 'is bigger than Chinese classics', and 'if we really want to save the nation, we will have to start from the novel, from the reform of the novel'.[4] Liang Qichao added: 'USA, Britain, Germany, France, Austria, Italy, Japan and other countries have been progressing in politics day by day, which is to a great extent due to political novels.' He took the 'novel as the spirit of a nation'. Liang proposed to translate all the foreign scholars' works on the current political situations of China one after another. [5] The writings of Yan Fu, Liang Qichao and others not only improved the status of novel in the society, but also made preparations for the translation of foreign novels, although they did not put their ideas into practice. Lin Shu was the one who turned their ideas into reality. Lin Shu's ideas were similar to these early reformists. In the postscript to *Hong jiao hua jiang lu* (*Beatrice*), he stated that some were ignorant and ill-informed as their education was hampered by pedants so that they were muddled in their life, while others who were clear-headed benefited from novels, not from pedants.[6] He wrote novels because he considered that the 'novel has sufficient appeal for readers'.[7] He favoured foreign novels because 'Western novels contain either philosophical reasoning or human experiences. They are not carelessly written.'[8]

---

[1] Yan Fu 严复 and Xia Suiqing 夏穗清，'Ben guan fuyin xiaoshuo yuanqi'本馆附印小说缘起 (The Origin of Printing Novels in This House), in A Ying, 1960, p.12.

[2] Liang Qichao 梁启超，'Yi yin zhengzhi xiaoshuo xu'译印政治小说序(The Preface to the Translation and Publication of Political Novel', in Liao Qichao, Yinbishi wenji 饮冰室文集(The Collected Works of Yinbishi), Vol. 3, Zhonghua shuju, Taibei, 1961, p.34.

[3] Liang Qichao, 'Lun xiaoshuo yu qun zhi guanxi'论小说与群治关系(On the Relation between Novel and Governance of the Masses', Yinbishi wenji 饮冰室文集(The Collected Works of Yinbishi), Vol. 1, Zhonghua shuju, Taibei, 1951.

[4] A Ying, 1960, p.12.

[5] Liang Qichao, 1961, p.34.

[6] Lin Shu, Hong jiao hua jiang lu 红礁画浆录 (Beatrice), Shangwu yinshuguan, 1906.

[7] Lin Shu, Ying xiaozi huoshan baochou lu 英孝子火山报仇录(the preface to Montezuma's Daughter), Shangwu yinshuguan, 1905.

[8] Ibid.

He appreciated the role and influence of foreign novels in terms of national political success and failure. Lin Shu's aim of translation was indirectly to warn the nation of its peril: 'I cannot help giving my cry for the people due to the situation: our nation will fall into slavery soon'.[1] For this reason, he began to translate *Uncle Tom's Cabin*. It may be said that Lin Shu's translated foreign novels were not only well received at that time, but also inspired the reformist zeal for saving China. As Lu Xun stated, novels can help people 'find both the society and themselves'',[2] for it was easy for them to associate the contents of Lin Shu's translated works with the reality and issues facing China.

However, in the process of his translation, he also gradually recognized the artistic value of foreign novels, which helped to dispel his prejudices against the art of the Western literature. As a well-known master of classical Chinese prose, Lin Shu held the prose of Sima Qian, Ban Gu, Han Yu and Liu Zongyuan in esteem, regarding them benchmarks for all the prose in China. He highly praised *The Dream of the Red Chamber* too: 'As for Chinese novels, nothing but *The Dream of the Red Chamber* could be regarded as reaching the peak of perfection'.[3] But he did not blindly worship Chinese culture. After his translation of Dickens's *David Copperfield*, he was full of praise for Dickens's artistry, thinking that Dickens's works were equal to *Records of the Grand historian* and *The Dream of the Red Chamber*. He also commented on Scott's *Ivanhoe*: 'foreshadowing, connections, tonal modification and composition can be seen everywhere, which is very similar to the works of our ancient prose writers', and Scott's novel could equate with Sima Qian's *Records of the Grand Historian*.[4] He was fond of Harggard's prose, thinking that Harggard's prose, like Han Yu's prose, contained hints foreshadowing later developments, and his usage was the same as the usage in *Records of the Grand historian*. After finishing his translation of Harggard's *Allan Quatermain*, he sighed in admiration, 'What a striking

[1] Lin Shu, 1982, p.206

[2] Lu Xun, 'Wenyi yu zhengzhi de qiantu' 文艺与政治的歧途 (The Divergence between Literature and Art and Politics), Ji wai ji 集外集, in Lu Xun Quanji, 1973, p.477.

[3] Feng Qi,, 1998, p.186.

[4] Lin Shu, Sakexun jie hou yingxiong Lue 萨克逊劫后英雄略(Ivanhoe), Shangwu yinshuguan, Shanghai, 1914, p.1.

similarity between Western works and Sima Qian's *Records of the Grand historian*!'[1] Lin Shu often mentioned foreign writers and famous Chinese literary writers such as Sima Qian in the same breath, and placed foreign novels on a par with *Records of the Grand historian* and *The Dream of the Red Chamber*. This had a great influence on Chinese intellectual circles at that time. Before Lin's translation, very few foreign literary works had been introduced into China, so the Chinese readers knew very little about foreign literature. As Zheng Zhenduo admitted that the intelligentsia of the time thought that the backwardness of China was merely its corrupted political structure, but Chinese literature was the highest and finest in the world; until Lin Shu introduced Western literature into China, Chinese intellectuals did not knew that so-called literature also existed beyond China, where there were also literary writers who could compare favourably with the first-rate Chinese writers.[2]

Lin Shu's appraisal basically helped to establish the status of foreign literature in China. His translations not only attracted a great number of readers, but also inspired many people to become engaged in literary translation. Lin Shu's translations therefore have a pioneering significance in the history of modern Chinese literature. The vast amount of literary translations imported both new ideological contents and new techniques of expression in China. The new techniques of expression inspired Chinese literati to break from the artistic form of traditional Chinese novel. This laid the groundwork for the development of the new Chinese literature from1917 onward. During the period of the New Culture Movement, a radical change took place in the literary creation, particularly the creation of vernacular novel in China. As Lu Xun pointed out, the historical reasons for this change were 'the social demands' and 'the impact of Western literature'.[3] It is argued that Lin Shu's translations were a crucial forerunner of China's modern literature.

In retrospect, it is not hard to find that Lin Shu and his translations have been berated largely because of his attitude towards the constitutional reforms of 1998 and the New Culture Movement as well as his free translation method. Although there appeared positive assessment of Lin Shu, the dominant

[1] Lin Shu, Feizhou yan shui chou cheng lu 斐洲烟水愁城录(Allan Quatermain), Shangwu yinshuguan,1905, p.1.
[2] Zheng Zhenduo, 1970, p.1229.
[3] Lu Xun, "'Caixie Jiao' Xiaoyin"《草鞋脚》小引，Lu Xun quanji 鲁迅全集 (Complete Works of Lu Xun), Vol.6, Renmin wenxue chubanshe, 1981, p.20.

assessment is negative. In the negative views, Lin Shu was a conservative or a reactionary 'old fogy' and the leading opponent of the New Culture Movement. Conversely, my argument is that in historical and cultural context, Lin Shu advocated and endorsed the constitutional reforms along with the advanced intellectuals such as Kang Youwei, Liang Qichao and Yan Fu. Therefore, he ought to be seen primarily as a figure with reformist ideas rather than with conservative or reactionary ideas, even though he disapproved the Republican Revolution. Objectively, his political attitude is one matter while his contribution and achievement in translation is another. Some see Lin Shu as an opponent of the New Culture Movement, but I argue conversely that Lin Shu was a pioneering figure of the New Culture Movement and modern Chinese literary translation. His introduction of Western ideas and literature in China by his translations enlightened the May Fourth generation of intellectuals and to some extent contributed to the occurrence of the New Culture Movement.

In short, Lin Shu was a reformist and a constitutional monarchist who in retrospect was berated and judged on his political views. This is now changing. Some critics have seen him as a pioneer in terms of the core concepts that were later central to China's New Culture Movement and May Fourth Movement. This cultural context is crucial to our re-evaluation of Lin Shu's translations.

Chapter 4

Lin Shu in Cultural Context

This chapter focuses on Lin Shu's translations in the cultural context of China. Examining Lin Shu and his translations in the cultural context of that time help us to understand their significance and contributions. First we investigate Lin Shu's translation activities, including his choice of and response to the original, his translation output and translation practice, and then, substantiate our arguments through a case study: Lin Shu's translation of *Le Dame aux Camélias*. This chapter links the two dimensions of this study: cultural context and a close comparative analysis of relevant texts.

1. Lin Shu's Translations in Cultural Context

There are three noticeable features in Lin Shu's translations: Lin Shu's choice of and response to the original, translation, and output translation practice. It may be said that these feature were closely linked to the cultural context of early modern Chinese translation.

(1) Lin Shu's Choice and Response

As stated in Chapter 2, Toury believes that translation is designed to fulfil the needs of the target culture by introducing into that culture a version of something existing in a source culture, which – for one reason or another – is deemed worthy of introduction into the target culture.[1] Toury's argument may be used partly to explain the reason for Lin Shu's success and influence in translation. The popularity of Lin Shu's translations to some extent indicates the need of Chinese culture (as a recipient culture) and the cultural interest and expectation of the Chinese reading public. As a matter of fact, in the process of choosing and responding to the originals, Lin Shu acted as both a reader and a translator/writer as argued earlier in Chiapter 2. As a reader, his reading interest and expectation would be the same as most of the Chinese readers', and as a translator/writer, he intuitively knew what the target culture needed and what

---

[1] Toury, 1995, p.166.

interested the readers. Therefore, he wrote a lot of prefaces or postscripts for his translations to express his translation motive and his feelings about the originals. Through reviewing his writings and inspecting his choice and response to the original, we can detect that the relations between Lin Shu's translations and his trans-cultural context.

It is an arguable question: what role did Lin Shu play as to the choice of the original? How did Lin Shu's preference influence his choice of the originals? It is generally thought that the choice of the originals was entirely dominated by his collaborators owing to Lin Shu's ignorance of foreign languages. Zheng Zhenduo thought that because Lin Shu did not understand any foreign language, the selection of original works was completely in the hands of the oral collaborators with whom he worked. Zheng described Lin Shu and his collaborators' choice of the originals: 'those oral interpreters just knew to pick a book at random and then read it. They felt it a good story, and orally relayed it to Lin Shu, and then Lin Shu wrote it down.'[1] According to Zheng, Lin Shu played an entirely passive role in the process of choosing the originals. This may be an unreasonable assumption. Compton's view seems more reasonable. He believed that as far as selection of works to be translated is concerned, 'Lin could have had a role in spite of his ignorance of foreign languages'. His reasons are that firstly, Lin Shu had the option of translating or not translating works brought to him; secondly, Lin might have been inspired to translate more works by a particular author after his initial introduction to him; finally, in at least one case, Lin was inspired to translate a work after seeing an earlier version of the same novel.[2] It is possible that the collaborators played a dominant role in collecting the originals, but Lin was unlikely to play a passive role in choosing among originals the collaborators had collected for translation. As Compton states, 'Lin Shu had the option of translating or not translating works brought to him'. In view of Lin Shu's personality of 'obstinacy'[3] and his prestige, Lin probably persisted in his own consideration and judgement in choosing the original for translation, and his consideration and judgement was perhaps respected by the collaborators, for most of them were Lin Shu's admirers or

---

[1] Zhend Zhenduo, 1970, p.1225.

[2] Copmton, R.W., 1971, pp.189-190.

[3] Lin Shu 林纾, 'Leng Hongsheng zhuan' 冷红生传 (A Brief Biography of Leng Hongsheng), Weilu wenji 畏庐文集 (Collected Essays of Lin Shu), Shangwu yinshuguan, Shanghai, 1928, p.25.

students. From Lin Shu's prefaces or postscripts, we can see his initiative in choosing the originals. The preface to his translation of *Joan Haste* shows that he was motivated to choose and translate *Joan Haste* by his dissatisfaction with Pan Xizi's incomplete version (discussed later in this chapter). For a foreign work that the readers and he were interested in, he would sometimes seek it on his own initiative to translate it. In the preface to his translation of *Benita* by Haggard (*Gui yi jin ji*), Lin said that, after hearing from Yan Fu that theology was in vogue in the West and there was a book that vividly describes ghosts in detail, he wanted to find the book for translation.[1] When he saw his translations of several Dickens's works were well received by the readers, Lin Shu told the readers in his preface to *Xiaonü Naier zhuani* (*The Old Curiosity Shop*) that Dickens's works were too many to be translated in time. He asked the readers to wait patiently, and promised that he would continue to translate Dickens's works to refresh the readers.[2] These prefaces of Lin Shu not only indicate that Lin Shu did not passively accept the originals brought to him by his collaborators, but also reveal his motives for choosing the originals.

<u>In Search of Similarities</u>

Why did Lin Shu's translations have such strong appeal to the Chinese readers? The reasons most probably relate to the subject matter, content and style of his translated works, which were readily identified and accepted by the Chinese readers. It may be seen from his prefaces and postscripts to his translations that the above-mentioned aspects, especially the subject matter, of foreign works and their relations to the needs of the target culture or the reception of the Chinese readers was one of Lin Shu's main considerations. As Toury says, 'After all, as much as translation entails the retention of aspects of the source text, it also involves certain adjustments to the requirements of the target system', the novelty of a translated work 'derives from the target culture itself, and relates to what that culture is willing (or allowed) to accept vs. what it feels obliged to submit to modification or even totally reject.'[3]. Obviously, in Lin Shu's translations, some inherent factors in the source works were truthfully introduced in order to influence or change the Chinese culture while some

---

[1] Zhu Xizhou, 1923, p.34.
[2] Ibid., p.6.
[3] Toury, 1995, p.166.

modifications were also made in order to make the translation acceptable to the target readers. To do so, Lin Shu sought identical aspects between the ST and the TT. For instance, in the preface to *Xiaonü Naier zhuan*(*The Old Curiosity Shop*), Lin Shu identified something in common between Chinese literature and foreign literature in literary expression: despite the differences in subject matter, plot and characters, the various expressions of feeling in the work all roots in human nature, and therefore 'it is an eternal truth, no matter who they are, the Chinese or foreigners, cannot overstep it.'[1] In Lin's eyes, it was impossible to change this common feeling, in China or elsewhere. In the postscript to *Honghan nülang zhuan* (*Colonel Quaritch, V.C.*), after comparison between Sima Qian's *Records of the Grand historian* and Haggard's *Colonel Quaritch, V.C.*, Lin Shu stated, 'There are foreshadowing lines in Haggard's works. The usage is the same as one in *Records of the Grand historian*.'[2] In the preface to *Bingxue yinyuan* (*Dombey and Son*), Lin Shu believed that the plots of *Zuo zhuan* (*Zuo Commentary*) and *Records of the Grand historian* were conceived as ingeniously as Dickens's works.[3] More concretely, Lin Shu made a comparative analysis of the literary techniques used in *Feizhou yanshui chou cheng lu* (*Allan Quatermain*) and Sima Qian's *Records of the Grand historian*, pointing out the similarities, wondering: 'how alike is the Westerners' works to Sima Qian's *Records of the Grand historian* in writing style!'[4] More important is that Lin Shu identified the themes or ideological contents of the originals that concerned the Chinese readers at that time (discussed in detail in the preceding chapter). Lin Shu's efforts in search of the similarities between the ST and the TT contributed much to the Chinese readers' enthusiastic reception.

Without question, there are similarities and differences between target culture and source culture. Generally, the similarities are readily accepted by the target culture whereas the reception of the differences mostly depends on target readers' expectations. In China's period of transition from the traditional to the modern, the differences may attract more attention and be more favorably received by some readers, but they may also be rejected and opposed by

---

[1] Feng Qi, 1998, p.185.
[2] A Ying, 1960, 252.
[3] Ibid., 265.
[4] Ibid, 216..

conservative readers. Therefore, when Lin Shu chose the originals, the receptive conditions of the target culture were certainly taken into his account.

Literary Subject Matters

Love is a predominant subject matter in Lin Shu's translated works. As Lin Shu stated, 'the first reason why fiction can move readers is to depict the sentiment between men and women.'[1] In the West and China, there are a great number of love stories. A new high tide in love stories sprang up in the early Republican period. It was originated from the late Qing, and closely related to the translated novels of that time. This high tide of the love story was actually initiated by Lin Shu's translation of *La Dama aux Camélias*. In the Chinese readers' eyes, *La Dama aux Camélias* was a love story. It fascinated the Chinese readers. Why was this Western love story so well received in China? What is the cultural basis of the reception?

In the Chinese society of the late Ming and the early Qing, Confucian ethical codes were highly emphasised. The conflict between love and a patriarchal society became more intense. However, the stories of 'talent meets beauty' of the period expressed the yearning for a true love rather than the constraints of the patriarchal society. These love stories were thus frequently romanticized, in which the conflict between a young couple in free love and their parents is rarely seen. Lin Shu's choice and translation of *La Dama aux Camélias* showed his courage and insight. *La Dama aux Camélias* conveys the idea centring around individuality, which is antagonistic to a patriarchal clan system. The work speaks of true love, and attributes the reason for the lovers' tragedy to the father, for he interferes in their love to uphold the reputation of the family. At that time, Song Cen, a Chinese critic, made a comparison between *La Dama aux Camélias* and *The Dream of the Red Chamber*, calling the former 'a foreign *The Dream of the Red Chamber*'[2] In fact, as for as ideas are concerned, *La Dama aux Camélias* goes a step further in comparison to *The Dream of the Red Chamber*. The latter depicts the love between a young man and a young girl who are well-matched in social and economic status, whereas in the former Armand

---

[1] Zhu Xizhou, 1923, p.36.
[2] .Song Cen 松岑, 'Lun xieqing xiaoshuo yu xin shehui zhi guanxi'论写情小说与新社会之关系(On the Relations between Romantic Fiction and New Society), in New Fiction, No.17, 1905..

falls in love with a courtesan. In the eyes of Armand's father, it is a disgrace to the reputation of his family, so he strangles their love while Marguerite displays her noble character through her self-sacrifice, setting off the baseness, imperiousness and cruelty of Armand's father. Lin Shu deleted and changed some dialogues that were contrary to orthodox Chinese ideas, but basically, he truthfully rendered the novel. Therefore, Western humanist spirit of the original attacked the ideas of the patriarchal clan system existing in Chinese society of the time. This attack coincided with the needs of the generation of reformist intellectuals.

Lin Shu's translation of Haggard's *Joan Haste* brought a stronger shock to the traditional Chinese idea of 'filial obedience'. The rulers of the Qing dynasty advocated governing the nation with filial piety. But in *Joan Haste*, the male protagonist Henry openly goes against his father's will, and is not ready to accept an arranged marriage, while Joan also openly reprimands her father for abandoning her. The lovers, who are not in accordance with filial obedience and have an illegitimate child, are commended as positive characters in the novel. They get married for the sake of love instead of fame, wealth and social position, and are more noble-minded, pure and sincere than all the people around them. Joan criticizes her father's wrongdoing of abandoning her, exhibiting her moral integrity through her spirit of self-sacrifice. Lin Shu's version of *Joan Haste* caused strong repercussions among the Chinese reading public at that time. In *Joan Haste*, Joan is pregnant before her marriage. It was due to this episode in his complete version that Lin Shu was reproached by conservative scholars fifty years ago. Prior to Lin Shu's translation, there had been another version of *Joan Haste* by Pan Xizi, but the translator only translated the first half of the novel, omitting the depiction of Joan Haste's passionate love for Henry, her pregnancy and her illegitimate child in order to preserve Joan's virginity. Lin Shu deemed it regrettable, thus producing a complete version of the novel.[1] Yin Bansheng, a conservative Chinese scholar, after reading the two versions, believed that Pan Xizi deliberately made omissions of the original in order to convey Joan's moral integrity while Lin Shu truthfully rendered the whole work in order to convey her licentiousness and degradedness.[2] Even reformists felt it difficult to accept

[1] Lin Shu, Jiayin xiaozhuan 迦茵小传 (Joan Haste), Shangwu yinshuguan, Beijing, 1981, p.1.
[2] A Ying, 1960, pp.285-287.

the ideas in Lin Shu's version. For example, Jin Tianhe, a vigorous advocate of feminism, attacked Lin Shu, 'instigates men to visit prostitutes and violate the will of their fathers as Armand does while instigating women to have a premarital pregnancy and break their virginity as Joan Haste does.' He worried that the courtesy of holding and kissing a lady's hand would be in vogue in China. China would rather follow the ancestors' teachings, and strictly enforce autocracy in order to control relations between men and women.[1] In addition, Zhong Junwen, another reformist, criticized Lin Shu: 'Where Pan Xizi tried to cover up for Joan, Lin Shu always tried to make up for to display her ugliness. How disgraceful it is!'[2] These attacks came from the reformists who advocated translating and learning from foreign novels rather than the diehards who cherished conservative ideas at that time. It shows how great shock these translated novels of Lin Shu brought to Chinese culture.

As a young man, Lin Shu was called 'an unconstrained scholar'. He satirized some sanctimonious Chinese scholars: 'It looks as if they were superficially refined, courteous and urbane, yet privately harbored beautiful women in mind, and did not dare to take action',[3] which perhaps partly explains why Lin Shu could accept and had the courage to translate love stories like *La Dame aux Camélias* and *Joan Haste*. In fact, to suit the Chinese readers, Lin Shu often made deletions and changes. For instance, the depiction of the lovers' lovemaking in *Joan Haste* was omitted in his translated work so that the readers more or less feel that the appearance of Joan's child is too unexpected. This seems to indicate that Lin Shu gave consideration to the acceptability of translation among the target culture and readers. However, these translated works of Lin Shu provided a new cultural idea: as long as it is a true love, in spite of going against the current moral principles, it should be affirmed and commended. The significance of this new idea lies that it not only carried forward the tradition of yearning for a true love in Chinese literature but also conferred a new meaning to Chinese love stories. It spurred the Chinese writers of love stories, not only to inherit the tradition of romantic literature, but also to

[1] Song Cen, 1905.
[2] Yan Bansheng 寅半生,'Du Jiayin xiaozhuan liang yiben hou'读《迦茵小传》两译本后（After Reading the Two Version of Joan Haste）, Game World, No.11, 1907.
[3] Lin Shu, Xianghu Xian Ying 橡湖仙影 (Dawn by R.Haggard), Shangwu yinshuguan, Shanghai, 1906.

have an eye to reality, exposing the conflicts and contradictions between love and reality. Individuality was highlighted. Anyway, in the period of the transition from the traditional to the modern, there existed rivalry between new and old cultures as well as new and old ideas. Undoubtedly, the translations of Lin Shu met the requirements of the modern Chinese culture and modern Chinese reading public, despite the fact that they were resisted by traditional culture. It indicates that these translated works of Lin Shu actually changed the Chinese readers' cultural and moral concepts: the readers could accept such a woman who falls in love with a married man if she cherishes a true love for him as well as accept a woman who is pregnant before marriage provided she has a noble mind. In other words, the readers began to be more concerned with a woman's feeling and spirit than her behavior, which greatly contributed to the women's emancipation in the May 4th New Culture movement.

As far as the reception of the original is concerned, Lin Shu actually assumed two roles simultaneously: both as a reader and as a translator. As argued, literary translation is a rewriting. As a reader/translator, Lin Shu, in his own way, applied his knowledge and brought his experience of life into play so as to throw himself into the process of the re-writing. According to Lin Shu's 'A Brief Autobiography of Leng Hongsheng', a beautiful and talented prostitute named Zhuang fell in love with him due to his learning and character, and wanted to meet with him, yet Lin Shu declined her request. His neighbors laughed at him and believed that he was an eccentric. Lin Shu sighed, 'I am not a man who is hostile to love, but I am a parochial man who is apt to be jealous. In case I love a woman, I will never change my mind until death. If it is really true, people may not understand this then; therefore I would rather refrain early from this relation… I like writing books; my translation of *La Dame aux Camélias* is particularly full of mournfulness and affection. I often laugh and say when reading it. Now that I have such a description in my translation, can it be said that a wooden and stubborn man like me is hostile to love?' [1] Perhaps, it is from Armand's ardent feeling for Marguerite that Lin Shu identified his own affection, which might be one of the reasons for his acceptance of the original. According to Gao Mengdan, one of Lin Shu's friends, when Lin Shu was 46, his wife Liu Qiong died of an illness. Lin Shu cherished a deep love for her, so he grieved. When Wang Shouchang returned from Paris with A.Dumas fils's novel

---

[1] Feng Qi, 1998, p.171.

La Dame aux Camélias, and invited him to translate this novel, he agreed immediately, as the sentimental tone of the work coincided with his state of mind at that time. In the process of translating this novel, Lin Shu devoted all his feelings. Whenever translating the most sorrowful episodes, he and his collaborator wailed together face to face.[1] In *A Critical View on Translation*, Zhou Yi and Luo Ping point out, 'Among all Lin Shu's translated works, the successful and well-received ones to a certain extent indicate the identification of the sentimental tone of the originals to Lin Shu's life situations and experiences, and that the translator poured his feelings into his translations.'[2] It seems that Lin Shu's personal experiences of life and feeling influenced his acceptance of the original.

Similarly, Lin Shu's prefaces and postscripts to his translated works also clearly manifest his motives of translation. Among them, the most important is to save the nation from subjugation and ensure its survival. It was imperative for the political, social and national culture of China at that time. In agreement with Liao Qichao's advocacy of political fiction, Lin Shu also paid attention to the social function of fiction, translating several political novels. Joseph Blotner states: 'As an art form and an analytical instrument, the political novel, now as ever before, offers the reader a means for understanding important aspects of the complex society in which he lives, as well as a record of how it evolves.'[3]

Lin's translation of Stowe's *Uncle Tom's Cabin* was widely read in China. It is a work against slavery. Indeed, it won the popularity and success in stirring up the public feeling against slavery in the United States and their anxiety for the destiny of the nation. Stowe wrote this novel during the Civil War in order to liberate the black slaves in the south of USA. Stowe declared in her preface that 'The object of these sketches is to awaken sympathy and feeling for the African race, as they exist among us; to show their wrongs and sorrows, under a system so necessarily cruel and unjust as to defeat and do away with the good effects of all that can be attempted for them.' The book did more than awaken sympathy, arousing the growing anti-slavery sentiment in the north, creating in part the political climate from which the Civil War grew. Thereupon, Blotner believed,

---

[1] Zuo Shunsheng, 1926, p.12.
[2] Zhou Yi and Luo Ping, 1999, p.127.
[3] Blotner, Joseph, The Political Novel, Greewood Press, Westport, 1955, p.1.

'*Uncle Tom's Cabin* is a prime example of the novel as political instrument both in intent and effect.'[1] But the effects of the novel were beyond America, and reached China. When Lin Shu translated this novel, Chinese labourers were being abused in USA. The Chinese readers read this novel and associated it with the precarious situation of the Chinese nation, thus causing a sensation throughout China. In the postscript to his translation of *Uncle Tom's Cabin*, Lin Shu clearly stated his motives: to contribute to bestirring the Chinese readers and saving the nation from subjugation to ensure its survival.[2]

From French writer G. Bruno's *Le tour de la France par deux enfants*, Lin Shu saw the reasons for developing industry to save the nation. He made this clear in the preface:

> Alas! Should we defend our country by troops? Yet the picked troops are not auspicious. Should we promote diplomacy by diplomatic language? Yet the national strength is so weak that it would be of no avail even if there were Zichan and Duanmuci's diplomatic language. [3] And the writings related to etiquette, moral integrity and righteousness existing in name only are not enough to empower the country. What can the country be empowered by? In my opinion, by knowledge, by students, by students who have lofty aspirations, especially by all the students who are experts in industry.[4]

It is evident that Lin Shu had the target culture and readers in mind. As a reader (or an audience), he knew what the target culture needed as well as what the target readers needed to know. As a translator, he aimed at introducing new ideas and factors that had not existed or been seldom found in Chinese culture to facilitate modernization. For example, from Haggard's *Beatrice*, Lin Shu recognized the issue of women's rights. In the novel, without tolerating his wife's arrogance and imperiousness toward him, the male protagonist falls in love with a gifted lady. They deeply love each other, but not in a promiscuous manner until the lady's death. For this reason, in the preface, Lin Shu said:

---

[1] Ibid., p.10.

[2] Lin Shu, 1981, p. 204.

[3] Zichan 子产, a senior official of Zheng State of the Spring and Autumn Period of China (770-746 B.C.), and Duanmuci 端木赐, one of Confucius's followers.

[4] Feng Qi, 1998, pp.181-182.

Alas! Freedom of marriage is a policy of benevolence. If it can be achieved, women will no longer sigh for their withered marriages throughout their life. ... To promote women's rights we need to initiate girl's schools. The affairs that exceed what is proper happen occasionally, but from the viewpoint of saving the nation, we should have an eye to great events. If someone merely seizes on some trifles, and regards them as malpractices of political reforms, and thus tries to suffocate the principles of being civilized, he is ignorant of political reforms. I am afraid that in case this book is published, everyone censures it as the licentiousness of Western customs and habits, and thereby hold back the promotion of establishing girl's schools, and still standing by the principle: a woman without ability is really a woman of virtue. This is not my long-cherished wish. [1]

Women's rights were a critical issue in Chinese culture in the transitional period. The reason for Lin Shu's acceptance and translation of the original *Beatrice* was to make readers concerned with women's rights. Certainly, Lin Shu's efforts in this respect preceded the May Fourth New Culture Movement. Chinese culture in the transitional period from traditional to modern showed two opposite inclinations: pioneering and conservative. When Lin Shu introduced pioneering ideas into the culture by translation, the pioneering ideas were more or less restricted by the conservative factors in the culture so that Lin Shu had to make some alterations of the original in order to make it acceptable in the culture, but at the same time, Lin Shu imported new concepts and ideas, which challenged conservative or negative aspects of the Chinese culture, thus bringing about changes to it.

Apart from the love story and political fiction, Lin Shu translated other types of fiction such as the historical novel, the adventure novel, the detective novel and so on. No matter what type of fiction he worked on, Lin Shu always expected that his translations could play a social role in the target culture, influencing and changing it. As a translator, Lin Shu had a strong sense of cultural mission: he expected to change the existing culture by translation. His target/culture-oriented translations were decided by the political, social, cultural and personal conditions of that time. As Toury argues:

---

[1] Ibid., pp.180-181.

After all, translations always come into being within a certain cultural environment and are designed to meet certain needs of, and/ or occupy certain 'slots' in it. Consequently, translators may be said to operate first and foremost in the interest of the culture into which they are translating, however they conceive of that interest. In fact the extent to which features of a source text are retained in its translation, which, at first sight, seems to suggest an operation in the interest of the source culture, or even of the source text as such, is also determined on the target side, and according to its own concerns: features are retained, and reconstructed in target-language material, not because they are 'important' in any *inherent* sense, but because they are assigned importance, from the recipient vantage point.[1]

Among the realistic novels translated by Lin Shu, the most conspicuous is Charles Dickens's works. In a humorous and satirical style, Dickens depicted the characters living in the lower strata of the English society, thus turning people's attention to social reform. Lin Shu reproduced Dickens's narrative style. The orphan David's ups and downs in life (*David Copperfield*), the corrupt orphan asylum, which actually became a place for training thieves (*Oliver* Twist), the Dombeys' family matters reflecting the change of England after the railways were built (*Dombey and* Son), the scene in which Nell dies in a desolate house (*The Old Curiosity Shop*), the conditions of village schools (*Nicholas Nickeby*) and so on were presented before the Chinese readers through Lin Shu's writings. In Lin Shu's time, there appeared several works of 'Reprimanding Fiction' with a realistic style, such as Li Boyuan's *The Bureaucrats: a revelation*, Wu Jianren's *Strange Events Witnessed in the Last Twenty Years*, and Zeng Pu's *Flowers in the Sinful Sea (Nie hai hua)*, but none of them gave so lively a portrayal of the real life of ordinary people as Dickens did in his novels. Lin Shu endorsed Liang Qichao's views on the political and social functions of fiction. He thought that 'Dickens took pains to select some long-standing defects of society present among the lower classes and dramatize them in novels, so that his government would find out them and put them right.'[2] He regretted that there were no writers like Dickens in China. Therefore, one of his motives of translating this novel was to let the Chinese

---

[1] Toury, 1995, p.12.
[2] Lin Shu, 'Preface to Oliver Twist', in Denton, Kirk A., edited, Modern Chinese Literary Thought: writings on literature 1893-1945, Stanford University Press, 1996, p.82.

readers/writers follow the example of Dickens to reflect the abuses of the society, and attract the rulers' attention to them. In his preface to *Kuairou yusheng shu(David Copperfield)*, he more clearly stated his motive for translating Dickens's novels:

Dickens's *David Copperfield* depicts lower-class society in various ways. …The malpractices among the common folk during the time when England was half-civilized are clearly exposed to the readers' eyes. When reading this novel, we Chinese should realize that society could be improved if a system of education is rigorously instituted. There is no need for us to be so enamoured with the West as to assume that all Europeans seem to be endowed with a sense of propriety and a potential for talent, and are superior to Asians. If readers of my translation reach a similar conclusion, I will not have translated this novel in vain.[1]

The introduction to Western realism through Dickens and Toistoy's works in China inspired more modern Chinese writers to be engaged in realistic writing. Lin Shu's translations of Conan Doyle's *Beyond the City* (*She nüshi zhuan*) in 1908, *Gambling the Son-in-law in Comet* (*Huixing duoxu lu*) in 1909,[2] *A MP Manipulated by His Wife* (*Zhenfen yiyuan*) in 1909,[3] John Oxenham's *God's Prisoner* (*Tian qiu chanhui lu*) in 1908, Montesquieu's *Lettres persanes* (*Yu yan jue wei*) in 1915 and L.N.Toistoy's *Childhood, Boyhood and Youth* (*Xianshen shuofa*) in 1918 also drew on social reality. *Gambling the Son-in-law in Comet* (*Huixing Duoxu Lu*) exposed an ugly social phenomenon in London. In the preface to the translated novel, Lin Shu stated, 'Why has someone called it a filthy novel? We may take this book as a warning.'[4] Dickens's *Oliver Twist* is also a realistic novel. It exposes the ugliness in the lower society. In the preface, Lin Shu believed that the reason for the power of Britain was that it could reform and mend its ways by referring to the social maladies exposed in the works of the novelists such as Dickens. If there were such novelists like Dickens in China, it would be of much help in

---

[1] Denton, 1996, p.86.
[2] The title and author of the original remain unknown. The English title here is translated by me.
[3] The title and author of the original remain unknown. The English title here is translated by me.
[4] Zhu Xizhou, 1923, p.12.

improving the Chinese social reality.[1]

Literary Genres

To meet the requirements of the development of Chinese fiction and the Chinese reading public, as well as to expand the influence and function of fiction in Chinese society, Lin Shu also translated other types of fiction, including both popular genres such as adventure stories, detective stories and ghost stories, and serious fiction such as the historical novel and the military novel. Snyder said, 'novels can be read in two ways: for pleasure and for profit.'[2] In fact, Lin Shu's translation of foreign fiction of all types, popular fiction in particular, and all combined pleasure with awareness that the content may reveal aspects of political and social life.

Lin Shu's translated works of detective fiction includes A.C.Doyle's *A Study in Scarlet*, M.M.Dodkin's *The Quest of Paul Beck* and E.P.Oppenheim's *The Secret*, and Arthur Morrison's *Martin Hewitt*. Along with other translators, Lin Shu brought about the popularity of detective fiction in China. In 'On the Chinese Translations of English Detective Novels during the Period of the Late Qing and the Early Republic', Kong Huiyi analyses the reasons for the popularity of detective fiction. She points out that on the one hand, the popularity of detective fiction in China was actually inseparable from the fact that detective fiction was very popular in all parts of the world, and for the intellectuals in the West, detective fiction was a literature of amusement; on the other hand, detective fiction in both content and form struck the Chinese readers as new, 'the new science and technology frequently mentioned in the detective novels — train, underground, telegram and so on — all were the things the Chinese people of the 19th century admired'[3]. Therefore, if the objective of translating foreign novels is to fill the gaps in the target culture, this type of fiction naturally attracted the Chinese readers who were assimilating foreign knowledge with great eagerness. Moreover, the logical ways in the Western detective works are similar to the Chinese 'Fiction of Detection'(Gong'an xiaoshuo). Yet in general, the description in the Western detective novel is more subtle and meticulous, and the case is more complicated and, and so more attractive to the

---

[1] Ibid.

[2] Snyder, Richard C., 'Editor's Foreword' in Blotner, 1955, p.v.

[3] Wang Hongzhi, 2000, p.93.

Chinese readers.

However, Lin Shu's consideration for translating Western detective stories might differ a little from the others. In the preface to his translation of Arthur Morrison's *Chronicles of Martin Hewitt* (*Shen shu gui cang lu*), Lin Shu mentioned the importance of detectives to the Western judicial process and emphasised the necessity of introducing Western detectives into China. He argued that 'China's judicial system was far inferior to the West'.[1] The main problem was that 'no lawyers pleaded for the accused and no detectives looked into the case of the accused', which led to a number of wrong cases. In his view, 'if Western detective stories could be popular in China, it would make the courts at different levels know how to improve the judicial system and make use of lawyers and detectives to decide a case'.[2] In addition, he argued that setting up 'law schools to train men as qualified lawyers and detectives' would gradually establish a fairer judicial system. If this were true, 'the detective stories would have a great achievement to their credit'.[3]   This seems to show that Lin Shu had interests beyond a detective story itself in Conan Doyle's works. He translated Doyle's seven works of fiction, but only one among them is really a detective story. The others seem to be little related to detective activities. For instance, *Beyond the City* is related to the issue of women's emancipation, *Uncle Bernac* is seen as an unauthorized biography of Napoleon, and *The White Company* is a historical novel. In fact, if we carefully examinine Lin Shu's choice of the subject matters of the originals, it is not hard to see Lin Shu's likings: it is commonly acknowledged that, as far as the process of detecting a case is concerned, Conan Doyle's short stories are far better than his novels. But Lin Shu translated his novel *A Study in Scarlet*, and a half of the story is irrelevant to the process of detecting the case. In *A Study in Scarlet*, Conan Doyle incorporates a detective story with an adventure story. It is the latter that attracted Lin Shu. Lin Shu's other translations of Conan Doyle's works are adventure fiction or historical fiction. It explains that Lin Shu had definite social purposes in choosing or accepting the original.

Lin Shu's introduction of Western adventure fiction filled in the gaps in available Chinese fiction. Among Lin Shu's translated works of adventure

---

[1] Zhu Xizhou, 1923, p. 47
[2] Ibid.
[3] Ibid.

fiction, *Lubinxun piaoliu ji* (*Robinson Crusoe* by Defoe) was the most popular. It is a story of a man shipwrecked alone on an island. Defoe, employing a first-person narrator, created a realistic frame for the novel. The account of a shipwrecked sailor conveys both the human need for society and the equally powerful impulse for solitude. But it also offered a dream of building a private kingdom, a completely self-made, self-sufficient Utopia. By giving a vivid reality to a theme with large mythical implications, the story has fascinated generations of Western readers. Similarly, after rendered by Lin Shu into Chinese, it has also fascinated generations of the Chinese readers. Why could the hero of the novel have such an appeal to Lin Shu that he decided to translate the work? In his preface to *Lubinxun piaoliu ji* (*Robinson Crusoe*), he gave a clear explanation: traditional Chinese culture emphasizes the doctrine of the golden mean of Confucianism, and sets it up as a doctrine that a man should adhere to in his whole life. This might have made the Chinese people lack a pioneering and adventurous spirit. Lin Shu attempted to change this by introducing Robinson Crusoe, a hero of adventure. In the preface, he argued,

> The English man Robinson, because he is not willing to accept the golden mean as a doctrine of his conduct, travels overseas alone by boat. As a result, he is wrecked in a storm, and was caught in a hopeless situation on a desert island. There he walks and sits alone, lives like a primitive man. He does not go back to his native country until twenty years later. From ancient times to the present, no book has recorded this incident. His father originally wishes that he could be a man who behaves according to the doctrine of the golden mean, but Robinson goes against his will, and in consequence, pioneering extraordinary undertakings. Thereupon, the adventurous people in the world, who are nearly devoured by sharks and crocodiles, are all inspired by Robinson.[1]

Apparently, Lin Shu hoped that his compatriots could, through reading his translation, learn the pioneering and adventurous spirit from the hero Robinson to revitalize the Chinese nation. In addition, Lin Shu also translated other adventure fictions such as J.D.Wyss's *Der schweizerische Robinson*, Haggard's *Allan Quatermain*, *The People of the Mist* and *King Solomon's Mines*.

---

[1] Lin Shu, Lubinxun piaoliu ji 鲁滨逊漂流记 (Robinson Crusoe), Shangwu yinshuguan, Shanghai, 1934, p.1.

Literary Style and Technique

As quoted in Chapter 2, Andre Lefevere asserts that translation is a rewriting of an original text, and that rewritings can influence a target culture.[1] In his choice and acceptance of the source text, proceeding from his consideration for the needs of the target culture, while importing new ideas by translation, Lin Shu introduced new literary concepts, styles, forms and techniques, which gave rise to a great change in both the Chinese readers' understanding of foreign literature. He therefore promoted the development of Chinese literary writing and the transition of Chinese literature from traditional to modern.

In the prefaces and postscripts, Lin Shu frequently made comparative comments on the similarities and differences between the originals and classical Chinese literary works. He sought the similarities between both in order that readers would not reject his translated works on the basis of the differences. He also demonstrated the differences between both in order that the readers could realize the significance of these differences in terms of the development of Chinese culture or literature.

As regards a novelist's literary talent, Charles Dickens is the novelist whom he had the greatest esteem for. In his preface to *The Old Curiosity Shop*, Lin Shu made a comparison between *The Old Curiosity* Shop and *The Dream of the Red Chamber*,

> Among Chinese novels, the best is *The Dream of the Red Chamber*. The author narrates the riches and honours on earth, sighing with emotion on the ups and downs of human feelings, and the description is deliberate and gorgeous and the composition is well-knitted, all of which are acclaimed as the acme of perfection. Moreover, the work is spiced with idlers, countrywomen, villains, and ends with wastrels; therefore the author is regarded to be good at description. Nevertheless, there is more refined taste than popular taste in this novel after all, yet not all the readers are interested in the refined taste. Dickens's works dismissed the pattern of celebrities and beautiful ladies, especially describing the evils, deceit and cruelty of lower-level of society. The ending unexpectedly, like castles in the air, make the audiences laugh or cry, too excited to control themselves for the

---

[1] Lefevere, 1991, p.XI.

moment, from which it can be clearly seen that the author's conception of the novel is circumspect and farsighted.[1]

Viewing the differences between the two famous works, Lin Shu affirmed the great artistry of *The Dream of the Red Chamber* and the profound realistic spirit of Dickens's novels. He concludes that this realistic spirit is insufficient in traditional Chinese literature. In the preface to his translation of *David Copperfield* (*Kuai rou yusheng shu*), Lin Shu also compared Dickens's *David Copperfield* with *Water Margin*, another classical Chinese novel. He discussed the similarities and differences between these two novels in the depiction of characters and structure. They both 'briefly depicting several dozen men, each of them appearing in an orderly fashion with individual characteristics'. The differences are: in *David Copperfield*, 'searching backward section by section for it, they will find that there has indeed been an account of this character or a source for the episode, but in *Water Margin*, 'when the author finally reaches the latter part of his novel, the characters pour out into the scene like a pack of coyotes, no longer distinguishable from one another', 'his spirit has failed to endure long enough to penetrate the entire novel'. [2] Lin Shu's comments are not without reason. Traditional Chinese novels have their own developmental context and course. Most traditional Chinese novels have an interesting plot, but pay little attention to the compactness of structure, as originally the story are not written on paper for reading but told to the audiences. It does mean that the Chinese novel has a different structure, and actually reflects the features of oral literature. Therefore, Lin Shu came to a conclusion: literature must pay attention to structure, though there are differences between Chinese and Western literature. It is Lin Shu's intention to introduce the strong points of the source literature to counteract the weaknesses of Chinese literature.

Lin Shu also translated historical novels, among which Scott and A.Dumas pere's works were especially well known. Scott's works drew their materials from the Crusades. Scott's *Ivanhoe* is Lin Shu's favourite work. It is one of the first to attempt to deal with the Middle Ages in a historically accurate manner. The author's artistic talent in this novel made a strong impression on Lin Shu. As a reader and a translator, Lin Shu readily accepted and rendered this work.

---

[1] Feng Qi, 1998, p.186.
[2] Denton, 1966, p.85.

Wolfgang Iser says, 'the study of a literary work should concern, not only the actual text but also, and the equal measure, the actions involved in responding to the text.'[1] Lin Shu's translation of *Ivanhoe* is an appropriate case in this respect. The process of Lin Shu's translation is actually also one of reading and interpretation according to his personal experience and feeling. His translated work is the outcome of his responding to the original text as well as the extension of his reading of the source text. Lin Shu's reading and interpretation were clearly reflected in his preface to *Ivanhoe*. In the preface, Lin Shu first placed Scott and the great Chinese writers Sima Qian and Ban Gu on a par, drawing an analogy between Scott and classical Chinese writers in the composition of a novel. In fact, Lin Shu brought the reading of *Ivanhoe* into the context of the target culture. In the preface, in comparison with Chinese literature, Lin Shu summarizes eight strong points of the novel in literary expressions such as structure, characterization, language, theme and style, which actually embody Lin Shu's own cultural reading and interpretation of the original text. Lin Shu made a brief comparison between Ban Gu's *History of the Former Han Dynasty: A Story of the Oriental Manqian (Han shu: dongfang manqian zhuan)* and *Ivanhoe*, believing that Ban Gu's description of Manqian's speaking to the dwarf and pulling out the sword to cut the flesh was more brilliant than Sima Qian's. Lin Shu said, 'In the eyes of a conservative person like me, there is certainly no humour in Western literature; but when describing the clown Wamba, Scott could fully express the sense of humour with just a few words, which consequently sets the reader roaring with laughter. His literary talent is not inferior to Ban Gu.' Lin Shu also remarked in the preface, 'Europeans had discriminated against the Jews for a long time, and tried to make them lose their family fortune, even dogs and lackeys also insulted them. Europeans were not sympathy with their sufferings; on the contrary, they held that it was a self-evident truth and the will of Heaven. But whenever the country needed, money was often borrowed from them. The Jews living in Europe were always preoccupied with the insecurity'.[2] It may be Lin Shu's summary of the ideas of the original, but he added, 'the Jew only knew his own home, but didn't know his country, taking his life with gold, and until his death he did not know what

---

[1] Iser, Wolfgang, *The Act of Reading: a theory of aesthetic response*, Routledge and Kegan Paul, London, 1978, pp.20-21.
[2] Lin Shu, 1914, p.2

the country was. If the people of yellow race really read this novel, it must be sufficient to cause their alertness.'[1] Here Lin Shu related the fate of the Jew to the possible fate of the Chinese as a warning. It may be said to be his feeling after reading the novel. Lin Shu's translation of *Ivanhoe* won the acclaim of Mao Dun and other famous Chinese scholars. His preface seemed to demonstrate his belief that his translated works could not only attract the Chinese readers but also arouse their patriotic feeling.

In short, it is proposed that Lin Shu's choice and acceptance of the originals was far from being passive, and to some extent, they reflected his own preference and judgement. His prefaces and postscripts evidently convey both his translation motives and orientation to the target culture. The subject matters, genres and styles of the originals were taken into consideration in his translations. More significantly, Lin Shu's comments in his prefaces and postscripts also involve cross-cultural and comparative literary criticism. He also recognized the source culture in a perspective of target culture, attempting to put the source culture in the garb of the target culture. He sought the similarities between both to make them readily accepted by the target readers as well as highlihgting the differences to import new ideological and artistic factors into the target culture and vitalize target culture.

(2) The Output of Lin Shu's Translations

As Kirk A. Denton states, Lin Shu is 'significant primarily as China's first and most prolific translator of Western novels'[2] Together with Yan Fu, Lin played a key role in the introduction to Western culture during the transition of Chinese culture from traditional to modern. Leo Ou-Fan Lee added to this: Lin Shu is 'the first major translator of Western literature and left an unsurpassed record of some 180 translated works'.[3]

Of the major literary translators in the period of the late Qing and the early Republic, Lin Shu was the 'most prolific' as the following table illustrates:

---

[1] Ibid.
[2] Denton, 1996, p.66.
[3] Lee, Leo Ou-Fan, 1973, p.44

Table / Figure 4:1 Output of Translated Novels in China[49]

Translator	Output of Translated Novels
Lin Shu	180 or so
Bao Tianxiao	80 or more
Zhou Shoujuan	30 or more
Zhou Guisheng	21 or more
Wu Tao	20 or more
Wu Jianguang	8 or more
Zhou Zuoren	7
Zeng Pu	6 or more
Lu Xun	5
Liang Qichao	3
Su Manshu	2

By comparison, Lin Shu's translations of foreign novels top the above-mentioned translators' records in amount. Scholars of different periods have different estimates of the total number of Lin Shu's translated works:

Table / Figure 4:2 Scholars' Estimates of Lin Shu's Translations

Estimator	Year	Number
Zheng Zhenduo	1924	156
Zhu Xizhou	1929	182
Han Guang	1935	171
Ma Tailai	1981	184
Yu Jiuhong	1982	181

Western scholars such as Denton claims that Lin Shu's translated works are close to 200.[1] Evidently, the number of Lin Shu's translated works is still a debatable question. According to Zheng Zhenduo's statistics, 156 of Lin Shu's translated works include 132 published, 24 unpublished. In 1935, Han Guang corrected Zheng's statistics: Lin Shu had 171 translated works including unpublished works. Later scholars mostly followed his statistics. Yet there is a problem in Han Guang's estimate. Lin Shu sometimes separated a foreign work

---

[1] Denton, 1996, p.66.

into two books, which ought to have been reckoned as one, but Han Guang counted them separately. In his statistics, Zhu Xizhou's estimate the same estimate as Han Guang's; besides, the figure in his list of Lin Shu's translated works is fewer than 182. Ma Tailai offered a new statistics: Lin Shu had 184 translated works, including 137 offprints, 23 unpublished works, and 8 manuscripts; yet Ma Tailai's estimate includes non-literary works like *Minzhong xue* (Ethnology) and *Ouzhou Tongshi* (*Comprehensive History of Europe*). On my own investigation, Lin Shu translated 181 foreign literary works, including 18 unpublished translated works in the twenty-five years before his death. (See Appendix: List of Lin Shu's Translated Work). Up to now, none of the Chinese translators has outstripped Lin Shu in translation output. As Qian Zhongshu said, Lin Shu's translated novels were one of his great discoveries at the age of twelve, and attracted him into a new world beyond *Water Margin*, *The Journey to the West* and *Strange Stories from Liaozhai*).[1] Thus, the contribution of Lin Shu as a pioneer of cross-cultural translation in China should not be underrated.

(3) Lin Shu's Translation Practice

Looking back at Lin Shu's translation practice, we can see that it differs noticeably from today's translation practice, but was a common practice in the early modern literary translation in China. In this section, I will examine in details how Lin Shu conducted his translation.

Joint translation

Joint translation was a common practice in early modern Chinese translation, especially in literary translation. The translators who were proficient in foreign language while were good at literary creation were very few.[2] The fact was that most of the persons who were good at literary writing knew no or little foreign languages while most of the persons who had a good command of foreign languages were not good at literary writing. Thus, to learn of the west, some literary writers collaborated on translating foreign works with the scholars who knew foreign languages. This was some early Chinese translators' common

---

[1] Qian Zhongshu, 1981, p.22.
[2] Guo Yanli, 1998, p.49

practice, particularly before 1907. [1] For example, Liang Qichao's translations of *Romantic Encounters with Two Fair Ladies* (*Jiaren qiyu*) and *Deux Ans de Vacances* (*Shiwu xiao haojie*), Wu Jianren's *The Strange Tale of Electricity*(*Dishu qitan*) and Bao Tianxiao's early translations were the products of joint translation. Lin Shu's case was the most typical.

Although the majority of scholars treat Lin Shu as a translator in their works, some don't think that Lin Shu was a translator in a strict sense. Lin Shu knew no foreign languages. On translating, he had to depend on the oral interpretation of his collaborators who knew foreign language. It seems that his collaborator orally interpret the original in vernacular Chinese, then Lin Shu wrote them down in classical Chinese. It is regarded that the act of translating the original was actually assumed by Lin's collaborator, and thus the true translator should be the collaborator rather than Lin Shu, as Compton believed:

On the strictest sense of the word, Lin Shu was not a translator at all. The act of translation, 'the giving of the sense or equivalent of, as a word or an entire work, in another language,' was the work of the assistant.[2]

Compton's judgement was according to the linguists Punk and Wagnalls' definition of translation in *Standard Dictionary* (international edition, 1958).[3] It is really an arguable question. In fact, what Punk and Wagnalls emphasize is expression in a target language. It shows that reading the original emphases a right understanding of the original, while translating lays stress on how to reproduce effectively the original in a target language. Even in the light of this linguistic definition, Lin Shu also should be regarded as a translator. Lin Shu's translations were realized in classical Chinese – 'another language'. It is because of his excellent classical Chinese that his translations achieved great success. Therefore, Lin Shu played a decisive and final role in the realization and success of the joint translation. Normally, a translator should be bilingual, and translation is a bilingual activity, yet Lin Shu's case is exceptional. He was a monolingual translator. His translation also involved a bilingual activity, but this bilingual activity was conducted through his collaboration with others who knew source languages. In addition, in most cases, a translator's abilities in

---

[1] Ibid., p.52.
[2] Compton, 1971. p.132.
[3] Ibid., p.170.

source language and target language are not equal. As for translation, the demands for the two languages are not equal too. It may be sufficient for a reader to have a correct understanding of the source language, but the translator is demanded not merely to be able to read the target language but also to be more able to write it in an excellent expression. In fact, writing is more difficult than reading. A person who can read a novel may not write a novel. However, literary translation must take shape in a writing form. In Lin Shu's case, the collaborators only offered their reading experience and oral explanations or interpretations of the original, which do not form a finished translation at all. Yet Lin Shu finalized it in the form of translation. One instance may clarify this point. Wei Yi, one of Lin Shu's collaborators, did his own translations of Dickens's works, for example, but his translations attracted little attention. His ability in the target language is one of the reasons. Unlike Lin Shu, the collaborator was not skilled at literary writing. Thus it can be seen that Lin Shu is the key to finalizing the translation. Here, we have no intention of belittling the role of his collaborators in the translating process. Without them, of course, the translations could not be realized all the same. What we want to argue is that Lin Shu played an indispensable and dominant role in the whole translation process.

As a matter of fact, the two roles of a translator, a reader and a writer, were assumed by Lin Shu (as a writer) and his collaborators as a reader/interpreter. This kind of collaboration in translation, particularly in literary translation ought be accepted as an act or activity of translation. In some cases, this joint translation can produce a better result and effect. Even today, there are advocates of Lin Shu's way of joint translation. For example, there is a passage in the Buddhist Textbook edited by Malaysian Buddhist Association, regarding how to translate Buddhist scriptures into English:

> In the early Republican period, the Fujianness Lin Shu was famous for translating foreign novels, but he did not understand English, so he often collaborated with Chen Jialin on translation. Chen first orally accounted for the meaning of the word or sentence, and then Lin Shu wrote it into Chinese. Unexpectedly, he thus became well-known. If we cannot find a

person who has a good command of both Chinese and English, as well as of Buddhism, we can follow the example of Lin Shu's way.[1]

However, the joint translation like Lin Shu's may be exceptional in today's view, but it was a common phenomenon in early modern Chinese translation. If we examine the cultural context of early modern Chinese translation, maybe we would not be surprised at the translational practice of Lin Shu.

Paraphrase or Free Translation

The translators of this period consisted of two groups: the translators who knew foreign languages such as Zhou Guisheng (1873–1936), Chen Hongbi and the translators who knew no or little foreign language such as Lin Shu, Liang Qichao and Bao Tianxiao (1876–1973). Both groups mainly adopted paraphrase or free translation in order to make their translation acceptable to the Chinese readers. Free translation was a common practice in the early literary translation of early modern China.

In the early stage of translation, for the sake of the needs of political propaganda and enlightenment, the translators transformed theme, structure and characters in an original work so that the translation became quite different from the original. For instance, according to Liang Qichao's account in the preface to his translation of Jules Verne's *Deux Ans de Vacances*, when *Deux Ans de Vacances* was originally translated into English, the English translator stated in the preface to his translation that he adopted the form of English novel, translating its meanings rather than its words. When translating this novel into Japanese on the basis of the English version, Morita Shiken (Sentian Sixuan) also stated that he turned it into a Japanese literary style while retaining its original meaning. When Liang Qichao and his collaborator translated this novel into classic Chinese on the basis of the Japanese version, Liang Qichao said: 'O n translating this work now, I worked it completely in the form of traditional Chinese fiction. I am confident that my translation is better than Morita's

---

[1] Malaysian Buddhist Association, (Comp. & ed.), Intermediate Buddhist Textbook, Chapters 22-24, (Online) Available:
http://www.mybuddhist.com/Buddbase/E-Book/Medium-Chapter22-24.htm
(2002, June 8).

original.'[1]   It is clear that the three translators tried to do their translations for target readers. In addition, other translations of the early period such as Su Manshu's translation of *Les Miserable* (*Beican shijie*), Wu Jianren's translation of *Strange Tales about Electricity* (*Dianshu qitan*),[2] Zhou Guisheng's translation of *Sherlock Holms* (*Xieluoke fusheng zhentan an*) are similar to Liang's free translation. Some of them read more like a creative work than a translation.

With the publication of Lin Shu's of translation of *La Dame aux Camélias* in 1899, Chinese literary translators tried to retain the spirit and style of the original while having the Chinese readers in mind. Lin Shu's translations were the most typical and representative in this respect. Lin Shu's translation was not only imitated by other Chinese writers and translators such as Zhu Ziqing, Lu Xun and Zhou Zuoren but also taken as a model or criterion for literary translation into classical Chinese by publishers of that time. Zhang Yuanji(1866–1959), a noted Chinese publisher, said, as far as the translation of foreign literature was concerned, only Lin Shu's translation in classical Chinese was ideal. Shangwu Yishuguan (The Commercial Press) always paid the highest contribution fees to Lin Shu.[3] It is true that the great impact and cultural significance of Lin Shu's translations as well as his translation method seemed to prove his success in translation in the early modern period. After 1907, as more translators who had studied abroad and knew foreign languages began to be involved in translation, literal translation appeared and the faithfulness of translation was further emphasized. Wu Tao (? –1912) and Chen Jialin (1874- ?) were known for the translation of Russian Literature, Zeng Pu and Wu Jianguang (1866–1943) were known for the translation of French literature, Su Manshu, Ma Junwu (1881–1940) and Gu Hongming (1875-1928) were known for the translation of poetry. Other young scholars and translators were Lu Xun, Zhou Zuoren, Hu Shi, Liu Bannong, Zhou Shoujuan (1895-1968), Li Shizeng (1881-1973), etc. They had a good knowledge of foreign languages, and some of them were well versed in foreign literature. All they concerned themselves with the loyalty of the target text to the source text. In *A Collection of Foreign Short Stories* (*Yuwai xiaoshuo ji*), Lu Xun and Zhou Zuoren consciously advocated

---

[1] Liang Qichao, Postscript to the first chapter of Collected Works and Essays of the Ice-Drinkers' Studio, vol. 11, Zhonghua shuju, Beijing, 1989, p.5.
[2] The Japanese writer Kikuchi Yuho (菊池幽芳)'s novel.
[3] Shi Meng 时萌, Zeng Pu yanjiu 曾朴研究(A Study of Zeng Pu), Shanghai guji chubanshe, Shanghai, 1982, p.49.

literal translation.[1] However, it is a fact that free translation enjoyed an advantage in the whole early modern period. In particular, the translated works of Lin Shu as a representative of free translation were well received and exerted a great impact in many respects. By contrast, the translated works of Lu Xun and Zhou Zuoren as a representative of literal translation were coldly treated at that time. After their translation *A Collection of Foreign Short Stories* was published, only 20 copies were sold.[2] This phenomenon can only be explained from a perspective of target/culture-oriented translation.

Most of the translators in this period paid more attention to the target text and readers than to the source text. They often made abridgments, omission, modification or addition of the source text for the Chinese readers' acceptance. A critic named Tie said: 'in my opinion, a translator should add his own words in his translation, if necessary, he might as well add or omit something.'[3] In addition, most of the translators preferred sinicizing the names of characters and places as well as allusions in the source. In his 'The translator's Foreword' to *Da chuxi (Great New Year's Eve)*[4], Xu Zhuodai (1880-1961) said, 'the original names, I am afraid, are rather difficult to remember, so they have been changed into Chinese-style names so that it is easy for women and children to recognize them.'[5] Yin Bansheng said in his comments on the transliteration of the original names, 'if the name of a character is transliterated into more than 5 words or so, it will easily make readers fed up. If they are changed to Chinese names, they will be more fascinating.'[6] These views were shared by many translators at the time. Sinicization was also applied to structure, namely, adapting the source text to the forms of traditional Chinese fiction. Having their eyes on readers' acceptance, the translators of this period deliberately translated foreign novels in

---

[1] See Lu Xun 鲁迅, Yuwai xiaoshuo ji 域外小说集(A Collection of Foreign Short Stories) in Lu Xun quanji 鲁迅全集(The Complete Works of Lu Xun), Vol.11, Renmin wenxue chubanshe, 1973, p.185-187.

[2] Lu Xu, Lu Xun shujian 鲁迅书简(Lu Xun's Letters), Chaoyang chubanshe, Hong Kong, 1973, p.11.

[3] Tie 铁，'Tie weng jin yu'铁瓮烬余, in A Ying, 1960, p.428.

[4] German writer J. Zschokke's novel. The original title is unknown, and the English title is translated according to Chinese title.

[5] Guo Yanli, 1998, p. 37.

[6] Yin Bansheng 寅半生, 'Xiaoshuo xianping'小说闲评, in A Ying, 1960. p.477.

zhanghui style.[1] For instance, Lu Xun's translated scientific novel *Yue jie lüxing*（*Cing semaines en Ballon*）in 1903[2] was divided into twenty-eight chapters (回). The title of the first chapter is '悲太平会员怀旧，破寥寂社长贻书'(Feeling sad for peace, the members thought fondly of the past time; to divert himself from boredom, the chairman sent the letter) . In the beginning of this chapter, Lu Xun wrote: '今且不说，单说那独立战争时，合众国，有一麦列兰国，其肖府名曰......'(Let us now turn to during the war of independence, there was a state named Maryland in the United States, and its capital is Baltimore...). The ending sentence of this chapter) is: '正是：壮士不廿空岁月，秋鸿何事卜庭除。究竟为着甚事，且听卜回分解'(It is proved that the heroic men were not willing to idle away their time; for what was the letter delivered to the courtyard? But the reason will be told in the following chapter).[3] These translated novels, except for new content, has no difference in form from traditional Chinese novels. Noticeably, Lin Shu adopted the form and style of the original novel in his *Chahuanü yishi* instead of the *zhanghui* style of the traditional Chinese novel. After Lin's early translations, more and more translators and novelists began to abandon the *Zhanghui style* and adopt the style of Western novel. This change became more obvious in the translated novels after 1907. It indicated that the structure and form of the foreign novel had gradually been accepted by the Chinese translators, and finally developed into the main style and form in the creation of the modern Chinese novel.

2. Case Study: *Bali chahuanü yishi*—Transfiguring Chinese Fiction

In this section, a comparative study and analysis of Lin Shu's *Bali Chahuanü yishi* (*La Dame aux Camélias*) is conducted to deepen the understanding of Lin Shu's relations to the cultural context of modern China.

---

[1] A type of traditional Chinese novel with each chapter headed by a couplet giving the gist of its content.

[2] It is Jules Verne's novel, but Lu Xun indicated the name of the author is an American writer (查理士.培仑). This translation of Lu Xun was based on a Japanese version of Jules Verne's work.

[3] The Complete Works of Lu Xun, 1973, Vol. 16, p.13 and p.18

The appearance of Lin Shu's first effort *Bali chahuanü yishi* was a significant event in the history of Chinese literature. The significance lies in the fact that it initially brought about a change in the developing trend of Chinese literature, particularly in Chinese romantic fiction. According to Yuan Jin's research,[1] there were two high tides of romantic fiction in China: the first, known as 'the fiction of the gifted scholars and beautiful ladies', appeared in the period of the late Ming and early Qing, the second in the early Republican period. The second high tide of romantic fiction originated from the translated works of fiction in the late Qing which began with Lin Shu's translation of *La Dame aux Camélias*. The publication of *Bali chahuanü yishi*, a Western romantic novel, deeply moved a great number of Chinese readers and offered them a distinct impression from traditional Chinese romantic fiction. As Lawrence Wong points out that *Bali chahuanü yishi* cast the most profound influence on the literary scene of the late Qing and early Republican period, introducing Chinese novelists and readers to many new literary techniques; as a result, the traditional Chinese romance began to lose much of its appeal.[2] In reality, *Bali chahuanü yishi* facilitated the transformation of Chinese romantic fiction from tradition to modernity. As Yu Jin believes, this transformation of traditional Chinese romantic primarily involved ideological content, characterization, and literary form.[3]

(1) Ideological Content

Why was Lin Shu's translation of *La Dame aux Camélias* so well received at that time? One of the major reasons is that it imported a new ideology, a new moral concept and a new sentimental world that traditional Chinese literature lack, thus challenging the emotional world of the Chinese reading public.[4]

The romantic fiction in the late Ming and early Qing periods mostly presented the conflict between love and the patriarchal system. As stated, the

---

[1] Yuan Jin, 'The Influence of Translated Fiction on Chinese Romantic Fiction', in *Translation and Creation: Readings of Western Literature in Early Modern China: 1840 –1818*, ed. David Pollard, 1998, pp.283-302.

[2] Wong, Lawrence, 'Lin Shu's Story-retelling as shown in His Chinese Translation of La Dame aux Camélias, babei, .44:3, 1998, p.208.

[3] Yuan, Jin, 'The Influence of Translated Fiction on Chinese Romantic Fiction', in David Pollard, 1998, pp.283. My discussion in this section has absorbed Yuan's main views.

[4] Refer to Guo Yanli, 1998, pp.278-190.

most popular at that time were stories of   "talent meets beauty". Lu Xun summarized the pattern of this type of fiction: 'The stories dealt with talented scholars and beautiful girls, with refined romantic actions, as well as failures and successes in the examinations and other changes of fortune. Since they started with many misadventures but always ended happily, they were known as 'pleasant tales.' [1] The most representative of these stories is *Yu jiao li* (*Jade-Charming-Pear*). We compare *Bali chahuanü yishi* as a modern work with *Jade-Charming-Pear*, a representative work in traditional Chinese fiction.

Jade-Charming-Pear, a novel in twenty chapters with no author's name, is also called *The Strange Story of Two Beauties* (*Shuang mei qiyuan*). The novel embraces traditional Chinese ideas on marriage and love, and underscores a patriarchal authority. In other words, the father's authority over his children's marriage is taken for grant. On deciding the marriage, the father was indifferent to the children's feelings. His criterion for choosing a son-in-law was to look at whether he is a talented scholar. For instance, the patriarchal Bai Xuan, impressed by the young scholar Liu's brilliant talent, decided to marry both his daughter and niece to Liu. He says to his daughter and niece:

'…there I happened to meet this young man Liu, who is from Nanjing too and a true gentleman… Struck by his good looks and learning, I am sure that he will soon distinguish himself as a scholar in the Imperial Academy…   I intend to marry Hongyu to him — only I am afraid my niece might think that it is unfair on her if I do so. However, if I married my niece to him, my daughter might well call me an unnatural father. It is quite out of the question, though, to find another scholar as good as this one….These two cousins are deeply attached to each other. They are bosom friends, quite inseparable. So I will offer both girls to him. This has put me in a good humor over this.'

The girls were transfixed after they heard it, gazing at each other in speechless dismay.[2]

The father had made up his mind to marry the beautiful girls to a man whom they were unfamiliar with, but the girls dare not utter a word in spite of their

---

[1] Lu Xun, 1982, p.222.
[2] Yu jiao li 玉娇梨 (Jade-Charming-Pear), Chunfen wenyi chubanshe, Shenyang, 1981, p 288.

private love for Su Youbai, another young man. This marital arrangement complies with the traditional Chinese formulation: 'Arrange a match by parents' order and on the matchmaker's word'. How did the young men think about their marriage? In the novel, Yang Tingzhao, an official, said that his son would not consider marriage until he gained the title of *Jinshi*. Su Youbai also asserted that 'If I could not marry a incomparable beauty, it would be vain for me to live in this world, and no point in reading so many books and being a talented scholar.' Evidently, they pursued their study for both scholarly honour and a beauty. This idea actually became a dominant theme in the Ming and Qing romantic fiction.

Bali chahuanü yishi broke through this pattern and theme in existing Chinese romantic fiction. The patriarch is no longer in position to decide his son's love and marriage. This novel also involves the conflict between the father's will and the son's love, but stresses that love is higher than the patriarch will and the family fame. When Armand fell in love with Marquette, he never felt misgivings about his father's opposition. When his father attempted to interfere in his intimacy with Marquette, what was Armand's reaction? In Chapter Nineteen, Armand's father arrived in Paris. It was naturally a bad news for Armand and Marguerite. They foresaw trouble. Though the author described that they 'looked at each other', Armand's first reaction was to say to Marguerite, 'fear nothing'. The dialogue between Armand and his father in Chapter Twenty of the translation is quoted below:

<u>Lin Shu's Translation:</u>

父曰：'尔有昵一女子名马克格尼尔者，与之深契乎？'
余对曰：'有之。'
父曰：'尔知此妇何等人也？'
余对曰：'勾栏中人耳。'
父曰：'尔即为此妇人，遂忘冬至家省父及妹乎？'
余对曰：'如父所言。'
父曰：'尔甚爱此妇人乎？'
余对曰：'父知之矣。彼能使儿忘其家庭应为之事，此儿所以服于父前也。。'
父似不料余无粉饰之言，诘词似穷，……。
……

128

父厉声曰：'尔亦知吾不耐见尔所为乎？'
余曰：'儿自忖向未尝败坏其家声，故偶有所错，尚可恃以自盖。'
父曰：'然则尔变易其所为之时至矣。'
余曰：'父言何为？'
父曰：'尔之所为，正所以能败其家声者也。'
余曰：'父言，儿不知所指。'
……

父曰：'凡为人父所以怒子，正欲其不为狭邪耳。今尔所为，纵未败裂，不久将自坏。'
余曰：'冤哉翁也。'
父曰：'吾阅历深于尔，天下惟贞洁之女乃有真情尔。如漫郎之与德凯尔之情，今时移俗易，不能仍蹈其既往之辙，坚不自改。而今须决计去尔所昵之马克。'
余曰：'其自憾其私心，竟至违背吾父之言。'
父曰：'我必使尔去之。'
余曰：'向有省马概岛以居勾栏之人，今无矣。即使马克为国法所驱入于此岛，儿亦将方舟从之。明知其过，特情不自禁，不复强为支历。'
……

父怒曰：'吾始劝尔，今则勒令去也。吾不欲家庭中见此不肖之事　　。'
……

余曰：'儿此时年纪，在律不必专受一人之号令。'
父哑然无语。[1]

Lin Shu's translation in English:[2]

My father asked: 'Is it true that you are living with a woman called Marguerite Gautier?'

---

[1] Lin Shu, 1931, pp.61-64.
[2] All the quoted passages from Lin Shu's translations in this book are literally rendered back into English by me. My English translation of all the quoted passages from Lin Shu's Bali Chahuanü yishi in this book have referred to Ji Mi, Mao Xueli, Gao Yuan and Yu Yan's Chinese-English Bilingual textbook chahuanü 茶花女 /Camille, Foreign Language Teaching and Research Press, 1998.

I answered: 'Yes.'

'Do you know what this woman is?'

'A kept woman.'

'And it is for her that you have forgotten to come and see your sister and me this year?'

'Yes, father, I admit it.'

'You are very much in love with this woman?'

'You see it, father, since she has made me fail in duty toward you. I humbly ask your forgiveness to-day.'

My father, no doubt, was not expecting such categorical answers, for he seemed to reflect a moment.

...

'But you must realize,' continued my father, in dryer tone, 'that I, at all events, should not permit.'

'I have said to myself that I have done nothing contrary to the respect which I owe to the traditional probity of the family, so even if I make an accidental mistake I can correct it by myself.'

'Then, the moment is come when you must live otherwise.'

'Why, father?'

'Because you are doing things which outrage the respect that you image you have for your family.'

'I don't follow your meaning.'

...

'Why a father is angry with his son. Because he always wants to rescue his son from evil. You have not done any harm yet, but you will do it.'

'Father, you are wronging me!'

'I know more of life than you do. There are no entirely pure sentiments except in perfectly chaste women. Every Manon can have her own Des Grieux, and times are changed. It would be useless for the world to grow older if it did not correct its way. Your will leave your mistress.'

'I am very sorry to disobey you, father, but it is impossible.'

'I will compel you to do so'

'Unfortunately, father, there no longer exists a Sainte-Marguerite to which courtesans can be sent, and, even if there were, I would follow Mlle. Gautier if you succeeded in having her sent there. Perhaps I am in the wrong, but I can only be happy as long as I am the lover of this woman.'

…

My father said to angrily: 'Just now I begged you; now I command you. I will have no such scandalous doings in my family. Pack up your things and get ready to come with me'

'Pardon me, father,' I said, 'but I shall not come.'

'And why?'

'Because I am at an age when no one any longer obeys a command.'

My father was left without an argument.

From this dialogue, we can clearly see that the son openly went against his father's will, and argued with his father in favour of his love for Marguerite. It was very unique in the eye of the Chinese readers as well as very rare in traditional Chinese fiction. Like *Jade-Charming-Pear*, the patriarch played a key role in the marriage and love of young generation, yet the difference is that in *Jade-Charming-Pear*, the father's will was never challenged. Although the girls were aware that the elder's will and decision would shatter their hope for true love, they had no intention of revolting at all, merely 'gazing at each other in speechless dismay', and giving tacit consent to his arrangement. The dominant role of the patriarchal father is quite evident. In *Bali chahuanü yishi*, patriarchal authority was boldly challenged. The opinions of Armand and his father were divided on love. His father represented traditional views: the honour or fame of the family was the most important, and 'there is no entirely pure sentiments except in perfectly chaste women', and 'a son should obey his father's will'. These views are actually very close to traditional Chinese ethical and moral concept, and therefore, easily recognisable to the Chinese readers. While Armand's view was diametrically opposed to his father's, he showed respect to his father, but regarded his love for Marguerite as superior to anything else. In other words, Armand thought that his individual right of pursuing love and happiness was more important than his father's authority and the family fame. To safeguard his right, he stressed four points in his arguments: first, his love for Marguerite surpassed his feeling for his father and sister; second, his love for Marguerite surpassed the reputation of his family; third, there were 'entirely pure sentiments in courtesans; fourth, at his age, he had the legal right to decide his own life and disobeyed anyone else's command. These ideas, focusing on humanism, were anti-traditional and fresh for the Chinese readers, as well as new in the romantic fiction of China. In addition, unlike the male protagonist in *Jade-Charming-Pear* who hankered for scholarly honour and official rank, Armand wholeheartedly pursued his love. Obviously *Bali Chahuanü yishi* is very different from *Jade-Charming-Pear* in theme. However, Lin Shu was unlikely to separate his writing from the historical and cultural context in China. He had to pay regard to both the constraints of the target culture and the response of the Chinese readers. Thereupon, when translating the passages quoted above, Lin Shu made some alteration of Armand's radical statements so as to make them more easily accepted by his readers in a given culture. For instance, when his father interrogated him, he was aware that conflict would be unavoidable:

The French original:
Les passions rendent fort contre les sentiments. J'étais prêt à toutes les luttes, même contre mon pere, pour conserver Marguerite.[1]

English translation:
Passions are formidable enemies to sentiment. I as prepared for every struggle, even with my father, in order that I might keep Marguerite.

Armand's inner soliloquy was omitted by Lin Shu, possibly because he was aware that the Chinese readers of the time would feel it difficult to totally accept the open assertion: 'prêt à toutes les luttes, même contre mon pere '(prepared for every struggle, even with my father) just in order to keep a courtesan. It seemed to Lin Shu, also as a father, that the assertion went to extremes, much as the traditional ideas prejudiced Armand's father against the young couple's love. As well Lin Shu omitted Armand's assertion 'après tout, que m'importe!'(After all, what does it (his father's attitude or advice) matter to me?) in Chapter Twenty, because it was difficult alike for Lin Shu to approve the assertion referring to his experience of life.

In his life, Lin Shu often gave advice to his sons. According to Zhu Bisen's *A Biography of Lin Qinnan*, while living in Hangzhou from 1899 to 1992, and witnessing the corrupts of Chinese officialdom, Lin Shu was determined never to set foot in the officialdom. As he said in *Shu juan ti chuanqi (Romance of Shu-Juan-Ti*, 1917), 'whenever mentioning the two characters 'zuo guan'(being an

---

[1] Dumas fils, 1939, p.181.

official), as it were, a fierce disease is attacking me.'[1] Nor is this all. He also advised his son not to be an official. But one day his eldest son Lin Gui, who had been absolutely obedient to him, told him that he was going to be an official in the northeast of China. Evidently the son's will went against the father's will. However, instead of forcing his son to obey his will, Lin Shu persuaded him by reason, though his son did not accept his advice in the end. Later Lin Shu specially wrote ' A Letter to My Son' to advise his son how to be a good official. In the end of the letter, he said: 'whenever necessary, I will send you a letter to offer my advice. You may mount this letter, and hang it on the wall in your study as a motto.'[2] This shows that Lin Shu attached importance to a father's advice, so he must feel it difficult to accept the assertion of Armand. The omissions revealed his attitude, but the anecdote illustrates that Lin Shu paid more attention to convincing his son by reason, which was clearly embodied in his treatment of the original passage. In fact, Lin Shu's attitude was the same as the majority of the educated the Chinese readers' at that time. Indeed, on translating *La Dame aux Camélias*, Lin Shu succeeded in finding the point of equilibrium between the new ideas from Western literature and the existing traditional Chinese ideas. It is undoubtedly one of the reasons why his version of *La Dame aux Cameliasi* was so well received at that time.

Lin Shu's translation of *La Dame aux Camélias* imported new ideas, which influenced Chinese writers to break through the ideological content of the novel, and encouraged them to write about romantic love in conflict with traditional ethical codes. According to Yuan Jin's research, the late Qing novel, Fu Lin's *Qin hai shi (A Rock in a Savage)* in 1906, Xu Zhenya's *Yu li hun (The Soul of Jade Pear Flower)* in 1912–13 and so on were obviously influenced by Lin Shu's version of *La Dame aux Camélias*. Fu Lin's *A Rock in a Savage* lashed out at the arranged marriage under the system of patriarchal autocracy, and criticized Mencius's position: a marital match should be arranged by parents' order and the matchmaker's word, thinking it 'merciless and rude'. He also said, 'as far as marriage is concerned, both a man and a woman have the right to decide for themselves, how can the parents and the matchmakers intervene in it?', 'since

[1] Lin Wei 林薇, Lin Shu xuanji 林纾选集(Selected Works of Lin Shu), Sichuan renmin chubanshe, Chendu, 1985, p.311.
[2] Lin Shu, Weilu xuji 畏庐续集(Collected essays of Lin Shu, second series), Shangwu Yishuguan, Shanghai, 1917, p.18.

Mencius said so, in China, an ordinary young couple in love had to yield to the pressure from the parents' autocracy; as a result, among 100 couples, 99 had an unhappy marriage.' [1] In *The Soul of Jade Pear Flower*, Xu Zhenya called himself 'an oriental Duma', declaring that his aim was to write a novel in imitation of Lin Shu's *Bali chahuanü yishi*. *The Soul of Jade Pear Flower* is a story about "a widow's love", which, in comparison with the courtesan's love, more seriously violated the traditional ethical code. It is said that the story was from Xu's personal experience. Conceivably, it was because of the inspiration and encouragement from the translated novel of Lin Shu that Xu Zhenya dared to take his personal experience as the subject matter of his novel. In *The Soul of Jade Pear Flower*, he persisted in depicting the widow and the youth in love as positive characters, a couple with true love, self-sacrifice and high moral integrity. Again under the influence of *The Soul of Jade Pear Flower*, the romantic novel with a western ideological content flourished in the early Republican period. Criticizing the arranged marriage by the family and longing for a free love and marriage of one's choice constituted a component of the May Fourth new literature. However, in the final analysis, *Bali chahuanü yishi* played a key role in the change of Chinese romantic fiction.

(2) Characterization

In characterization, *Bali Chahuanu yishi* changed the pattern of 'Talent meets beauty' in traditional Chinese romantic fiction, highlighting the characters' 'spirit of self-sacrifice' and their 'consciousness of remorse'.[2] In traditional fiction, it is rare to describe: between a man and woman, one side sacrificed oneself, even one's life for the interest of the other side. But in *Bali chahuanü yishi*, the female protagonist sacrificed herself for her lover's interest, mainly for the interest of her lover's family. Due to Armand's father's persuasion, Marguerite made up her mind to sacrifice herself for Armand's prospects and the fame of his family, and suddenly left Armand. As Armand did not know the cause, he misunderstood her, so took a series of vindictive acts. In consequence, Marguerite suffered a greater mental torture and agony.

---

[1] Yuan Jin, 'The Influence of Translated Fiction on Chinese Romantic Fiction' in *Translation and Creation: readings of western literature in early modern China, 1840 – 1918*, ed. David Pollard, 1998, pp.285-286.

[2] Pollard, 1998. p.290

Before she died, she told the reason why she suddenly left him in her diary. In the diary, she gave an account of the conversation between Armand's father and her, which manifests her spirit of self-sacrifice:

Lin Shu's Translation:

> (翁)谓余曰，以翁垂老之年，不能眼睁睁观其子为一妇人，尽破其产。余虽极美，何得以一人之美，陷一精壮有用之少年。余只得以一言辩之，谓余自与亚猛交，从未逾格，费其一金。于是，尽出质贴及还债之收条，举以示翁。余尽弃家具，正欲同亚猛赁小屋自活，良不欲多所糜费耳。且告翁以余二人安乐投契事，未尝纵恣浪游。
>
> ……
>
> …当知，心契此人而此人身旁犹有家室，此人身上，犹有伦纪。……须任正事，方为成人。…… 尔爱亚猛之心甚挚，尤当思所以保全亚猛者。[1]

Lin Shu's translation in English:

The old man said to me that as in his old age he could not any longer allow his son to ruin himself over me; that I was beautiful, it was true, but I ought not to make us of my beauty to spoil the future of a young man. At that, there was only one thing to do, to show him the proof that since I was your mistress I had spared no sacrifice to be faithful to you without asking for more money than you had to give me, I showed him the pawn ticket, the receipts of the people to whom I had sold what I could not pawn. I told him of my resolve to part with my furniture in order to rent a small house and live with you without being a too heavy expense. I told him of our happiness, and that we were leading a quieter and happier life.

…

But remember that there is not only the mistress, but the family; that besides love there are duties; …if a person attends to his duties, he will become a real man. …You love Armand; prove it to him by the sole means which remains to you of yet proving it to him, by sacrificing your love to his future.

---

[1] Lin Shu, 1931, p.81.

M. Duval made use of Marguerite's love for Armand to persuade her to give up her love with both hard and soft tactics. She was aware that what M. Duval had said was a fact despite his overriding family interest, and that she had to make a decision. But before this, she wanted to convince M. Duval of her true love for Armand:

Lin Shu's translation:

余于是拭泪问翁曰：'翁能信我爱公子乎？'

翁曰：'信之。'

'翁能信吾情爱不为利生乎？'

翁曰：'信之。'[1]

Lin Shu's translation in English:

I said to your father, wiping away my tears, 'Do you believe that I love your son?'

M. Duval said: 'Yes.'

'With a disinterested love?'

M. Duval said: 'Yes.'

After hearing M. Duval's answers, Marguerite felt relieved to have changed his prejudice against her, as this 'may encourage my good intention, and show my chastity' (可以鼓舞其为善之心，即以贞洁自炫于人). Finally, she determinedly told M. Duval,'I took an oath that I would never get his son in trouble!' (立誓不累公子!'). Here Lin Shu changed the original. The original is 'me fera forte contre mon amour, et qu'avant huit jours votre fils sera retourné auprès de vous, peut-être malheureux pour quelque temps, mais guéri pour jamais'[2](will make me strong against my love, and that within a week your son will be once more at your side, perhaps unhappy for a time, but cured forever). This change was motivated to emphasize Marguerite's good intention and chastity so as to highlight her self-sacrifice, and present a more readily

---

[1] Lin Shu, 1931, p. 83.

[2] Dimas fils, 1939, p.234.

acceptable image in the Chinese readers' mind. Self-sacrifice usually means the loftiness of morality. It is these women's lofty spirit of self-sacrifice that served as a foil to the selfishness and baseness of the aristocrats around them and that aroused the Chinese readers' sympathy for the women who violated the ethical code.

Under the influence of *Bali chahuanü yishi*, *Jiayin xiaozhuan(Joan Haste)* and other translated works, this spirit of self-sacrifice was widely applied in the characterization by the Chinese writers during the early Republic. For instance, in Chapter Five of Su Manshu's *Duan hong ling yan ji* (*The Lonely Swan*, 1912) , the author described Sanlong's sacrifice of becoming a monk in order not to encumber his fiancée. In *The Soul of Jade Pear Flower*, the widow Liniang committed suicide so that Juanqian and Mengxia could marry. In Bao Tianxiao's *Bu guo* (*Redemption*, 1916), the male protagonist sacrificed his personal prospects to save the fallen female protagonist. It is because of such noble sentiment that their acts were accepted by the Chinese readers even though they transgressed traditional ethical codes. Like *Bali chahuanü yishi*, this spirit of self-sacrifice was so prominent that most of the romantic novels had a grievous sentiment and a tragic ending.

In addition, characters' repentance in the fiction of the early Republican period is also a sign of the influence of *Bali chahuanü yishi*. Classical Chinese fiction is short of repentance, but in *Bali chahuanü yishi*, the male protagonist Armand told his whole love story with a repentant heart. These descriptions of repentance intensified the psychological conflict of the characters, enriching their inner world, and making them more authentic as romantic and heroic characters.

(3) Literary Form

Lin Shu's *Bali chahuanü yishi*, along with his other translated novels, also conspicuously changed in the narrative mode and literary technique of the Chinese novel. The changes in narrative mode are primarily embodied in narrator and narrative time. As far as the narrator is concerned, traditional Chinese novels developed out of '*huaben*', the script for story-telling in the Song and Yuan folk literature. From this beginning, Chinese fiction uses a third-person narrator to narrate a story in an omniscient and omnipotent narrative way. Admittedly, this narrative mode has its strong points: it can freely and objectively describe the story, and the narrator can enjoy a larger narrative space. But Lin Shu's version of *La Dame aux Camélias* brought in a new narrative mode. The novel adopts a first-person narrator. In fact, there are two first-person narrators in the work: one is the author Dumas, the other is the male protagonist Armand. The former directly recounted the story of Marguerite in the beginning of the novel; then the latter told the story in the form of recall, which is the mainstay of the novel. In the last, the female protagonist Marguerite was designed to narrate how Armand's father compelled her to break off her relations to Armand on the pretext of his son's prospects and his daughter's marriage, and her desolation and sufferings from longing for Armand during her illness. In the other translated novels of Lin Shu, such as *Kuai rou yusheng shu(David Copperfield)*, *Haiwai xuan qu lu(Gulliver's Travels)* , a first-person narrator was used as well. The use of first-person narrator enhanced the authenticity of the story. To the readers who had got used to the narration of the third-person narrator in traditional Chinese novels, this new narrative mode, had artistic appeal, and influenced the writing of the novel of that time. Many Chinese writers adopted a first-person narrator such as Wu Jianren 's *Ershi nian mudu zhi guai xianzhuang (Strange Events Witnessed in the Last Twenty Years)*, Su Manshu's *Duan hong ling yan ji (The Lonely Swan)*, Wu Shuangre's *Yuannie jing (Mirror of Evil Injustice)*. In the period of the early Republic, at least more than ten writers used a first-person narrator, introduced through *Bali chahuanü yishi*.

In narrative technique, the influence of *Bali chahuanü yishi* was evident as well, especially in the use of flashback, letters and diaries. The major feature of traditional Chinese literature is a linear narrative. Before Lin Shu's *Bali chahuanü yishi*, the narrative in a traditional Chinese novel was basically chronological. But in *Bali chahuanü yishi*, the author first related what was happening after Marguerite's death, and then let Armand traced back his love with Marguerite in the form of flashback. The use of flashback in *Bali chahuanü yishi* attracted the Chinese writers' interest so that soon, Chinese novelists began to use flashback in their works, e.g. Fu Lin's *Qin Hai Shi (A Rock in a Savage)* and Xu Zhenya's *Yu li hun (The Soul of Jade Pear Flower)*. Besides, *Bali chahuanü yishi* also introduced letters and diaries into Chinese literary narrative. In classical Chinese fiction, letters were hardly ever used to expose a character's inner world. However, in *Bali chahuanü yishi*, Lin Shu translated the letters and diaries in *La Dame aux*

Camellias, as well showing their important effects in the novel. In Chapter Four, Armand showed Marguerite's letter to 'Duma'. It was the letter that Marguerite had written to Armand when critically ill. It can actually stimulate the readers' curiosity: what happened to the heroine? What relations are there between the hero and the heroine? It is the letter that triggers the story of Marguerite. Chapters Twenty-Five, Twenty-Six and Twenty-Seven are composed of Marguerite's diaries and Julie Duprat's letters to Armand. These diaries and letters not only clarify why Marguerite suddenly left Armand, but also vividly expose her inner feeling and true love for Armand, displaying her self-sacrifice. No wonder the readers were so deeply moved to tears. The use of letters and diaries in *Bali chahuanü yishi* also directly influenced the Chinese writers at that time. For instance, Xu Zhenya, imitating *Bali chahuanü yishi*, used letters and diaries in his novel *The Soul of Jade Pear Flower*, in which these letters and diaries served to exhibit the character's inner world, making the work a great success. Apart from *The Soul of Jade Pear Flower*, *Bali chahuanü yishi* also inspired more Chinese writers to try to write a epistolary novel, e.g. Bao Tianxiao's *Feilai zhi riji* (*A Unexpected Diary*) and Zhou Shoujuan's *Zhuzhu riji* (*Zhuzhu's Diary*).[1] In reality, the letters and diaries were mainly used to reveal the character's psychological activity, e.g. Wu Jianren's *Hen hai* (*Sea of Woe*) and Bao Tianxiao's *Bu guo*(*Redemption*), and Chinese novelists hence began to show a strong interest in a character's psychological description in their works.[2] Indeed, the first story in vernacular Chinese fiction, Lu Xun's 'Kuangren riji' (A Madman's Story), adopts the diary as a psychological narrative.

Indeed, The translation *of La Dame aux Camélias* is quite representative in Lin Shu's translations. Apart from its ideological influence, as Lawrence Wong asserts that in view of its peculiar approach, of its influence on Chinese writers, of its role in shaping the taste of a whole generation of readers, above all, of its possible contribution to a deeper understanding of literary translation in the late-Qing and early-Republican period in general and of Lin Shu's later translations in particular, it will be worthwhile examining some of the major features of *Bali Chahuanü Yishi*.[3]

---

[1] Guo Yanli, 1998, p.503.
[2] Pollard, 1998, p.296.
[3] Wong, Lawrence, 'Lin Shu's Story-retelling as Shown in His Chinese Translation of La Dame aux Camélias, babel, 44:3, 1998, p.209.

It is necessary to understand Lin Shu's role and influence in trans-culture context. Lin Shu was the most prolific and influential translator in Chinese literary translation. His translations initiated an epoch of literary translation unequalled in the history of Chinese translation. Lin Shu based his translations on the needs for Chinese culture and readers of that time, which was clearly embodied in his choice, response to the originals and his specific translation goals. The prefaces and postscripts are evidence. Through his translations, Lin Shu introduced new cultural and literary forms into China, promoting a transition of Chinese literature from tradition to modernity. In this chapter, the case study focuses on the influence of *Bali chahuanü yishi* on Chinese fiction. The appearance of Lin Shu's translation *Bali chahuanü yishi* caused an upsurge in the late Qing literary translation. It also greatly influenced the creation of Chinese romantic fiction in the early Republican period. The influence was mainly embodied in both ideology and literary style of the novel. To some extent, it caused traceable changes in Chinese fiction. These changes in the novels of the early Republic became a key link between late Qing Fiction and the May Fourth new fiction. As Yuan Jin states in 'The Influence of Translated Fiction on Chinese Romantic Fiction', Lin Shu's *Bali chahuanü yishi* and others can be regarded as 'essential stepping stones in the progress to the new style of fiction that was to appear in the May Fourth period.'[1]

---

[1] Ibid.,p.301.

Chapter 5

Poetic Equivalence

In this chapter I challenge a crucial criticism of Lin Shu's translations: their alleged lack of fidelity or faithfulness to the original. I claim conversely that there is faithfulness in Lin's translation. The claim is based on a close comparison between the source and target texts. From such comparisons I argue that Lin Shu translated the spirit, content and style of the original works, rather than seeking a superficial and technical imitation. This faithfulness is primarily embodied in poetic equivalence between the source and target literary texts. The chapter discusses poetic equivalence in Lin Shu's translation in terms of spirit and style, expression and sincization.

1. Poetic Equivalence and Lin Shu

The concept of poetic equivalence proposed in this study, although it is first coined and used in this study, evolves from the concept of dynamic equivalence. It lays special emphasis on the equivalence between the source and target texts in literary and aesthetic effect, and is closely related to the dynamic equivalence theory in translation studies. Before the emergence of target-oriented translation theory, the theory of equivalence was dominant in translation studies. It covers two basic orientations in translation: formal equivalence and dynamic equivalence. Dynamic equivalence is based upon 'the principle of equivalent effect'. A translation of dynamic equivalence is not so concerned with matching the target language message with the source language message, but with the dynamic relationship. It aims at complete naturalness of expression, and tries to relate the target reader to modes of behaviour relevant to the context of his own culture.[1] According to Nida, 'during the past fifty years, there has been a marked shift of emphasis from the formal to the

---

[1] Nida, Eugene, Toward A Science of Translation, with Special Reference to Principles and Procedures involved in Bible Translating, E. J. Brill, Leiden, 1964, p.159

dynamic dimension.'[1] It is obvious that a translation of dynamic equivalence pays considerable attention to the target text and cultural context. The concept of poetic equivalence particularly applies to literary translation studies. It is concerned with the equivalence of literary or aesthetic effect between target literary text and source literary text. Its final goal is target readers' acceptance.

This study is designed to view Lin Shu's translations from a target-oriented perspective with a view to challenge the criticism that Lin's translations lack faithfulness to the originals. I therefore apply the theory of equivalence into the assessment of the truthfulness of Lin's translations. According to the theory of equivalence, I argue that Lin Shu's translations are closer to the translation in terms of dynamic equivalence or, rather, poetic equivalence. The faithfulness of his translations is primarily embodied in rendering or retaining the spirit, content, artistic style and, sometimes, the form of the original.

To achieve poetic equivalence, besides an excellent command of source language, a translator must have an excellent grasp of target language, and have a profound understanding of target literary or aesthetic tradition. As far as Lin Shu is concerned, his fame as a translator partly rests on his outstanding skill in classical Chinese. This language is very different from colloquial or written English in the source texts and there can therefore never be a close equivalence in both linguistic levels between the ST and TT. However, classical Chinese has a two-millennia history as a literary language of great depth, concision and richness that Lin Shu exploited to the full. Lin Shu's linguistic skills ensured that his translations not only effectively render the spirit, content and artistic style of the original, but also realize the naturalness of expression and achieve the 'equivalent effects', or rather, a poetic equivalence.

Without doubt, it is impractical or impossible to require Lin Shu to engage himself in the translation of formal equivalence, not only because Lin Shu had to rely on his collaborators' oral interpretation, but also because he was a literary writer rather than a linguist. Lin Shu based his translation strategy on target culture and readers: he was an expert in classical Chinese, a writer of high literary attainments and a scholar who had Chinese culture at his fingertips. He was primarily concerned with his country and people. All these determined his translation orientation towards the target culture and readers as well as his

[1] Ibid., p.160.

approaches to the ST that facilitated target readers' acceptance. Thus he produced translations in such a way that were acceptable as literature to the recipient culture.

Lin Shu was also a poet and a painter. His writings and paintings clearly reflected his pursuit of the classical Chinese arts. One of the main differences between classical Chinese aesthetics and classical Western aesthetics according to Zhou Laixiang is that the former pays more attention to expression, namely, expressing a writer, a poet or a painter's feelings and ideas while the latter pays more attention to reproduction or imitation, namely, imitating or reproducing what happens in reality. [1] Harold Osburne argues that Western classical aesthetics is basically naturalistic, whereas classical Chinese aesthetics is non-naturalistic. He believes that classical Chinese literature and art emphasize how a work can express a spirit and sentiment rather than reproduce a superficial resemblance. [2] Indeed, valuing likeness in spirit above likeness in appearance is one of the features of classical Chinese aesthetics, clearly reflected in classical Chinese paintings. Let us look at Lin Shu's following painting:

---

[1] Zhou Laixiang 周米祥, 'Dongfang yu xifang gudian meixue lilun bijiao' 东方与西方古典美学理论的比较(A Comparison between the Eastern Classical Aesthetics and the Western Classical Aesthetics), in Cao Shunqing 曹顺庆, (ed.), Zhong xi bijiao meixue wenxue lunwen ji 中西比较美学文学论文集(Collected Essays on Chinese and Western Comparative Aesthetics and Literature),   Sichuan wenyi chubanshe, chengdu, 1985, p. 17.
[2] Osburne, Harold, Aesthetics and Art Theory: an historical introduction, Longman, Harlow, 1968, p.15.

In this work, Lin Shu painted Lushan Mountain, the waterfall in the mountain, the Yangtze River, two men boating on the river. They are not faithful to the real landscape of Lushan Mountain, but express the painter's emotion, aspiration and interest with the codes of landscape painting. Valuing likeness in spirit above likeness in appearance in classical Chinese aesthetics most probably influenced Lin Shu's attitude towards literary translation: preferring likeness in spirit to likeness in linguistic form, or rather, preferring poetic equivalence to formal equivalence.

However, this is not to say that Lin Shu untruthfully dealt with the original texts on purpose in order to cater to the reading public. On the contrary, he strove to seek poetic equivalence between his translation and the original. His statement in his preface to *Robinson Crusoe* evidently shows his growing respect for the integrity of the original:

> From the many references to religion in the book, it might seem that the translator is rather partial to that faith. To think that would be mistaken: the translator did not write the book. An author can expound his personal viewpoint and give play to his imagination without limit. A translator, to the contrary, relates a given story: how can he interpolate his own opinions? When I came across religious sentiments in this book, how could I as a translator shun them and weed them out? Hence I preserved them just as they were.[1]

In addition, in some cases, the translator adapted the source text in order to be truthful to the original in spirit, content, sentiment and style. Popovic argued that instead of accusing translators of ignorance or unfaithfulness, they resort to shifts precisely because they are attempting to render faithfully the content of the original despite the differences between the languages.[2] Therefore, it is not proper simply to attribute all Lin Shu's adaptations of the original to

---

[1] Lin Shu, Lubinxun piaoliu ji 鲁滨逊漂流记(Robinson Crusoe), Shangwu yishuguan, Shanghai, 1934, p.2.
[2] Popovic, Anton, 'The Concept "Shift of Expression" in Translation Analysis' in Holmes, James S., (ed.), The Nature of Translation: Essays on the Theory and Practice of Literary Translation, Publishing House of the Slovak Academy Bratislava , Mouton, The Hague & Paris, 1970, pp.78-87.

untruthfulness. As Popovic explained:

> It is not the translator's only business to "identify" himself with the original: that would merely result in a transparent translation. The translator also has the right to differ organically, to be independent.... Between the basic semantic substance of the original and its shift in another linguistic structure a kind of dialectic tension develops along the axis of faithfulness-freedom.[1]

From this perspective, Lin Shu translations at least made known that Lin Shu tried to make his translation truthful to the spirit and artistic style of the original rather than to its words and sentences. As George Chapman stated, a translator must attempt to reach the "spirit" of the original and avoid word for word renderings.[2] It is reasonable to regard Lin Shu's translation as a free translation in this sense. As Han Guang stated:

> In the times that Lin Shu translated *La Dame aux Camélias* and Yan Fu translated *On Evolution*, if adopting literal translation rather than free translation in Chinese to translate the books, undoubtedly the Chinese readers would only have a look, and then would go away. Therefore, the advantage of Lin Shu's translations is that the readers can immediately comprehend them, and find no faults in incompatibility and awkwardness.[3]

Thus, Lin Shu's free translation method can be seen as based on poetic equivalence.

2. Spirit and Style

For the sake of the target readers, Lin Shu's translations do not stick to the words and sentences in the source text, but try to convey the overall spirit, including the ideas, sentiments, atmospheres, and literary style of the original text. In this respect, Lin Shu's translations of *La Dame aux Camélias* and *Uncle Tom's Cabin* and others are good examples. Dumas's *La Dame aux Camélias* is the

---

[1] Popovic, Anton, 'The Concept "Shift of Expression" in Translation Analysis' in Holmes, James. S, 1970, p.80.
[2] Chapman, George, Epistle to the Reader in Bassnett, Susan, Translation Studies, Routledge, London and New York.1991, p.55.
[3] Han Guang, 1935, pp.33-34.

most celebrated and most popular expression of what Susan Sontag calls 'the sentimental fantasy', which captured the imagination and represented the sensibility of many 19th century writers, artists and readers.[1] The sentimental effects that Lin Shu's Chinese version conveyed are as powerful as the ones in the original. Yan Fu once remarked that Lin Shu's version thoroughly broke the hearts of China's young people in love.[2] Mao Dun believed that Lin Shu's translation of *Ivanhoe*, except for several minor errors, considerably preserved the sentiment and style of the original; the characterization in the translation was the same as in the original.[3]

Although Lin Shu did not stick to the original word for word or sentence for sentence, and indeed adapted the original in consideration of the target culture and the target readers, he preserved the spirit and style of the original on the whole. An example is taken from *Sakexun jie hou yingxiong lue* (*Ivanhoe*) to support this statement. In Chapter Twenty-Three, there is a depiction of the dual between Ivanhoe and Bois-Guilbert for a decision on whether the Jewish girl Rebecca is innocent or not:

The original:

The trumpets sounded, and the knights charged each other in full career. The wearied horse of Ivanhoe, and its no less exhausted rider, went down, as all had expected, before the well-aimed lance and vigorous steed of the Templar. This issue of the combat all had foreseen; but although the spear of Ivanhoe did but, in comparison, touch the shield of Bois-Guilbert, that champion, to the astonishment of all who beheld it, reeled in his saddle, lost his stirrups, and fell in the lists.

Ivanhoe, extricating himself from his fallen horse, was soon on foot, hastening to mend his fortune with his sword; but his antagonist arose not. Wilfred, placing his foot on his breast, and the sword's point to his throat, commanded him to yield to him, or die on the spot. Bois-Guilbert returned no answer.

---

[1] Sontag, Susan, Illness As Metaphor, Farrar, Straus & Giroux, New York, 1977, p.5.
[2] Yan Fu 严复, Yan Fu ji 严复集 (A Collected Works of Yan Fu), Zhonghua shuju, Beijing, 1986, p.365.
[3] Zheng Zhenduo, p.161

"Slay him not, Sir Knight," cried the Grand Master, "unshriven and unabsolved—kill not body and soul! We allow him vanquished."

He descended into the lists, and commanded them to unhelm the conquered champion. His eyes were closed—the dark red flush was still on his brow. As they looked on him in astonishment, the eyes opened—but they were fixed and glazed. The flush passed from his brow, and gave way to the pallid hue of death. Unscathed by the lance of his enemy, he had died a victim to the violence of his own contending passions.

"This is indeed the judgment of God," said the Grand Master, looking upwards—"*Fiat voluntas tua!*" [1]

<u>Lin Shu's translation:</u>

筘声一振，二骑飞腾，挨梵诃人马皆乏，一触即踣，然挨梵诃槊锋适及白拉恩盾上，而白拉恩亦立蹶于马下。挨梵诃疾起，出剑谋地斗，而白拉恩偃卧弗动。挨梵诃以剑抵其喉门："尔不降者，立死。"教主曰："勿杀，吾尚未有救罪之书；惟吾辈许汝为胜可尔。"于是教主下座，去白拉恩面具；额上紫脉偾起，二目狞视，实无伤，为怒气所激而死。众皆太息曰："是殆天意也！"[2]

<u>Lin Shu's translation in English:</u>

The trumpet sounded, and the two riders charged each other at full speed. Ivanhoe and his horse were so weary that they had no sooner run into the opponent than they went down. However, when Ivanhoe's spearhead just touched the shield of Bois-Guilbert, Bois-Guibert fell from his house right away. Ivanhoe was swiftly on foot, and drew his sword and sought to fight on the ground, but Bois-Guilbert was lying motionlessly. Ivanhoe placed the sword's point tot his throat, saying:'if you don't yield me, you will die on the spot.' The grand master cried: "Slay him not! My edict for shriving him is not ready. We allow you to win a victory.' The grand master descended and unhelmed Bois-Guilbert. The dark red veins protruded on his brow. His eyes opened—but stared hideously. Unscathed, he had died a victim to the

[1] Scott, Walter, 1931, p.438
[2] Lin Shu, 1930, p. 281.

violence of his own contending passions. Everyone signed and said with regret: 'This is indeed the judgment of God.'

After a comparative reading the two quotations above, the readers would most probably share Zheng Zhenduo's view: 'Although we are less likely to read his translated text against the original text word for word, and think that he correctly rendered each word, if reading the translated text after reading the original text without a break, we would feel that the sentiment and style of the original were not changed at all.'[1] In the translation, Lin Shu did not follow the word order and sentence structure of the original; instead, he made some alterations. For example, 'the trumpets' was rendered as '笳', an ancient Chinese instrument whose function in the ancient Chinese battle was the same as 'the trumpet' in the ancient Western battle. 'As all had expected', 'this issue of the combat all had foreseen', 'to the astonishment of all who beheld it' and so forth were omitted. 'The dark red flush was still on his brow' was altered into '额上紫脉偾起'(the dark red veins protruded on his brow). In the last line, 'said the Grand Master' was changed into '众皆太息曰'(everyone signed and said with regret). Nevertheless, on the whole, the translation is very close to the original in content, sentiment, style, and even sometimes in sentence structure. Let us compare one of passages quoted above:

> The original: Ivanhoe, extricating himself from his fallen horse, was soon on foot,
> Lin Shu's translation: 挨梵诃疾起
> Lin Shu's translation in English: Ivanhoe was swiftly on foot

> The original: hastening to mend his fortune with his sword
> Lin Shu's translation: 出剑谋地斗
> Lin Shu's translation in English: drew his sword and sought to fight on the ground

> The original: but his antagonist arose not
> Lin Shu's translation: 而白拉恩偃卧弗动
> Lin Shu's translation in English: but Bois-Guilbert was lying motionlessly

---

[1] Qian Zhongshu, 1981, p.15.

148

The original: Wilfred, placing his foot on his breast, and the sword's point to his throat

Lin Shu's translation: 挨梵诃以剑抵其喉门

Lin Shu's translation in English: Ivanhoe placed the sword's point tot his throat, saying:

The original: commanded him to yield to him, or die on the spot

Lin Shu's translation: '尔不降者，立死。'

Lin Shu's translation in English: 'if you don't yield to me, you will die on the spot.'

In the translation, except 'extricating from his fallen horse' (this omission is reasonable, because there are such descriptions as 'reeled in his saddle, lost his stirrup' in the preceding paragraph), 'placing his foot on his breast' was omitted and 'commanded him to yield him, or die on the spot' was changed into the direct speech '尔不降者，立死' (if you don't yield me, you would die on the spot) the whole passage mimics the original in sentence structure.

If we compare Lin's most important translated texts such as *Bali Chahuanü yishi*(*La Dame aux Camélias*), *Heinu yu tian lu* (*Uncle Tom's Cabin*), *Kuai rou yusheng shu*(*David Copperfield*) with original texts, we can accept the statements by Mao Dun. In Mao Dun's opinion, Lin Shu's translation of *Ivanhoe* considerably preserved the sentiment and style of the original, and the characterization in the translation was the same as in the original. [1] For examole, in Chapter Twenty-One of *David Copperfield*, we can compare the portrayals of the servant Littimer in both Dickens' original and Lin Shu's version:

The original:

There was a servant in that house, a man who, I understood, was usually with Steerforth, and had come into his service at the University, who was in appearance a pattern of respectability. I believe there never existed in his station a more respectable-looking man. He was taciturn, soft-footed, very quiet in his manner, deferential, observant, always at hand when wanted,

---

[1] Zheng Zhenduo, p.161.

and never near when not wanted; but his great claim to consideration was his respectability.[1]

Lin Shu's Translation:

司蒂尔福司家有老仆，恒侍主人赴大学。老仆颇凝重，不类斯仆，言笑弗苟，行事轻便，举止安贴，见客至有礼。每欲有需，彼必侍立；意不属彼，则彼亦远引，然亦无委琐卑屈之状。[2]

Lin Shu's translation in English:

There was an old servant in Steerforth's house, who always served his master at the University. This old servant was in appearance a pattern of respectability, unlike those servants in lower position. He was taciturn, soft-footed, quiet in his manner, deferential, observant, always at hand when wanted, and never near when not wanted; but did not lose his respectability.

The translated text is mostly faithful to the original text in both content and form. Nearly each sentence in the original can find its correspondent one in the translation. For example, 'there was a servant in that house' / '司蒂尔福司家有老仆', 'come into his service at the University' / '恒侍主人赴大学', 'a man…who was in appearance a pattern of respectability. I believe there never existed in his station a more respectable-looking man' / '老仆颇凝重，不类斯仆', 'taciturn' / '言笑弗苟', 'soft-footed' / '行事轻便', 'very quite in his manner' / '举止安贴', 'deferential' /见客至有礼', 'observant, always at hand when wanted' / '每欲有需，彼必侍立', 'never near when not wanted' / '意不属彼，则彼亦远引', 'but his great claim to consideration was his respectability' / '然亦无委琐卑屈之状'. Although Lin Shu made some minor adaptations, e.g. omitting the parentheses 'I understood' and 'I believe', adding the adjective '老' (old) before the noun '仆' (servant), and slightly adjusted the word order somewhere, on the whole, the translation is very close to the original.

---

[1] Dicken, Charles, The Personal History of David Copperfield, Oxford University Press, London, 1948, p.299.
[2] Lin Shu, Kuai rou yusheng shu 块肉余生述 (David Copperfield), Shangwu yinshuguan, Beijing, 1981, p.175.

In Chapter Three, there is a description of David Copperfield's impression on Ham when Copperfield met Ham for the first time:

<u>The original:</u>

He was dressed in a canvas jacket, and a pair of such very stiff trousers that they would have stood quite as well alone, without any legs in them. [1]

<u>Lin Shu's translation:</u>

汉姆…，衣帆布之衫，裤坚硬如铁，即无股承之，亦足自立于地。[2]

<u>Lin Shu's translation in English:</u>

Ham…, dressed in a canvas jacket, and his trousers are so stiff as iron. Without any thighs in them, they would have stood quite as well alone.

Lin Shu's translation truthfully reproduced both the meaning and the humorous style of the original. 'Very stiff' was rendered as '坚硬如铁'(stiff as iron), which, though exaggerated, is correlated to '即无股承之，亦足自立于地'(without any thighs in them, they would have stood quite as well alone), thus creating an humorous effect. When Mr. Peggotty walked back into the ship after washing himself in a kettleful of hot water, Dickens wrote:

<u>The original:</u>
He soon returned, greatly improved in appearance; but so rubicund, that I couldn't help thinking his face had this in common with the lobsters, crabs, and crawfish — that it went into the hot water very black and cam out very red.[3]

<u>Lin Shu's translation:</u>
少许入船，垢尽，颜色奇绛，余自思螃蟹龙虾，如沸即红，渔兄之状，得无如虾蟹耶。[4]

<u>Lin Shu's translation in English:</u>
Soon he entered the boat, the dirt on his face had been washed off, and the

---

[1] Dicken, 1948,p.29.
[2] Lin Shu, Kuai rou yusheng ji (David Copperfield), 1981, p.16.
[3] Dickens, 1948, p. 32.
[4] Lin Shu, 1981, p. 18.

colour of his face was unusually rubicund. I couldn't help thinking that crabs and lobsters turn red the moment they are put into the hot water. Could it be said that the fisherfolk looks like the crabs and lobsters?)

In the translation, instead of sticking to the sentence structure of the original, Lin Shu added '得无如虾蟹耶'(Could it be said that the fisherfolk looks like the lobsters and crabs?). Thus the translation truthfully conveys the humour of the original. As Walter Benjamin remarks, 'The task of the translator consists in finding that intended effect upon the language into which he is translating which produces in it the echo of the original.'[1] This remark is quite applicable to Lin Shu's case. Lin Shu not only properly reproduced Dickens's vivid portrayal of the servant in an extraordinary language, but also displayed his linguistic style: succinct, sprightly and rhythmical, which was more suitable for educated Chinese readers. Indeed, Lin Shu could translate the humorous style in Dickens's novels, although he did not always stick to the original word for word.

Another typical example may be seen in Chapter Forty-One of *David Copperfield*, where there is a humorous description of the hairstyle of Traddles:

<u>The original:</u>
> Excellent fellow as I know Traddles to be, and warmly attached to him as I was, I could not help wishing, on that delicate occasion, that he had never contracted the habit of brushing his hair so very upright. It gave him a surprised look – not to say a hearth-broomy kind of expression – which, my apprehensions whispered might be fatal to us.
>
> I took the liberty of mentioning it to Traddles, as we were walking to Putney; and saying that if he would smooth it down a little –
>
> 'My dear Copperfield,' said Traddles, lifting off his hat, and rubbing his hair all kinds of ways, 'nothing would give me greater pleasure. But it won't.'
>
> 'Won't be smoothed down?' said I.
>
> 'No,' said Traddles. 'Nothing will induce it. If I was to carry a half-hundredweight upon it, all the way to Putney, it would be up again the moment the weight was taken off. You have no idea what obstinate hair mine is, Copperfield. I am quite a fretful porcupine.'
>
> I was a little disappointed, I must confess, but thoroughly charmed by

---

[1] Benjamin, Walter, Illuminations, Trans. Harry Zohn, Harcourt, Brace & World, New York, 1968, p.67.

his good-nature too. I told him how I esteemed his good-nature; and said that his hair must have taken all the obstinacy out of his character, for he had none.[1]

Lin Shu's transltion:

忲老特尔司者良友也，今兹有不满余意事，则额上壮发突起，为可厌也。

道中余告吾友，胡以不刷平此发。

吾友闻言，去冠伏其发久，言曰："我亦思伏此发，乃终不受令，奈何？"

余曰："终不卜乎？"

友曰："吾以百镑物压之令伏，及去重，发付翘起。考伯菲而乃不审吾发之倔强，乃类豪猪。"

余思吾友此状，何令两姑见之。然友之驯善可人，吾又何忍峻责，因曰："君之德性良，而一生之刚果之气悉钟此壮发，故和平至此。"[2]

Lin Shu's translation in English:

Traddles was a good friend of mine. At the moment, what dissatisfied me was that the strong hair stands upright on his head. It was disagreeable.

On the way, I asked my friend why he did not smooth down his hair.

After hearing it, my friend lifted off his hat and pressed his hair for a long time, saying: 'I also think of trying to smooth down my hair, but it does not obey me. What can I do?'

I said: 'Can't it be smoothed down in all events?"

My friend said: 'if I was to carry a hundredweight on it to force it obedient, it would be up again the moment the weight was taken off. My dear Copperfield, you have no idea what obstinate hair mine is. It is similar to a porcupine.'

I thought of how I could let my two aunts see this hair shape of the fellow. But charmed by his good nature, I was not hardhearted enough to blame him, so I said: 'You have a good nature. All the disposition of your obstinacy has been absorbed into your strong hair. For this reason, you can be mild and peaceful till now.'

---

[1] Dickens, 1948, p.591.
[2] Lin Shu, 1981, p.330.

A contrastive reading of the translation and the original shows that the former is not the same as the latter in word order or sentence sequence at all. But when we read the translation after finishing reading the original, we find that the translation faithfully renders the humour in the original. In the translation, on the one hand, Lin Shu retained the concision of classical Chinese writing, omitting some words and phrases that seem inappropriate or superfluous to expressions in classical Chinese and abridging the wordy descriptions (contrary to the habit of the Chinese readers). For instance, the first sentence 'Excellent fellow as I know Traddles to be, and warmly attached to him as I was' in the original was abridged into '忒老特尔司者良友 也'(Traddles was a good friend of mine). On the other hand, however, after a contrastive reading of the translation and the original, we can also feel that the style of humour in the original remains intact in the translation. In the translation, Lin Shu combined free translation with literal translation to render the style of the original. '去冠伏其发久' is practically the literal translation of 'lifting off his hat, and rubbing his hair all kinds of ways', while '我亦思伏此 发，乃终不受令，奈何？ '(I also thought of trying to smooth down my hair, but it does not obey my order. What can I do to it?) is the free translation of 'Nothing would give me greater pleasure. But it won't.' The sense of humour in the original was not decreased in the translation. In this way, there is equivalence in effect between the target and source texts. Retaining the style and sentiment rather than word and sentence in the original embodies the faithfulness in Lin Shu' translations.

3. Expression in Literary Language

As is stated, Lin Shu was a master of classical Chinese. This is embodied in his extraordinary ability to use classical Chinese in translation. This ability assured his success in rendering the spirit and style of the original, even in details, when he had an accurate understanding of the original. Bates argues that a bilinguist never exists, in a true sense, and that if a person can only be really proficient in one language, a translator can only take his mother language as his

154

language for translation.[1] He adds that truthfulness should be based on spirit instead of surface. Since the translator can master his native language as proficiently as the original author can, or even more proficiently than the original author can, so it is possible that a translation is as lasting as the original is, or even surpasses the original. [2] In Qian Zhongshu's view, sometimes Lin Shu's ability to apply the target language surpassed the original author's ability in the source language. He said, 'It is my first finding that I prefer reading Lin Shu's translated text to Haggard's original text. The reason is very simple: Lin Shu's Chinese writing is far better than Haggard's English writing.' [3] He illustrated his view with the following example:

The original:
What meanest thou by such mad tricks? Surely thou art mad. (*Allan Quatermain*, Chapter 5)[4]

Lin Shu's translation:
汝何为恶作剧？尔非痫当不如是。（斐洲烟水愁城录，第五章）[5]

Lin Shu's translation in English:
Why did you play such a prank? You must be mad.

Qian Zhongshu thought that Haggard's sentence, mixing up ancient English and modern English, was 'nondescript', 'ridiculous' and 'disagreeable'; whereas Lin Shu's translation was 'sprightly'.[6]

Qian Zhongshu's conclusion is that Lin Shu's ability to apply the target language is far better than Haggard's ability to write in the source language. This conclusion is arguable, as Qian Zhongshu's native language was Chinese after all, though he had studied English Literature at Oxford University and in China for many years. However, one point in Qian Zhongshu's view may be confirmed, namely, Lin Shu's ability in the target language is extraordinary. It is this ability

---

[1] E. Stuart Bates, Modern Translation, cited in Liao Qiyi 廖七 ·, Dangdai Yingguo fanyi lilun 当代英国翻译理论(Contemporary Translation Theories in UK), Hubei jiaoyu chubanshe, Wuhan, 2001, p.19.
[2] Ibid.
[3] Qian Zhongshu, 1981, p.45.
[4] Ibid.
[5] Ibid.
[6] Ibid.

that largely ensured the success of his translations and made them win a great number of readers.

In fact, Qian Zhongshu's conclusion in some cases may be supported by Waley's views on Lin Shu. The English scholar Waley, after his contrastive reading of Dickens's works and Lin Shu's translations, believes that Lin Shu succeeded in using classical Chinese to translate Dickens's works. In his translations, Lin Shu retained and transmuted the humor in Dickens's novels. Lin Shu replaced all the over-elaboration, the over-statement and uncurbed garrulity in the originals with a precise, economical style. Waley continues: 'every point that Dickens spoils by uncontrolled exuberance, Lin Shu makes quietly and efficiently.'[1]

Another example of Lin Shu's ability in the target language can be seen in the beginning of Chapter Three of *Uncle Tom's Cabin*. Eliza was standing in the verandah, rather dejectedly looking after the retreating carriage when George came to her place:

The original:

...A hand was laid on her shoulder. She turned, and a bright smile lighted up her fine eyes.[2]

Lin Shu's translation:

背上有人以手拊之，意里赛回眸一盼，瓠犀灿然，……[3]

Lin Shu's translation in English:

Someone clapped her on the shoulder. She turned around and looked rapidly, and then smiled brightly.

Here without doubt, the translation is very truthful to the original and further, in the presentment of Eliza's surprising and pleasant expression on seeing her husband George, Lin Shu's description is very picturesque and impressive. '回眸一盼，瓠犀灿然' corresponds very well to 'She turned, and a bright smile lighted up her fine eyes' in conveying the meaning and vividness of the original, though the sentence structure was altered. '回眸一盼'(she turned around and

---

[1] Waley, Renditions, No. 5, 1975, p.30.
[2] Stowe, Harriet Beecher, Uncle Tom's Cabin, Houphton Mifflin Company, Boston and New York, 1952, p.16.
[3] Lin Shu, Hei nu yu tian lu (Uncle Tom's Cabin), 1981, p. 9.

looked rapidly) and '皓犀灿然'(its original meaning is 'her teeth are so white, crystal-clear', which is often used to describe a beauty's bright smile in classical Chinese literature), and here is used to describes Eliza's bright smile) are refined Chinese description, implying a pleasant surprise and a finally fulfilled expectation. '回眸一盼' is correlated to '皓犀灿然'. Both are close to the original, reproducing its succinctness and vividness while retaining the elegance of classical Chinese.

Long Yuhong and Tong Liqiang's translation of the passage is quoted for comparison:

Long and Tong's translation:
有人从后面走来，把手搭在了她的肩膀上。她转回身，两眼顿时发出多彩的光辉，美丽的笑容浮现于脸上。[1]

English translation of Long and Tong's translation:
Someone walked towards her from the back, put his hand on her shoulder. She turned, and her eyes immediately emitted colorful brilliance, and a beautiful smile gradually rose on her face.

Differing from Lin Shu, Long and Tong have a good command of the English language and translated *Uncle Tom's Cabin* in modern vernacular Chinese. Their translation is however much inferior to Lin Shu's, and their Chinese expression is relatively mediocre, even inapt. In their translation, Long & Tong's '有人从后面走来'(Someone was walking toward her from the back) is actually a superfluous addition. '顿时'(immediately) seems to contradict '浮现' (gradually rose), as according to the original, both '多彩的光辉'(colorful brilliance) and '美丽的笑容'(beautiful smile) should happen 'immediately'. It may be proper to use 'brilliant' in the description of a person's happy look in English, yet '多彩的光辉'(colorful brilliance) is hardly used in modern Chinese, as it appears to be too exaggerated. Besides, the adjective '多彩的' (colorful) is an inapt use as well, as the meaning of the adjective cannot be found from the original. Thus it can be seen that Lin Shu's ability in classical Chinese surpassed Long & Tong's

---

[1] Long Yuhong 龙雨虹 and Tong Liqiang 仝立强, Tangmu shushu de xiaowu 汤姆叔叔的小屋 (Uncle Tom's Cabin), Dazhong wenyi chubanshe, 2000, (Online) Available: http://www.shuku.net:8080/novels/foreign/ tmssdxw/tmssdxw03.html (2002, June 8).

ability in modern Chinese. It could be one of the reasons why Lin Shu's translation was widely read while Long and Tong's one is little known to the Chinese readers.

Lin Shu not only preserved the spirit and style of the original in some of his important translated works, but he also skillfully used the target language to make his translation more vivid and more attractive to the target reading public. This skill is evident in characterization as well as the portrayal of scenery, thus creating a poetic equivalence between the target and source texts. In the first chapter of his translation *Sakexun jie hou yingxiong lue (Ivanhoe)*, there is a splendid representation of the scenery:

The original:

The sun was setting upon one of the rich grassy glades of that forest, which we have mentioned in the beginning of the chapter. Hundreds of broad-headed, short-stemmed, wide-branched oaks, which had witnessed perhaps the stately march of the Roman soldiery, flung their gnarled arms over a thick carpet of the most delicious green sward; in some places they were intermingled with beeches, hollies, and copsewood of various descriptions, so closely as totally to intercept the level beams of the sinking sun; in others they receded from each other, forming delights to lose itself, while imagination considers them as the paths to yet wilder scenes of silvan solitude. Here the red rays of the sun shot a broken and discoloured light, that partially hung upon the shattered boughs and mossy trunks of the trees, and there they illuminated in brilliant patches the portions of turf to which they made their way. A considerable open space, in the midst of this glade, seemed formerly to have been dedicated to the rites of Druidical superstition; for, on the summit of a hillock, so regular as to seem artificial, there still remained part of a circle of rough unhewn stones, of large dimensions. Seven stood upright; the rest had been dislodged from their places, probably by the zeal of some covert to Christianity, and lay, some prostrate near their former site, and others on the side of the hill. One large stone only had found its way to the bottom, and in stopping the course of a small brook, which glided smoothly round the foot of the eminence, grave, by its opposition, a feeble voice of murmur to the placid and elsewhere silent streamlet.[1]

<u>Lin Shu's translation:</u>

大树林中，一口斜阳方落，回光倒影纤草之上；千百巨橡，臃肿无度，瘿周其身，虬枝怒挐如仙龙撙。树之年代，当罗马大兵入国时，固已见之矣。群橡之中，苍藤荄生，荆棘杂出，几于阳光无能射入；人迹既稀，长日幽静，而树影所不及者，则细草廉纤，斜阳如画矣。此外有草碛一区绝旷。尚有残石半堆，似庙祀妖神之坛坫，而石状倾颠，似基督徒教门吕炽后，毁出之者。地有小山，溪流抱之；复有巨石亘路，流触石而过，声琤琤然，它处则否。[2]

<u>Lin Shu's translation in English:</u>

One large stone only had found its way to the bottom, and in stopping the course of a small brook, which glided smoothly round the foot of the eminence, grave, by its opposition, a feeble voice of murmur to the placid and elsewhere silent streamlet

In the great forest, the sun was setting, shining upon the find grassy grades. There were hundreds of tall oaks with great circumference, numerous gnarls and wide branches like a dragon stretching its arms. The trees were seen as early as the Roman soldiery marched into this country. In the oaks, old vines trailed and brambles grew thickly so that the level beams of the sinking sun were intercepted. There it was secluded and quiet all day long. In the places without shades of trees, there were tenuous grass and picturesque slanting sunrays. Besides, in a considerable open space, there remained part of a circle of rough unhewn stones, which seemed to be the rite of a temple for offering sacrifices to gods. The stones were askew, which seemed to be dislodged after the Christianity prevailed. A hill was surrounded by a brook, and a large stone had found its way to the bottom. The streamlet touched and flowed by the stone, gurgling, which could not be heard elsewhere.

---

[1] Scott, Walter, Ivanhoe: a romance, J. M. Dent & Sons Ltd, London and Tpronto, 1931, pp.27-28.

[2] Lin Shu, Sakexun jiehou yingxiong lue 撒克迅劫后英雄略 (Ivanhoe), Shangwu yinshuguan, 1930, pp.27–28.

In the English text, the depiction of the scene in the forest is full of color and sound, very impressive, which exhibits Scott's outstanding ability to observe the nature and apply the language. As a master of classical Chinese, Lin Shu also showed his extraordinary ability in classical Chinese to reproduce the linguistic and literary style of the original. '大树林中，一日斜阳方落，回光倒影纤草之上' can compare favorably with 'the sun was setting upon one of the rich grassy glades of that forest'; '千百巨橡，臃肿无度，瘿周其身，虬枝怒拏如伸龙臂'(There were hundreds of tall oaks with great circumference, numerous gnarls and wide branches like a dragon stretching its arms) may rival 'Hundreds of broad-headed, short-stemmed, wide-branched oaks…flung their gnarled arms over a thick carpet of the most delicious green sward'. Especially, '虬枝怒拏如伸龙臂' used to render 'flung their gnarled arms over a thick carpet of the most delicious green sward' not only present the original scene, but also deeply impressed the Chinese readers. '…流触石而过，声琤琤然'(The streamlet touched and flowed by the stone, gurgling) is matchable to 'a small brook, which glided smoothly round the foot of the eminence, grave, by its opposition, a feeble voice of murmur to the placid', the wording and sentence structure of both are different but equally satisfactory in effect; for example, '声琤琤然' corresponds well to 'a feeble voice of murmur' in meaning. The contrast demonstrates that Lin Shu's translation reproduces both a dynamic equivalence and a poetic equivalence.

Thus it can be seen that the equivalence between Lin Shu's translation and the original is embodied in spirit, content and sentiment as well as literary effect and style, rather than word order and sentence structure. In consequence, as I mentioned above, when readers read the corresponding sections or the whole text of Lin Shu's translation after reading a paragraph, a chapter or the whole text of the original, they are hardly aware of the differences between Lin Shu's translation and the original or aware of Lin Shu's obvious changes of the original in content, sentiment and literary style in many cases. This point is supported by such Chinese scholars as Zheng Zhenduo, Mao Dun and Qian Zhongshu's experience in comparative readings of Lin Shu's most important translated works. The sentiment in *Bali chahuanü yishi* (*La Dame aux Camélias*), the humorous style in *Kuai rou yusheng shu* (*David Copperfield*) and the grief and indignation *Hei nu yu tian ju* (*Uncle Tom's Cabin*) impressed their Chinese readers as deeply as the originals would have impressed their readers.

4. Sinicization

In terms of translation, sinicization means to try to indigenize a translated text or description so as to make it read more like a Chinese one for the acceptance of the Chinese readers. Sinicization was a common phenomenon in the translations of early modern China. Sinicization embodies Lin Shu's target orientation in translation and his skills in poetic equivalence in the translation process. In this section, I focus on Lin Shu's linguistic style or diction and literary style, examining in considerable detail how Lin Shu sinicized the original. First, the use of classical Chinese in translation is a most important step to achieve sinicization. Classical Chinese is the product of the traditional Chinese culture, whereas modern Chinese is partly produced from the influence of Western culture interacting with the Chinese language. Lin Shu achieved his sinicization by transforming the original into a Chinese linguistic and literary style.

First of all, let us look at how Lin Shu sinicized the original letters in his translations. In Lin Shu's time, educated people attached importance to letter writing. As a rule, they wrote a letter in classical Chinese rather than in vernacular Chinese, for classical Chinese is a written language while in most cases vernacular Chinese is used in spoken Chinese. However, most of the foreign novels Lin Shu translated are in their original vernacular language. Therefore when translating them, Lin Shu had to transform the vernacular linguistic style of the source text into a classical linguistic style in the target text, considered a refined and elegant style. Lin Shu's translation of the letter in the original can show this alteration to letter writing. If we compare the note Joan Haste wrote to Henry in the original with Lin Shu's Chinese version, the distinction is obvious:

The original:

Dear Sir Henry Graves,

Thank you for the kind message you sent asking after me. There was never much the matter, and I am quite well again now. I was very sorry to hear of the death of Sir Reginald. I fear that it must have been great shock to you, Perhaps you would like to know that I am leaving Bradmouth for good and all, as I have no friends here and do not get on well; besides, it is time that I should be working for my own living. I am leaving without telling my aunt, so that nobody will know my address or be able to trouble me to come back. I do not fear, however, but that I shall manage to hold my own in the world, as I am strong and active, and have plenty of money to start with. I think you said that I might have the books which you left behind here, so I am taking them with me as a keepsake. If I live, they will remind me of the days when I used to nurse you, and to read to you out of them, long years after you have forgotten me. Good-bye, dear Sir Henry. I hope that soon you will be quite well again and happy all your life. I do not think that we shall meet any more, so again good-bye.

> Obediently Yours
> Joan Haste[1]

Lin Shu's translation:

亨利勋爵足下：前此医者寓君言，来省吾病，语极温婉慈爱，足见深心。唯吾病殊不剧，今且勿药。闻老勋爵奄逝，闻之悲梗万状，此亦君生平祸难之第一遭，悲戚必且更甚，至念至念。吾今日将谋去白拉墨斯，以此间孑然无朋友之助，孤飘一女子，何由可立？且贫女年事已及，应自图活于外，然实未尝与阿姨谋之，且无人知我所向，必难见诇。至吾一身远出，凭其壮岁体质，料不为风寒所中，而腰囊亦硕，足以为客。君去年归时，所留箧中书卷，君诺赐我，吾即携书同行，用为记念。吾一日生者，每于风前展卷，必一一忆及病蹶趋走之时；且展此一篇，就榻读之为君排闷。想后此数年，君必积渐忘我。然吾对遗篇，仍复不能遗君。君今勿念，吾行矣。用此留别，愿君清恙早瘳，一生安乐；唯此后谅无再见之期，书此以为永诀。侍儿迦茵. 赫司德笺上。[2]

Lin Shu's translation in English:

Dear Sir Henry [literally translated into 'beneath of the feet of Sir Henry']: Not a long ago, the doctor passed your message to find out the state of my illness, in which your words were so kind that I could feel your deep sympathy. My condition is better, and I don't have to take medicine now. I

---

[1] Haggard, H. Rider, Joan Haste, Longmans, Green, and Co., London, 1895, p. 214.

[2] Lin Shu, Jiayin xiaozhuan 迦茵小传 (Joan Haste), Shangwu yishuguan, Beijing, 1981, pp. 133–134.

felt very sad to hear of the death of Sir Seginald. It is the first disaster in your life, you must be deeply grieved, and so I worry very much about you. I will leave Bradmouth now. Here I am loner and have no friend to help me. What will I, a helpless girl, live by? Beside I have grown to womanhood, therefore I should be working for my own living. I am leaving without consulting with my aunt. Nobody knows where I am going, so it will be difficult to detect my address. As for my lonely long journey, I do not fear by virtue of my good health that I would catch cold. I have plenty of money with me, which is sufficient to support me as a traveller. When you returned last year, you said that I might have the books that you left in the case. Therefore, I am taking them with me as a keepsake. If I live, whenever I open one of the books, it will remind me of the days when I used to nurse you and read them for you beside bed. Many years later, you will have gradually forgotten me, but whenever I see the book you left, I will think of you. Do not worry, and I am leaving. Good-bye. I hope that you will recover your health as early as possible and will be happy all your life. I do not think that we shall meet again, so I write this letter to say good-bye.

Obediently Yours, Joan Haste [literally, submitted by your servant Joan Haste]

Except for linguistic style, e.g. self-depreciatory expression and elegant diction, Lin's Chinese version closely relays the meaning and even sentence order of the English version, but the latter reads really like a note, expressed in simple phrases while the former reads more like a formal letter, expressed in classical style. The translation embodied Lin Shu's style of writing, and had much appeal for the Chinese readers. It can be seen from the comparison that the style of the target language has more different linguistic codes than the simple vernacular style of the source language, but successfully impressed the Chinese readers with epistolary style. As far as diction is concerned, 'Dear Sir Henry Grave', for example, was rendered into '亨利勋爵足下'. '足下' (beneath your feet) is a self-depreciatory expression in a classical Chinese letter. Like 'Dear', it is a polite appellation, yet not a self-depreciatory expression. Similarly, in the end of the letter, Lin Shu rendered the name of the sender into '侍儿迦茵笺上'(submitted by your servant Joan), in which both '侍儿' and '笺上' are self-depreciatory expressions as well. Other Chinese additions are '座下', '(beneath your seat), '顿

首'(touch the ground with my head), '惠鉴'(be kind enough to read). This Chinese code cannot be found in the original, and it belongs to the form of classical Chinese letter-writing, and so gains functional equivalence between Chinese readers and Western readers' concepts of epistolary style. It shows that different diction in the source and target texts can also achieve functional equivalence.

Another example of sinicization by Lin Shu is his treatment of the scriptures in the original. He always attempted to locate a corresponding style in his translations. In Chapter Twenty-Two of *Uncle Tom's Cabin*, for example, Tom sang the hymns to Eva:

The original:
Oh, had I the wings of the morning,
I'd fly away to Canna's shore;
Bright angles should convey me home,
To the new Jerusalem.

…

I see a band of spirits bright,
That taste the glories there;
They all are robed in spotless white,
And conquering palms they bear.[1]

Lin Shu's translation:
谁副吾翼兮，
吾将向彼迦南之滨。
天神幡幢纷而我前导兮，
吾将止彼基督自由之京。
……
吾仰睹天女衣裙之明丽兮，
若有银云为之被也。
长裙缟然其如鹤兮，
执杨枝其依依也。[2]

Lin Shu's translation in English:

[1] Stowe, 1952, p.290.
[2] Lin Shu, 1981, p.124.

Who would give me the wings?
I'd fly away to Canna's shore;
Gods's fluttering flags would lead me
To the free capital of Jesus.

...

I look up at the bright skirts of the fairy maidens,
Like robbing themselves in glorious clouds
The long skirts are as white as a crane's feather
The willow branches in their hands are swaying.

Lin Shu translated the Christian hymns in the poetic style of *sao*. *Sao* refers to the Chinese poet Qu Yuan (340-278 B.C.)'s long poem, *Li sao*. The poetic style became so well known that it inaugurated a classical poetic style that many later Chinese poets imitated. Lin Shu thought that this poetic style was most suitable for the translation of Christian hymns. In fact, he sinicized them so that the Chinese readers could be impressed by the holy style of the hymns from Lin Shu's translation. Similar cases may also be seen in Lin Shu's other translations such as *Sakexun jiehou yingxiong lue (Ivanhoe)*.

In addition, traditional Chinese prose depicts an ancient cosmology, and therefore classical Chinese literature emphasizes the link between landscape and humanity. Lin Shu is a master of the portrayal of scenery. He always translated the descriptions in a typical classical Chinese style so that the Chinese readers felt that they were reading a depiction of Chinese scenery rather than exotic scenery. In fact, Lin Shu's depiction of scenery in classical Chinese can compare favourably with the original depiction, even though some alterations were made. Let us compare the following passages from Chapter Twenty-Two of *Uncle Tom's Cabin*:

The Original:

It is now one of those intensely golden sunsets which kindles the whole horizon into one blaze of glory, and makes the water another sky. The lake lay in rosy or golden streaks, save where white-winged vessels glided hither and thither...[1]

Lin Shu's translation:

---

[1] Stowe, 1909, p.289.

方夕阳始落，红霞弥空，倒印入水，似水中别成一天。而水之回澜，舍白色风帆外，均闪闪作金线。[1]

<u>Lin Shu's translation in English:</u>
Now when the sun is setting, it kindles the whole horizon into a blaze of red glory, and is mirrored in water, which looks like another sky. The returning ripples on the lake, white-winged vessels, are flashing like golden streaks.

This translation basically retains the features of the scenic depiction in the original, but instead of following the linguistic style in the original, Lin Shu stylized the scenic depiction into classical Chinese, e.g., turning the long sentences into short poetic phrases in lively rhythm. As a result, it reads like a sinicized scenic depiction. Actually, the scenic depictions like this are quite common in   classical Chinese prose and poetry

The translation of the scenic depiction in Rip Van Winkle, *The Sketch Book* also exhibited Lin Shu's mastery of the scenic depiction in classical Chinese:

<u>The original:</u>
Every change of season, every change of weather, indeed, every hour of the day, produces some change in the magical hues and shapes of these mountains, and they are regarded by all the good wives, far and near, as perfect barometers. When the weather is fair and settled, they are clothed in blue and purple, and print their bold outlines on the clear evening sky; but, sometimes, when the rest of the landscape is cloudless, they will gather a hood of grey vapors about their summits, which, in the last rays of the setting sun, will glow and light up like a crown of glory.

At the foot of these fair mountains, the voyager may have descried the light smoke curling up from a village, whose shingle-roofs gleam among the trees, just where the blue tints of the upland melt away into the fresh green of the nearer landscape. [2]

<u>Lin Shu's translation:</u>

---

[1] Lin Shu, 1981, p.123.
[2] Irving, Washington, Rip Van Winkle, Heinemann, London, 1905, p.1; also see The Sketch book, Twayne, Boston, 1978.

四时代谢，及旦晚阴晴，山容辄随物候而变；凡之村庄中承家之妇恒视此山若寒暑表焉。若在晴稳时，则山色青紫驳露，接于蔚蓝之中，空翠爽肌；或天淡无云，则峰尖如被云巾，蓊然作白气，斜日倒烛，则片云肖幻为圆光，周转圆顶，如仙人之现其圆明焉者。山跌之下，村人炊烟缕缕而上，树阴辄山楼角及瓦缝，隐隐若画。[1]

Lin Shu's translation in English:

Every change of four seasons, every change from morning to evening and well as from fine to cloudy produces some changes in the hues and shapes of these mountains. Therefore all the housewives in the village always regard them as barometers. When the weather is fair and settled, they are clothed in blue and purple, which is interweaved with the blue sky. The scene is spacious, emerald and cool. Or when it is cloudless, the summits vapour as if they were covered with a white, cloudy hood. In the rays of the setting sun, the cloud sheet changes into a round light round the summit just like a celestial being in the halo. At the foot of these mountains, the light smoke curling up from a village may be descried, and the eaves of roofs and the rows of tiles appear from the trees are faintly visible like a painting.

By comparison, Lin Shu's translation is quite close to the original. In the Chinese version, Lin Shu gave full play to his talent for scenic depiction in classical Chinese. As a result, the scenery in his translation was imbued with a strong Chinese colour so that the Chinese readers read it as classical Chinese prose. Lin Shu's sinicized scenic portrayal embodies the style and features of Tang and Song prose, for which he had the greatest esteem. As Qian Boji said, 'Lin Shu's prose remains the style of the Tang and Song prose.'[2] Lin Shu was especially good at lyrical prose.[3] Let us look at the famous Song poet, Ouyang

---

[1] Lin Shu, Fi zhang lu 拊掌录 (The Sketch Book), Shangwu yinshuguan, Beijing, 1981, p.5.

[2] Qian Boji 钱博基, 'Lin Shu de guwen'林纾的古文(Lin Shu's Classical Prose'), Xiandai Zhongguo wenxueshi 现代中国文学史(A History of Modern Chinese Literature), Shijie shuju, 1933, p.145.

[3] Yu Ling 舆龄, 'Lin Qinnan zhuanlue'林琴南传略(A Brief Biography of Lin Qinnan), in Zhu Chuanyu 朱传誉, (ed.), Lin Qinnan zhuanji ziliao 林琴南传记资料(Biographical Materials on Lin Qinnan), Tianyi chubanshe, Taipei, 1981,p.786.

Xiu's (1007-1072) scenic depiction in his well-known prose 'Zuiweng ting ji'(The Old Drunkard's Pavilion Notes):

The original:

若夫日出而林霏开，云归而岩穴暝，晦明变化者，山间之朝暮也。野芳发而幽香，佳木秀而繁阴，风霜高洁，水落而石出者，山间之四时也。朝而往，暮而归，四时之景不同，而乐亦无穷也。[1]

English translation:

When the sun rises, the mist in the trees is dispelled, and when the cloud returns, the cliff becomes dark. This shift between bright and dark is caused by the change from morning to evening in the mountains. The wild flowers grow with a delicate fragrance, and the beautiful trees are dense with shades. The wind is high and the frost is pure. When the water subsides the rocks emerge, which caused by the shift of the four seasons. Go in the morning and return in the evening. Due to the difference of scenery in each season, it is a great delight.

By comparison with the poetic description of Lin Shu, the two writers depicted different sceneries in detail, but the depictions have equal styles and effects. Lin Shu's '四时代谢，及旦晚阴晴，山容辄随物候而变'(Every change of four seasons, every change from morning to evening and well as from fine to cloudy produces some changes in the hues and shapes of these mountains) and '若在晴稳时，则山色青紫驳露，接于蔚蓝之中，.....或天淡无云，则峰尖如被云巾，蓊然作白气，斜日倒烛，则片云直幻为圆光'(When the weather is fair and settled, they are clothed in blue and purple, which is interweaved with the blue sky. ...when it is a find day, the colour of the mountain is variegated, green here and purple there, linked up to the blue sky, ...or when it is cloudless, the summits vapour as if they were covered with a white, cloudy hood. In the rays of the setting sun, the cloud sheet changes into a round light round the summit just like a celestial being in the halo) compare favourably with Ouyang Xiu's '日出而林霏开，云归而岩穴暝，晦明变化者，山间之朝暮也'(When the sun rises, the mist in the trees is dispelled, and when the cloud returns, the cliff becomes dark. This shift between bright and dark is caused by the change from

---

[1] Ouyang Xiu 欧阳修, Ouyang Xiu ji 欧阳修集(A Collection of Ouyang Xiu's Works), Heluo tushu chubanshe, Taipei, 1975, pp.110-111.

morning to evening in the mountains) and '朝而往，暮而归，四时之景不同，而乐亦无穷也'(Go in the morning and return in the evening. Due to the difference of scenery in each season, it is a great delight). In the translation, Lin Shu's linguistic style, such as parallelism, short and pithy sentence structure, metaphor and lively rhythm, in reality inherited from the style of the Tang and Song prose. Therefore, it may be said that the scenic depictions in Lin Shu's translations are a true sinicization.

Lin Shu's sinicization is also obvious in the choice and use of some Chinese words that were functionally equivalent to the words in the original. In Lin Shu's translation of *Ivanhoe*, we can find a great number of examples: 'squire' was rendered into '奴了'(lackey), 'the robbers' into '绿林之盗'(the robbers in the greenwood), 'trumpet' into '胡笳'(an ancient Chinese instrument), 'Friar', and 'Father' into '道人'(Taoist priest), 'chapel' into '庵'(Buddhist convent), 'horse-litter' into '竹轿'(bamboo litter), 'Father' into '老僧人'(the old Buddhist monk), 'woman' into '巾帼'(kerchief) and so on. The practice of Lin Shu exemplifies Nida's 'dynamic equivalence' or 'functional equivalence'. Nida illustrated his views on equivalent translation through translation of 'white as snow'. In Nida's view, if the target readers have never seen snow, and if there is no such a word as 'snow' in the target language, but they are familiar with 'frost', then 'frost' may convey the meaning of 'snow'. Hence 'white as snow' becomes 'white as frost'. Otherwise, if the phrase is literally translated, it will result in a 'zero message'. Lin Shu's treatment of the foreign words that did not exist in Chinese language tallied with Nida's position.

Therefore, Lin Shu's translations, especially his most influential translations, such as *Bali chahunü yishi*（*La Dame aux Camélia*）, *Hennu yu tian lu(Uncle Tom's Cabin)*, *Kuai rou yusheng shu(David Copperfield)*, *Sakexun jie hou yingxiong lue(Ivanhoe)* should be regarded as dynamically and peotically true to the originals. As Zheng Hailing states, 'After all Lin Shu was a veteran writer in the literary world of China; with the help of others, he actually made his translations basically close to the originals, and added the finishing touch or gilding refined gold, translating more than one hundred Western classical works.'[1] Pollard also thinks that apart from abridgements, translations into classical Chinese on the whole stayed close to the original, although verbal correspondence could not be looked for where the translation depended on oral interpretation, as in Lin

---

[1] Zheng Hailing, 2000, p.34.

Shu's case.[1] It is worth noting that these remarks on the truthfulness of Lin Shu's translation have appeared only recently. It indicates that today's scholars are reassessing Lin Shu's translations. This chapter primarily discusses the 'truthfulness' of Lin Shu's translation. Poetic equivalence, a fresh concept, is used to explain the 'truthfulness' of Lin Shu's literary translation. Trough a number of examples from his translated texts, I demonstrate that the truthfulness of Lin Shu's translation lies in poetic equivalence rather than formal equivalence between the target and source texts. This chapter examines how Lin Shu achieved poetic equivalence in terms of the spirit and style, literary expression and sinicization. In this chapter, I argue that poetic equivalence is similar to Nida's principle of correspondence, but is beyond his dynamic equivalence. It lays special stress on literary or aesthetic equivalence. Poetic equivalence in Lin Shu's translations particularly refutes the claim of 'unfaithfulness' in Lin's translation. Classical Chinese aesthetics influenced Lin Shu's translation strategy: seeking poetic equivalence in his translation. Lin Shu's extraordinary ability in classical Chinese made his translations outstanding in terms of poetic equivalence. His target-oriented sinicization of the original was in reality his efforts to seek poetic equivalence between his translation and the original at a linguistic level. It is the contribution of this study to apply poetic equivalence to the analysis of Lin Shu's translated texts.

---

[1] Pollard, 1998, p.15.

Chapter 6

Beyond Equivalence

As discussed in Chapter 5, the 'truthfulness' of Lin Shu lies primarily in poetic equivalence between the original text and his translated text, but on the other hand, Lin Shu's translation method sometimes is 'beyond' equivalence for various reasons. In other words, it is not his only goal to seek equivalence, dynamic or functional. His 'beyond equivalence' in translation actually shows his close attention to the target culture and readers. In regard to the content, spirit and style, Lin Shu's translations are mostly truthful to the originals, but he often made adaptations of the originals especially for the needs of the target culture and the acceptance of his readers. Lin Shu's adaptation of the source text, including omission, addition and abridgment, is considered an unacceptable practice by some critics. However, in terms of target/culture/reader-oriented translation theories, Lin Shu's adaptation is feasible and acceptable. In this chapter, through a comparative analysis of the ST and the TT, I examine how Lin Shu dealt with the ST for the sake of the Chinese culture and readers, focusing on four aspects of adaptation: omission, addition, alteration and abridgment.

1. Adaptation

In *Translation and Creation*, Pollard quotes the view of the Chinese translator of a Japanese novel titled *Zui qiongzhe* (*The Poorest of the Poor*): 'If a translation sticks to the surface features of the original which have no connection with our country's politics or customs, so making it as dull as ditch-water, what value will it have, and why should the reader spend his other energy reading it?' Pollard concludes: 'If the purpose of the novel is to move the readers' feelings, and the reader cannot relate to it, then it fails in its purpose. And the logic applies to translation as much as to creation.'[1]

---

[1] Pollard, David, (ed.), Translation and Creation: Readings of Western Literature in Early Modern China: 1840 –1818, John Benjamins Publishing Company, Amsterdam/Philadelphia, 1998, pp.12-13.

In Lefevere's view as well, truthfulness or 'fidelity' in translation is not just a matter of matching on the linguistic level. Rather, it involves a complex network of decisions to be made by translators on the level of ideology and poetics.[1] As Bassnett and Lefevere argue (see the relevant discussion in Chapter 2), translation is a rewriting of an original text: rewriting (1) reflects a certain ideology and a poetics; (2) in its positive aspect, helps in the evolution of a literature and a society; (3) introduces new concepts, new genres, and new devices.[2] In this sense, Lin Shu's translation is rewriting.

As discussed above, Lin Shu had his eyes on the target culture and readers rather than truthfulness or fidelity to the words and language of the original. For this reason, Lin Shu made changes to the originals, including omission, addition, alteration and abridgment. This is controversial. From the viewpoints of linguistic translation or source-oriented translation theory, Lin Shu's adaptation is an unacceptable act. However, from the viewpoint of target-oriented translation theories, now that Lin Shu's translation aimed at the needs of Chinese culture and the acceptability of the target readers, his adaptations are worth affirming and exploring, and may be used as a case to support cultural translation studies.

Toury points out the translations are intended to cater for the needs of a target culture.[3] In order to meet the needs of the target culture and the acceptance of the target readers while preserving the spirit and style of the original, Lin Shu made varying types of adaptations to the original.

Adaptation, on the one hand, means to use a natural, easy and smooth target language to express the content of the original, and on the other hand, it means actual 'translingual practice'[4] — the annexation of the source culture in the original to the target culture to a different extent. The advantage of the adaptation approach lies in the fact that 'it can make the readers realize that different cultures holding the same ideas can produce equally satisfactory result,

---

[1] Lefevere,1992, p.xi.
[2] Ibid.
[3] Toury, 1995, p.28.
[4] The phrase comes from Liu, Lydia He, Translingual practice: literature, national culture, and translated modernity--China, 1900-1937, Stanford University Press, ,Stanford, 1995.

while making the translation more tally with the reading habit of the target readers, making the target language more easier and more smooth.'[1]

For example, in the second chapter of his translation of *La Dame aux Camélias*, Lin Shu described Marguerite's appearance this way:

> <u>The original:</u>
>
> Grande et mince jusque'à l'exagération, … Son cachemire, dont la pionte touchait à terre, laissait échapper de chaque côté les larges volants d'une robe de soie, … qu'il fût, … mettez des yeux noirs surmontés de sourcils d'un arc si pur qu'il semblait; voilez ces yeux de grands cils qui, …la teinte rose des joues; … Les cheveux noirs comme du jais, ondés naturellement ou non, s'ouvraient sur le front en deux larges bandeaux, et se perdaient derrière la tête, en laissant voir un bout des oreilles, auxquelles brillaient deux diamants…[2]
>
> <u>Lin Shu's translation:</u>
>
> 马克长身玉立，御长裙， 倦倦然，描画不能肖。虽欲故状其丑，亦莫知为辞。修眉媚眼，脸犹朝霞，发黑如漆覆额，而仰盘于顶上，结为巨髻。耳上饰二钻，光明四射。[3]
>
> <u>Lin Shu's translation in English:</u>
>
> Marguerite was tall, slim and graceful, thin. Her cashmere reached to the ground. She looked a little tired, of which I could not give a depiction. I could find no fault even if I want on purpose. The two black eyes, surmounted by eyebrows of so pure a curve that it seemed as if painted; the rosy hue of the cheeks; the hair black as jet, waving naturally or not, was parted on the forehead in to large folds, and draped back over the head, leaving in sight just the tip of the ears, in which there glittered two diamonds.

Lin Shu's description is succinct and refined, easy and smooth, typically showing a linguistic style of classical Chinese. Dumas's Western-style description was transformed into a typical Chinese style so that the reader reads it as if he was reading a Chinese description.

---

[1] Xu Jun, 2001, p.380

[2] Dumas fils, 1939, p.31.

[3] Lin Shu, 1981, p.3.

In Chapter Fourteen of *Uncle Tom's Cabin*, there is a depiction of the landscape:

<u>The original:</u>

The slanting light of the setting sun quivers on the sea-like expanse of the river; the shivery canes, and the tall, dark cypress, hung with wreaths of dark, funeral moss, glow in the golden ray.[1]

<u>Lin Shu's translation:</u>
日脚斜穿云罅而出，直射江上芦港。芦叶倒影，万绿荡漾于风漪之内，景物奇丽，江光如拭。[2]

<u>Lin Shu's translation in English:</u>
The slanting rays of the setting sun piece through clouds, and are directly radiated on the reeds in the river. The leaves of the reeds are reflected in water, and all the green plants undulate in the winds and ripples. The scenery is peculiarly beautiful, and the bright river looks like a cleaned mirror.

<u>Long and Tong's translation:</u>
夕阳的余辉，照耀着密西西比河那宽阔的河面，一圈圈乌黑的苔藓，挂在两岸随风摇曳的甘蔗和黑藤萝树上，在晚霞的映照下，闪闪发光。[3]

<u>English translation of Long and Tong's translation:</u>
The light of the setting sun shines on the broad surface of Mississippi river, and wreaths of pitch-black moss hang in the canes and cypresses on the both banks swaying with the wind.

Lin Shu's depiction exhibits a Chinese style of literary writing, as much he did not closely keep the wording of the original; yet it can really reproduce the literary effect nearly as much as in the original text. Lin Shu's translation of 'the slanting light of the setting sun' into '日脚斜穿云罅而出'(The slanting rays of

[1] Stowe, 1952, p.159.
[2] Lin Shu, 1981, pp. 66–67.
[3] Long Yuhong and Tong Liqiang, 2000, (Online)
Available:http://www.bookbar.net/wgwx/cp/tmss/014.htm (2002, July, 5).

the setting sun piece through clouds) is both accurate and more picturesque. In the depiction, Lin Shu changed canes and cypress into '芦'(reeds), probably as he thought that the Chinese readers were more familiar with reeds than canes and cypresses. Long and Tong's translation, superficially follows the wording of the original, yet carefully examining it, it is hard to find that they could not reproduce the meaning of 'the slanting light'. The plant '黑藤萝'(cypress) in their translation is unfamiliar to most of the Chinese readers. According to the original, it is the cypress but not the canes that 'hung with' '一圈圈乌黑的苔藓'(wreaths of dark funeral moss), yet in their translation, both the canes and the cypress hung with '一圈圈乌黑的苔藓'. Besides, '两岸'(on the both banks) was fabricated too, and is not found in the original. However, Lin Shu's '万绿荡漾于风漪之内， 景物奇丽，江光如拭'(all the green plants undulate in the winds and ripples. The scenery is peculiarly beautiful, and the bright river looks like a cleaned mirror) embraces the meaning of the original depiction, but differs in detail. Lin Shu's translation was more acceptable to the Chinese readers at that time, as it has no sign of Europeanized Chinese, and its effect is by no means inferior to the effect of the original.

It is a fact that there are many faults in Lin Shu's translations partly due to the speed of his translation, partly due to the faults of his collaborators. What I discuss here mainly refers to his intentional adaptation, and from my analysis, this reveals Lin Shu's conscious orientation to the target culture and readers.

2. Omission

In literary translation, omission is a common practice, and sometimes is a strategy that a translator adopts for such reasons as the needs of the target culture, the acceptance of readers, current social, political or historical conditions, or the verbosity and untranslatability of the original text. Besides, the original text may not be flawless, and the translator may make adaptations or omissions of the original to correct any perceived errors or contradictions in the original. For instance, of the manuscript of Swift's *Gulliver's Travels*, the publisher Richard Sympson thought it necessary to make omissions.

This volume would have been at least twice as large, if I had not made bold to strike out innumerable passages relating to the winds and tides, as well as to the variations and bearings in the several voyages; together with the minute descriptions of the management of the ship in storms, in the style of sailors: likewise the account of the longitudes and latitudes; wherein I have reason to apprehend that Mr. Gulliver may be a little dissatisfied: but I was resolved to fit the work as possible to the general capacity of readers.[1]

Through proofreading and revision of the author's manuscript, Sympson 'struck out innumerable trivial details' in the manuscript', as in his opinion, 'a little too circumstantial' is 'the only fault' of the novel.[2] Like editors, target-oriented and reader-oriented translators are also likely to make some adaptations, among which omission is one of the translator's main strategies. Omission is often found in Lin Shu's translations. As we have seen in the preceding chapters, in some scholars' eyes, Lin Shu's strategy of omission is totally unacceptable, deviating too far from the source text. But if we use target-culture and reader-oriented criticism as a guide, Lin Shu's omissions may be understandable and acceptable, and can be treated as part of the process in cultural oriented translation.[3] Lin Shu's omissions were based on a number of considerations. They include (1) overcoming 'cultural default' (2)simplification for succinctness and (3)treatment of religious materials.

(1) To Overcome 'Cultural Default'

'Cultural default' is described as the absence of relevant cultural background knowledge shared by the author and the intended readers.[4] In terms of literary translation, what is transparent to the SL readers in the form of cultural default is often opaque to the TL reader, the translator included. The cultural defaults in the original, without the proper adaptation of the translator, will undoubtedly perplex the TL readers, thereby damaging the translational effect. In order to resolve the problem of cultural default, Lin Shu often used omission as one of his translation strategies. In the first chapter of *David Copperfield*, the description of 'a caul' is such an example:

---

[1] Sympson, Richard, 'The Publisher to the Reader' in Swift, Jonathan, Gulliver's Travels, Appletree Press Limited, Belfast, 1976, pp.25-26.

[2] Ibid., p.25.

[3] Toury,　p. 166, and Lefevere, 1992,　p. 63.

[4] Wang Dongfeng, 'Cultural Default and Translation Compensation', in Culture and Translation, ed. Guo Jianzhong, Zhongguo duiwai fanyi chuban gongsi, Beijing, 2001, p234.

I was born with a caul; which was advertised for sale, in the newspapers, at the low price of fifteen guineas. Whether sea-going people were short of money about that time, or were short of faith and preferred cork-jackets, I don't know, all I know is, that there was but one solitary bidding, and that was from an attorney connected with the bill-broking business, who offered two pounds in cash, and the balance in sherry, but declined to be guaranteed from drowning on any higher bargain...and ten years afterwards the caul was put up in a raffle.... The caul was won, I recollect, by an old lady... she was never drowned ...[1]

Caul as a cultural default in the passage necessarily makes it difficult for the Chinese readers with little or no knowledge of the English culture, especially the English culture of Dickens's times, to understand the coherent cultural implication. For instance, why did the caul go so far as to be advertised for sale in a newspaper? Why were the expected buyers the sea-going people? Why were the caul and the cork-jacket mentioned in the same breath? Why did the attorney decline 'to be guaranteed from drawing'? Why would the old lady never be drowned after buying the caul? Certainly, whether all these questions are clear or not directly influences the translation of the sentence 'an attorney ... declined to be guaranteed from drowning on any higher bargain'. If the background of 'caul' is not made clear, it will be difficult to translate the semantic relations in this sentence. It is worth noting that Lin Shu omitted the whole passage in his translation as his resolution of the cultural default. The reasons for Lin Shu's omission could be these: Lin Shu and his collaborators did not understand the cultural background of 'caul', or they believed that the implication of 'caul' in the English culture was neither understandable nor acceptable to the Chinese reading public of that time. The omission of this passage was of no importance to the characterization of the protagonist. The most important thing might be to avoid causing the readers' perplexity (including the translator's own perplexity) so as to make his translation more acceptable.

---

[1] Dickens, Charles, The Personal History of David Copperfield, Oxford University Press, New York and Toronto, 1948, pp.1-2.

In Chapter Fourteen of *La Dame aux Camélias*, when describing Armand's jealousy of Marguerite's relation with Comte de G., the author refers to Othello:

The original:

…et au lieu de croire à sa lettre, au lieu d'aller me promener dans toutes les rues de Paris, excepté dans la rue d'Antin; au lieu de passer ma soirée avec mes amis et de me presenter le lendemain à l'heure qu'elle m'indiquait, je faisais l'Othello, je l'espionnais, et je croyais la punir en ne la voyant plus.[1]

Lin Shu's translation:

何不至戏园游，而必径至恩谈。何不存故交，而必私侦妆楼之下。[2]

Lin Shu's translation in English:

Why had I to go the Rue d'Antin instead of going to the theatre for fun? Why had I to spy near her house instead of staying with my friends?

Lin Shu omitted 'je faisais l'Othello'(I was acting Othello). This omission was actually for the sake of 'cultural default'. Shakespeare's tragedy *Othello* has been a widely-known drama in the West since it appeared, where Othello murdered his wife, Desdemona, due to his jealousy, so Othello became a synonym of 'jealousy' and was merged into Western culture afterwards. However, before Lin Shu introduced Shakespeare's works, the Chinese readers were totally ignorant of Shakespeare, let alone Othello and the implication of Othello. To deal with this 'cultural default', Lin Shu had two alternatives: annotation or omission. Lin Shu chose the latter, because he did not want the annotation to distract readers' interest. He translated for common educated readers rather than literary scholars.

Similarly, in *Uncle Tom's Cabin*, there are several passages of discussing ghosts, in which the author quoted the line from Shakespeare's *Hamlet*:

The original:

'The sheeted dead
Did squeak and gibber in the streets of Rome.'[3]

---

[1] Duma fils, 1939, p.141.
[2] Lin Shu, 1931, p.44.
[3] Stowe, 1952. p.471.

In his translation, to overcome the cultural default, Lin Shu not only deleted this quotation, but also omitted the passages of abstractly discussing the question of ghosts. Ghost stories exist in both traditional Chinese literature and traditional Western literature, yet between them there are differences. Traditional Chinese literature shows more interest in a ghost story itself than the question of ghosts, whereas traditional Western literature not only pays attention to the story, but also probes 'pneumatology' and the question of ghosts. Therefore, in his translation of the chapter, Lin Shu retained the story of ghosts while omitted the abstract discussion of ghosts, as inimical to the Chinese readers' interest, for instance,

The original:
...this is a striking fact in pneumatology, which we recommend to the attention of spiritual media generally.[1]

After all, let a man take what pains he may to hush it down, a human soul is an awful ghostly, unquiet possession, for a bad man to have. Who knows the metes and bounds of it? Who knows all its awful perhapses, —those shudderings and tremblings, which it can no more live down than it can outlive its own eternity! What a fool is he who locks his door to keep out spirits, who has in his own bosom a spirit he dares not meet alone,--whose voice, smothered far down, and piled over with mountains of earthliness, is yet like the forewarning trumpet of doom![2]

If Lin Shu had retained these discussions in his translation, it would have presumably confused and distracted his readers.

In fact, Lin Shu's omissions on the basis of cultural default mostly appeared in his treatment of religious matters in *Uncle Tom's Cabin*. This point will be discussed later in this chapter. In short, Lin Shu's intentional omissions were mainly based on his consideration for target readers.

(2) Simplification for Succinctness

One of the main differences between classical Chinese language and the Western literary language lies in the fact that the former stresses the abundance

---

[1] Ibid.
[2] Ibid., p.472.

of the meaning or implication of a single word, the succinctness of sentences, and the rhythm, smoothness and elegance of writing while the latter pays attention to the accuracy of word usage, the detailedness and concreteness of depiction. Classical Chinese is exclusively a written language. Classical Chinese writing lays stress on expression, namely, expressing one's emotion and aspiration, rather than reproducing the real life that traditional Western literature emphasizes. As Zhou Laixiang claims: 'Both the East and the West emphasize the combination of reproduction and expression, but the West lays particular stress on reproduction, imitation and realism, while the East on expression, lyricism and the voice of aspiration.'[1] Classical Chinese writing lays particular stress on the combination of formal beauty but pays little attention to grammatical structure, unlike Western language writing that sets store by morphology, syntax and tense. As a result, in traditional Chinese literature, classical Chinese was most often used in the writing of lyrical prose or essay while vernacular Chinese was more often used in the writing of novel. In this sense, it may be said that classical Chinese is not suitable for a detailed description of real life. Nevertheless, Lin Shu was the first person who succeeded in applying classical Chinese to the translation of western novels.

Since Lin Shu used classical Chinese in the translation of foreign novels, he tried to bridge the gap between classical Chinese and Western literary language. On the one hand, he extended or strengthened the narrative function of classical Chinese to adapt itself to a realistic description; on the other he tried to make his translation more succinct than the original by simplification to fit the habit of the Chinese readers. To fit his translated works 'as much as possible to the general capacity' of the Chinese readers, Lin Shu omitted some descriptions in the original text that he regarded 'too circumstantial'.[2]

In the Chapter one of *David Copperfield*, Dickens gave a detailed description of the temperament of the doctor who comes to deliver a child:

The original:

He was the meekest of his sex, the mildest of little man. He sidled in and out of a room, to take up the less space. He walked as softly as the Ghost in

---

[1] Zhou Laixiang 周来祥, 'Dongfang yu xifang gudian meixue lilun de bijiao' 东方与西方古典美学理论的比较(A Comparison between the Classical Aesthetic Theories in the East and the West), in Cao Shunqing, 1985, p.17.

[2] Sympson, Richard, 'The Publisher to the Reader' in Swift, 1976, p.26.

Hamlet, and more slowly. He carried his head on one side, partly in modest depreciation of himself, partly in modest propitiation of everybody else. It is nothing to say that hadn't a word to throw at a dog. He couldn't have *thrown* a word at a mad dog. He might have offered him one gently, or half a one, or a fragment of one; for he spoke as slowly as he walked; but he wouldn't have been rude to him, and he couldn't have been quick with him, for any earthly consideration.[1]

Lin Shu translated the passage consisting of 126 words into 11 Chinese characters:

Lin Shu's translation:

医生平惋不忤人，　亦不叱狗。[2]

Lin Shu's translation in English:

The doctor was meek and mild, propitiating everyone else, and he couldn't have thrown a word at a dog as well.

In the Chinese version, Lin Shu only translated the doctor who 'was the meekest', 'in the modest propitiation of every body else', and 'couldn't have thrown a word' at a dog', as Lin Shu was dissatisfied with the author's long-worded description. In the original, the author used a number of words to describe the meek disposition of the doctor, but this long-worded description is not applicable to classical Chinese. If the whole description was translated in detail into classical Chinese, the translation would be rather awkward. However, owing to the wide embracing and rich implication of classical Chinese, Lin Shu's description with eleven characters accommodates the plot requirements of the 126 English words, in spite of the lack of the details. It shows the difference between Western literary writing and classical Chinese literary writing and their respective feature.

'Westminster Abbey', the last part of Washington Irving's *The Sketch Book of Geoffrey Crayon, Gent.* recounts the detail of the author's visit to the cloisters and graves of Westminster Abbey. It is considered a fine piece of writing which meditates on the past in the light of the present. Lin Shu only used one page to

---

[1] Dickens, 1948, pp.9-10.
[2] Lin Shu, Kuai rou yusheng shu (David Copperfield), Shangwu yishuguan, 1981, p.7.

vividly represent the scenic and emotional presentation in about nine pages of the original text. His translation preserves both the essence and literary effect of the original text. I compare the first three passages of the original and their translated text. Lin Shu merged the three passages in the original into one passage, abridging 27 English lines in the original into 8 Chinese lines. It is another evidence of simplification. How did Lin Shu simplify the original text in his translation? Striking out some adjectives, adverbs and adverbials, Lin Shu concentrated the original text and especially made it more suitable to classical Chinese expression.

The original:

Passage 1:

On one of those sober and rather melancholy days, in the latter part of Autumn, when the shadows of morning and evening almost mingle together, and throw a gloom over the decline of the year, I passed several hours in rambling about Westminster Abbey. There was something congenial to the season in the mournful magnificence of the old pile; and, as I passed its threshold, seemed like stepping back into the regions of antiquity, and losing myself among the shades of former ages.

Lin Shu's translation:

一日为萧晨，百卉俱靡，秋人寡欢之时，余在惠斯敏司德寺游憩可数句钟。当此荒寒寥瑟之境，益以阴沈欲雨之秋天，可云两美合矣！余一入寺门，已似托身于古昔，与地下鬼雄款语。[1]

Lin Shu's translation in English:

On a sober and melancholy days, when all flowers withered and the people in the autumn were depressed and cheerless, I rambled about Westminster Abbey for several hours. There was something congenial between the desolate and bleak place and the dismal autumn. I passed the threshold as if I had stepped back to the regions of antiquity, and chatting with those great ghosts.

In Lin Shu's version, the original sentence 'on one of those sober and rather melancholy days, in the latter part of Autumn, when the shadows of morning

---

[1] Lin Shu, Fu zhang lu 拊掌录 (The Sketch Book), Shangwu yishuguan, Beijing, 1981, p.54.

and evening almost mingle together, and throw a gloom over the decline of the year' was concentrated into '一日为萧晨，百卉俱靡，秋人寡欢之时'. The Chinese character '萧' accommodates the meaning of the English words 'sober', 'melancholy', 'gloom' and 'decline'. ' 百 卉 俱 靡 '(all flowers withered) corresponded to 'in the latter part of Autumn' and 'the decline of the year', although the word '百卉' cannot be seen in the original, but it is a reasonable derivation. The Chinese sentence with 7 characters '已似托身于古昔', corresponds to the English sentence with 18 words 'seemed like stepping back into the regions of antiquity, and losing myself among the shades of former ages'. It lacks the poetic flow of the English but presents the moody elegance of traditional Chinese poetry.

<u>The original:</u>
Passage 2:
I entered from the inner court of Westminster Abbey, through a long, low, vaulted passage, that had an almost subterranean look, being dimly lighted in one part by circular perforations in the massive walls. Through this dark avenue I had a distant view of the cloisters, with the figure of an old verger, in his black gown, moving along their shadowy vaults, and seeming like a spectre from one of the neighboring tombs. The approach to the abbey through these gloomy monastic remains prepares the mind for its solemn contemplation. The cloisters still retain something of the quiet and seclusion of former days. The gray walls are discolored by damps, and crumbling with age; a coat of hoary moss has gathered over the inscriptions of the mural monuments, and obscured the deaths heads, and other funereal emblems. The sharp touches of the chisel are gone from the rich tracery of the arches; the roses which adorned the key-stones have lost their leafy beauty; every thing bears marks of the gradual dilapidations of time, which yet has something touching and pleasing in its very decay.

<u>Lin Shu's translation:</u>
门内列两道至修广，上盖古瓦，阴森如履地洞；修墉之上，作圆窦通漏光。是中隐隐见一僧，衣黑衣，徐行若魅。余一人既入是中，决所见必皆厉栗之状，即亦无怖。墙壁年久，莓苔斑驳，泥土亦渐

削落；壁上碑版，隐隐亦悉为苔纹所封；而镌刻之物，觚棱渐挫，但模糊留其形式而已。[1]

<u>Lin Shu's translation in English:</u>
In the interior, there was a long, wide vaulted passage covered by the ancient tiles. It was so gloomy as if I were walking in a subterrane. The dim light leaked through the circular perforations in the massive walls. Through it I had a distant view of the figure of a monk, in his black gown. He moved quietly and slowly like a specter. Entering the abbey, I supposed that what I would see must have been some shivery sight, but wasn't horrible. The walls were variegated by moss and crumbling with age. The inscriptions of the mural monuments had been slightly covered with a coat of hoary moss. The sharp touches of the chiseled objects were gradually worn; nothing was more than their rough contour.

The second passage with 14 lines in the original was simplified into 6 lines in the Chinese version. Lin Shu simply used the two characters '门内' (in the interior) to render the sentence 'I entered from the inner court of Westminster School', as 'I passed its threshold' has been mentioned in the preceding passage. '是中隐隐见一僧，衣黑衣，徐行若魅' (Through it I had a distant view of the figure of a monk, in his black gown. He moved quietly and slowly like a specter) corresponds to 'through this dark avenue I had a distant view of the cloisters, with the figure of an old verger, in his black gown, moving along their shadowy vaults, and seeming like a spectre from one of the neighboring tombs', in which particularly '徐行若魅'(moving quietly and slowly like a spectre), omitting 'along their shadow vaults' and ' from one of the neighbouring tombs', is more succinct but retains the original meaning. Lin Shu also omitted the last sentence of the passage 'every thing bears marks of the gradual dilapidations of time, which yet has something touching and pleasing in its very decay', because preceding it, there is a detailed description of the 'marks of the gradual dilapidations of time'. He wrote '墙壁年久，莓苔斑驳，泥土亦渐削落；壁上碑版，隐隐亦悉为苔纹所封；而镌刻之物，觚棱渐挫，但模糊留其形式而已' (The walls were variegated by moss and crumbling with age. The inscriptions of the mural monuments had been slightly covered with a coat of hoary moss. The sharp touches of the chiseled objects were gradually worn,

---

[1] Ibid, p.55.

nothing was more than their rough contour), so it is unnecessary to render the last sentence.

<u>The original:</u>
Passage 3:
The sun was pouring down a yellow autumnal ray into the square of the cloisters; beaming upon a scanty plot of grass in the centre, and lighting up an angle of the vaulted passage with a kind of dusky splendor. From between the arcades, the eye glanced up to a bit of blue sky or a passing cloud; and beheld the sun-gilt pinnacles of the abbey towering into the azure heaven.

<u>Lin Shu's translation:</u>
黄口布地，四围仍阴悄动人，高墙修直，仰望蔚蓝，直类井底 观天；而本寺塔尖直上，半在云表。[1]

<u>Lin Shu's translation in English:</u>
The sunshine was pouring down a yellow ray to the ground. There was a kind of dusky splendor all around. The tall walls were very upright, and the eyes glanced up to the blue sky just like looking up at the sky from the bottom of a well. The pinnacles of the abbey towered into midair.

In the translation, '黄口布地'(The sunshine was pouring down a yellow ray to the ground) corresponds to 'The sun was pouring down a yellow autumnal ray into the square of the cloisters; beaming upon a scanty plot of grass in the center', where the character '地'(the ground) is the simplification of 'the square of the cloisters' and 'upon a scanty plot of grass in the center'. '四围仍阴悄动人' (There was a kind of dusky splendor all around) is equal to 'lighting up an angle of the vaulted passage with a kind of dusky splendor', replacing the concrete description with a general one but retaining the original meaning.

Through a contrastive reading, it is clear that we cannot inflexibly check the translated text against the original text word for word or sentence for sentence. The translation indeed embraces the content and style of the original text. The proof-reader Yan Jicheng commented on the translated text:

It is one of Irving's favourite writings in all his life, which can most fully express the author's temperament, and was much praised by the writers of

---
[1] Ibid.

that time. It is pity that the translator made too many deletions. If making up the deficiency, I am afraid that it would decrease the charm and imposing manner of the original and translated texts. Fortunately, this type of writing about meditating on the past originally has no well-knit and complete composition, it seems that there is no harm in making a little abridgement and deletion. ... As for the spirit and sense of beauty in the original text, this translated text can keep them intact. We cannot but regard it as the top grade in Lin Shu's translations.[1]

Indeed, Lin Shu's simplification of the original was not whimsical. He tried to make his translation as close to the original as possible while fit in with the modes of classical Chinese expression and the habit of the Chinese readers. Lin Shu preferred changing a long sentence in the original into one or more short sentences, which carried the rhythmic flow of Chinese writing.

(3) Treatment of Western Religious Materials

In his translation, Lin Shu often made omissions of religious matters in the original. Now let us first look at how Lin Shu and his collaborator Wei Yi dealt with the religious materials in his translation of *Uncle Tom's Cabin*. In his introductory remarks on the translation of the novel, Lin Shu stated two points regarding the religious materials:

First, Lin Shu wrote that 'the writer is an American, and Americans are devout Christians. Their talk is all bound up with religion. The translators, however, are not Christians but they have to convey the religious message nevertheless. They plea for understanding from those who are enlightened and educated'. Second, he wrote that 'a considerable part of the novel is about matters relating to the Church. Wei Yi has omitted the trivial details for the convenience of the readers. It is hoped that the translators will not be castigated for these omissions.' [2]

But Lin Shu thought that the novel focuses primarily on the black slaves, although it also covers other topics. Evidently, Lin Shu preserved some religious materials in the translation. As Cheung said, 'much of the ST religious material is retained, giving the impression that the translators had indeed tried to be

---

[1] Ibid, p.74.
[2] Lin Shu, 1981, p.2.

'faithful' to the ST'.[1] Generally, Lin Shu's retainment of religious materials can be seen in the following cases: the protagonist undergoes a religious crisis, direct reference to God or the Lord, the character quotes the Bible or sings a hymn to express his feeling, and a character's views are based on a moral and religious standpoint.[2] All these are related to characterization in the novel. In other words, this retention relates to characterization. Lin Shu was a writer, so he was clear of this point. However, more important is Lin Shu's omissions of religious information. In the introductory remarks of his translation, Lin Shu indicated that Wei Yi omitted some trivial details while they translated the novel.[3] However, Lin Shu was a celebrated scholar in the literary world while Wei Yi was an ordinary junior scholar unknown to the public at that time, so Lin Shu's opinion was presumably dominant. It should be said that it was on Lin Shu's advice that Wei Yi made the omissions. In other words, Wei Yi's omission probably reflected Lin Shu's preference and consideration to a certain extent.

According to Cheung's findings, the omission of the religious materials in Lin Shu and Wei Yi's translated text can be categorized as follows: (1) The narrator's interpolations relating to religions; (2) Quotations from the Bible or religious hymns; and (3) Passages describing the influence of the Christian behaviour of the central characters. [4] In this study, examples have been found and cited below to support this argument.

In Chapter Forty of *Uncle Tom Cabin*, the author narrated that Legree cruelly beat Tom, in which the author described Tom in the suffering nearly as the embodiment of Christ Jesus's spirit. Tom said to his master Legree:

> Mas'r, if you was sick, or in trouble, or dying, and I could save ye, I'd give ye my heart's blood; and, if taking every drop of blood in this poor old body would save your precious soul, I'd give 'em freely, as the lord gave his for me. Oh, Mas'r! don't bring this great sin on your soul! It will hurt you

[1] Cheung, Martha P.Y., 'The Discourse of Occidentalism? Wei Yi and Lin Shu's Treatment of Religious Materal in Their Translation of Uncle Tom's Cabin, in Pollard, 1998, p.129.
[2] Ibid., pp.129-130.
[3] Lin Shu, 1981, p.2.
[4] Ibid., pp.131-132.

more than 't will me! Do the worst you can, my troubles' will be over soon; but if you don't repent, yours won't never end!¹

Then the author interpolated a passage to eulogize the spirit of Christ Jesus:

> Of, old, there was One whose suffering changed an instrument of torture, degradation, and shame, into a symbol of glory, honor, and immortal life; and, where his spirit is, neither degrading stripes, nor blood, nor insults, can make the Christian's last struggle less than glorious.²

At last, to coordinate closely with the above descriptions, the author had Tom at the moment of his life to praise the spirit of Christ Jesus:

> He poured forth a few energetic sentences of that wondrous One, — his life, his death, his everlasting presence, and power to save.³

Obviously, in this chapter the author was motivated to advocate the spirit of Christ Jesus through Tom's sufferings and death. But Lin Shu omitted nearly all of them. Only in the first passage quoted above, Lin Shu translated 'my troubles' will be over soon; …yours won't never end' (吾之苦恼， 只此须臾， 尔之凶祸，将无穷期也). The author's interpolations relating to the religion were thoroughly omitted by the translators. Descriptions that touch lightly on the religion were frequently omitted or abridged. In Chapter Twenty-Two, the author gave a concrete depiction of Tom's religious vision of Eva's religious feeling:

> He loved her as something frail and earthly, yet almost worshipped her as something heavenly and divine. He gazed on her as the Italian sailor gazes on his image of the child Jesus, — with a mixture of reverence and tenderness; and to humor her graceful fancies, and meet those thousand simple wants which invest childhood like a many-colored rainbow, was Tom's chief delight.

The description was totally omitted, although it does not involve any religious activity itself. However, the omission may be reasonable, because for the unchristian Chinese readers, it was quite difficult to understand Tom's religious

---

¹ Stowe, 1952, p.461.
² Ibid.
³ Ibid., p.463.

188

vision and the feeling of the little girl Eva. This is an issue of cultural default as well.

From these omissions, Lin Shu's motive of translating the novel is revealed as he stated in the foreword and postscript of his translation. As a reader (or an audience), Lin Shu was very clear about what the target culture and readers need while as a translator, he was also clear about how to meet the needs. It seemed to be his intention to make his work of translation serve as a warning to his compatriots, making them conscious of the national calamity and crisis, alerting them the need to strengthen the country, and rousing their national spirit. As Cheung points out, if Mrs Stowe was motivated by humanitarian and religious reasons to write, then Li Shu and Wei Yi were clearly motivated by political and patriotic reasons to translate, particularly by their anxiety about the fate that awaited the Chinese if they became a people without a nation.[1]

Another instance of omission is seen in Chapter Three of *La Dame aux Caméllias*, after comparing Marguerite's death with Manon's death, the author dwelt at great length on his religious views: indulgence and pardon. For instance,

The original:

Je suis tout simplement convaincu d'un principe qui eŝt que: Pour la femme á qui l'éducation n'a pas enseigné le bien, Dieu ouvre Presque toujours deux sentiers qui l'y ramènent; ces sentiers sont la douleur et l'amour. Ils sont difficiles; celles qui s'y engagent s'y engagent s'y ensanglantent les pieds, s'y déchirent les mains, mais elles laissent en même temps aux ronces dela route les parures du vice et arrivent au but avec cette nudité dpmt pm me rpigot [ass devant le Seigneur.

...Il ne s'agit pas de metre tout bonnement à l'entrée de la vie deux poteaux, portant l'un cette inscription: *Route du bien*, l'autre cet avertissement: *Routedu mal*, et de dire à ceux qui se présentent: Choisissez; il faut, comme le Chriŝt, montrer des chemins qui ramènent de la seconde route àla première ceux qui s'étaient laissé temter par les abords; et il ne faut pas surtout que le commencement de ces chemins soit trop douloureux, ni paraisse trop impenetrable.

Le chriŝtianisme eŝt là avec sa merveilleuse parabole de l'enfant

[1] Ibid., pp.137-138.

prodigue pour nous conseiller l'indulgence et le pardon. Jésus était plein d'aour pour ces âmes blesses par les passions des hommes, et don't il aimait à panser les plaies en tyrant le baume qui devait les guérir des plaies elles-mêmes. Ainsi, il disait à Madeleine: "Il te sera beaucoup remis parce que tu as beaucoup aimé", sublime pardon qui devait éveiller une foi sublime. Pourquoi nous ferions-nous plus rigides que le Chriŝt? Pourquoi, nous en tenant obŝinément aux opinions de ce monde qui se fait dur pour qu'on le croie fort, rejetterions-nous avec lui des âmes saignantes souvent de blessures par où, comme le mauvais sang d'un malade, s'épanche le mal de leur passé, et n'attendant qu'unemain amie qui les panse et leur rende la convalescence du Cœur?[1]

English translation of the original:

I am quite simply convinced of a certain principle, which is: for the woman whose education has not taught her what is right. God almost always opens two ways which lead thither, the ways of sorrow and of love. They are hard; those who walk in them walk with bleeding feet and torn hands, but they also leave the trappings of vice upon the thorns of the wayside, and reach the journey's end in a nakedness which is not shameful in the sight of the Lord.

... It is not a question of setting at the outset of life two sign-posts, one bearing the inscription 'the Right Way', the other the inscription 'The Wrong Way', and of saying to those who come there, 'choose'. One must needs, like Christ, point out the ways which lead from the second road to the first, to those who have been easily led astray; and it is needful that the beginning of these ways should not be too painful nor appear too impenetrable.

Here is Christianity with its marvellous parable of the Prodigal Son to teach us indulgence and pardon. Jesus was full of love for souls wounded by the passions of men; he loved to bind up their wounds and to find in those very wounds the balm which should heal them. Thus he said to the Magdalen: 'Much shall be forgiven thee because thou hast loved much', a sublimity of pardon which can only have called forth a sublime faith.

---

[1] Dumas fils, 1939, pp. 40-41.

Why do we make ourselves stricter than Christ? Why, holding obstinately to the opinion of the world, which hardens itself in order that it may be thought strong, do we reject, as it rejects, souls bleeding at wounds by which, like a sick man's bad blood, the evil of their past may be healed, if only a friendly hand is stretched out to lave them and set them in the convalescence of the heart?

Here the author seemed to be delivering a religious sermon to his readers. For the Western readers, it might be normal. However, for most of the Chinese readers of the late Qing and the early Republic, it was inexplicable. For example, if these passages were translated, the Chinese readers might raise a series of questions: what is the meaning of 'the ways of sorrow and of love' God opens? Why are the ways hard? What dose 'those who walk in them' 'reach the journey's end in a nakedness' mean? Why isn't this situation shameful in the sight of the Lord? What is the Christian parable of the Prodigal Son about? Who is the Magdalen? The readers who lacked the cultural context of Christianity, would lead to frustration when reading these passages regarding Christianity.

It is because of his consideration for the Chinese readers' interest that Lin Shu omitted the narratives regarding religion in the chapter.

3. Addition

As mentioned in the preceding chapters, in many cases, it is neither possible nor necessary to translate word for word. In the process of translation, a translator makes additions in accordance with either the correspondence principle or the needs of the target culture and the readers' reception. Lin Shu orientated his translation towards the Chinese culture and readers, so addition is unavoidable. Toury argues for the necessity of addition as a new feature in translation:

It may also entail the reshuffling of certain features, not to mention the addition of new ones in an attempt to enhance the acceptability of the translations as a target literary text, or even as a target literary text of a particular type. ... the added features may occupy central positions within the translation (when looked up as a text in its own right), even serving as markers of its own literariness despite their having no basis in the original.[1]

Addition can be found in many places in Lin Shu's translations. Lin Shu's omissions included individual words, sentences or even passages, but in most cases, Lin Shu's additions simply involved words and sentences. As a supplement, they aimed at intelligibility and readability. Lin Shu's additions were heavily based on the considerations of (1) to make up 'a perceived lack' in the original text, (2) to embellish the original text and (3) to bridge the gap between the source and target cultures, to be discussed next.

(1) To Make Up 'a Perceived Void' in the Original Text

Lin Shu was a literary writer, and his literary impulse was often activated in the process of his translation, supplementing the original so as to make the translated text more appealing to his readers. In 'Lin Shu's Translations', Qian Zhongshu said, 'When Lin Shu found a perceived void in the original text, he always liked to add here and polish there so as to make the wording more concrete, the scene more vivid, the whole description more substantial.'[2] Examples of this kind are very common in his translations.

For instance, in the Chapter Three, Part Two of *Gulliver's Travels*, the king 'could not forbear taking me up in his right hand, and stroking me gently with the other'. In his translation, Lin Shu added '如抚小弥猴' (like stroking a macaque),[3] which is not completely 'loyal' to the original text, but more vivid and concrete, and foreshadows the section describing that Gulliver is held by the monkey in Chapter Five. In Chapter Five, Part Two of *Gulliver's Travels*, the queen wanted Gulliver to try out his sea-voyage skill, but Gulliver replied that he could not find a proper boat in the country. There is only 'the queen said' in the original text, but Lin Shu translated it into '皇后闻言，笑曰' (After hearing what I said, the queen said with a laugh).[4] The addition enlivens the Queen's character. The addition like this, frequently seen in his translations, mostly

---

[1] Toury, 1995, p.171.
[2] Qian Zhongshu, 1981, p.26.
[3] Lin Shu, Haiwai xuan qu lu 海外轩渠录 (Gulliver's Travel), Vol.1, Shangwu yishuguan, Shanghai, 1915, p..23.
[4] Lin Shu, Haiwai xuan qu lu (Gulliver's Travels), Vol.2, p.34.

appeared in the description of the interaction between characters, making the dialogue in the original more lively in Chinese because of adding the words like '欢笑'(with a laugh) , '愤怒'(angrily), '疑惑'(doubtedly).[1]

There is another example in Chapter Twenty-Four of *David Copperfield*. The drunken David happened to meet Agnes in the theatre, and spoke to her so thickly that Agnes felt ashamed of David's behavior. The original is: 'saw her shrink into her corner, and put her gloved hand to her forehead'.[2] Lin Shu rendered it into '安尼司则瑟缩座隅，以手扶头，状似避余'[3](Agnes shrank into her corner, and put her hand to her forehead as if she was dodging me), adding '状似避余'(as if she was dodging me). Obviously, it is an additional remark. Then the author described that the drunken David left the theatre for home: 'I[David] stepped at once out of the box-door into my bedroom.'[4] Two different Chinese translators respectively translated it into '我从包厢门的那儿一步就跨进了我卧室'[5](I stepped in a step out of the box-door into my bedroom) and '我一踱出厢座的门，就进入了我的卧室'(As soon as I stepped out of the box-door, I entered my bedroom',[6]- while Lin Shu translated it into '不审何故，一举踵即及余寓'[7](I could not see why, as soon as I stepped out, I arrived at my bedroom).The formers evidently adopted literal translation, which may perplex the Chinese readers: how could David step at once of the box-door into his bedroom? Yet in Lin Shu's translation, he added '不审何故'(I could not see why). This addition not only was of some help to the readers' understanding, but also implied David's drunkenness.

Similarly, in the beginning of Chapter Twenty-Two, *Ivanhoe*, the Jew Issac in the castle heard someone's steps on the dungeon stairs, and then the wicket opened. The author described:

[1] Refer to 'Translation as Intervention and Subversion: reevaluating Lin Shu's literary Translation via Guiliver's Travels',
http://english.nccu.edu.tw/conference/shan.htm, 2001.

[2] Dickens, 1948, p.363.

[3] Lin Shu, Kuai rou yusheng shu (David Copperfield), 1981, p.205.

[4] Dickens, 1948, p.363.

[5] Zhang Guruo 张谷若, Dawei kebofei 大卫. 科波菲(David Cooperfield by C. Dickens), Shanghai yiwen chubanshe, Shanghai, 1980, p.538.

[6] Dong Qiusi 董秋斯, Dawei kebofeier 大卫.科波菲尔(David Cooperfield by C. Dickens), Renmin wenxue chubanshe, Beijing, 1958, p.422.

[7] Lin Shu, Kuai rou yusheng shu (David Copperfield), 1981, p.206.

<u>The original:</u>

The bolts screamed as they were with drawn – the hinges creaked as the wicket opened.[1]

<u>Lin Shu's translation:</u>

时门之上下拴均锈启之，格格有声。[2]

Lin Shu's translation in English

Then both the top and bottom bolts became rusty. They creaked as the wicket opened.

In the translation, Lin Shu added '均锈'(both... became rusty) to explain why '格格有声'('screamed' and 'creaked') could happen. For today's Chinese readers, this addition is unnecessary, but it might be necessary for the ordinary Chinese readers who knew little about mechanism in Western castles and dungeons at that time.

In Lin Shu's translations, such additions are too numerous to cite one by one. The above examples serve to demonstrate his method.

(2) To Embellish the Original Text

Embellishing the original text reflects the creative impulse of Lin Shu as a literary writer. Critics have admitted that Lin Shu was able to convey Dickens' humor in his translations. In fact, sometimes, Lin Shu added his own humorous color to intensify Dickens's humor. Qian Zhongshu remarked,

If a person with the ability or confidence in literary writing is engaged in literary translation, it will be hard for him to control his impulse of literary creation as Lin Shu did.[3]

Qian Zhongshu cited an example to support his argument. In Chapter Thirty-Three of *Nicholoas Nickeby*, there is a descriptive passage when Squeers said to Ralph:

<u>The original:</u>

---

[1] Scott, Walter, 1931, p.206.
[2] Lin Shu, 1981, p.130.
[3] Ibid., p. 28.

.... My son, Sir, little Wackford. ... Ain't he fit to bust out of his clothes, and start the seams, and make the very buttons fly off with his fatness. Here's flesh!" cried Squares, turning the boy about, and indenting the plumpest parts of his figure with divers pokes and punches, to the great discomposure of his son and heir. "Here's firmness, here's solidness! Shy you can hardly get up enough of him between your finger and thumb to pinch him anywhere.

... on his father's closing his finger and thumb illustration of his remark, he uttered a sharp cry, and rubbed the place in the most natural manner possible.

'Well,' remarked Squeers, a little disconcerted, 'I had him there; but that's because we breakfasted early this morning, and he hasn't had his lunch yet. Why you couldn't shut a bit of him in a door, when he's had his dinner. Look at them tears, Sir,' said Squeers, with a triumphant air, as Master Wackford wiped his eyes with the cuff of his jacket, 'there's oiliness!' [1]

Lin Shu's translation:
'此为吾子小瓦克福 ...... 君但观其肥硕，至于芙能容衣。 其肥乃口
共，至于衣缝裂儿铜纽断。' 乃按其子之首，处处以指戟其身， 口：
'此肉也。' 又戟之曰：'此亦 肉， 肉韧而坚。今吾试引其皮，乃附
肉不能起。' 方司圭尔引皮时，而小瓦克福已大哭，摩其肌曰：'翁乃
苦我！' 司圭尔先生曰：'彼尚未饱。若饱食者，则力聚而气张，虽
有瓦屋，乃不能壁其身。...... 君试观其泪中乃有牛羊之脂， 由食
足也。'

Lin Shu's translation in English:
'This is my son, little Wackford.... You can see that he is so fat that no clothes fit him. He is getting fatter and fatter, with the result that he has busted out his clothes and made the brass buttons fly off.' Then he pushed his son's head down, ceaselessly poking his son's body, and said: 'Here is flesh.' Then he poked again: 'Here is flesh too. The flesh is firm and solid. Now I am trying to pull the skin up, but I cannot as the skin sticks in the flesh.' When Mr. Squeers pulled the skin, little Wackford cried loudly, rubbing the place and said: 'You have hurt me!' Mr Squeers said: 'You

---

[1] Dickens, Charles, The Life and Adventures of Nicholas Nickleby, University of Pennsylvania Press, Philadelphia, 1982, pp. 327-328.

haven't had enough yet. If you eat your fill, the energy gathering inside would make his body swell. Even if there is a roofed house, it cannot accommodate his body. … You can see the grease of oxen and sheep in his tears, it is because he eats too much.'

Lin Shu vivified the original description by translation. In his translated passage, Lin Shu added '乃按其子之首'(push his son's head down), '力聚而气张'(the energy gathering inside would make his body swell), '牛羊之脂，由食足也'(… the grease of oxen and sheep, it is because he eats too much) and so on. This intensified the humorous effect of the original description. It is worth noting that Dickens only wrote that little Wackford 'uttered a sharp cry, and rubbed the place in the most natural manner possible'; whereas in the translated passage Lin Shu groundlessly inserted a word of complaint '翁乃苦我'(you have hurt me). However, if only Squeers was soliloquizing, the Chinese reader would felt that the character little Wackford seemed to be too stiff and coldly treated.

In Chapter Seven of *La Dame aux Camélias*, when Armand, who had fallen in love with Marguerite, was told that Marguerite was very ill and was dying, the author wrote about Armand's first reaction: 'Le coeur est étrange; je fus presque content de cette maladie'[1](The heart is a strange thing; I was almost glad at hearing it). In the translation, Lin   Shu added, '初闻心怔忡不能自己,继又喜病深客寡'[2](When I heard it first, I could not help worrying about her, and then I became glad because very few men would visit her when she was very ill). Apart from '喜'(glad) based on the original, the extra words were added by Lin Shu. In comparison with the original, the addition seems necessary, as it reveals Armand's contradictory and mixed feeling when hearing that Marguerite was very ill. Otherwise, the Chinese reader might be bewildered: how could he feel glad since he heard that Marguerite was very ill and was dying? And he/her might feel that Armand's 'glad' reaction seems unreasonable. Thus the addition clarifies Armand's reaction and feeling. As well, in Chapter Thirteen, Armand arranged a tryst with Marguerite that night, but he received a note from her, in which Marguerite told him that she would not meet with him until next noon owing to her sickness. After reading the note, his first thought was that Marguerite was deceiving him, so Armand was deep in agony. The original is:

---

[1] Dumas fils, 1939, p.76.
[2] Lin Shu, 1931, p.17.

'Une sueur glacée passa sur mon front, car j'aimais déjà trop cette femme pour que ce soupcon ne me bouleversât point'[1](A cold sweat broke out on my forehead, for I already loved this woman too much not to be overwhelmed by the suspicion). Lin Shu's translation is: '额上汗出如蒸，不知马克此人，何以镂吾肝而镌吾肺',[2] in which '镂吾肝而镌吾肺'(cut my liver and lungs with a burin) was used to describe Armand's agony from jealousy. Compared with the original, the addition intensified Armand's agony according to Chinese equivalents. In the context, the intensification creates a stronger emotional effect in Chinese.

Another example of Lin Shu's literary impulse is in Chapter Seven of *Uncle Tom's Cabin*, where the author described how Eliza felt when she fled from home. She was forced to leave 'the only home she had ever known', and parting with the friends 'whom she loved', parting 'from the place where she had grown up'.[3] In the translation, Lin Shu added '意此次之逃，能否自脱，又能否竟至坎拿大？' (Can Eliza make her escape successfully this time? Can she arrive in Canada smoothly?) and '长路漫漫，茫无归宿，惨戚盖万状矣'(It would be a long journey, on which she did not know where to stay. The situation was extremely miserable).[4] The addition here aims to emphasize the possible dangerous and difficult situation that confronted Eliza upon her escape so as to touch off readers' concern with the fate of Eliza and her son. In fact, the fate of Eliza is one of the important threads of the story. Therefore, Lin Shu's addition is not contrary to the plot of the novel. However, Lin Shu did not halt but went further. To prevent the readers from misreading Eliza's leaving without saying good-bye to her mistress, Lin Shu added again, '主母恩意素厚，今乃不告而去，自绝于素所姅幪之人，自觉此心过于凉薄'[5](The mistress's kindness to me is very deep. Now I went away without saying good-bye to her and alienated myself from the person who had done me favours, so I feel that I am too ungrateful). This emphasizes the positive image of Eliza. These examples show that Lin Shu was always ready to make some additions where he thought it necessary in order to embellish the original and help the readers achieve a better understanding and appreciation of the original.

---

1 Dumas fils, 1939, p.133.
2 Lin Shu, 1939, p.41.
3 Stowe, 1952, p.56.
4 Lin Shu, Hei nu yu tian lu (Uncle Tom's Cabin), 1981, p.22.
5 Ibid.

(3) To Bridge the Cultural Gap

In Lin Shu's times, a period of transition from tradition to modernity in China, the Chinese readers hoped to learn about Western culture. But the existing Chinese culture sometimes hindered this learning. Therefore, cultural shock and clash had to be minimized as much as possible. Lin Shu used addition as a way to bridge the gap between the two very different cultures.

For instance, in Chapter Nine of the *La Dame aux Camélias*, there is a description of Marguerite's boudoir, where Gaston introduced Armand, Marguerite held out her hand, and Armand kissed it.

The original:
El elle me tendit sa main que je baisai.[1]

English translation of the original:
she held out her hand, which I kissed

Lin Shu's translation:
举皓腕，余即耳亲之 （此西俗男女相见之礼也）[2]。

Lin Shu's translation in English:
When she held out her hand, I kissed it (this is Western etiquette observed and practiced by a gentleman and a lady when both meet)

It involves Western etiquette: a Western lady stretches her hand for a gentleman to kiss when they first meet, particularly in a social occasion. For the Chinese readers of Lin Shu's time who were not familiar with the Western etiquette, this practice was most probably rather odd. It is also a cultural default. To reduce the cultural shock the Chinese readers was likely to experience, Lin Shu added a brief explanatory note on the practice: '此西俗男女相见之礼也'(this is Western etiquette observed and practised by a gentleman and a lady when both meet).

In addition, let us look at how Lin Shu handled Western musical notation. In the chapter, Marguerite invited Gaston to play Weber's *à la Valse* with the piano. She followed every note on the music, accompanying it in a low voice. She sang out: 'Ré, mi, ré, do, ré, fa, mi, ré.' On translating the musical notes, Lin

---

[1] Dumas fils, 1939, p. 85.
[2] Lin Shu, 1931, p.21.

Shu had to transliterate the sounds as: '海咪海朵海发咪海'. Of course, it was almost impossible for the Chinese readers to understand them without a footnote, so Lin Shu added a short note: '即华音工尺上四合声也' [1] (namely, the Chinese music that is composed of the four notes: gong, chi, shang, si). Hence, the Chinese readers not only learned about the distinctions between Western and Chinese musical notation, but might also wonder at the similarity between them. Again, when translating the word 'champagne', Lin Shu transliterated it as '香槟'(xiangbin). Certainly, to most of the Chinese readers at that time, champagne was something they had never seen before; thereupon, Lin Shu added the note: '酒名'(the name of an alcohol). Most probably, Xiangbin(香槟), the transliterated Chinese name of champagne, was first invented by Lin Shu and is still used today.

In Chapter Fifteen of *Uncle Tom's Cabin*, St. Clare married a wealthy girl. The author narrated, 'the married couple were enjoying their honeymoon'.[2] Lin Shu translated it into 彼夫妇在蜜月期内，两情忻合无间'(During the honeymoon, the married couple were on very intimate terms with each other).[3] 'Honeymoon' in the original was a new concept for the Chinese reader. Lin Shu was believed to be the first person who translated 'honeymoon' literally into '蜜月'. Since this word was introduced into China, it has become a common everyday word, especially now in China. However, for the Chinese readers of Lin Shu's time, '蜜月'(honeymoon) was a new thing and required an explanation. Lin Shu defined it in brackets: '蜜月者，西人娶妇时，即挟其妇游历，经月而归'(honeymoon means that when a western man marries a woman, he will travel with her, and return in a month). Through his translation and additional explanations, the Chinese readers began to be familiar with this practice and started to imitate this Western custom.

Again, in Chapter Sixteen of *Uncle Tom's Cabin*, there is a conversation in which St. Clare showed a contemptuous attitude toward his wife Maire who made a fuss about an imagined illness and was full of prejudice against black slaves:

---

[1] These are the musical notation Chinese musicians used to use, which consist of seven sounds: he (合), si (四), yi (·), shang (上), chi (尺), gong (工), fan (凡). They accord with C, D, E, F, G, A, B or Do, Re, Mi, Fa, So, La, Si in Western musical notation.

[2] Stowe, 1952, p.171.

[3] Lin Shu, Hei nu yu tian lu (Uncle Tom's Cabin), 1981, p.71.

<u>The original:</u>

St. Clare whistled a tune.

'St. Clare, I wish you would n't whistle,' said Marie; 'it makes my head worse.'

'I won't,' said St. Clare. 'Is there anything else you wouldn't wish me to do?'

'I wish you would have some kind of sympathy for my trials; you never feeling for me.'

'My dear accusing angel!' said St. Clare.

'It's provoking to be talked to in that way.'

'Then how will you be talked to? I'll talk to order, — any way you'll mention, — only to give satisfaction.'[1]

<u>Lin Shu's translation:</u>

圣格来愀然翕其唇，噫气作微啸。

媚利曰：'圣格来，何啸为！吾头涔涔，不耐此声也。'

圣格来曰：'诺。凡吾所为，何者可以当君意？'

媚利曰：'吾但愿君能悉吾胸臆中莫言之隐恫可尔。'

圣格来曰：'难哉，吾恩及儿也。'(恩及儿者，天女也，为女中最妍丽无匹之人。圣格来盖隐讽媚利为不可瞻仰之天人，实深恶之。)

媚利曰：'此称谓足动吾气。'

圣格来曰：'此称既不愿受，何者方当君意？今尽君言之，无不如命。'[2]

<u>Lin Shu's translation in English:</u>

St. Clare rounded his lips, whistling a tune.

Maire said: 'St. Clare, why are you whistling? I am having a headache, and cannot bear this sound.'

St. Clare said: 'I won't. Why can whatever I do always dissatisfy you?'

Maire said: 'I wish you would thoroughly understand the trials in my heart.'

St. Clare said: 'It is too difficult, my dear angel!'[Angel, a female celestial, is the most beautiful among the female celestials. Here St. Clare

---

[1] Stowe, 1952, p.197.
[2] Lin Shu, Hei nu yu tian lu (Uncle Tom's Cabin), 1981, p.83.

used it to satirize Marie as an unreachable woman in Heaven, which actually expressed his detestation of her]

Maire said: 'It is provoking to be talked to in that way really.'

St. Clare: 'Now that you don't like it, what can satisfy you? Please completely speak out, I'll talk to order.'

From the dialogue, readers can perceive the disharmony between St. Clare and Marie, especially St. Clare's dislike of Marie. In the dialogue, he called his wife 'my dear accusing angel', which implied an ironical tone. Nevertheless, how did the Chinese readers at that time understand it? Most of them never heard of 'angel', so a series of questions might arise: What is the 'angel'? Why does St.Clare call his wife 'angel' now that he disliked his wife so much? Such possible questions from readers made Lin Shu feel it necessary to make additions. Therefore, he added in brackets'恩及儿者，天女也，为女中最妍丽无匹之人。圣格来盖隐讽姆利为不可瞻仰之天人，实深恶之'(Angel, a female celestial, is the most beautiful among the female celestials. Here St. Clare used it to satirize Marie as an unreachable woman in Heaven, which actually expressed his detestation of her). Evidently, Lin Shu's addition was to bridge the gap between the Western and Chinese cultures and terminology, and clear away obstacles in the receptive process of the target readers.

In brief, some of Lin Shu's adaptations were motivated by his knowledge of his own culture and readership. Omissions and additions clarify the source text in terms of the target culture. The success of Lin Shu's translations demonstrates his masterly mediation between texts and between cultures.

4. Alteration

In Toury's view, the introduction of a source text 'into a target culture always entails some change.'[1] Alteration means that a translator alters the original text for some specific purposes and artistic effects. Lin Shu was no exception. In the process of his translation, Lin Shu often made alterations of the source text according to the readers' prospective responses, the needs of the target culture, and even his literary judgments. His alterations of the ST can be

---

[1] Toury, 1995, p.27.

categorized under four overlapping headings: (1) to heighten the readers' impression, (2) to re-write the original text, and (3) intervention into translation.

(1) To Heighten the Readers' Impression

Often, Lin Shu altered a description in the original text when it was not enough to impress Chinese readers with an artistic effect. At the end of Part Two of *Gulliver's Travel*, Gulliver was rescued from the sea by a seaman. Gulliver asked whether the captain or the crew had seen any prodigious birds:

<u>The original:</u>
He answered, that discoursing this matter with the sailors while I was asleep, one of them said he had observed three eagles flying towards the north; but remarked nothing of their being larger than the usual size; which I suppose must be imputed to the great height they were at: And he could not guess the reason of my question.[1]

Lin Shu's alteration of the above passage is as follows:

船主曰：此事方君寝时，吾已与舵工论及矣。舵工曰：吾见之鹰，其大无比，鼓翅北去，较诸常鹰殊巨。吾以舵工之言为诞。彼鹰横绝九霄，自下测之，安知其巨。余知此理，船长未能悟也。[2]

<u>Lin Shu's translation in English:</u>
The captain answered: "I have discoursed this matter with the sailors while you were asleep. One of the sailors said: 'the eagle I had observed was gigantic, fluttering towards the north, being exceptionally larger than the usual size.' I suppose that what the sailor said is absurd. The eagle was traversing the great height flying when they measured it underneath. How could they know that the eagle was so gigantic?

In the original, the sailor said that the eagles he had observed were 'remarked nothing of their being larger than the usual size', but Lin Shu changed it into 'the eagle I had observed was gigantic, fluttering towards the north, being exceptionally larger than the usual size'. Here Lin Shu altered the text for visual effect, which could impress the readers more deeply. Moreover, the alteration

---

[1] Swift, Jonathan, Gulliver's Travels, Appletree Press Ltd, Belfast, 1976, pp.131-132.
[2] Lin Shu, Haiwai xuan qu lu (Gulliver's Travels), 1915, p.59.

corroborates Gulliver's adventures and visions, and causes the Chinese readers' cultural association with Zhuangzi's description of 'the great roc'(大鹏) in his 'Xiaoyao you'(A happy Excursion):

The original:

北冥有鱼，其名为鲲。鲲之大，不知其几千里也。化而为鸟，其名为鹏。鹏之背，不知其几千里也。怒而飞，其翼若垂天之云。是鸟也，海运则将徙于南冥。南冥者，天池也。[1]

English translation of the original:

In the Northern Ocean there is a fish, called Kun. Kun is too gigantic to know how many thousand *li* its size is. Kun changes into a roc, called Peng. People do not know how many thousand *li* its back is in breadth. When exerting itself to fly, its wings stretch like clouds overspreading the sky. When the sea moves, the roc prepares to remove to the Southern Ocean. The Southern Ocean is the Lake of Heaven.

After reading Lin Shu's alteration, the Chinese readers were likely to associate it with the great roc in Zhuangzi's 'A Happy Excursion', thus achieving a deeper impression of the gigantic eagle in the translation. It is true that Lin Shu, who mastered traditional Chinese culture, took delight in inserting classical Chinese hints and allusions between the lines in his translations so as to arouse the educated Chinese readers' cultural association and enhance the acceptability of his translation.

In Chapter Three of *David Copperfield*, there is a talk between David and Emily in the beach:

The original:

'No,' replied Emily, shaking her head, 'I'm afraid of the sea.'
'Afraid!' I said, with a becoming air of boldness, and looking very big at the mighty ocean. 'I an't!'[2]

Lin Shu's translation:

女摇首曰：'否，吾其畏水。'
余插手于腰间，言曰：'汝乃畏海，吾固弗畏。'[1]

---

[1] He Peixiong 何振雄 and Chen Bingliang 陈炳良, Selections from Chinese Literature, Vol. 1, Hong Hong University Press, 1983, p.79.
[2] Dickens, 1948, p.34.

Lin Shu's translation in English:
The girl shook her head and said: "I am too afraid of the sea."
With arms akimbo, I said: "You are afraid of the sea, but I am not."

In the translation, Lin Shu altered 'with a becoming air of boldness' into '插手于腰间'(with arms akimbo). Emily witnessed or heard that his father and others had been devoured by the sea, so she said: 'I am afraid of the sea', whereas David lacked a deep understanding of the danger of the sea, so he wanted to flaunt his boldness before Emily. To highlight his flaunty 'air of boldness', Lin Shu replaced 'with a becoming air of boldness' with '插手于腰间', a more physical description, thus deeply impressing the readers.

In 'Rip Van Winkle' of *The Sketch Book*, the author depicted how Rip Van Winkle, a simple good-natured fellow, played with the children in the village:

The original:
The children of the village, too, would shout with joy whenever he approached. He assisted at their sports, made their playthings, taught them to fly kites and shoot marbles, and told them long stories of ghosts, witches, and Indians. Whenever he went dodging about the village, he was surrounded by a troop of them, hanging on his skirts, clambering on his back, and playing a thousand tricks on him with impunity; and not a dog would bark at him throughout the neighbourhood.[2]

Lin Shu's translation:
李伯之处儿中，亦水乳，百窘不见忤状，且助之戏，告以古红人之事迹，小儿听者津津然。于是李伯每出，则群儿引襟而行，履迹相续，或直趣其背，拈其须，虽狎弗怒。至于狞狗见之，亦嗫而弗吠。
[3]

Lin Shu's translation in English:
Rip was among the children like milk mingling with water. Although he was very often embarrassed, he was never annoyed; instead, he joined their

[1] Lin Shu, Kuai rou yusheng shu, 1981, p.19.
[2] Irving, 1905, p.12.
[3] Lin Shu, Fu zhang lu 拊掌录(The Sketch Book), Shangwu yishuguan, Beijing, 1981, p.6.

games and told them the story about Red Indians, and the children listened to it with keen interest. Consequently, whenever Rip walked out, a troop of children followed him, hanging on his skirts and treading on his heels, or clambering on his back playing tricks, and fingering his beard.

It may be seen from the comparison that Lin Shu's depiction of Rip in the translation is as lively as in the original, but he also made some alterations. For instance, he altered 'the children of the village, too, would shout with joy whenever he approached' into '李伯之处儿中，亦水乳，百狎不见怍状'(Rip was among the children like milk mingling with water. Although he was very often embarrassed, he was never annoyed). Lin Shu used '水乳' in describing Rib's harmonious relationship with the children to emphasis Rib's good nature. '津津然'(with keen interest) was added to describe the children's strong interest in the stories Rib told. 'Hanging on his skirts' was rendered into '引襟而行，履迹相续'(hanging on his skirts and treading on his heels) and 'clambering on his back' into '肖趣其背，拈其须'(clambering on his back playing, and fingering his beard). The additions '履迹相续'(treading on his heels) and '拈其须'(fingering his beard) made the scene of the mutual amusement between Rib and the children more picturesque.

(2) To Re-write the Original Text

Lin Shu often re-wrote the original texts so that his own ideas permeated the lines of his translated texts. As a result, through partly altering or mostly extending the meaning of the original texts, the translated texts to some extent became an expression of Lin Shu or the Chinese readers' ideas.

The instance in the beginning of *La Dame aux Camélias* is quoted again to exhibit Lin Shu's traditional bias towards the written language:

The original:
Mon avis est qu'on ne peut créer des personages que lorsque l'on a beaucoup étudié les hommes, comme on ne peut parler une langue qu'à la condition de l'avoir sérieusement apprise.

Lin Shu's translation:
小仲马曰：凡成一书，必详审本人性情，描画始肖， 犹之欲成一国之书，必先习其国语也。

Lin Shu's translation in English:

Dume said: it is impossible to produce a book until one has carefully studied men's temperament and how to describe them in a right way, just as it is impossible to produce books of a country until the country's language has been seriously acquired.

In the translation, the original clause 'comme on ne peut parler une langue qu'à la condition de l'avoir sérieusement apprise'(as it is impossible to speak a language until it has been seriously acquired' was altered into '犹之欲成一国之书，必先习其国语也' (as it is impossible to produce books of a country until the country's language has been seriously acquired). Though Lin Shu's version, if judged according to the view of linguistic translation, deviated from the original, Lin Shu's alteration is a cultural preference for literary writing over spoken language. In his eyes, a writer should play a more important role in shaping the national spirit and culture than a linguist, so the mastery of the written language was an essential prerequisite for writing a book. Lin Shu's alteration was almost constantly related to China's long literary tradition.

To give another example, in Chapter Eleven of *Uncle Tom's Cabin*, Mr. Wilson found George and gave him a well-meaning advice. Mr Wilson as a Christian repeatedly cited the Bible to persuade George to obey his master while George, who believed in freedom rather than Christianity, waged a tit-for-tat debate with Mr Wilson. Lin Shu's translation of this chapter is quite truthful to the original. It faithfully reproduced the emotion and atmosphere of the debate between Mr Wilson and George, perhaps because the ideas expressed in the chapter coincided with Lin Shu's. However to make his translation more understandable to his readers, Lin Shu altered the original. For example, Mr.Wilson said, 'the apostle says, "let every one abide in the condition in which he is called."'[1] In order to make his readers readily understand the meaning of the apostle as well as highlight the view of the apostle (the highlight shows Lin Shu's disapproval of the view), Lin Shu wrote:

圣经之语：' 天生是人，居何等级，　即须其等级，勿来分外之获。'[2]

---

[1] Stowe, 1948, p.123.
[2] Lin Shu, Hei nu yu tian Lu (Uncle Tom's Cabin), 1981, p.50.

In this Chinese version, first, Lin Shu changed 'the apostles' (使徒传) into 'Bible'(圣经), as the Chinese readers at that time might be more familiar with the Bible than with 'the apostles'; and then elucidated the original as 'when a person is born in a certain social estate, he should abide in the estate and should never have any inordinate demands'. On the surface, the Chinese version has the same meaning as the original, but in the Chinese cultural context, due to offering a more concrete explanation, it becomes more acceptable, and the translation implies the translator's negative inclination to the teaching from the apostles.

Besides, on mentioning law, George argued:

> What laws are there for us? We don't make them, — we don't consent to them, — we have nothing to do with them; all they do for us is to crush us and keep us down. Haven't I heard your Four-of –July speeches? Don't you tell us all, once a year, that governments derive their just power from the consent of the governed? Can't a fellow *think*, that hears such things? Can't he put this and that together, see what it comes to?[1]

Lin Shu altered the passage as follows:

> 若言法律，而吾之义属何条？凡言法律者，律其国民向法，尤必须与国民公定，必众诺之，而后其法乃立。今彼私立之法，必令吾辈陷身入地，更无自见天日之时。吾尚忆礼拜堂牧师之言曰：'凡统辖天下之柄者，是天下人举而奉之，非统辖者敢自诩能同辖也。'[2]

<u>Lin Shu's translation in English:</u>
With regard to the law, its aim is to discipline the citizen towards the law. Therefore it is particularly necessary to make it with the citizen publicly, and have their approval, and then establish the law. Now the law is made in private, which has caught us into the hell so that we have lost all hope of seeing the light of day. I still remember what the priest said that 'a ruler should be elected and supported by all the people, how dare he consider himself to be a qualified ruler?'

---

[1] Stowe, 1952, p.124.
[2] Lin Shu, Hei nu yu tian Lu (Uncle Tom's Cabin), 1981, p.50.

This Chinese version is a typical free translation, in which Lin Shu transformed the personal statement 'we don't make them, — we don't consent to them, — we have nothing tot do with them' into an impersonal statement '凡言法律者，律其国民向法，尤必须与国民公定，必众诺之，而后其法乃立(with regard to the law, its aim is to discipline the citizen towards the law. Therefore it is particularly necessary to make it with the citizen publicly, and have their approval, and then establish the law). By this transformation, Lin Shu sublimated the personal statement into a collective principle regarding the law. Similarly, he changed 'your Four-of-July' speeches into a clergyman's speeches as well, thus generalizing Mr. Wilson's personal speech '凡统辖天下之柄者，是天下人举而奉之，非统辖者敢自诩能同辖也'(A ruler should be elected and supported by all the nationals, how dare he consider himself to be a qualified ruler?). Thus the clergyman's speech or sermon aims not to express his personal view but to relay or interpret the beliefs and ideas from Bible or the church. It is through such alterations that Lin Shu expressed his own political ideal about constitutionalism, a concern of many Chinese intellectuals at that time such as Kang Youwei and Liang Qichao.

Sometimes, Lin Shu transmitted the mood of the original while ignoring the sentence structure and word order. For example, the description of seclusion on an evening in Paris in *La Dame aux Camélias*.

The orignal:
Un soir, nous étions reŝés à las fenêtre plus tard que de coutume; le temps avait été magnifique et le soleil s'endormait dans un crepuscule eclatant d'azur et d'or, Quoique nous fussions dans Paris, la verdure qui nous entourait semblait nous isoler du nonde, et à peine si de temps en temps le bruit d'une voiture troublait notre converstion.[1]

English translation of the original:
One evening we had sat at the window later than usual; the weather had been superb, and the sun sank to sleep in twilight dazzling with gold and azure. Though we were in Paris, the verdure which surrounded us seemed to shut us off from the world, and our conversation was only now and again disturbed by the sound of a passing vehicle.

---

[1] Dumas fils, 1939, pp.67-68.

Lin Shu virtually re-wrote this description in the translation as follows:

一日天气晴朗，晚霞一片，在浓树之外，与蔚蓝天相映发，神爽气清。虽居巴黎辗轱之下，而所居隐于树间，青叶翠阴，不类人境，隐隐闻马车声若在空际。[1]

<u>Lin Shu's translation in English:</u>
It was a bright day. There was a stretch of sunset glow, which, beyond the dense trees, added radiance and beauty to the blue sky and was very refreshing.　Although I lived in the downtown area in Paris, but my dwelling was hided among the trees, under their green leaves and shades, as if not among people. Indistinct sounds of horses and carriages might be heard just as if they came from the horizon.

In the translation, Lin Shu seems to borrows phrases and '意境' (poetic imagination) from the work of one of China's most famous poets, Tao Yuanming(alias Tao Qian，365–427). Lin's Version seems to end with the early phrase of Tao's poem:

结庐在人境，
而无车马喧。
问君何能尔，
心远地自偏。[2]

<u>English translation of the poem:</u>
I make my home among people,
Yet there are no sounds of horse and carriages.
You ask me how this is possible,
I say, when the heart is detached the place is remote.

Reading Lin's translation, an educated Chinese reader would enter Tao Yuanming's wondrous landscape of detachment and bliss. Lin Shu omitted quite a few of the original concrete images and activities such as 'the window', 'the sun', 'conversation' and so on. He added '不类人境'(as if not among people), that introduces us to Tao Yuanming's poetic imagination, albeit in

---

[1] Lin Shu, 1931, p.14.
[2] Tao Qian 陶潜, Jingjie xiansheng ji 靖节先生集(A Collected Works of Tao Yuanming), Heluo tushu chubanshe, Taibei, 1975, p.27.

some what changed words. By comparing the source text with the target text, it is clear that it is a typical target-oriented free translation. Lin Shu' re-writing linked his translation of *La Dame aux Camélias* to the great works of Chinese poetry over two millennia. This is poetic equivalence that moves beyond poetic equivalence.

Again, in the beginning of *Robinson Crusoe*, the father advised him to abandon his idea of adventure overseas. The original is as follows:

The original:

He asked me what reasons more than a meer wandring inclination I had for leaving my father's house and my native country, where I might be well introduced, and had a prospect of raising my fortune by application and industry, with a life of ease and pleasure. [1]

Lin Shu's translation:

吾儿，汝宗旨安在？胡为霍霍如是？设汝果好游，则必远离尔父及尔钓游之地。不知此地固僻，然汝若弗行，则亦足以使汝增长其学问，更助汝以先畴所积，则汝之功用，亦将无穷。[2]

Lin Shu's translation in English:

My son, what is your goal? Why do you suddenly want to do this? if you really love travelling, you will certainly be far away from your father and the place where you have amused yourself since your childhood. I don't know if it is an out-of-the-way place, but if you don't leave here, it would be enough to broaden your knowledge, and also you will be supported from the accumulated family property. In that case, you will enjoy the fortune and have a life of ease.

This translation is a re-writing too. Lin Shu made conspicuous alterations of the original. First, to avoid the monotony, Robinson's self-narrative was changed into his father's words, namely, from indirect speech into direct speech. 'He asked me what reasons more than a meer wandering inclination I had for leaving my father's house and my native country' was shifted into a conditional sentence '设汝果好游，则必远离尔父及尔钓游之地'(if you really love travelling, you will certainly be far away from your father and the place where

---

[1] Defoe, Daniel, The life and Adventure of Robinson Crusoe, 1965, Penguin Books, pp..27-28.
[2] Lin Shu, 1934, p.2.

you have amused yourself since your childhood). The 'native country was replaced with '钓游之地'(the place to fish or swim[1]), which added a local delight. Besides, Lin Shu added the conditional sentence '然若弗行......'(if you don't leave here, ...), '足以使汝增长其学问，更助汝以先畴所积'(it will be enough to broaden your knowledge, and also you will be supported from the accumulated family property'. Obviously, the alteration changed the original, but still retained its meaning, as from the context, those added words should be what the father wanted to say. In his translation of the father's long talk to Robinson over the doctrine of the mean, he retained the views of the original while making alterations so that it is hard to made a contrastive reading.

These re-writings of the original demonstrate Lin Shu's literary heritage and his standpoint as a Chinese reader by extension to a collective Chinese readership. He assumed two roles: translator and writer. Whatever the role is, his standpoint is toward the target culture and readers all the same.

(3) Intervention into Translation

Intervention into translation is seen in a number of Lin Shu's translations where he was inclined to acting as a commentator to express himself or as the voice of his generation of intellectuals. *Gulliver's Travel* is one example. In chapter Two, of Part I, the king issued an imperial commission to oblige the villages round the city to supply food and drink to Gulliver. The author wrote:

For the due payment of which his majesty gave assignment upon his treasury. For this prince lives chiefly upon his own demesnes; seldom, except upon great occasions raising any subsidies upon his subjects, who are bound to attend him in his wars at their own expense.[2]

Lin Shu's translation:
时呈帝府藏允实， 不苟敛于百姓。荀非战事，无就民间征发者，而民亦乐以资助国家也。[3]

Lin Shu's translation in English:

---

[1] It is a literal translation. In fact, it means 'hometown'.
[2] Swift, 1976, p.39.
[3] Lin Shu, Haiwai xuan qu lu(Gulliver's Travels), Vol.1, 1915, p.14.

Then the emperor's treasury was replenished, so he did not extort heavy taxes and levies from his people. Without any wars, there is no wartime draft, so the people are ready to aid the country financially.

In this translation, which does not completely tally with the original, Lin Shu gave voice to his own political views. The readers of the late Qing would be deeply impressed, as during the late Qing period, the Qing Court was forced to pay an immense amount of indemnity due to the repeated defeats of China in the wars against the foreign powers. Hence, the Qing government had to extort heavy taxes and levies from the people. Lin Shu's alterations in the translation obviously aimed at the political and social reality of China to evoke the Chinese readers' sympathy and provoke their reflection on China.

Another example from *Gulliver's Travel* comes in Chapter Six of Part II, on talking to the king of Brobdingnag about English parliament consisting of House of Peers and House of Commons, Gulliver only said:

And these two Bodies make up the most august Assembly in *Europe*, to whom, in Conjunction with the Prince, the whole Legislature is Committed.[1]

Yet Lin Shu made use of the subject under discussion to put over his own ideas:

此两院人，欧洲之国力，系属于是。 借之以通上下之情，立宪之源，即出于此。[2]

Lin Shu's translation in English:

It is the reason why the members of the two Houses are regarded as the power of every European country. By them, the upper levels and the lower levels can be linked up. They are the source of constitutionalism.

Lin Shu, an advocate of constitutional monarchy, attributed the power and prosperity of Europe to the two Houses' '通上下之情'(the upper levels and the lower   levels can be linked up), and regarded it as '立宪之源' (the source of constitutionalism). He extended his translation to political reforms within the context of strengthening the country against the intrusion of the foreign powers.

---

[1] Swift, 1976, p.117.
[2] Lin Shu, Haiwai xuan qu lu(Gulliver's Travels), Vol.2, 1915, p.42.

212

In Chapter Seven of Part II, after his advice was rejected by the king of Brobdingnag, Gulliver disappointedly commented:

> Great allowances should be given to a king who lives wholly secluded from the rest of the world, and must therefore be altogether unacquainted with the manners and customs that most prevail in other nations: The want of which knowledge will ever produce many prejudices, and a certain *narrowness of thinking*, from which we and the politer countries of Europe are wholly exempted. And it would be hard indeed, if so remote a prince's notions of virtue and vice were to be offered as a standard for all mankind.[1]

Lin Shu's translation:

以此国立于世界之外，遂不审地球上尚有他国。我国虽有人利，彼盖未尝一见。见既弗广，所施于政体者，遂偏执不可浚沦。且深斥吾欧之文明为多事。[2]

Lin Shu's translation in English:

This country is wholly secluded from the world, so is ignorant of other countries existing on the globe. Although there are great advantages in my country, he has never seen them personally. On enforcing the governmental system, he becomes very bigoted, reprimanding the civilization of our Europe for too much trouble.

In the translation, Lin Shu seemed to point out through Gulliver's comment that the rulers had a very narrow view while refusing to come to their senses, which disappointed the reformists, who were inclined to introduce foreign political systems. The alterations in the Chinese version such as '我国虽有人利，彼盖未尝一见' (Although there are great advantages in my country, he has never seen them personally), '所施于政体者，遂偏执不可浚沦' (on enforcing the governmental system, he will become very bigoted) clearly show that Lin Shu made use of translation to express his own ideas.

In the postscript to his translation of *Uncle Tom's Cabin*, Lin Shu declared that his reason for translating this novel was to 'encourage bestirring ourselves, loving our nation and protecting our race from subjugation'.[3] Hence, he

---

[1] Swift, 1976, p.122.
[2] Lin Shu, Haiwai xuan qu lu(Gulliver's Travels), Vol.2, 1915, p.48.
[3] Lin Shu, Hei nu yu tian lu (Uncle Tom's Cabin), 1981, p.204.

frequently made use of the subject in his translations to put over his own ideas. In Chapter Nine, Mary argued with her husband Mr. Bird about how to treat escaped slaves. She was clearly in sympathy with Abolitionism:

The original:

'Well; but is it true that they have been passing a law forbidding people to give meat and drink to those poor colored folks that come along? I heard they were talking of some such law, but I didn't think any Christian legislature would pass it!'

'Why, Mary, you are getting to be a politician, all at once.'

'No, nonsense! I wouldn't give a fig for all your politics, generally, but I think this is something downright cruel and unchristian. I hope, my dear, no such law has been passed.'

...

'And what is the law? It don't forbid us to shelter those poor creatures a night, does it, and to give 'em something comfortable to eat, and a few old clothes, and send them quietly about their business?'[1]

Lin Shu's translation:

马利亚曰："吾闻院中得新规约，凡黑奴逸出，投奔人家者，例不得假以须臾之息，当立遣之，此意确否？吾思文明之国，法当不如此。"

钵特曰："尔妇人，何由发此伟论？"

马利亚不顾而唾，曰："国有此例，终与公理不和，吾故不觉多口。然丈夫既处议院，具有权力，能革此例，讵不称快人心。"

......

马利亚曰："所云旧典者，合理之谓也。既不合理，何尚云典！......"

Lin Shu's translation in English:

Mary said: "I hear that the congress has passed a new law forbidding people to permit escaped black slaves to stay in their house even for a moment, and repatriating them right away. Is it true? I think that the law of any civilized country should not act like this."

Mr Bird said: "You are a woman, why do you have such an informed opinion?"

---

[1] Stowe, 1952, p.88.

Mary ignored his ridicule and said: "If there is really such a law, it will go against the generally acknowledged truth after all, so I was not aware that I spoke out of turn. Since my husband is a member of the congress and has the power, if you can help abolish this law, it will give people much gratification."

…

Mary said: "In terms of the passed law, it should be reasonable. Since it is not, why should it be called 'law'?"

In translating Mary's argument, Lin Shu made some alterations. For example, 'I didn't think any Christian legislature would pass it' was altered to '吾思文明之国，法当不如此'[1](I think that the law of any civilized country should not act like this), in which, '文明之国，法..'(the law of a civilized country) replaces 'any Christian legislature' to lay stress on political issues while revealing his disapproval of the discriminatory policy of the American government on the Chinese labourers.[2] Similarly, 'I think this is something downright cruel and unchristian' was translated into '果有此例，终与公理不合'[3](if there is really such a law, it will go against the generally acknowledged truth after all), in which Lin Shu replaced 'unchristian' with '与公理不合'(go against the general acknowledged truth), thus switching 'Christian' principles to a universal principle concerning human rights. Lin Shu wholly altered the last quotation above into '所云旧典者，合理之谓也。既不合理，何尚云典?'(In terms of the passed law, it should be reasonable. Since it is not, why should it be called 'law'?). In the translation, Lin Shu shifted a specific law into law in general, universalising this issue. These shifts easily caused the readers' association with or reflection on the imperfect law of China at that time, which is one of Lin Shu's motives, as in his eyes, China's judicial system was much far inferior to that of the West. These alterations of Lin Shu apparently demonstrated his political intervention into translation.

The most obvious instance of Lin Shu's intervention into translation can be seen in his translation of George's letter in Chapter Forty-Three of *Uncle Tom's Cabin*. In the translation, he added:

---

[1] Lin Shu, Hei nu yu tian Lu (Uncle Tom's Cabin), 1981, p.34.
[2] See Lin Shu's preface and postscript to Hei nu yu tian lu (Uncle Tom's Cabin).
[3] Lin Shu, Hei nu yu tian Lu (Uncle Tom's Cabin), 1981, p.35.

Lin Shu's translation:

须知有国之人与无国者，其人民苦乐之况，何啻霄壤。吾今回念同
种之羁绊于美洲，禽犴兽辱，无可致力，脱吾能立一国度，然后可
以公法公理，向众论申，不致坐听白人夷灭吾种。......盖欲振刷国
民之气，悉力保种，以祛外侮。吾至死不懈也。[1]

Lin Shu's translation in English:

It must be understood that the happy situation of the people with their
country and the suffering situation of the people without their country are
poles virtually apart. I think now of our compatriots who are being fettered
and mal-treated in America, but I am incapable of action. If I can leave to
establish a country, in that way, I will can appeal to the nations by the
generally acknowledged laws and truth so as not to sit still waiting for the
white men's extermination of our race. ... To bestir the nationals, go all out
to protect our race and drive out the humiliation imposed by the foreign
powers, I will make unremitting efforts until death.

This statement cannot be found in the original; it was made by Lin Shu himself
rather than George. It is clear that Lin Shu made use of George's letter to
express his own ideas. It also can be confirmed by the statement in his
postscript to the translation of the novel:

I translated this book with Mr Wei in order not to win readers' gratuitous
tears by skilfully telling a tragic story, but to cry out for the Chinese because
our nation is being reduced to the status of slavery. ... May I ask that our
Chinese have a country? Reading George's letter to his friend, I find it
means that the people without a country can be maltreated by the civilized
people. ... But the Japanese also belong to the yellow race. When the
Americans insulted the Japanese women, the Japanese flew into a rage,
doing all they could to struggle in the American court meanwhile setting up
an organization for the struggle. How brave the Japanese were! If our
Chinese have their rulers, could it be said that they don't know that their
nationals are innocent but being humiliated and starved to death? The
relation between the high and the low as if they respectively belonged to
different countries. It is shameful to mention the poor national dignity!

[1] Ibid., p.203.

Now the political reforms have just started when I have finished translating this book. All the people are abandoning old learning while pursuing new learning. Although my translated book is unrefined and meagre, it is enough to contribute to bestirring ourselves and saving the nation from subjugation to ensure its survival.[1]

The view expressed in his translation of George's letter is exactly the same as one in his postscript. Thus, Lin Shu made use of a subject in the original as a pretext for his own opinion. This method is typical of his intervention into translation. Such alteration deviated from the original, so it is likely to be censured by linguistic critics. But it reflects a target culture orientation, and this orientation is central to target-oriented criticism and theory.

It is clear that Lin Shu's alterations show his own attitude and motives, substantiated by his views in the prefaces to his translations. His practice tallied with Yan Fu and Liang Qichao' views on the novel, i.e. a novel can influence the rise and fall of a nation.[2] Lin Shu's translated novels were a vehicle for Chinese nationalism and constitutional reforms at that time. In short, Lin Shu first attempted to intervene the target text (translation), and then use the target text to intervene the target culture by evoking the Chinese readers' sympathy and reflection.

5. Abridgement

Abridgement can be frequently seen in Lin Shu's translations. Here abridgement means that Lin Shu tried to make his translation more succinct than the original. The reasons for abridgement are very much as already mentioned above. A further reason is that Lin Shu tried to make his translation accord with the habit of Chinese literary expression as closely as possible so that Chinese readers readily accepted it. As a matter of fact, the process of abridging the target text may be regarded as a process of re-writing or concentration. Unlike a tape-recorder, Lin Shu did not passively or mechanically record his

---

[1] Lin Shu, 1981, p.204.
[2] Xia Zhiqing 夏志清, 'Xin xiaoshuo de tichang zhe: Yan Fu yu Liang Qichao'新小说的提倡者：严复与梁启超(The Promoters of New Novel: Yan Fu and Liang Qichao), Ren de wenxue 人的文学(Humanist Literature), Chuwenxue, Taibei, 1977, p.79.

collaborator's oral interpretation of the original text word for word or sentence for sentence. In this process, apart from turning vernacular Chinese into literary Chinese, Lin Shu also re-composed and re-wrote the original text. This is one of the reasons that Chinese scholars are always ready to attribute the translations resulting from the joint efforts of Lin Shu and his collaborators to Lin Shu's name, terming his translated works of fiction 'Lin yi xiaoshuo'(Lin Shu's Translated Novels) as a genre.

As discussed in Chapter 5, overall, literary description in classical Chinese is more succinct and poetic. This style led to his readers' acceptance. However, more often, Lin Shu abridged the original when he felt that something in the original was unsuitable for his readers' acceptance. For example, in Chapter Seven of *Joan Haste*, the author described Emma's religious piety in the church service through Henry's observation:

The original:

Henry, watching Emma's face, saw it change and glow as she followed those immortal words, till at the fifty-third verse and thence to the end of the chapter it became alight as though with the effulgence of a living faith within her. In deed, at the words " for this corruptible must put on incorruption and this mortal must put on immortality," it chanced that a vivid sunbeam breaking from the grey sky fell full upon the girl's pale countenance and spiritual eyes, adding a physical glory to them, and for one brief moment making her appear, at least in his gaze, as though some such ineffable change had already overtaken her, and the last victory of the spirit was proclaimed in her person.[1]

Lin Shu's translation:
亨利静观爱玛，凝神壹志，似出其精神，直与天接。此时适有阳光射窗而入，直注爱玛之面，亨利觉此人清超宁肃，已非俗间闺秀所有。[2]

Lin Shu's translation in English:
Henry quietly watched Emma. She was so engrossed that her soul appeared out of her body and connected directly with Heaven. Just then, a sunbeam,

---

[1] Haggard, H. Rider, Joan Haste, Longmans, Green, and Co., London, 1985, p.59.
[2] Lin Shu, Jiayin xiao zhuan 迦茵小传 (Joan Haste), Shangwu yinshuguan, Beijing, 1981, p.38.

through the window, fell full upon Emma's countenance. Henry felt that this girl's mind is spiritual and peaceful, which is hardly seen in worldly girls.

In the original, the author gave a detailed description of Emma's preoccupation with the lessons from the Bible, in which the author mentions the chapter Emma was listening to, quotes the words, portrays Emma's reflection and countenance on her face.... All its detailed description is abridged into '凝神壹志，似出其精神，肖与天接' (was so engrossed that her soul appeared out of her body and connected directly with Heaven). Lin Shu's Chinese version erased the Christian detail. Certainly, readers who lived in a non-Christian country or were ignorant of Western Christianity readily accept such alteration. In Lin Shu's translations, the passages involving Christianity were often abridged or altered, as stated before.

Another case in point is Lin Shu's treatment of the description of the religious activity in the Chapter Four of *Uncle Tom's Cabin*. The focus of the chapter is on the description of the joyous atmosphere in Tom's house, particularly on the activity of worship: singing hymns, preaching, reading the *Book of Revelation* and so forth, which were designed to foil and forebode Tom's pressing adversity. The description takes up 20 pages or so, but Lin Shu abridged all the passages regarding religious activity into one sentence:

<u>Lin Shu's translation:</u>
一日傍晚，汤姆为邻人筵饮，宾主歌呼，方极酣嬉。[1]

<u>Lin Shu's translation in English:</u>
One evening, Tom entertained his neighbours at a banquet. The host and guests both sang and spoke loudly in the greatest delight.

The focus of the translated text was shifted on the second section of the chapter describing the trade of the black slaves between Shelby and Heley in Shelby's house, which actually takes up only one page in the original, yet takes up more than 1/2 of the whole chapter (merely 1/13 in the original text). It is clear that Lin Shu' focus was on the question of black slaves rather than on religion.

---

[1] Lin Shu, Hei nu yu tian lu (Uncle Tom's Cabin), 1981, p.13.

In Chapter Three of *David Copperfield*, we can also find the instances of Lin Shu's abridgment for other reasons. When Peggotty talked to David about the disposition of his kindhearted brother, the author described:

<u>The original:</u>
He was but a poor man himself, said Peggotty, but as good as gold and as true as steel - those were her similes. The only subject, she informed me, on which he ever showed a violent temper or swore an oath, was this generosity of his; and if it were ever referred to, by any one of them, he struck the table a heavy blow with his right hand (had split it on one such occasion), and swore a dreadful oath that he would be 'gormed' if he didn't cut and run for good, if it was ever mentioned again. It appeared, in answer to my inquiries, that nobody had the least idea of the etymology of this terrible verb passive to be gormed; but that they all regarded it as constituting a most solemn imprecation. [1]

But Lin Shu abridged this passage into:

我兄甚贫，然乐善好施，且不欲以善自鸣。[2]

<u>Lin Shu's translation in English:</u>
My brother is very poor, but love to do philanthropic things while never wanting to preen himself by it.

Lin Shu's abridgment here avoids literally translating Peggotty's similes 'as good as gold and as true as steel'. In Western culture, 'gold' may be associated with 'good', and 'steel' with 'true', but there are no such associations in traditional Chinese culture. If the similes were literally translated, it would certainly confuse Chinese readers. So is the oath 'be gormed'. Let's quote another Chinese translator's literally translations of them: 'as good as gold and as true as steel' was translated into '他像金子一样好，像钢一样纯'(as good as gold and as pure as steel) and 'be gormed' into '高埋'. [3] These literal translations certainly

---

[1] Dickens, Charles, *Personal History of David Copperfield*, Oxford University Press, London, 1949, p.39.
[2] Lin Shu, 1981, p.19.
[3] Dong Qiusi 董秋斯, *Dawei keibofeier* 大卫·科波菲尔(*David Copperfield*), Renmin wenxue chubanshe, 1962, p.41.

baffle the Chinese readers, because it is hard for them to see any internal relations between 'gold' and 'good' as well as 'steel' and 'true'. As far as the meaning of '尚埋'(gormed) is concerned, I believe, it is little known to most of the Chinese readers. Another reason for the abridgment was to simplify the complicated and verbose sentence structure. In the original, the author used many words and complex sentences to describe Mr Peggotty's will: he hated people to mention his philanthropic deeds. Nevertheless, Lin Shu just used a few Chinese characters, e.g. '且不欲以善自鸣' to render the meaning of the whole description. It may be envisaged as well that it would have frustrate the Chinese readers if the description had been literally translated. The instances of the abridgment for simplification can be easily seen in Lin Shu's translations. However, in the final analysis, Lin Shu's abridgment is for the acceptance of the Chinese reading public.

Lin Shu's strategy of translation aims to retain the spirit and style of the original as faithfully as possible, while adapting where necessary for the sake of the target culture and readers. This discussion of Lin Shu's adaptation is divided into five categories: adaptation, omission, addition, alteration and abridgment for explanatory purpose. In fact, they are interrelated. Lin Shu's practice may not be regarded as a model for today's literal translators, but as a phenomenon of cultural translation in a specific period, it should be acknowledged that Lin Shu's practice was reasonable and acceptable to his audience. In Lin Shu's times, the Chinese readers were more concerned with the new contents, subject matters, literary style and techniques, as well as with the readability of a translation rather than with whether a translation is faithful to the original or translating itself. Indeed, to enhance the acceptability of his translations, Lin Shu's adaptation of the original actually embraces, 'reshuffles'(Toury's word) certain features, adding new features, though there is no basis in the original sometimes.[1] Lin Shu's efforts to seek equivalence beyond equivalence show his consistent orientation towards the target culture.

---

[1] Toury, 1995, p.171.

Chapter 7

Conclusion:

An Exemplar of Chinese Literary Translation

The translational practice of Lin Shu has been a controversial topic. Source-oriented translation theory cannot effectively explain it. However, target /culture-oriented translation theories provide us with a new insight to it, laying a theoretical foundation for our re-evaluation of Lin Shu and his translations. On the basis of the theories and empirical analysis in the thesis, it is concluded that Shu was the father of modern Chinese literary translation.

Lin Shu initiated China's literary translation undertakings. Along with Yan Fu's social science translations, Lin's translations of foreign literature reshaped the ideas of the intellectuals of his time in China, but also changed, diversified and enriched Chinese culture and literature. Later generations of modern Chinese writers, to varying extents, benefited from the influence of Lin Shu's translations. Therefore, in terms of output and impact, Lin Shu's contributions and achievements in translation are inestimable.

The reasons why Lin Shu's translations exerted such an enormous cultural impact and why Lin Shu had such a great achievement in literary translation are that they met the needs of the Chinese culture and the demands of the Chinese readers of his time. Lin Shu was both a reader and translator/writer, intuitively knew what the Chinese culture needed and what his Chinese readers demanded, as well as what kind of translation could impress or influence his readers. This was demonstrated in his choice of the originals and his treatment of the source texts (as analyzed in Chapters 4, 5 and 6). Furthermore, his prefaces and postscripts to his translations, as Chapter 4 indicates, clearly show that his translations entirely focused on the target Chinese culture and readers.

For the most part, Lin Shu adopted free translation. No doubt, it was determined by both the historical and cultural conditions of his time and his personal circumstances, but more importantly, by Lin Shu's incessant attention to the needs of the Chinese culture and readers. As targe/culture-oriented translation theories indicate, on the one hand, the target culture can influence a translator's translation strategy (refer to Toury's views in Chapter 2); on the other hand, a translator's works can also influence the target culture. These two factors heavily affected Lin Shu's translation strategies and methods. Lin Shu's translations, without sticking to the word and sentence structure of the original text, retained the spirit and style of the original. In fact, I argue that Lin Shu's translation methods may be more properly called 'poetic equivalence'. In other words, Lin Shu primarily sought a poetic equivalence rather than a literal equivalence or even dynamic equivalence between the ST and the TT. Sometimes, as textually analysed in Chapter 6, his translations also go beyond equivalence, showing his inclination to the target culture and readers. The acceptability and influence of his translations in the Chinese literary world testify the effectiveness and success of his translation methods.

Lin Shu also occupied an important position in the history of modern Chinese literature. Lin Shu was not only an initiator of Chinese literary translation, but also a pioneering figure of the May Fourth New Culture Movement. As discussed in Chapters 1, 3 and 4, Lin Shu introduced new ideas, new literary content, style and techniques into China through his translations and writings. These exerted a huge impact on both the occurrence of the May Fourth movement and its promoters as well as on later generations of modern Chinese writers. Through his literary writings and translations, Lin Shu helped break through the modes of traditional Chinese literature, and promoted the transition of Chinese literature from the traditional to the modern. Previous political criticisms totally ignored Lin Shu's literary achievement and status in the respect.

The assessment of Lin Shu as a translator ought to be conducted from cultural, literary and translational angles rather than from a purely political angle. The main problem in the previous assessment of Lin Shu lies in the fact that political judgment superseded other judgments, thus becoming the dominant criterion of assessing Lin Shu and his translations. Only from cultural, literary and translational views, can Lin Shu's translations be properly understood. Moreover, as stated in Chapters 2, 5 and 6, the assessment of translation ought to include cultural consideration and translational influence in the target language rather than solely linguistic equivalence. In the final analysis, the ultimate goal of translation is to realize cultural exchange, and particularly to serve the target culture and readers. In this sense, Lin Shu's achievements can only be assessed through theories that incorporate cultural variables and target influence.

The translational phenomenon of Lin Shu deserves careful consideration. It may also help to illustrate some important issues in translation studies. Firstly, whether literary translation succeeds depends heavily on the target readers' response and the cultural influence of the translated works rather than literal equivalence between the ST and the TT as illustrated by Lin Shu in this Study. A literary translation that is not accepted by its readers or has no or little influence should be considered unsuccessful. Secondly, a translator must really understand and take into consideration the needs of the target culture, the demands and reception of the target readers and the factors of the target linguistic culture into consideration. Therefore, a literary translator seeks poetic equivalence and beyond rather than a formal correspondence as shown in the case of Lin Shu. Literary translation is primarily a re-writing or re-creating cultural activity rather than a pure linguistic exchange act.

To conclude, Lin Shu was undoubtedly an initiator of modern Chinese literary translations as well as a pioneer of the New Culture Movement. Lin Shu's translations exerted a huge impact on Chinese culture and literature, brought a substantial change in the creation of fiction, influenced generations of modern Chinese writers, and inspired other Chinese scholars to embark on literary translation. Examined in its given cultural context, Lin Shu's translation practice and strategy were also successful, and fitted in with the needs of the Chinese culture and readers at that time. Therefore, along with the application of target/culture-oriented translation theories to translation studies and the emergence of the re-assessments of the historical events and figures of modern China, Lin Shu's achievement and contributions as well as his status as a literary translator in the history of Chinese translation should be affirmed to the fullest extent. This is the goal of this study in recasting Lin Shu.

Bibliography

Abdulla, Adnan K., 1999, 'Aspects of Ideology in Translating Literature', *Babel*, 45:1, pp.1-18.

Adams, Robert M., 1973, *Proteus, His Lies, His Truth: Discussions of Literary Translation*, Norton, New York.

Ames, Roger T., Chan Sin-wai, Mau-sang Ng, (ed.), 1991, *Interpreting Culture through Translation: A Festschrift for D.C. Lau*, Chinese University Press, Hong Kong.

A Ying 阿英, 1973, *Wanqing xiaoshuoshi* 晚清小说史(*A History of Late Qing Fiction*), Zhonghua shuju, Hong Kong.

—— (ed.),1960, *Wanqing wenxue congchao: xiaoshuo xiqu yanjiu juan* 晚清文学丛钞：小说戏曲研究卷(*Late Qing Critical Papers on Fiction and Drama*), Zhonghua shuju, Shanghai.

Amos, Flora Ross, 1973, *Early Theories of Translation*, Octagon Books, New York.

Baker, Margaret John, 1997, Translated Images of the Foreign in the Early works of Lin Shu (1852-1924) and Pearl S. Buck (1892-1973): Accommodation and Appropriation, Ph.D thesis, University of Michigan.

Baker, Mona, 1992, *In Other Words : A Coursebook on Translation*,: Routledge, London and New York.

—— (ed.), 1997, *Encyclopedia of Translation Studies*, Routledge, London and New York.

—— 2000, 'Towards a Methodology for Investigating the Style of a Literary Translator', *Target* 12:2, pp.241-266.

Barnstone, Willis, 1993, *The Poetics of Translation: History, Theory, Practice*, Yale University Press, New Haven.

Bassnett, Susan, 1980, *Translation Studies*. Methuen, New York.

—— and Lefevere, André, (eds), 1990. *Translation, History and Culture*, Pinter, London.

—— 1991, *Translation Studies*, Routledge, London and New York.

—— 1993, *Comparative Literature: A Critical Introduction*, Blackwell Publishers, Oxford, UK and Cambridge MA.

—— (ed.), 1997, *Translating Literature*, D.S. Brewer, Cambridge.

—— and Lefevere, André, 1998, *Contructing Cultures: Essays on Literary Translation*, Multilingual Matters, Clevedon, Philadelphia, Toronto, Sydney and Johannesburg.

—— and Trivedi, Harish, (eds), 1999, *Post-Colonial Translation: Theory & Practice*, Routledge, London and New York..

Bell, R. T., 1987, 'Translation Theory: Where Are We Going?', *Meta,* 32:4, pp.403-415.

—— 1991, *Translation and Translating: Theory and Practice,*: Longman, London and New York.

Benjamin, Walter, 1968, *Illuminations*, Trans. Harry Zohn, Harcourt, Brace & World, NewYork.

Bingxin 冰心, 1984, *Binxin xuanji* 冰心选集 (*Selected Works of Bingxin*), Vol.2, Sichuan renmin chubanshe, Chengdu.

Bishop,John L., 1965, *Studies in Chinese literature*, Harvard University Press, Cambridge, Mass.

Bloom, Alfred, 1981, *The Linguistic Shaping of Thought: A Study in the Impact of Language on Thinking in China and the West*, Lawrence Erlbaum Association, Hillsdale, N.J.

Blotner, Joseph, 1955, *The Political Novel*, Greewood Press, Westport.

Boase-Beier, Jean and Holman, Michael, (eds.), 1999, *The Practices of Literary Translation: Constraints and Creativity*, St. Jerome, Manchester.

Booth, A. D., (ed.), 1958, *Aspects of Translation*, Secker and Warburg, London.

Booth, Wayne C., 1983, *The Rhetoric of Fiction*, The University of Chicago Press, Chicago and London.

Bowker, Lynne, (ed.),1998, *Unity in Diversity?: current trends in translation studies*, St. Jerome, Manchester.

Brower, R. A., (ed.), 1959, *On Translation*, Harvard University Press, Cambridge, Mass.

Brown, Calvin S., 1956, *The Reader's Companion to World Literature*, New American Library, New York.

Brownlie, Siobhan, 2002, An Investigation of Methodological Issue in Descriptive Translation Research: drawing on a case study of the English translations of texts by Jean-Fracois Lyotard, PhD thesis, University of Queensland.

Budick, Sanford and Iser, Wolfgang, (eds.), 1996, *The Translatability of Cultures:Figurations of the Space between*, Stanford University Press, Stanford, Calif.

Campbell, Duncan, 1998, 'In Defence of the Humble Art of Translation', *Asia Quarterly*, October, from the web site: www.vuw.ac.nz/ asianstudies/ publications/ quarterly.html.

Cao Shunqing 曹顺庆, (ed.), 1985, *Zhong xi bijiao meixue wenxue lunwen ji* 中西比较美学文学论文集 (*Collected Essays on Chinese and Western Comparative Aesthetics and Literature*), Sichuan wenyi chubanshe, Chengdu.

—— 2000, *Zhongwai wenxue kua wenhua bijiao* 中外文学跨文化比较 (*A Comparative Study across Culture between Chinese Literature and Foreign Literature*), Beijing shifan daxue chubanshe, Beijing.

Cazaminan, Louis, 1955, *A Short Hisotry of French Literature*, Clarendon Press, Oxford.

Chan Sin-wai and Pollard, David E., (eds.), 1995, *An Encyclopaedia of Translation: Chinese-English, English-Chinese*, Chinese University Press, Hong Kong.

Chang, Nam Fun, 2001, 'Polysystem Theory: Its Prospect as A Framework for Translation Research', *Target*, 13:2, pp.317-332.

Chao, Y. R.,1976, *Aspects of Chinese Sociolinguistics: Essays*, Stanford University Press, Stanford.

Chen Fukang 陈福康, 2000, *Zhongguo yixue lilun shigao* 中国译学理论史稿 (*A History of Chinese Translation Theory*), Shanghai waiyu jiaoyu chubanshe, Shanghai.

Chen Hongwei, 1999, 'Cultural Differences and Translation', *Meta*, 44:1, pp.121-132.

Chen Penxiang 陈鹏翔, (ed.), 1976, *Fanyi shi . Lun fanyi* 翻译史翻译论 (*A History of Translation / On Translation*), Hongdao wenhua shiye youxian gongsi, Taipei.

Ch'en Shou-yi, 1961, *Chinese Literature: A Historical Introduction*, The Ronald Press Company, New York.

Chen Yugang 陈玉刚, 1989, *Zhongguo fanyi wenxue shigao* 中国翻译文学史稿 (*A Draft History of China's Translation Literature*), Zhongguo duiwai fanyi chuban gongsi, Beijing.

Chen Yuankai 陈元恺, 1987, *Ershi shiji Zhongguo wenxue yu shijie* 二十世纪中国文学与世界 (*Chinese Literature and World in the Twentieth Century*), Shanxi renmin chubanshe, Xi'an.

Chen Zizhan 陈子展, 2000, *Zhongguo jindai wenxue zhi bianqian* 中国近代文学之变迁 (*The Changes of Early Modern Chinese Literature*), Shanghai guji chubanshe, Shanghai.

Chesterman, Andrew, 1997, *Memes of Translation: the Spread of Ideas in Translation Theory*, John Benjamins Publishing Company, Amsterdam/ Philadelphia.

—— 1998, *Contrasting Functional Analysis*, John Benjamins Publishing Company, Amsterdam/Philadelphia.

—— Gallardo, San Salvador and Gambier, Yves, (eds.), 2000, *Translation in Context: Selected Papers from EST Congress, Granada 1998*, John Benjamins Publishing Company, Amsterdam/Philadelphia.

Cheung, Martha, 1998, 'The Discourse of Occidentalism? Wei Yi and Lin Shu's Treatment of Religious Material in Their Translation of *Uncle Tom's Cabin*', in David Pollard, (ed.), *Translation and Creation: Readings of Western Literature in Early Modern China, 1840-1918*, John Benjamins Publishing Company, Amsterdam/Philadelphia, 1998, pp.127-149.

—— 2000, 'Power and Ideology in Translation Research in Twentieth Century China: An Analysis of Three Seminal Works', Paper presented at the Conference on Research Models in Translation Studies, University of Manchester, Manchester.

Chow Tse-tsung, 1960, 'Lin Shu', in Howard L. Boorman, (ed.), *Men and Politics in Modern China: 50 Preliminary Biographies*, Columbia University Press, New York.

—— 1960, *The May Fourth Movement: Intellectual Revolution in Modern China*, Harvard University Press, Cambridge.

Church, Richard, 1951, *The Growth of the English Novel*, Methuen, London.

Cicero, 1959, *De optimo genere oratorum*, trans. H.M Hubbell, Leob Classical Library, Heinemann, London.

Compiling group of *Zhongguo jindai shi*, (comps. and eds.), 1988, *Zhongguo jindai shi* 中国近代史 (*A History of Early Modern China*), Zhonghua shuju, Beijing.

228

Compiling Group of the Seven Universities and Colleges in Southern China, (comps. & eds.), 1979, *Zhongguo xiandai wenxueshi* 中国现代文学史 (*A History of Modern Chinese Literature*), Changjiang wenyi chubanshe, Wuhan.

Compton, Robert W., 1971, A Study of the Translations of Lin Shu, 1852 – 1924, Ph.D thesis, Stanford University.

Crystal, D., 1976, 'Current Trends in Translation Theory' *The Bible Translator*, 27:3, pp.322-329.

David, M. D., 1993, *The Making of Modern China*, Himalaya Publishing House, Bombay.

de Bary, William Theodore, Bloom, Irene and Adler, Joseph, (eds), 1961, *Sources of Chinese Tradition*, Columbia University Press, New York & London.

Defoe, Daniel, 1965, *Robinson Crusoe*, Penguin Books, London.

Delisle, Jean, 1988, *Translation: An Interpretative Approach*, trans., P. Logan & M. Creery, University of Ottawa Press, Ottawa.

—— and Woodsworth, Judith, (eds.), 1995, *Translators Through History*, Benjamins Publishing Company, Amsterdam & Philadelphia.

Denton, Kirk A., (ed.), 1996, *Modern Chinese Literary Thought: Writings on Literature, 1892-1945*, Stanford University Press, Stanford.

Dickens, Charles, 1879, *Dombey and Son*, Chapman and Hall, London.

—— 1948, *The Personal History of David Copperfield*, Oxford University Press, London.

—— 1950, *The Life and Adventures of Nicholas Nickleby*, Oxford University Press, London.

—— 1966, *Oliver Twist*, Clarendon Press, Oxford.

—— 1967, *The Old Curiosity Shop*, Oxford University Press, London and New York.

Dingwaney, Anuradha and Maier, Carol, (eds), 1995, *Between Languages and Cultures: Translation and Cross-cultural Texts*, University of Pittsburgh Press, Pittsburgh.

Dolezelova-Velingerova, Milena, 1980, *The Chinese Novel at the Turn of the Century*, University of Toronto Press, Toronto.

Dove, George N., 1997, *The Reader and the Detective Story*, Bowling Green State University Press, Bowling Green.

Eco, Umberto, 1979, *The Role of the Reader*, Indiana University Press, Bloomington.

—— 1984, *Semiotics and the Philosophy of Language*, Indiana University Press.

—— 2001, *Experiences in Translation*, University of Toronto, Toronto.

Ellis, Roger and Oakley-Brown, Liz, (eds.), 2001, *Translation and Nation : towards a cultural politics of Englishness*, Multilingual Matters, Clevedon, England ; Tonawanda, NY.

Eoyang, Eugene Chen, 1993, *The Transparent Eye: Reflections on Translation, Chinese Literature, and Comparative Poetics*, University of Hawaii Press, Honolulu.

—— and Lin Yao-fu, (eds.), 1995, *Translating Chinese Literature*, Indiana University Press, Bloomington.

Even-Zohar, Itamar, 1981, 'Translation Theory Today: A Call for Transfer Theory', *Poetics Today*, 2(4), pp.1-7.

—— and Toury, Gideon, (eds.), 1981, *Translation Theory and Intercultural Relations*, (a special issue of) *Poetics Today*, 2(4).

—— 1990, *Polysystem Studies*, (a special issue of) *Poetics Today*, 11(1).

—— 1997, 'The Making of Culture Repertoire and the Role of Transfer', *Target*, 9(2), pp.355-363.

—— 1997, 'Factors and Dependencies in Cultures: A Revised Outline for Polysystem Culture Research', *Canadian Review of Comparative Literature*, 24:3, p.15-34.

Fairbank, John King, 1992, *China, A New History*, The Belknap Press of Harvard University Press, Cambridge, Massachusetts, London.

Fan Boqun 范伯群 and Zhu Donglin 朱栋霖, (eds.), 1993, *1898-1949 Zhongwai wenxue bijiao shi*1898-1949 中外文学比较史(*A History of Comparison between Chinese Literature and Foreign Literature*), Jiangsu jiaoyu chubanshe, Nanjing.

Fan Shouyi, 1999, 'Highlights of Translation Studies in China Since the Mid-Nineteenth Century', *Meta*, 44:1, pp.27-43.

—— 1999, 'Translation of English Fiction and Drama in Modern China: Social Context, Literary Trends, and Impact', *Meta*, 44:1, pp.154-177

Feng Qi 冯奇, (ed), 1998, *Lin Shu pingzhuan ji zuopin xuan* 林纾评传及作品选(*A Critical Biography of Lin Shu and His Selected Works*), Zhongguo wenshi chubanshe, Beijing.

Feng Shigang 冯世刚, 1981, yiyi zhiyi zhuziyi '意译、直译、逐字译'(*Free Translation, Literal Translation and Word for Word Translation*), Fanyi tongxun 翻译通讯(*Translation Bulletin*), No.2, pp7-8.

Fish, Stanley, 1980, *Is There a Text in This Class?: The Authority of Interpretive Communities*, Harvard University Press, Cambridge.

230

Franke, W., 1967, *China and the West*, trans., R.A. Wilson, Harper Torchbooks, New York.

Fuery, Patrick John, 1997, *Cultural Studies and the New Humanities: Concepts and Controversies*, Oxford University Press, Oxford and New York.

Gálk, Marián, 1980, *The Genesis of Modern Chinese Literary Criticism (1917-1930)*, Curzon Press, London.

Gao, Wanlong, (ed.), 1990, *Ershi shiji waiguo wenxue liubian* 二十世纪外国文学流变(*Thedevelopment of the Twentieth Century Foreign Novel*), Huanghe chubanshe, Jinan.

—— 1997, 'Development of American Literary Criticism', *Youth Thinkers*, No.5, pp.38-44.

—— 1998, 'Literary Relations between China and the west', *Journal of Shandong Normal University*, No.6, p.23-30.

Gentzler, Edwin, 1993, *Contemporary Translation Theories*, Poutledge, London and New York.

Gile, D.,1991, 'Methodological Aspects of Interpretation (and Translation) 、Research', *Target*, 3:2, pp.151-174.

Giles, H. & Pwesland, P. F., 1975, *Speech Style and Social Evaluation*, Academic Press, London and New York.

Grierson, H.J.C, 1949, *Criticism and Creation: Essays and Addresses*, Chatto and Windus, London.

Guerin, W.L., Labor, E., Morgan, L., Reesman, J.C. and Willingham, J.R., 1992, *A Handbook of Critical Approaches to Literature*, Oxford University Press, New York and Oxford.

Guo Jianzhong 郭建中, (ed.), 2000, *Wenhua yu fanyi* 文化与翻译 (*Culture and Translation*), Zhongguo duiwai fanyi chuban gongsi, Beijing.

Guo Moruo 郭沫若, 1997, *Shaonian shidai* 少年时代 (*My Early Youth*), Renmin wenxue chubanshe, Bejing.

Guo Songtao 郭嵩焘，1984, *Lundun yu Bali riji* 伦敦与巴黎日记(*A Diary in London and Paris*), Yuelu shushe, Changsha.

Guo Yanli 郭延礼, 1998, *Zhongguo jindai fanyi wenxue gailun* 中国近代文学翻译概论 (*The Modern Translated Literature of China: An Introduction*), Hubei jiaoyu chubanshe, Wuhan.

—— 2001, *Zhongguo jindai wenxue fazhan shi* 中国近代文学发展史(*A History of Early Modern Chinese Literature*), Gaodeng jiaoyu chubanshe, Beijing.

Guo, Yangsheng, 2001, 'English Literature in China', from the website: http:// educ.queensu.ca/~landl/web/archives/vol22papers/yangsheng.htm.

Haggard, H. Rider, 1895, *Joan Haste*, Longmans, Green, And Co., London.

Halliday, M. A. K., 1979, Language as Social Semiotic: the Social Interpretation of Language and Meaning, Edward Arnold, London.

Halverson, S., 1997, 'The Concept of Equivalence in Translation Studies', *Target*, 9:2, pp. 207-233.

Han Dihou 韩迪厚, 1969, *Jindai fanyi shihua* 近代翻译史话(*A History of Early Modern Translation*), Chenguang tushu gongsi, Hong Kong.

Han Guang 寒光, 1935, *Lin Qinnan* 林琴南, Zhonghua shuju, Shanghai.

Hao, Fu, 1999, 'On English Translation of Classical Chinese Poetry', *Babel*, 45:3, pp.227-243.

Hardwick, Lorna, 2000, *Translating Words, Translating Culture*, Duckworth, London.

Hart, Roger, 1999, 'Translating Worlds: Incommensurability and Problems of Existence in Seventeenth-Century China', *Positions*, vol. 7, No.1, pp.95-128.

Hatim, Basil, 1997, *Communication across Cultures: Translation Theory and Contrastive Text Linguistics*, University of Exeter Press, Devon.

—— and Mason, I., 1990, *Discourse and the Translator*, Longman Inc., New York.

Hermans, Theo, (ed.), 1995, *The Manipulation of Literature: Studies in Literary Translation*, Croom Helm, London and Sydney.

Hewson, Lance and Martin, Jacky, 1991, *Redefining Translation : the Variational Approach*, Routledge, London.

—— (ed.),2002, *Crosscultural Transgressions: Research Models in Translation Studies II: Historical and Ideological Issues* , St. Jerome Publishing, Manchester.

Hodge, B., & Louie, K., 1998, *The Politics of Chinese Language and Culture: the Art of Reading Dragons*, Routledge, London and New York.

Holland, Norman, 1968, *The Dynamics of Literary Response*, Oxford University Press, New York.

Holmes, James S., (ed.), 1970, *The Nature of Translation: essays on the theory and practice of literary translation*, The Hague: Mouton.

—— Lambert, J. & Broeck, R. V. d., (eds.), 1978, *Literature and Translation: New Perspectives in Literary Studies*, Acco, Aleuren and Belgium.

232

—— 1988, *Translated!: papers on literary translation and translation studies*, Rodopi, Amsterdam.

Horace, 1965, *On the Art of Poetry*, *Classical Literary Criticism*, Penguin Books, Harmondsworth.

Horizon Publishing Co. (eds.), 1975, *Essays on May Fourth Movement*, The Horizon Publishing Co., Taipei.

Hsia, Chih-Tsing, 1968, *The Classic Chinese Novel: A Critical Introduction*, Columbia University Press, New York.

—— 1971, *A history of Modern Chinese Fiction*, Yale University Press, New Haven.

Hsu, Immanuel C. Y., 1990, *The Rise of Modern China*, New York: Oxford University Press, New York.

Hu Shi 胡适, 1986, *Hu Shi gudian wenxue yanjiu lunji* 胡适古典文学研究论集 (*Hu Shi's Research Essays on Classic Chinese Literature*), Shanghai guji chubanshe, Shanghai.

—— 1930, *Hu Shi wencun* 胡适文仔 (*The Selected Essays of Hu Shi*), Vol.2, Yadong Tushuguan, Shanghai.

Hu Ying, 1995, 'The Translator Transfigured: Lin Shu and the Cultural Logic of Writing in the Late Qing', *Positions*, 3:1, pp.69-96.

Huang Jiade 黄嘉德, 1940, *Fanyi lun ji* 翻译论集 (*Essays on Translation*), Xifeng she, Shanghai.

Huang Long 黄龙, 1988, *Fanyi xue* 翻译学 (*Translatology*), Jiangsu Jiaoyu chubanshe, Nanjing.

Hung, Eva, 1999, 'The Role of the Foreign Translator in the Chinese Translation Tradition, 2nd to 19th Century', *Target*, 11:2, pp.223-244.

Huxley, Thomas H., 1989, *Evolution & Ethics*, Princeton University Press, Princeton.

Ingarden, Roman, 1973, *The Literary Work of Art: An Investigation on the Borderlines of Ontology, Logic and Theory of Literature*, Northwestern University Press, Evanston.

Iser, Wolfgang, 1978, *The Act of Reading: A Theory of Aesthetic Response*, Routledge and Kegan Paul, London.

Ivir, V., 1981, 'Formal Correspondence vs. Translation Equivalence Revised, *Poetics Today*, 2:4, pp.51-59.

Jin, Di. and Nida, E. A., 1984,. *On Translation With Special Reference to Chinese and*

English, China Translation Publishing Corporation, Beijing.

Jin, Di, 1997, 'What is a perfect translation?' *Babel*, 43:3, pp.267-272.

Jin Lihua 金莉华, 1995, *Fanyixue* 翻译学*(Translatology)*, Sanmin shuju, Taipei.

Kaltenmark, Odile, 1984, *Chinese Literature*, Walker and Company, New York.

Katan, David, 1999, *Translating Cultures : an Introduction for Translators, Interpreters and Mediators*, St. Jerome Publishing, Manchester.

Ke Ping, 1999, 'Presuppositions and Misreadings', *Meta*, 44:1, pp.133-143.

Kelly, L. G., 1970, 'Cultural Consistency in Translation', *The Bible Translator*, No.21, pp. 170-175.

—— 1979, *The True Interpreter: A History of Translation Theory and Practice in the West*, St Martins Press, New York.

Kloepfer, R., 1981, 'Intra- and Intercultural Translation', *Poetics Today*, 2:4, pp.29-37.

Koller, W., 1995, 'The Concept of Equivalence and the Object of Translation Studies', *Target*, 7:2, pp.191-222.

Kong Huiyi 孔慧怡, 1999, *Fanyi, wenxue, wenhua* 翻译·文学·文化*(Translation, Literature, Culture)*, Beijing daxue chubanshe, Beijing.

Kong Li 孔立, 1981, *Lin Shu he Lin yi xiaoshuo* 林纾和林译小说*(Lin Shu and His Translated Novels)*, Zhonghua Shuju, Beijing.

Kong Qingmao 孔庆茂, 1998, *Lin Shu zhuan* 林纾传*(A Biography of Lin Shu)*, Tuanjie Chubanshe, Beijing.

Lane-Mercier, Gillian, 1997, 'Translating the Untranslatable: The Translator's Aesthetic, Ideological and Political Responsibility', *Target* 9:1, pp.43-68.

Larson, Mildred L., (ed.), 1991, *Translation: Theory and Practice, Tension and Interdependence*, State University of New York at Binghamton, Binghamton, N.Y.

—— 1998, *Meaning-based Translation : A Guide to Cross-language Equivalence*, University Press of America, Lanham.

Larson, Wendy, 1991, *Literary Authority and the Modern Chinese Writer: Ambivalence and Autobiography*, Duke University Press, Durham and London.

Latourette, Kenneth Scott, 1964, *The Chinese, Their History and Culture*, Macmillan, New York.

Lee, Leo Ou-fan, 1965, 'Lin Shu and His Translations: Western Fiction in Chinese Perspective', *Papers on China*, Vol. 19, pp.159-193.

234

—— 1973, *The Romantic Generation of Modern Chinese Writers*, Harvard University Press, Cambridge, Massachusetts.

Lefevere, Andre, (ed), 1970, 'The Translation of Literature: An Approach', *Babel*, No.17, pp.75-80.

—— 1976, 'Western Hermeneutics and Concepts of Chinese Criticism', *Tamkang Review*, No.6/7, pp.159-169.

—— 1981, 'Translated Literature: Towards an Integrated Theory', *Bulletin of the Midwest Modern Language Association*, 14:1, pp.86-96.

—— 1984, 'Translations and Other Ways in Which One Literature Affects Another', *Symposium*, No.38, pp.127-142.

—— 1992, *Translating Literature: Practice and Theory in a Comparative Literature Framework*, Modern Language Association of America, New York.

—— 1992, *Translation, Rewriting, and the Manipulation of Literary Fame*, Routledge, London and New York.

—— 1992, *Translation/History/Culture*, Routledge, London and New York.

Leppihalme, Ritva, 1997, *Culture Bumps: An Empirical Approach to the Translation of Allusions*, Multilingual Matters Ltd, Clevedon.

Leuven-Zwart, K. M. V., 1989, 'Translation and Original: Similarities and Dissimilarities, Part 1', *Target*, 1:2, pp.151-181.

—— 1990, 'Translation and Original: Similarities and Dissimilarities, Part 2' *Target*, 2:1, pp.69-95.

Levenson, Joseph R., 1958, *Confucian China and Its Modern Fate: The Problem of Intellectual Continuity*, University of California Press, Berkeley.

Li, C. N.,1982, 'The Gulf Between Spoken and Written Language: a case study in Chinese' in Tannen, D., (ed.), *Spoken and Written Language: Exploring Quality and Literacy*, Ablex Publishing, Norwood and New Jersey, pp. 77-88.

Li, Chien-nung, 1967, *The Political History of China, 1849-1928*, trans. Ssu-yu Teng and Jeremy Ingalls, Stanford University Press, Standford.

Li Defeng, 2000, 'Tailoring Translation Programs to Social Needs: A Survey of Professional Translators', *Target*, 12:1, pp.127-149.

Li Dian, 1998, 'Translating Bei Dao: Translatability as Reading and Critique', *Babel*, 44:4, pp.289-303.

Li Jingguang 李景光, 1983, Lin Shu yu xin wenhua yundong '林纾与新文化运动' (Lin Shu and the New Culture Movement), *Shehui kexue jikan* 社会科学辑刊(*The Collected Essays on Social Science*), No.4, pp.130-137.

Li, Tien-Yi, 1968, *Chinese Fiction: A Bibliography of Books and Articles in Chinese and English*, Far Eastern Publications, Yale University, New Haven.

Liang Qichao 梁启超, 1896, *Xixue shumu biao* 西学书目表 (*Booklist of Western Learning*), Yanglushi block-print edition, Shanghai.

—— 1913, *Liang Rengong wenji* 梁任公文集(*Collected Essays of Liang Qichao*), Vol.2, Sanda chubang gonsi, Hong Kong.

—— 1961, *Yinbishi Wenji* 饮冰室文集 (*The Collected Essays of Yinbi Study*), Vol.3, Zhonghua shuju, Taipei.

Liao Qiyi 廖七一, 2001, *Dangdai Yingguo fanyi lilun* 当代英国翻译理论 (*Contemporary Translation Theories in UK*), Hubei jiaoyu chubanshe, Wuhan.

Lin Shu 林纾, 1923, *Weilu wenji* 畏庐文集(*Collected Essays of Lin Shu*), Shangwu yinshuguan, Shanghai.

—— 1923, *Weilu xuji* 畏庐续集(*Collected Essay of Lin Shu, sequel*), Shangwu yishuguan, Shanghai.

—— 1923, *Welu san ji* 畏庐三集(*Collected Essays of Lin Shu, third volume*), Shangwu yinshuguan, Shanghai.

—— 1923, *Weilu shiji* 畏庐诗存(*Poems of Lin Shu*), Shangwu yinshuguan, Shanghai.

—— 1973, *Weilu wenji shicun lunwen* 畏庐文集·诗存·论文(*The Collection of Lin Shu's Poems and Essays*), Wenhai chubanshe, Taipei.

—— 1985, *Lin Qinnan wenji* 林琴南文集(*The Collected Works of Lin Qinnan*), Zhongguo shudian, Beijing.

—— 1990, *Lin Shu shi wen xuan* 林纾诗文选(*The Selected Poems and Essays of Lin Shu*), Huadong shifan daxue chubanshe, Shanghai.

—— 1993, *Lin Shu shi wen xuan* 林纾诗文选(*The Selected Poems and Essays of Lin Shu*), Shangwu yinshuguan, Beijing.

—— 1994, *Lin Shu fanyi xiaoshuo wei kan jiu zhong* 林纾翻译小说未刊九种 (*Lin Shu's Nine Unpublished Translated Novels*), Fujian renmin chubanshe, Fuzhou.

236

—— 1998, *Weilu xiaopin* 畏庐小品(*Lin Shu's Essays*), Beijing Chubanshe, Beijing.

Lin Wei 林微, 1985-1987, *Lin Shu xuanji xiaoshuojuan* 林纾选集·小说卷(*The Selected Works of Lin Shu: Novels*), Sichuan renmin chubanshe, Chengdu.

—— 1990, *Bainian chenfu: Lin Shu yanjiu zongshu* 百年沉浮：林纾研究综述 (*Vicissitudes in a Century: A Summary of Lin Shu Studies*), Tianjin jiaoyu chubanshe, Tianjin.

Lin Yiliang 林以亮, 1984, *Wenxue yu fanyi* 文学与翻译(*Literature and Translation*), Huangguan, Hong Kong.

Link, E. Perry, 1981, *Mandarin Ducks and Butterflies: Popular Fiction in Early Twentieth-century Chinese Cities*, University of California Press, Berkeley.

Liu, Chun-jo, 1964, *Controversies in Modern Chinese Intellectual History*, Harvard University Press, Cambridge.

Liu Jingzhi 刘靖之, 1996, *Shensi yu xingsi* 神似与形似(*Alikeness in Spirit and Alikeness in Appearance*), Shulin Chubanshe, Taipei.

Liu Miqing 刘宓庆, 1999, *Wenhua fanyi lungang* 文化翻译史纲 (*An Outline Theory of Cultranslation*), Hubei jiaoyu chubanshe, Wuhan.

Liu, Lydia H., 1995, *Translingual Practice: literature, national culture, and translated modernity – China, 1900 –1937*, Stanford University Press, Stanford & California.

Liu Shousong 刘绥松, 1956, *Zhongguo xin wenxue shi chugao* 中国新文学史初稿 (*First Draft of the History of New Chinese Literature*), Zuojia chubanshe, Beijing.

Liu Zongde, 1991, *Ten Lectures on Literary Translation*, Zhongguo duiwai fanyi chuban gongsi, 1991.

Lu Shukun 吕树坤, (ed.), 2002, *Lin Shu shici jiexi* 林纾诗词解析(*An Analysis of Lin Shu's Poems*), Jilin wenshi chubanshe, Changchun.

Lu Xun 鲁迅, 1971, *Lu Xun quanji* 鲁迅全集(*The Complete Works of Lu Xun*), Renmin wenxue chubanshe, Beijing.

—— 1973, *Lu Xun shujian – Zhi Riben youren Zengtian She* 鲁迅书简 - 致日本友人增田涉 (*Lu Xun's Letters to His Japanese Friend Masuda Wataru*), Chaoyang chubanshe, Hong Kong.

—— 1976, *A Brief History of Chinese Fiction*, trans. Yang Xianyi and Yang Gladys, Foreign Language Press, Beijing, third edition.

Luo Xinzhang 罗新璋, 1984, *Fanyi lunji* 翻译论集(*Essays on Translation*), Shangwu yinshuguan, Beijing.

Lyell, William A., 1976, *Lu Xun's Vision of Reality*, University of California Press, Berkeley, Los Angeles and London.

Ma Chunlin 马春林, 2001, *Zhongguo jindai wenxue geming shi* 中国近代文学革命史(*A History of the Early Modern Literary Revolution*), Liaoning daxue chubanshe, Shenyang.

Ma, Perry W., 1999, 'China's View of Europe: A Changing Perspective', *Europa*, 3:1, pp.38-41.

Malaysian Buddhist Association, (Comp. & ed.), *Intermediate Buddhist Textbook*, Chapters 22-24, Available from http://www.mybuddhist.com/Buddbase /E-Book/ Medium220-Chapter22-24.htm (2002, June 8).

Ma Tailai 马泰来, 1981, Lin Shu fanyi zuopin quan mu '林纾翻译作品全目'(A Complete List of Lin Shu's Translated Works), in Qian Zhongshu, et.al, *Lin Shu's Translations*, Shangwu yishuguan,, pp.60-101.

Ma Zuyi 马祖毅, 1998, *Zhongguo fanyi jianshi* 中国翻译简史(*A Short History of Chinese Translation*), Zhongguo duiwai fanyi chuban gongsi, Beijing.

Mao Shihui, 2001, 'Cultures Translated and Appropriated', *Translation Quarterly*, No.16-17, from the website: *China's Translation*(http://wgwx.tongtu.net).

Markins, Marian, (eds), 1993, *Collins Softback English* Dictionary, HarperCollins Publishers, Glssgow, 4th edn.

Martinet, H., 1983, 'Some Remarks About Translation and Style', *Papers and Studies in Contrastive Linguistics*, No.17, pp.85-91.

McDougall, Bonnie S., 1971, *The Introduction of Western Literary Theories into Modern China 1919 –1925*, The Centre for East Asian Cultural Studies, Tokyo.

—— & Louie, Kam, 1997, *The Literature of China in the Twentieth Century*, Bushbooks, Gosford, New South Wales.

Minford, J., 1987, 'Translation Studies and Sinology', Paper presented at the Conference on Translation Today, Hong Kong.

Mok, Olivia, 2001, 'Translational Migration of Martial Arts Fiction East and West', *Target*, 31.1, pp.81-102.

Mossop, Brian, 2001, *Revising and Editing for Translators*,. St. Jerome Pub, Manchester, UK and Northampton.

Munday, Jeremy, 2001, *Introducing Translation Studies : theories and applications*, Routledge, London and New York.

238

Mueller-Vollmer, Kurt and Irmscher, Michael, (ed.), 1998, *Translating Literatures, Translating Cultures: new vistas and approaches in literary studies*, Stanford University Press, Stanford.

Newman, A., 1980, *Mapping Translation Equivalence*, ACCO, Leuven.

Newmark, Peter, 1995, *Approaches to Translation*, Prentice Hall, Hertfordshire.

—— 1988, *A Textbook of Translation*, Prentice Hall, Hemel Hempstead.

—— 1989, 'Modern Translation Theory', *Lebende Sprachen*, No.1, pp. 6-8.

—— 1991, *About Translation*, Multilingual Matters, Clevedon and Philadelphia.

Nida, Eugene A., 1947, *Bible Translating: An Analysis of Principles and Procedures, with Special Reference to Aboriginal Languages*, American Bible Society.

—— 1954, *Customs and Cultures*, Harper, New York.

—— 1964, *Toward a Science of Translating: with Special Reference to Principles and Procedures Involved in Bible Translating*, E. J. Brill, Leiden.

—— and Taber, Charles Taber, 1969. *The Theory and Practice of Translation*. (United Bible Societies), E.J. Brill, Leiden.

—— and Reyburn, William, 1981, *Meaning Across Cultures*, No.4, American Society of Missiology Series, Orbis Books, New York.

—— 1982, *Signs, Sense and Translation*, University of Pretoria, Pretoria.

—— and De Waard, Jan, 1986, *From One Language to Another: Functional Equivalence in Bible Translating*, Thomas Nelson, Nashville, TN.

—— 2001, *Contexts in translating*, J. Benjamins Pub. Co., Amsterdam & Philadelphia. Nord, Christiane, 1997, *Translating as A Purposeful Activity: Functionalist Approaches Explained*, : St. Jerome Pub., Manchester, UK.

Olohan, Maeve, (ed.), 2000, *Intercultural Faultlines : research models in translation studies*, St. Jerome Pub., Manchester, UK and Northampton, MA.

Osburne, Harold, 1968, *Aesthetics and Art Theory: an historical introduction*, Longman, Harlow.

Pajares, Eterio and Romero, Fernando, 1997, 'Translating and the Reading Process', *Babel*, 43:4, pp.289-302.

Poddar, Prem, (ed.), 2000, *Translating Nations*, Aarhus University Press, Aarhus, Denmark.

Pollard, David, (ed.), 1998, *Translation and Creation: Readings of Western Literature in Early Modern China: 1840 –1818*, John Benjamins Publishing Company, Amsterdam/Philardelphia.

Porter, Stanley E. and Hess, Richard S., (ed.), 1999, *Translating the Bible: Problems and Prospects*, Sheffield Academic Press, Sheffield, England.

Qian Boji 钱博基, 1933, *Xiandai Zhongguo wenxueshi* 现代中国文学史(*A History of Modern Chinese Literature*), Shijie shuju, Shanghai.

Qian Zhongshu 钱锺书, 1975, 'Ch'ien Chung-Shu: Lin Ch'in-nan Revisited', trans., George Kao, *Renditions*, No.5, pp.8-21.

—— 1979, *Jiu wen si pian* 旧文四篇(*My Four Old Articles*), Shanghai Guji chubanshe.

—— A Ying 阿英，Zheng Zhenduo 郑振铎 and Ma Taiyuan 马泰元., 1981, *Lin Shu de fanyi* 林纾的翻译 (*The Translations of Lin Shu*), Shangwu yinshuguan, Beijing.

Reiss, Katharina, 2000, *Translation Criticism, the Potentials and Limitations: Categories and Criteria for Translation Quality Assessment*, trans., Erroll F. Rhodes, St. Jerome Pub., Manchester, UK; American Bible Association, New York.

Ritva, Leppihalme, 1997, *Culture Bumps: An Empirical Approach to the Translation of Allusions*, Multilingual Matters Ltd, and Clevedon, UK and Bristol, USA.

Robinson, Douglas, 1997, *Western Translation Theory*, St. Jerome Publishing, Manchester.

Rolston, David L.,1997, *Traditional Chinese Fiction and Fiction Commentary: Reading and Writing between the Lines*, Stanford University Press, Stanford, Calif.

Rose, Marilyn Gaddis, (ed.), 1996, *Translation Horizons: Beyond the Boundaries of Translation Spectrum*, State University of New York, Binghamton, USA.

—— 1997, *Translation and Literary Criticism: Translation as Analysis*, St. Jerome, Manchester, UK.

Schulte, R. and Biguenet, J., (eds.), 1992, *Theories of Translation: An Anthology of Essays from Dryden to Derrida*, University of Chicago Press, Chicago.

Schwartz, Benjamin, 1964, *In Search of Wealth and Power: Yen Fu and The West*, The Belknap Press of Harvard University Press, Cambridge and Massachusetts.

Scott, Walter, 1931, *Ivanhoe*, J. M. Dent and Sons Ltd, London and Toronto.

Sequeiros, Xosé Rosales, 1998, 'Degrees of acceptability in literary translation', *Babel*, 44:1, pp.1-14.

Shanghai Library, (ed.), 1980, *Zhongguo jin-xiandai congshu mulu* 中国近代现代丛书目录 (*The Catologue of Early Modern and Modern Series of Books*), Shangwu yinshuguan, Hong Kong.

Shi Meng 时萌, 1982, *Zeng Pu yanjiu* 曾朴研究 (*A Study of Zeng Pu*), Shanghai guji chubanshe, Shanghai.

Shuttleworth, Mark and Cowie, Moira, 1997, *Dictionary of Translation Studies*, St. Jerome Pub., Manchester.

Sima Changfeng 司马长风, 1975, *Xin Zhongguo Wenxueshi* 新中国文学史 (*A History of New China's Literature*), Zhaoming Chubanshe youxian gongsi, Hong Kong.

Simpson, E., 1975, 'Methodology in Translation Criticism', *Meta*, No.20, pp.251-262.

Simon, Sherry, 1996, *Gender in Translation: Cultural Identity and the Politics of Transmission*, Routledge, London and New York.

Smith, D. M. and Shuy, R. W., (eds), 1972, *Sociolinguistics in Cross-cultural Analysis*, Georgetown University Press, Washington.

Snell-Hornby, Mary, 1988, *Translation Studies: An Integrated Approach*, John Benjamins Publishing Company, Amsterdam/Philadelphia.

Sontag, Susan, 1977, *Illness As Metaphor*, Farrar, Straus & Giroux, New York.

Song, Yo-In, 1984, *Topics in Translation Studies*, Han Shin Pub. Co., Seoul.

Sorvali, Irma, 1996, *Translation Studies in a New Perspective*, P. Lang, Frankfurt am Main and New York.

—— 1998, 'The Translator as a Creative Being with special regard to the translation of literature and LSP', *Babel*, 44:3, pp.234-243.

Spiller, Robert E., 1957, *The Cycle of American Literature*, Macmillan, New York.

Stallknecht, Newton and Frenz, Horst, 1961, *Comparative Literature: Method & Perspective*, Southern Illinois University Press, London and Amsterdam.

Steiner, George, 1975, *After Babel : aspects of language and translation*, Oxford University Press, London and New York.

Steiner, T. R., 1975, *English Translation Theory 1650-1800*, Van Gorcum, Assen.

Stowe, Harriet Beecher, 1952, *Uncle Tom's Cabin*, Boughton Mifflin Company, Boston and New York.

Surburg, Raymond, 1997, 'The Influence of Eugene Nida On Bible Translators?' *The Christian News*, May 5.

Swift, Jonathan, 1976, *Gulliver's Travels*, Appletree Press Ltd, Belfast.

Taber, C. R., 1980, 'Sociolinguistic Obstacles to Communication Through Translation', *Meta*, 1:25, pp.421-429.

Tay, William, Chou, Ying-hsiung and Yuan Heh-hsiang, 1980, *China and the West: Comparative Literature Studies*, The Chinese University Press, Hong Kong.

Tagore, Amitendranath, 1967, *Literary Debates in Modern China 1918 – 1937*, The Centre for East Asian Cultural Studies, Tokyo.

Teng, Ssu-yu, Biggerstaff, Knight and Fairbank, John K., 1959, *Research Guide for China's Response to the West: A Documentary Survey 1839-1923*, Harvard University Press, Cambridge.

Tirkkonen-Condit, Sonja and Laffling, John, (eds), 1993, *Recent Trends in Empirical Translation Research*,: University of Joensuu, Joensuu.

Toury, Gideon, 1979, 'Interlanguage and Its Manifestations in Translation', *Meta*, 24:2, pp.223-231.

—— 1980, *In Search of a Theory of Translation*, Tel Aviv University, Tel Aviv.

—— 1981, 'Translated Literature - System, Norm, Performance: Toward a TT-Oriented Approach to Literary Translation', *Poetics Today*, 2:4, pp.9-27.

—— 1984, 'Translation, Literary Translation and Pseudotranslation' in Shaffer.E.S., (ed.), *Comparative Criticism*, Cambridge University Press, Cambridge, pp.73-85.

—— 1985, 'Aspects of Translating into Minority Languages, from the Point of View of Translation Studies', *Multilingua: Journal of Interlanguage Communication*, 4:1, pp.3-10.

—— 1985, 'A Rationale for Descriptive Translation Studies' in Hermans, Theo, (ed.), *The Manipulation of Literature: Studies in Literary Translation*, Croom Helm, London and Sydney, pp.16-41.

—— (ed.), 1987, *Translation Across Cultures*, (a special issue of) *Indian Journal of Applied Linguistics*, 8:2.

—— 1993, '"Translation of Literary Texts" vs. "Literary Translation": A Distinction Reconsidered' in Tirkkonen-Condit, Sonja and Laffling, John, (eds.), *Recent Trends in Empirical Translation Research*,: University of Joensuu, Joensuu, pp.10-24.

—— 1995, *In Descriptive Translation Studies and Beyond*, John Benjamins Publishing Company Compnay, Amsterdam / Philadelphia.

242

―― 1999, 'The Nature and Role of Norms in Literary Translation' in Venuti, Lawrence, (ed.), *The Translation Studies Reader*, Routledge, London and New York, pp.198-211.

―― 2000, 'My Way to Translation Studies: *Gideon Toury Interviewed by Miriam* Shlesinger, *Across Languages and Cultures*, 1:2, pp.275-286.

Tsien Tsuen-hsuin, 1953-1954, 'Western Impact on China through Translation', *Far Eastern Quarterly*, No.8, pp.307-322.

Tytler, Alexander Fraser, 1970, *Essay on the Principles of Translation*, Garland, New York.

―― 1978, *Essay on the principles of translation*, John Benjamins, Amsterdam.

Velingerov Milena Dolezelov, 1980, *The Chinese novel at the turn of the century*, University of Toronto Press, Toronto.

Venuti, Lawrence, (ed.), 1992, *Rethinking Translation: Discourse, Subjectivity, Ideology*, Routledge, London.

―― 1995, *The Translator's Invisibility: A History of Translation*, Routledge, London and New York.

―― 1998, *The Scandals of Translation: Towards an Ethics of Difference*, Routdlege, London and New York.

―― (ed.), 2000, *Translation Studies Readers*, Routledge, London and New York.

Vermeer, Hans J., 1998, 'Starting to Unask What Translatology Is About', T*arget*, 10:1, pp.41-68.

Wang Bingqin 土采钦, 1995, Wenhua fanyixue 文化翻译学 (*Cultural Translatology*), Nankai daxue chubanshe, Tianjin.

Waite, D.A., 1992, *Defending the King James Bible*, The Bible for Today Press, Collingswood, NJ.

Waley, Arthur, 1958, 'Notes on Translation', *The Atlantic Monthly*, the 100th Anniversary issue, pp.107-122.

―― 1975, 'Arthur Waley on Lin Shu', *Renditions*, No.5, Hong Kong University, pp.29-31..

Wang Dongfeng 土东风, 2000, Fanyi wenxue de wenhua diwei yu duzhe de wenhua taidu 翻译文学的文化地位与读者的文化态度(The Cultural Status of Translated Literature and the Cultural Attitude of Readers), *China Translation* 中国翻译, No.4.

Wang Hongzhi 土宏志, 2000, *Tanslation and Creation: on early modern Chinese translation of foreign fiction*, Beijing University Press, Beijing.

Wang Kefei 王克非, 1997, *Fanyi wenhua shilun* 翻译文化史论 (*A Critical History of Translational Culture*), Shanghai waiyu jiaoyu chubanshe, Shanghai.

—— and Fan Shouyi, 1999, 'Translation in China: A Motivating Force', *Meta*, 44:1, pp.7-26.

Wang Senran 王森然, 1924, Lin Shu xiansheng pingzhuan '林纾先生评传'(*A Critical Biography of Mr. Lin Shu*), in Wang Senran, *Jindai ershi jia pingzhuan* 近代二十家评传(*Critical Biographies of the Twenty Early Modern Writers*), Xingyan shudian, Beijing.

Wang Tao 王韬，1983, *Manyou Suilu* 漫游随录(*Jottings of Travel*), Yuelu Shushe, Changsha.

Warren, R., 1989, *The Art of Translation: Voices From the Field*, Northeastern University Press, Boston.

Wilfred L.Guerin, 1992, *A Handbook of Critical Approaches to Literature*, Oxford University Press, New York and Oxford.

Witherspoon, Alexander M., (ed.), 1951, *The College Survey of English Literature*, Harcourt, Brace & World, New York.

Wilss, W., 1984, *Translation Theory and its Implication*, Gunter Narr, Tübingen.

Wong, Lawrence, 1998, 'Lin Shu's Story-retelling as Shown in His Chinese Translation of *La Dame aux camélias*', *Babel*, 44:3, pp.207-233.

Wright, Arthur F., 1953, *Studies in Chinese Thought*, University of Chicago Press, Chicago.

Wu Jun 吴俊, (ed.),1999, *Lin Qinnan shuhua* 林琴南书话(*Lin Qinnan's Writings*), Zhejiang renmin chubanshe, Hangzhou.

Xie Tianzhen 谢天振, 1994, *Bijiao wenxue yu fanyi yanjiu* 比较文学与翻译研究 (*Comparative Literature and Translation Studies*), Yeqiang chubanshe, Taiwan.

—— 1999, *Yijie xuey* 译介学 (*Medio-translatology*), Shanghai waiyu jiaoyu chubanshe, Shanghai.

Xu Jun 徐均, 1992, *Wenxue fanyi piping yanjiu* 文学翻译批评研究(*A Study of Criticism on Literary Translation*), Yilin Chubanshe, Nanjing.

Xu Yuanchong 徐渊冲, 1984, *Fanyi de yishu* 翻译的艺术(*The Art of Translation*), Zhongguo duiwai chuban gongsi.

—— 1998, *Wenxue fanyi tan* 文学翻译谈 (*On Literary Translation*), Shulin Chubanshe, Taipei.

Xu Weize 徐维则, 1899, *Doxixue shulu* 东西学书录 (*Booklist of Eastern and Western Learning*), Jiangnan zhizaoju yishuguan, Shanghai.

Xu Zhixiao 徐志啸, *Jindai Zhongwai wenxue guanxi* 近代中外文学关系(*The Literary Relations between Early Modern China and Foreign Countries*), Huadong shifan daxue chubanshe, Shanghai.

Xue Suizhi 薛绥之 and Zhang Juncai 张俊才, 1982, *Lin Shu yanjiu ziliao* 林纤研究资料(*Research Materials on Lin Shu*), Fujian renmin chubanshe, Fuzhou.

Yan Chunde 阎纯德, 1981, 'Wusi de chan'er' 五四的产儿(A Newborn Baby of the May Fourth), *Xin wenxue shiliao* 新文学史料（*Materials Concerning New Literature*）, No.4.

Yan Fu 严复, 1986, *Yan Fu ji* 严复集 (*A Collected Works of Yan Fu*), Zhonghua shuju, Beijing.

Yang Zijian 杨自俭，(ed.), 1994, *Fanyi xin lun* 翻译新论(*A series of translation studies in China*), Hubei jiaoyu chubanshe, Wuhan.

Zang Zhonglun 臧仲伦，1991，*Zhongguo fanyi shihua* 中国翻译史话(*A History of Chinese Translation*), Shangdong jiaoyu chubanshe, Jinan.

Zeng Xianhui 曾宪辉, 1982, Lin yi xiaoshuo de diwei yu yingxiang '林译小说的地位与影响' (The Status and Influence of Lin Shu's Translated Novels), *Fujian shida xuebao* 福建师大学报(*Journal of Fujian Normal University*), No.4, pp.83-90.

—— 1999, *Lin Shu* 林纤, Chunfeng wenyi chubanshe, Shenyang.

Zhang Henshui 张恨水, 1982, *Xiezuo shengya huiyilu* 写作生涯回忆录 (*Memories of My Writing Career*), Renmin wenxue chubanshe, Beijing.

Zhang Jian, 1997, 'Reading Transaction in Translation', *Babel*, 43:7, pp.237-150.

Zhang Jinglu 张静庐, 1920, *Zhongguo xiaoshuoshi dagang* 中国小说史大纲 (*An Outline of the History of Chinese Fiction*), Taidong tushuju, Shanghai.

Zhang Juncai 张俊才, 1993, *Lin Shu pingzhuan* 林纤评传(*A Critical Biography of Lin Shu*), Naikai daxue chubanshe, Tianjin, 1992.

Zhang Ruoying 张若英, (ed.), 1935, *Zhongguo xin wenxueshi yundong ziliao* 中国新文学史运动资料（*Source Materials on the history of the New Literature Movement in China*）, Guangming shuju, Shanghai.

Zhang Yingji, (ed.), 1998, *China in a polycentric world : essays in Chinese comparative literature*, Stanford University Press, Stanford and Calif.

Zhao, Henry Y.H., 1995, *The Uneasy Narrator: Chinese Fiction from the Traditional to the Modern*, Oxford University Press, Oxford and New York.

Zheng Hailing 郑海凌, 2000, *Wenxue fanyixue* 文学翻译学(*Literary Translatology*), Wenxin chubanshe, Zhengzhou.

Zheng Shengtao 郑声涛, (ed.), 1994, *Fanyi yu wenhua jiaoliu: fanyi xue xin jiaocheng* 翻译与文化交流：翻译学新教程(*Translation and Cultural Exchange: A New Translatology Course*), Chengdu keji daxue chubanshe, Chengdu.

Zheng Zhenduo 郑振铎, 1970, 'Lin Qinnan xiansheng'林琴南先生(Mr Lin Qinnan), *Zhongguo wenxue yanjiu* 中国文学研究 (*Studies of Chinese Literature*), Guwen shuju, Hong Kong.

—— 1975, 'Cheng Chen-to: A Contemporary Appraisal of Lin Shu, trans., Diana Yu, *Renditions*, No.5, pp.

Zhou Yi 周仪 and Luo Ping 罗平, 1999, *Fanyi yu piping* 翻译与批评(*A Critical View on Translation*), Hubei jiaoyu chubanshe, Wuhan.

Zhou Zuoren 周作人, 1924, 'Lin Qinnan yu Luo Zhenyu'林琴南与罗振玉(Lin Qinnan and Luo Zhenyu), *Yusi* 语丝(*Thread of Talk*), No. 3.

—— 1933, *Zhitang wenji* 知堂文集(*The Selected Essays of Zhitang*), Tianhai shudian, Shanghai.

—— 1935, *Ku cha suibi* 苦茶随笔 (*Bitter Tea Jottings*), Beixin shuju, Shanghai.

—— 1974, *Zhitang Huiyilu* 知堂回忆录(*Zhitang's Reminiscences*), San Yu Stationery & Publishing Co., Hong Kong.

Zhu Bisen 朱碧森 1989, *Nü guo naner lei: Lin Qinnan zhuan* 女国男儿泪 — 林琴南传 (*The Man's Tears in the Women's State: A Biography of Lin Qinnan*), Zhongguo wenlian chuban gongsi, Beijing.

Zhu Chuanyu 朱传誉, (ed.), 1982, *Lin Qinnan zhuanji ziliao* 林琴南传记资料 (*Biographical Materials on Lin Qinnan*), Tianyi chubanshe, Taibei.

Zhu Xizhou 朱羲胄, 1949, *Chunjue Zhai Zhushu Ji* 春觉斋著述记 (*Works from the Chunjue Study*), Shijie Shuju, Shanghai.

List of Lin Shu's Translated Works[1]

Ai chui lu 哀吹录(1914), Honoré de Balzac (1799 – 1850, French)

Aiguo er tongzi zhuan 爱国二童子传(1907), *Le tour de la France par deux enfants*(1877) by G. Bruno(1833-1923, French)

Aiji jinzita poushi ji 埃及金字塔剖尸记(1905), *Cleopatra* (1889) by Henry Rider Haggard (1856-1925, British)

Aiji yiwen lu 埃及异闻录(1921), 路易原著(British)

Aisilan qingxie Zhuan 埃司兰情侠传(1904), *Eric Brighteyes* (1891) by Henry Rider Haggard

Bali Chahuanü Yishi 巴黎茶花女遗事(1899), *La Dame aux camélias* (1848) by AlexandreDumas fils (1824-1895, French)

Bali si yiren lu 巴黎四义人录(1901)

Bai furen gan jiu lu 白大人感旧录 (1917), *Monsieur Destrémeaux, roman psychologique*(1882) by Jean Richepin(1849 – 1926, French)

Bao zhong yingxiong zhuan 保种英雄传(unpublished)

Beike zhentan ji 贝克侦探谈(1909), *The Quest of Paul Beck* (1908) by M. McDonnel Bodkin (1850 – 1933, British)

Bingxue yinyuan 冰雪因缘(1909), *Dombey and Son* (1848) by Charles Dickens (1812 - 1870, British)

Bing yang gui xiao 冰洋鬼啸(1911)

Boxing lang 薄幸郎 (1911), *The Changed Brides* (1869) by Emma D. E. Southworth (1819 - 1899, American)

Buni di'erci zhanji 布匿第二次战纪(1903, *Second Punic War* by Thomas Arnold

---

[1] This list is based on different sources, heavily on Ma Tailai's 'The Complete List of Lin Shu's Translated Works', Yu Jiuhong's 'The Textual Research of Lin Shu's Translated Works' and Zhang Juncai's 'The Chronicle of Lin Shu's Works'. This list does not include Lin Shu's translated articles. If the author and title of the original are not indicated, it means that they remain unknown.

(1795 – 1842, British)

Buru gui 不如归(1908), 不如归(*Nami-ko*, 1904) by 德富健次郎 Kenjiro Tokutomi（1868 – 1927, Japanese）

Can chan ye sheng lu 残蝉曳声录(1912), 测次希洛(British)

Cang bo yan die ji 沧波淹谍记(1921), 卡文原著(British)

Chan chao ji 颤巢记(1919), *Der schweizerische Robinson* (1813) by Johann David Wyss (1743 – 1818, Swedish)

Chi lang huanying 痴郎幻影(1918), 赖其镗女士原著(British)

Dashi gugong yuzai 大食故宫余载(1907) , *The Alhambra* (1832) by Washington Irving (1783 - 1859, American)

De dajiang xingdengbao ou zhan chenbai jian 德大将兴登堡欧战成败鉴 (1922), *Hindenburg*(1921) by Edmond Buat (1868 – 1923, French)

Dianying loutai 电影楼台(1908), *The Doings of Raffles Haw* (1892) by Arthur Conan Doyle (1859 – 1930, British)

Dong ming ji (1921), *A Journey from This World to The Next*(1743) by Henry Fielding (1707 – 1754, British)

Dong ming xuji 洞冥续记(unpublished), *A Journey from This World to The Next*, book 19 (1743) by Henry Fielding

E gong mi shi 俄宫秘史(1921), 魁特原著（French）

Feizhou yanshui chencheng lu 斐洲烟水愁城录(1905), *Allan Quatermain* (1887) by Henry Rider Haggard

Fengzao huanghou xiao ji 凤藻皇后小记 (unpublished), by Berha M. Clay (? , American)

Fuzhang Lu 拊掌录(1907), *The Sketch Book of Geoffrey Crayon, Gent.*(1820) by Washington Irving

Ganlan xian 橄榄仙(1916), 巴苏谨原著(American)

Gaojiasuo zhi qiu 高加索之囚（1920）, *A Prisoner of the Caucasus*(1872) by Lev Nikolayevich Tolstoi (1828 – 1910,Russian)

Geleixida 格雷西达(1917)

Gongzhu yunan 公主遇难(1917)

Gu gui yi jin ji 古鬼遗金记(1912), *Benita* (1906) by Henry Rider Haggard

Guai dong 怪董(1921), 伯鲁大闪支原著（British）

Gui ku cang jiao 鬼窟藏娇(1919), 武英尼原著(British)

Guishan Langxia Zhuan 鬼山狼侠传(1905), *Nada the Lily* (1892) by Henry Rider Haggard

Gui wu 鬼悟(1921), by Herbert George Wells (1866 – 1946, British)

Haiwai xuanqu lu 海外轩桀录(1906), *Gulliver's Travels* (1726) by Jonathan Swift (1667 - 1745, British)

Hao shi shu lie 豪士述猎(1919), *Maiwa's Revenge* (1888) by Henry Rider Haggard

Hei lou qing nie 黑楼情孽(1914), *The Man Who Was Dead* (1907) by Arthur W. Marchmont (1852 - 1923, British)

Hei nu yu tian lu 黑奴吁天录(1901)，*Uncle Tom's Cabin* (1852) by Harriet Beecher Stowe (1811 - 1896, American)

Hei taizi nan zheng lu 黑太子南征录(1909), *The White Company* (1891) by Arthur Conan Doyle

Hen lü qing si 恨缕情丝(1918) , *The Kreutzer* Sonata (1889) and *Domestic Happiness* (1859) L. N. Tolstoi

Hen qi chou luo ji 恨绮愁罗记(1908), *The Regugees* (1893) by Arthur Conan Doyle

Hengli diliu yishi 亨利第六遗事(1916), *Henry VI* (1594 – 1623) by William Shakespeare (1564 - 1616, British)

Hengli disi ji 亨利第四纪(1916), *Henry IV* (1598 – 1960) by William Shakespeare

Hengli diwu ji 亨利第五纪(1925), *Henry V* (1600) by William Shakespeare

Honghan nulang zhuan 洪罕女郎传(1906), *Colonel Quaritch, V. C.* (1888) by Henry Rider Haggard

Hong jiao hua jiang lu 红樵画桨录(1906), *Beatrice* (1890) by Henry Rider Haggard

Hong qie ji 红箧记(1916), 希登希路原著(British)

Huangjin zhu mei lu 黄金铸美录（unpublished）, by Bertha M. Clay

Huaji waishi 滑稽外史(1907), *Nicholas Nickeby* (1839) by Charles Dickens

Huatielu zhanxue yu xing ji 滑铁庐战血余腥记(1904), *Waterloo: A Sequel to the Conscript* (1872) Erckmann-Chatrian

Hua yin 花因(1907), 儿拉德原著(British)

Huanzhu yan shi 环珠艳史(1920), 堪伯路原著(American)

Huangtang yan 荒唐言(1908), *Tales from Spenser, Chose from the Faerie Queene* (1890) by Sophia H. Maclehose (? - 1912, British)

Huiguo 悔过(1917)

Huixing duo xu lu 彗星夺婿录(1909), 却洛得倭康，诺埃克尔司原著 (British)

Hun zhong hua 溷中花(1915), *Le coupable* (1897) by Francois Coppée (1842 – 1908, French)

Huo mu yingxiong 霍目英雄(1922), 泊恩原著(British)

Jisi ci hu ji 玑司刺虎记(1909), *Jess* (1887) by Henry Rider Haggard

Jia mu lin 加木林

Jiayin xiaozhuan 迦茵小传(1905), *Joan Haste* (1895) by Henry Rider Haggard

Jian di yuanyang 剑底鸳鸯(1907), *The Betrothed* (1825) by Walter Scott

Jiang tao ji 僵桃记(1921), by Bertha M. Clay

Jiaotoulane 焦头烂额(1919), by Nicholas Carter (American)

Jin feng tie yu lu 金风铁雨录(1907), *Micah Clark* (1889) by Arthur Conan Doyle

Jin lü yi 金缕衣 (unpublished), by Berha M. Clay

Jin suo shen nü zaisheng yuan 金梭神女再生缘(1920), *The World's Desire* (1890) by Henry Rider Haggard

Jintai chunmeng lu 金台春梦录(1918), 丹米安和华伊尔原著（French）

Juedou de qi 决斗得妻(1917)

Jun qian suo yu 军前琐语 (unpublished), 马路亚. (French)

Kaiche yishi 凯彻遗事(1916), *Julius Caesar* (1623) by William Shakespeare

Kantebolei gushiji 坎特伯雷故事(1916 – 7), Tales from Chaucer in Prose(1870)

by Charles Cowden Clarke(1787 – 1877, British)

Kuairou yusheng shu 块肉余生述,(1908), *David Copperfield* (1850) by Charles Dickens

Leichade ji 雷差得记(1916), *Richard II* (1597) by William Shakespeare

Libise zhan xue yuxing ji 利俾瑟战血余腥记(1904), *The Conscript*(1871) by Erckmann-Chatrian (1822 – 1899,French)

Li gui fan bi ji 厉鬼犯跸记(1921), *Windsor Castle*(1843) by William Harrison Ainsworth (1805 – 1882, British)

Li hen tian 离恨天 (1913), *Paul et Virginie* (1787) by Bernardin de Saint-Pierre(1737 – 1814, French)

Lian xin ou Lü yuan 莲心藕缕缘(1919), *When Knighthood was in Flower*(1898) by Charles Major (1856 – 1913, American)

Lin yao 林妖(1917)

Lubinxun piaoliu ji 鲁滨逊飘流记(1905), *Life and Strange Surprising Adventures of Robinson Crusoe* (1719) by Daniel Defoe (1600 - 1731, British)

Lubinxun Piaoliu Xuji 鲁滨逊飘流续记(1906), *Farther Adventures of Robinson Crusoe* (1719) by Daniel Defoe

Luhua Yunie 芦花余孽(1909), *From One Generation to Another* (1892) by Henry Seton Merriman (1862 - 1903, British)

Luosha xiongfeng 罗刹雄风(1913), 希洛原著(British)

Luosha yinguo Lu 罗刹因果录(1914), L N. Tolstoi

Lu shi 赂史(1919), *The Phantom Torpedo-boats*(1905) by Allan Upward (1863 – 1921, British)

Luxien 路西恩(1917), *Lucerne* (1857) by L. N. Tolstoi

Lüxing Shuyi 旅行述异(1907), *Tales of a Traveller* (1824) by Washington Irving

Ma du 马妒(1921), 高尔忒原著（British）

Manhuang zhiyi 蛮荒志异(1906), *Black heart and White Heart, and Other Stories* (1900) by Henry Rider Haggard

Meigui hua 玫瑰花(1918 - 9), *The Rosary*(1909) by Florence L. Barclay(1862 – 1921, British)

Meizhou tongzi wanli xunqin ji 美洲童子万里寻亲记(1905), *Jimmy Brown Trying to Find Europe* (1889) by William L. Alden (1837 – 1908, American)

Mei ye 梅孽(1921), *Ghosts* (1881) by Henrik Ibsen (1828 – 1906,Norwegian)

Miao lang die xue ji 眇郎喋血记 (unpublished), by Baroness Emma Orczy (？)

Minzhong xue 民种学（1900）, Volkerkunde (Ethnology, 1988) by Michael Haberlandt (1860 – 1940, Germany)

Mo wai fengguang 膜外风光(1920), *Le voile du bonheur*(1901) by Georges Clémenceau(1841 – 1929, French)

Mo xia zhuan 魔侠传(1922), *Don Quixote de la Mancha*, I (1605) by Miguel de Cervantes Saavedra(1647 – 1616, Spanish)

Muma ling she 木马灵蛇(1916)

Napolun benji 拿破仑本纪(1905), *History of Napoleon Buonaparte* (1829) by John Gibson Lockhart (1794 - 1854, British)

Na yun shou 拿云手(1917)

Nü shi yin jian ji 女师饮剑记(1917), *A Brighton Tragedy*(1905) by Guy Boothby(1867 – 1905, British)

Nu xing xu qing 奴星叙情(unpublished), 洛沙子（French）

Ou kong bi bing lu 藕孔避兵录(1909), *The Secret* (1907) by E. Phillips Oppenheim (1866 - 1946, British)

Ou xi tongshi 欧西通史 (unpublished, the author is unknown)

Ou zhan chungui meng 欧战春闺梦(1920), 高桑斯原著(British)

Pinzei qing si ji 牝贼情丝记(1917), 陈施利原著(British)

Qinü geluzhi xiaozhuang 奇女格露枝小传(1916), *The Thane's Daughter*(1850) by Mary Cowden Clark (1809 – 1898, British)

Qing hai yi bo 情海疑波(1921), 道因原著(British)

Qing huan ji 情幻记(unpublished), by L. N. Tolstoi

Qing qiao hen shui lu 情桥恨水录(unpublished) , 斐尔格女士原著（British）

Qing tian bu hen lu 情天补恨录(1923), 克林登女士原著（American）

Qing tian yi cai lu 情天异彩录(1919), 周鲁倭原著（French）

Qing tie 情铁(1914)

Qing wo 情窝(1912), 威利孙(British)

Qing yi 情翳(1922), 鲁兰斯原著（American）

Qiu deng tan xie 秋灯谭屑(1916), *Thirty More Famouse Stories Retold* (1905) by James Baldwin (1841 – 1925, American)

Qiu fang ji shi 球房纪事（1920）, *Memoirs of A Marker*(1855) by L. N. Tolstoi

Ran cike zhuan 髯刺客传(1908), *Uncle Bernac* (1897) by Arthur Conan Doyle

Ren gui guantou 人鬼关头(1917), *The Death of Ivan Iliich*(1886) by L. N. Tolstoi

Rongma shusheng 戎马书生(1919), *The Lances of Lynwood* (1855) by Charlotte Mary Yonge (1823 - 1901, British)

Rou xang shu Xian 柔乡述险(1917), 利华奴原著(British)

Sakexun jie hou yingxiong lue 撒克逊劫后英雄略(1905), *Ivanhoe* (1820) by Walter Scott (1771 – 1832, British)

San qiannian yan shi ji 三千年艳尸记(1910), *She* (1886) by Henry Rider Haggard

San shaonian yu sishen 三少年遇死神(1916)

San zhong si fa 三种死法(1924), *Three Deaths*(1859) by L. N. Tolstoi

Shalisha nüwang xiaoji 沙利沙女士小记(1921), *The Island Mystery*（1918）by George A. Birmingham(1865 – 1950, British)

Shehui sheng ying lu 社会声影录(1917), *A Morning of a Landed Proprietor*(1856) and *Two Hussars*(1856) by L. N. Tolstoi

She nüshi zhuan 蛇女士传(1908), *Beyond the City* (1892) by Arthur Conan Doyle

Shengu meiren 深谷美人(1914), 倭尔吞原著(British)

Shen shu gui cang lu 神枢鬼藏录(1907), *Chronicles of Martin Hewitt* (1895) by Arthur Morrison (1863 - 1945)

Shen wo 神窝（unpublished）, 惠而东大人原著

Shi lin yi yue ji 石麟移月记(1915), 马格内原著(British)

Shi wan yuan 十万元(1919)

Shiren jie yi ru 诗人解颐语(1916), *Chambers's Complete Tales for Infants* by W. & R.

Chambers, Ltd (British)

Shizijun yingxiong ji 十字军英雄记(1907), *The Talisman* (1825) by Walter Scott

Shuang xiaozi xunxie chouen ji 双孝子巽血酬恩记(1907), *The Martyred Fool* (1895) by David Christie Murray (1847 - 1907, British)

Shuang xiong jiao jian lu 双雄较剑录(1910), *Fair Margaret* (1907) by Henry Rider Haggard

Shuang xiong yi si lu 双雄义死录(1921), *Ninety-three*(1874) by Victor Hugo (1902 – 1885, French)

Si kou neng ge 死口能歌(1917)

Taixi Gu Ju 泰西古剧 (1919), *Stories from the Opera*(1914) by Gladys Davidson(British)

Tao dawang yinguo lu 桃大王因果录(1917), 参恩女士原著(British)

Tiannu lihun ji 天女离魂记(1917), *The Ghost Kings* (1908) by Henry Rider Haggard

Tian qiu chanhui lu 天囚忏悔录(1908), *God's Prisoner* by John Oxenham (1852 - 1941, British)

Tie xia toulu 铁匣头颅(1919), *The Witch's Head* (1887) by Henry Rider Haggard

Tuerqi luan shi shimo 土耳其乱事始末 （1913）

Wang yan wang ting 妄言妄听(1919), 美森原著(British)

Wu ding kai shan ji 五丁开山记(unpublished), 文鲁倭原著

Wuzhong ren 雾中人(1906), *People of the Mist* (1894) by Henry Rider Haggard

Xiliya junzhu biezhuan 西利亚郡主别传(1908), *For Love or Crown* (1901) by Arthur W. Marchmont

Xilinna xiaozhuan 西林娜小传(1909), *A Man of Mark* (1890) by Anthony Hope (1863 - 1933, British)

Xi lou gui yu 西楼鬼语(1919), 约克魁迭斯原著(British)

Xiama cheng zha gui 夏马城炸鬼 (unpublished) by Henry Rider Haggard

Xiao you jing 孝友镜 (1918), *Le gentilhomme pauvre*(1851) by Hendrick Conscience(1812 – 1883,)

Xianshenshuofa 现身说法 (1918), *Childhood*(1852), *Boyhood*(1854) *and Youth*(1857) by L. N. Tolstoy

Xiang fu lian 想夫怜(1920), by Bertha M. Clay

Xiang gou qing yan 香钩情眼(1916), *Antonine* (1849, France) by Alexandre Dumas fils

Xianghu xian ying 橡湖仙影(1906), *Dawn* (1884) by Henry Rider Haggard

Xiaonü lü shuang ji 孝女履霜记（unpublished）, by Bertha M. Clay

Xiaonü naier zhuang 孝女耐儿传(1907), *The Old Curiosity Shop* (1841) by Charles Dickens

Xielian junzhu zhuan 蟹莲郡主传(1915), *Une fille du régent* (1845) by Alexandre Dumas, pere

Xieluoke qian kaichang 歇洛克奇案开场(1908), *A Study in Scarlet* (1887) by Arthur Conan Doyle

Xin tian fang ye tan 新天方夜谭(1908), *More New Arabian Nights: The Dynamiter* (1885) by Robert Louis Stevenson (1850 - 1907, British)

Xue hua yuanyang zhen 血华鸳鸯枕(1916), *L'Affaire Clémenceau* (1866) by Alexandre Dumas fils

Xuesheng fengyue jian 学生风月鉴(unpublished), by Alexandre Dumas, pere

Yanhuo ma 烟火马(1917), *The Brethren* (1904) by Henry Rider Haggard

Yao kun huan shou ji 妖髡缳首记(1923), *Carnival of Florence*(1915) by Marjorie Bowen (British)

Yi de bao yuan 以德报怨(1922), *The Bride of Llewellyn* (1864) by Emma D. E. Southworth

Yi hei 义黑(1913), 德尼罗原著(French)

Yi luo mai xin ji 伊罗埋心记(1920), *La boite d'argent* (1855) by Alexandre Dumas fils

Yisuo yuyan 伊索寓言(1903), *Aesop's Fables* by Aesop (Greek)

Yin bian yan yu 吟边燕语(1904), *Tales from Shakespeare* (1807) by Charlse Lamp (1775 - 1834, British)

Yingguo daxie hong fanlu zhuan 英国大侠红蘩露传(1908), *The Scarlet Pimpernel*

(1905) by Baroness Emma Orczy (1865 - 1947, British)

Ying nüshi yiseer liluan xiaoji 英女士意色儿离鸾小记(1901)

Yingti xiao haojie 鹰梯小豪杰(1916), *The Dove in the Eagle's Nest* (1866) by Charlotte Mary Yonge

Yingwu yuan 鹦鹉缘(1918), *Adventures de quatre femmes et d'un perroquet* (1846 – 47) by Alexandre Dumas fils

Ying xiaozi huoshan baochou lu 英孝子火山报仇录(1905), *Montezuma's Daughter* (1893) by Henry Rider Haggard

Yu hai lei bo 鱼海泪波(1915), *Pêcheur d'Islande*(1886) by Pierre Loti(1850 – 1923, French)

Yu lou hua jie 玉楼花劫(Book One, 1908), *Le Chevalier de la Maison-Rouge* (1846) by Alexandre Dumas, pere

Yu xue feng mao lu 雨血风毛录(unpublished), 汤沐林森 (American)

Yu xue liu hen 玉雪留痕(1905), *Mr. Messon's Will* (1888) by Henry Rider Haggard

Yu yan jue wei 鱼雁抉微(1915), *Lettres persanes*(1721) by Charles Louis de Secondat Montesquieu(1689 – 1755, French)

Yueshi yalubaite jishi 乐师雅路白忒纪事（1920）, *Albert*(1857) by L. N. Tolstoi

Yun po yue lai yuan 云破月来缘(1915), 鹘刚伟(British)

Zei shi 贼史(1908), *Oliver Twist* (1838) by Charles Dickens

Zha gui ji 炸鬼记(1921), *Queen Sheba's Ring* (1910) by Henry Rider Haggard

Zhifen yiyuan 脂粉议员(1909), 司丢阿忒原著(British)

Zhi jin ju hun 织锦拒婚(1916),

Zhong ru kulou 钟乳髑髅(1908), *King Solomon's Mines* (1885) by Henry Rider Haggard

□□ (the Chinese title is unknown), *The Gentle Grafter*(1904) by O. Henry(1862 – 1910, American)

□□ (unpublished, and the Chinese title was not decided), by Henry Riger Haggard